Finding
Emilie

Finding Emilie

LAUREL CORONA

G

GALLERY BOOKS

New York   London   Toronto   Sydney

G

Gallery Books
A Division of Simon & Schuster, Inc.
1230 Avenue of the Americas
New York, NY 10020

First Gallery Books trade paperback edition April 2011

GALLERY BOOKS and colophon are trademarks of Simon & Schuster, Inc.

For information about special discounts for bulk purchases,
please contact Simon & Schuster Special Sales at 1-866-506-1949
or business@simonandschuster.com

The Simon & Schuster Speakers Bureau can bring authors to your live event. For more information or to book an event contact the Simon & Schuster Speakers Bureau at 1-866-248-3049 or visit our website at www.simonspeakers.com

Designed by Davina Mock-Maniscalco

Manufactured in the United States of America

10   9   8   7   6   5   4   3   2   1

Library of Congress Cataloging-in-Publication Data is available.

ISBN 978-1-4391-9766-0
ISBN 978-1-4391-9767-7 (ebook)

"Common sense is not so common."
—Voltaire

For Jim and Lynn, in gratitude for their uncommonness

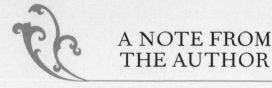

A NOTE FROM
THE AUTHOR

ON SEPTEMBER 3, 1749, shortly before her forty-third birthday, Gabrielle-Emilie le Tonnelier de Breteuil, the Marquise du Châtelet, gave birth to a baby girl, Stanislas-Adélaïde. Six days later, already back at her translation of and commentary on Newton's *Principia Mathematica*, Emilie du Châtelet complained of a headache, and within hours this charismatic and brilliant woman of letters was dead. This is a work of fiction about the daughter she left behind.

What actually happened to her baby, whom she named Stanislas-Adélaïde? Historical records indicate that she died of unknown causes before her second birthday, a fate shared with more than a quarter of the infants born in that era. She is buried beside her mother at Lunéville, France. We know little about Emilie's other daughter and first child, Gabrielle-Pauline, who moved to Italy after her marriage at sixteen. Sad but true: even if Emilie's baby had survived, we likely would know equally little about her.

In short, if Stanislas-Adélaïde had lived, it still would have been necessary to invent her. But what to invent? She was an inconvenient child about whom no one was likely to care much; and with no mother to protest on her behalf, she would almost certainly have gone directly from her wet nurse to a convent, where she would have lived out the rest of her days. I preferred to imagine the life Emilie du Châtelet would have wished for her second daughter—one in which she had the chance to follow her own dreams and her own mind, and to live a life as full and unique as Emilie's had been. That story is the one I chose to write.

On another note: the stories of Meadowlark and Tom, which are authored by Lili (as Stanislas-Adélaïde is called in the book) and appear as small excerpts throughout, can be read in full at the end of the novel.

"Judge me for my own merits, or lack of them, but do not look upon me as a mere appendage to this great general or that great scholar, this star that shines at the court of France or that famed author. I am in my own right a whole person, responsible to myself alone for all that I am, all that I say, all that I do. It may be that there are metaphysicians and philosophers whose learning is greater than mine, although I have not met them. Yet, they are but frail humans, too, and have their faults; so, when I add the sum total of my graces, I confess I am inferior to no one."

Emilie du Châtelet

PROLOGUE

Lorraine, Palais de Lunéville, 1 September 1749
To Florent-Claude, Marquis du Châtelet-Lomont
Commercy, Lorraine

My Dear Brother-in-Law,

Your last letter caused me such great distress that I have been unable to write until now. The post is leaving soon, and much as it pains me to dispense with the usual civilities, I will get directly to the matter at hand.

Your wife—who, I do not need to remind you, bears your name and that of my late husband—comports herself in a way that is truly beyond endurance. Shortly after my arrival two weeks ago, I laid out for you in great detail the affronts to propriety inflicted upon our most gracious host at the hands of your wife and the people she chooses as friends. I can only suppose that, being Polish, the duke does not understand our ways, although I cannot imagine that before he was deposed as king of even such a backward country, he would have permitted behavior as scandalous as I have witnessed here in Lunéville.

And what, my dear brother-in-law, do you have to say in response? "I have never been able to control my wife, and I find my happiness, and hers, is better served by not trying to do so." What kind of an answer is that for a retired army general, from one of the most respected and admired families in France? And surely I do not need to remind you that any true happiness comes in service to God's will, with which your wife seems entirely unacquainted despite her protestations to the contrary.

The sight of that reprobate Monsieur de Voltaire walking beside her in the garden and holding her parasol—for at the end of her lying-in she needs both hands to support her enormous stomach—has only been made worse in the last two days by the arrival of Monsieur de Saint-Lambert. That he is present at this time is shocking in its audacity, since surely you must be aware of the rumors arising—I shall put this as delicately as I can—from his journey to Cirey to visit your wife at a time consistent with the swollen condition I have described.

Perhaps it will be enough for you to ask for leave to return to Lunéville immediately. Though I am aware that your recent appointment as Grand Maréchal de Logis requires you to be in attendance to the duke at all times, I cannot imagine how such a journey would work a true hardship on the court. Since it is impossible for me to believe that such behavior was permitted while the court was in residence here, I can only assume that your wife has taken advantage of the duke's absence, and of course yours as well, to behave as if there are no rules at all.

That she has not taken to bed, and continues to work long hours in her study, is ample evidence of her lack of concern for her familial and social obligations. And on that last matter, her toilette, or rather lack of it, is sure in time to cause insolence among the servants. Though she always troubles herself to wear her diamonds, she rarely has her hair arranged suitably, and she often receives visitors with no further preparation than putting an apron over her dressing gown.

I would also like to discuss with you the future of the child, for Madame la Marquise speaks only of science, and seems to have made no plans at all for after the birth. I have no doubt you are sincere in lauding her for the attention she paid your children when they were young, but at forty-three, she has quite obviously changed. In fact, just last night at supper, she—laughingly, no less—told us that learning, gambling, and greed are the only pleasures left in life for a woman of her advanced years. I am sure she hardly intends—

The man has come for the post and I can say no more.

I remain your devoted sister-in-law,

Philippe-Charlotte, Baronne Lomont

Lorraine, Palais de Lunéville, 1 September 1749
To Florent-Claude, Marquis du Châtelet-Lomont
Commercy, Lorraine

My Dear Monsieur le Marquis,

I write to tell you how splendidly Emilie, your magnificent wife and my dearest friend, is managing these last days before the birth of your child. She is such a wonderful example for me, since, as I can now safely announce, I am expecting my first, which will be born in four months. I so hope the two are both boys, since it would be such a joy to see them playing together on visits to your estate at Cirey. Of course, I would prefer a little girl to dress up like a doll, but since the first order of business is to produce an heir, I will do my best to accede to my husband's wishes.

Oh dear, I realize I am writing the wrong kind of letter to a former general and gentleman of the court, but since there is no time to start anew, please ignore my silly ramblings.

Emilie still manages to walk daily, although slowly and not for very long. It is so pleasant being away from Paris, where appearing in public in such a state would be viewed as the height of vulgarity. Duke Stanislas has been a most gracious host to let us stay behind at his palace at Lunéville for Emilie's lying-in, and I assure you we have been watching over her most carefully. I imagine you have heard that the duke is quite serious about setting up a library and laboratory like the one she and Monsieur Voltaire created at Cirey, and she cannot stop talking about the exciting scientific progress that is possible when cost does not have to be so brutally considered.

I suppose she has written to tell you that Monsieur Voltaire arrived shortly after the court left for Commercy, and he was most disappointed to have missed the chance to see you, and to offer his plays for the court's entertainment. That will have to wait until Emilie is safely beyond childbirth and we can travel there to join you.

Perhaps the duke would not say this to you as Emilie's husband, but just before he moved the court to Commercy, he told me he found it quite remarkable that you allowed another man to live openly with your wife all these years and, knowing the nature of their relationship, still intercede for him whenever his pen gets him into trouble. And of course, as you know, when anything puzzles that dear man, he always asks, "Is it the French way?" as if that could satisfactorily explain even something as odd as a two-headed cow. Of course, when his question touched on the rather unusual role of Monsieur Voltaire in your wife's retinue, Emilie and I burst out laughing, though she stopped in seconds from the pain.

Her pain is worse in the last week, I must admit, since the baby has dropped so low and still refuses to come. Nevertheless she sits at her desk, full of anxiety about not finishing her book, and though I try to tell her that something as important as the deepest principles in nature can wait for a baby to be born, she shakes her head quite assuredly, and that is the end of the subject. I must reveal to you, monsieur, that when she speaks about her work, her face darkens—so unlike how it would light up in the past—and she admits she has premonitions that I will not discuss here for fear that putting them down in words may bring them to life.

In the evenings we perform plays in her bedroom—or rather all of us except Baronne Lomont, who keeps to herself from lack of enjoyment of our company. Though Emilie is too uncomfortable and weary to take part, she still enjoys these immensely, clapping and making remarks so bawdy, they would give no delight if they did not come from someone so charming. She cannot pull herself up to the card table in the parlor, so she rests on a daybed we have positioned nearby. She demands that Voltaire lift his hand over his shoulder so she can have a look at his cards, and when she likes them, she doubles his wagers with her own money. Last night it was Monsieur Saint-Lambert who had the honor of sitting in Voltaire's usual seat, since he is our newest arrival and Emilie is clamoring, as usual, for his undivided attention.

We wake up hopeful each morning and go to bed at night praying to be awakened to news that the hour of her deliverance has come. With a fourth child we are told it should be an easy birth, but there are, of course, difficulties that come with age, and no one can recall other such births to use for comparison.

It is time for me to go to my dear friend. She is grateful for my help with her work, since it is so difficult for her to fetch what she needs. I hope to write soon with joyous news.

Your devoted,
Julie, Madame de Bercy

Lorraine, Palais de Lunéville, 4 September 1749
To Florent-Claude, Marquis du Châtelet-Lomont
Commercy, Lorraine

Esteemed Monsieur,

I write in haste to inform you that today your wife was safely delivered of a daughter. The labor took only two hours and the baby appears healthy. She was taken immediately to the parish church for baptism, and then sent out to nurse. She is named Stanislas-Adélaïde and, to everyone's satisfaction, she resembles her mother.

I remain your devoted sister-in-law,
Philippe-Charlotte, Baronne Lomont

Lorraine, Palais de Lunéville, 11 September 1749
To Florent-Claude, Marquis du Châtelet-Lomont
Commercy, Lorraine

Dearest Monsieur le Marquis,

I know of no other way to get over this wretched moment than just to say what must be said.

Your beloved wife Emilie died suddenly last night, six days after giving birth. I expect you will put down this letter now and only pick it up later when you have had your first round of tears, but before you do, please let me say that this is also the worst moment of my own life. I can barely write I am so full of grief, and my tears have ruined several starts at this letter already. When you are ready to read again, I fear you will simply have to forgive the stains I am sure will fill its pages.

We do not know the cause. She did not complain of illness and in fact had set up a lap table so she could work on her papers in bed. Sometime around midday yesterday she complained she felt hot, but she did not appear exceedingly so, considering the brutal weather we have been having. Though we reminded her that cold was the worst possible remedy for fever, she insisted on having her favorite syrup in water with chunks of ice. Immediately after finishing it she put her hands to her temples, complaining of a sudden, excruciating headache and gasping for breath.

The physician whom the duke so graciously allowed to stay behind until the delivery gave her a hot tisane, which calmed her considerably. He sent for the best doctors from Nancy, who arrived shortly after nightfall. By then the pain and labored breathing had recurred several times, and we were all terribly frightened. She was given opiates and when she began to relax, the doctors told us the air would be better if there were fewer people in the room.

Monsieur Voltaire and Baronne Lomont left with the doctors and the rest of Emilie's company to have supper in an apartment across the courtyard. I was preparing to go with them, but Emilie wanted me and Monsieur Saint-Lambert to stay behind.

We spoke with her until she fell asleep, and then we went out into the hall so we could talk without disturbing her. After no more than a few minutes, we heard the most terrifying groans coming from her room. When we reached her bed, her covers were strewn as if she had been thrashing about, but our precious Emilie was completely still, and her eyes were rolled back in her head.

Monsieur Saint-Lambert had the presence of mind to put his hand to her chest to see if she was breathing. God save us all, I cannot describe the feeling in my heart when he said she was no more. He closed our darling's eyes, and we held each other in silence while the chambermaid ran across the courtyard to tell the others.

Within a few minutes we heard the cries of the other guests as they mounted the stairs. Oh, dear monsieur, such a doleful scene I pray I will never witness again! Voltaire flung himself upon her, sobbing that he had lost the better half of himself. When he left the room, he was shaking so badly he fell down the stone stairs, or perhaps he flung himself—it isn't clear—and he is now limping and rather battered about the face. He said terrible things to Saint-Lambert, accusing him of killing Emilie by his carelessness. As for Saint-Lambert, he has locked himself in his quarters and his valet reports the most terrible moans and laments coming from within.

It is left to the women to do what the situation demands. Baronne Lomont and I will shortly begin the sad process of laying out the body. We have sent for permission to raise a floor stone in the new parish church of Saint-Jacques so she may be laid to rest in a place she found so bright and lovely. But since the weather is so hot we must proceed quickly. Please, please, come yourself as soon as you can, and send word if you can ride here in time for the burial. We all need to share our profound loss with you and cover you with tears.

As ever, your devoted,
Julie de Bercy

Lorraine, Palais de Lunéville, 13 September 1749
To Florent-Claude, Marquis du Châtelet-Lomont
Commercy, Lorraine

My Dear Brother-in-Law,

We regret that it was necessary to commit your wife's body to the ground before you had leave to return, but as you said in your last letter, there is no reason to hasten for the dead, and there will be enough time later to do what is required of you. Madame de Bercy and I appreciate the trust you put in us to act in the best interests of the child, since your new position in the duke's service obviously precludes involvement yourself. I regret I had to make it forcefully clear to Madame de Bercy that a woman with child for the first time is scarcely in a position to take responsibility for another infant before the birth of her own. Madame de Bercy is of a nature far more sentimental than practical, and her tearful pleas not to send the child immediately to a convent, as you suggested, have worn me down to the point where I have agreed to bring Stanislas-Adélaïde back to Paris and serve as her guardian for the time being. Please do not come to Lunéville in search of us, for we are departing for Paris tomorrow.

I remain your devoted sister-in-law,
Philippe-Charlotte, Baronne Lomont

Paris, 8 April 1753
To Florent-Claude, Marquis du Châtelet-Lomont
Lorraine, Palais de Lunéville

Dearest Monsieur le Marquis,

I just received your letter in the post. Such wonderful news—oh, please forgive me for seeing someone else's ill health in that way!—that Baronne Lomont no longer feels she can serve as guardian for our beloved Lili. I thank you from the depths of my heart for overruling her decision that Lili be sent to a convent at such a tender age, when I am so willing to raise her myself. What a heartbreak that would have been! I love your darling Lili as much as I do my own Delphine-Anne, and the two girls—still just three years old!—have already shown signs of deep bonds in the few times the baronne has permitted Lili to visit.

In response to Baronne Lomont's concerns that your daughter will be corrupted by visitors to the salon I have recently begun, I promise you I will keep a watchful eye to ensure she is not made irresponsible or irreverent by exposure to modern thinking. I have given my word to the baronne that Lili will visit her regularly, so she can see for herself that the girl is not being introduced to men of poor character and insufficient loyalty to the king.

She claims that Lili will receive better instruction from her in the comportment so critical to making a good marriage, though I have not taken with the best humor her insinuation that I am not capable of this myself. I must admit, and surely you have noticed yourself, that the baronne's comportment is, to put it as kindly as I can, rather difficult to tolerate with good humor, and may not be the best model for Lili's own times. Still, in her own way, I am sure she loves the child and wants to ensure that she is not at a disadvantage in a world that can be most indifferent to the plight of the motherless.

Baronne Lomont and I have very little on which we agree, although our thoughts are united on the issue you raised, as to what

Lili should be told about her mother. As you know, I have the greatest admiration and deepest love for my dear friend, but her path is not one I think it is wise for any young girl to follow. The baroness and I have agreed that it is best that Lili not be told the more—oh, how shall I say it?—salacious details of her mother's life, and that her achievements in science should not overpower the more conventional view of what accomplishments are appealing in a woman. It is good to be bright and articulate, since it improves the quality of men's lives as well as our own, but I agree that a woman should glow and warm her surroundings, rather than blind others with her own light.

Baronne Lomont will also see to the transfer of the capital whose interest pays the stipend you so generously provide the child. She tells me it is more than adequate for Lili's needs at this time. She has made clear that you intend this stipend to serve in lieu of any personal contact with Lili. When she is old enough to ask questions, I will explain that although you do not write or visit, your stipend is the way you express your concern and love. Baronne Lomont tells me she has informed you that a dowry will need to be discussed when the time comes, so that Lili will have the protection that accompanies bringing at least a small measure of her own wealth to a marriage. But of course that can wait for another time. I must prepare Lili's quarters and tell my Delphine she is to have Lili as a sister!

As ever, your devoted,
Julie de Bercy

1

1759

"STOP WINNING all the time!" Delphine tossed her cards in the air in frustration that turned to laughter as they cascaded over Lili's head and fell around her on the bed. The two ten-year-old girls sat cross-legged in muslin nightdresses, curling their bare toes around ripples in the green velvet coverlet. Next to them, a small white dog snorted at the disturbance to his sleep.

Lili picked up the strewn cards and tapped the sides of the pack until they were aligned. "Want to play again? I told you how I do it."

Delphine sighed. "I know. You remember the cards we've already played. Me, it's king, queen, la-la-la."

"Well, you can't win at piquet if you don't know what's already happened."

"All of that remembering is like schoolwork. No more fun than doing sums." Delphine stood up on the bed behind Lili. "Want me to play with your hair? I'll get some combs and put it up just like Madame de Pompadour's." She picked up Lili's brown hair and crushed it in her hands on top of Lili's head. "Just like that," she said, pursing her lips and kissing the air in imitation of King Louis XV's mistress. "Where did you put your brush?"

Lili didn't answer. "They're arguing about something downstairs," she said, cocking her head. "Can you hear them?"

Delphine sniffed as she retrieved the brush from Lili's dressing table. "Who cares? Silly old men." While her back was turned, Lili hopped off the bed and tiptoed out into the upstairs hallway of Hôtel Bercy. The dog jumped down to follow her.

"Stanislas-Adélaïde! Come back here!" she heard Delphine scold. "You're practically naked!" Lili turned and put her finger to her lips. "I'm going to try to listen."

"Well, at least put on your robe! I can see the outline of your bottom under your chemise!" Ignored, Delphine gave a dramatic sigh and, throwing on her dressing gown, came out into the hallway. "It's freezing," she whispered, picking up the tiny bichon frise and holding it to her chest. "Look! Tintin is shivering, even with his fur coat." She nuzzled him. "Aren't you, *mon petit*?"

"Shh!" Lili held a finger to her lips. "They're talking about the Jansenists, I think. Or maybe it's the Jesuits. It's hard to hear." Lili stood by the railing at the top of the staircase and cocked one ear. "I thought I heard someone call Jesuits a plague on France, but that can't be right." She listened again. "Or maybe it was that there's no place for them in France, but that doesn't make much sense either." She looked at Delphine. "They're priests. How could anyone think there's no need for priests?"

"You'll need one soon enough if you catch your death of cold," Delphine said, prancing on her bare toes. "My feet are turning to ice."

The voices downstairs had quieted again to an indistinguishable murmur. Lili suddenly became aware of floorboards so cold they burned her toes and sent goose bumps up her arms and legs. "Race you to bed!" she said with a grin as she dashed past Delphine. The two girls leapt onto the soft pile of bedcovers, and Tintin joined in the jumble of arms and legs, licking their eyes and noses until they squealed.

"Time for your hair," Delphine reminded her. Lili sat up, with Tintin in her lap, and Delphine knelt behind her. Lili closed her brown eyes in contentment as Delphine brushed her hair, but Lili's ears remained focused on the murmuring downstairs. "I'd like to know what they're so passionate about, wouldn't you?"

"Who?"

"The men at Maman's salon."

"Unless it's about me, I don't really care," Delphine said. She sat back on her haunches. "It would be rather nice to be Maman, wouldn't it? So beautiful and kind that everyone comes to her salon because they're secretly in love with her."

She crawled around in front of Lili, shooed the dog away, and laid her head in Lili's lap. "My arm's tired. Tell me a story," she pleaded. "About a beautiful princess. I don't care which one."

"Don't you get tired of those? How about 'Puss and Boots,' or something else for a change?"

Delphine glared at her and said nothing.

"All right," Lili conceded. "If you promise that just one will put you to sleep."

"Promise."

Lili took a deep breath. "Once upon a time . . ."

Corinne, the girls' *femme de chambre,* gave a cursory knock on the door frame before coming in. "I beg your pardon, mam'selles," the young servant said with a quick curtsey. "Madame said I am to make sure you have a good sleep before you return to the abbey tomorrow." She went to the table and extinguished an oil lamp. "Madame says that you may sleep in one bed if you wish."

With a groan of annoyance, Lili wiggled out from under Delphine's head and lay down beside her. When Corinne had arranged the covers over them, she blew out the candles, and shut the door behind her. Lili immediately sat back up in the dark, and Delphine resumed her position on her lap.

"Once upon a time there was a king and queen who had no children for years and years. Finally they had a baby daughter, and they asked seven fairies to be the godmothers. But they forgot about one fairy, who was so old she rarely left her tower."

"An ugly fairy," Delphine murmured. "With one good eye."

"Mmm. When she arrived and saw there was no place for her at the christening banquet, she was angry, and she cursed the baby girl to die of a spindle prick before she could be married . . ." Lili stroked Delphine's forehead. "Sleepy yet?"

"Of course not. You barely started. But skip to the part about the dresses she wore."

"Let's say the princess was called . . ." Lili pretended to be choosing a name before coming up with the same answer she always did. "Princess Delphine." Delphine sighed her approval and wiggled deeper into Lili's lap. "A new dress magically appeared for her every morning, and her petticoats left a trail of sparkles behind her."

"Sparkles?"

"Well, they are magic dresses," Lili said. "Do you like it?"

"Oh yes," Delphine whispered. "Put the sparkles in every time."

"One day the beautiful princess was wandering through the palace and she saw an old woman spinning . . ."

By the time Lili reached the point where Sleeping Beauty was awakened from a hundred-year sleep, Delphine's breathing was shallow, and her head was heavy on Lili's lap. "The prince noticed right away that her gown was hopelessly out of style," Lili continued. "Even his grandmother would not have been seen in public wearing it." If Delphine were awake, they would have added detail after ugly detail to the dress, but her breathing did not change. "So the wolf went to the grandmother's house and tricked the little girl into getting into bed with him. Then he ate her up, and they all lived happily ever after." Lili waited a few seconds before transferring Delphine's head to a pillow and snuggling in next to her.

She heard the voices of two departing guests and the sound of horses' hooves in the street just beyond the courtyard of Hôtel Bercy. What could they care enough to argue about week after week? Certainly not fairy stories, or anything she and Delphine were taught at the convent. Tintin snored softly next to her, and Delphine murmured something in her sleep. Lili yawned and put her arm around her, and let her thoughts drift off into nothing.

* * *

A SPRING THUNDERSTORM had drenched the city overnight. The next morning Corinne held up the backs of Lili's and Delphine's skirts to avoid muddying their hems in the few steps to the carriage, and sent them off before Maman was awake. The sky was clearing, but one gray cloud after another drifted in front of the sun, darkening the coach bearing the two girls down the Rue Saint-Antoine toward the center of Paris.

Wrapped in the gloom that always overcame them on these mornings, neither girl said a word as the carriage made its way between the narrow rows of shops and houses lining the Pont Notre-Dame, and then rattled across the Île de la Cité and the Petit Pont to the far side of the Seine. Though their private room at the Abbaye de Panthémont was furnished at Maman's expense with soft bedcovers and a thick rug on the floor, life at home was as cozy as the thick warm *chocolat* and fresh-baked brioche they had eaten for breakfast that morning. Being at Hôtel Bercy meant not having to get up for prayers and going to sleep only when Maman remembered to send Corinne. It meant being asked what they would like for supper, and having a dog that would beg and roll over for the tiniest scrap smuggled from the dining room.

Delphine sniffled. "I hate Sister Thérèse." After a moment she added, "But not as much as I hate Sister Jeanne-Bertrand." Lili was silent, and Delphine went on. "I can't do anything well enough for them." She pinched her nostrils. " 'Ladies don't get ink on their fingers when they write,' " she said in an imitation of Sister Jeanne-Bertrand so perfect that Lili giggled in spite of her dark mood.

In Rue Saint André-des-Arts, the coach slowed to a stop. Obstructions in the streets were common enough that Delphine took no note. " 'A lady's quality can be seen in the way she signs her name,' " she continued in the same nasal tone. " 'Your handwriting is getting bigger. It must be all the same size, or you must start again.' "

Hearing the voices of a group of children in the narrow, unpaved street, Lili pulled back the curtain and peered out. Her eyes locked on a young man in a threadbare coat, but sporting a new hat in the latest style. He was swinging his walking stick at a group of ragged children, while one of them dangled just out of reach a book-size parcel tied with string.

"Give it back!" he shouted, as another boy with a dirty face and unkempt hair made a grab for the man's coat pocket. Two women in shabby dresses and soiled white caps watched the commotion from the doorway of a bakery, with no more interest than if they were watching birds peck for crumbs. Another passerby, older and slightly better dressed, grabbed one of the children and shoved him to the ground.

"Street scum!" he hissed, kicking the boy over and over again. "Get out of here before I knock your rotten little teeth out!" Neither woman made any move to intervene, but one of them shook a fist. "Leave him alone!" she said. "Can't you see he's got nothing in this world, and you so rich and all?"

The boy holding the parcel grinned and cocked his head as he danced backward down the street, and the others who had escaped the man's wrath followed slowly enough to convey they were not frightened in the least by anyone or anything. Lili's carriage started forward with a lurch, just as another coach passed in the other direction and sprayed thick, black mud onto the window where her face was pressed. Startled, Lili sat back, but she immediately leaned forward again to look out through the one spot that was not covered with slime. Splattered black from head to toe, including the new hat, the two men waved their fists in the air, cursing the world.

Lili giggled for a moment, before pressing her gloved fingers to her mouth so Delphine wouldn't notice. She was sure to turn the men's misfortune into something to joke about, and what happened really wasn't funny. The carriage had barely moved before stopping again, and Lili craned her neck to keep watching. The boy had gotten up and was now walking in their direction, showing no signs at all that he had just been kicked repeatedly in the ribs. He had his hands in his pockets and under his muddy cap he was grinning and bobbing his head as if he might be humming a tune.

He stopped for a moment to make sure the older man wasn't watching and then pulled a gold watch from his pocket. As he brushed a spot of mud from its surface, he looked up and saw Lili watching him from the carriage. With a smirk, he swung it by the fob for a moment just to make sure she saw. Then he stuck out his tongue and ran down an alley before the man had a chance to notice his pocket had been picked.

ALONG THE RUE de Grenelle, the tight squeeze of buildings and narrow streets gave way to more stately buildings and patches of tidy gardens as the street left the city and became a country road connecting the farming village of Grenelle with Paris. Just before the grounds of Les Invalides, the coach pulled up at the Abbaye de Panthémont. A porter and a young novice emerged from the imposing stone building, and the girls and their belongings were whisked inside.

Despite the chill lingering in the walls, the fire was unlit, as it was May. Lili unwrapped the copy of Madame d'Aulnoy's fairy tales she had brought from home. She opened it to the place she had left off, marked by a ribbon between the pages. "I wish I could stay here and read," she said, looking at the engraving of the sad and ragged princess Finette Cendron.

Delphine sighed as she unlaced her boots. Shivering in the musty cold, they changed out of their traveling clothes and into the simple dresses that were the uniform of the convent, before going out into the hallway.

"Time to say hello to Mother-Ugly," Delphine whispered softly enough not to be overheard. At one point in her life, Abbess Marie-Catherine had lost an eye, and though the embroidered black velvet patch she wore was tasteful, a one-eyed nun was enough to warrant horror, if not abject fear.

"Do you think she used to be a pirate?" Delphine had asked when they were eight and saw her for the first time.

"I'm quite sure not," Lili had said. "Maybe she was born that way. Maybe she had a tiny eye patch even then. A pretty white one to match her christening bonnet."

Delphine's eyes were huge. "Do you really think so?"

"Maybe a raven pecked her eye out," Lili went on. "You know, like the birds who ate Prometheus's liver."

"Over and over again," Delphine shuddered. She thought for a moment. "Do you think perhaps she was supposed to be born a Cyclops and some goddess had mercy on her and softened the curse?"

"Or maybe an evil wanderer in the streets of the Faubourg Saint-Germain scooped it out with a spoon."

Lili knew she had gone too far when she saw Delphine's face. "Things like that can't happen to us, can they?" Delphine had whimpered.

Lili rushed to reassure her that she just liked to make things up, and Delphine forced her to promise never to invent anything that involved people who might actually live in Paris.

A few minutes later, the two made the short visit required of returning girls, and before being turned away by a servant, they caught a glimpse of the abbess without her patch. Over the hollow cavity, her lids had been sewn together, and the scars formed what looked like stubby white eyelashes. The girls backed away in shock and ran to their room, where Delphine vomited into a washbasin and Lili retched in sympathetic dry heaves until her stomach was sore.

Still, Lili told Delphine later, when she had a chance to think about it some more, it wasn't fair to blame the abbess, because it was hard to imagine how losing an eye was her fault.

"I know," Delphine said, "but still, there should be something she can do not to bother people so much."

"Perhaps she could wear a hood that covered her whole face, with one hole for her good eye," Lili suggested. She meant it as a joke, but Delphine took all solutions seriously, including wearing shimmering veils like a harem girl, until Lili pointed out how unlikely that would be for a nun.

Finally Delphine dismissed the entire subject. "All I know is I would never let that happen to me," she said, touching each of her eyes tenderly. "I'd die first, wouldn't you?"

Wondering for a moment if losing an eye might give someone a secret, compensatory magic, Lili didn't respond. *Maybe that's the real reason the abbess is so frightening*, she thought. *She has a power we don't even know about.* "I think I'd have to wait and see," she finally replied. "It's probably a good idea to wait to see how desperate you really are."

THE AFTERNOON OF their return to the abbey, Lili and Delphine went with a few other girls to a wood-paneled study with large windows giving out onto a lawn bordered with tidy flowers and neatly clipped hedges. Sister Thérèse, their catechism nun, was leafing through one of the leather-bound books in an ornately carved bookcase.

"Good afternoon, madame," each girl said before taking her place on one of the couches arranged around a fireplace.

"*Bien*," the middle-aged nun said, coming over to her chair without sitting down. "Shall we pray?" The girls all stood up and crossed themselves, and Lili heard Delphine suppress a burp from their just-completed midday meal. "*In nomine Patris, et Filii, et Spiritus Sancti, Amen*," they murmured before droning an Ave Maria and a Pater Noster. Sister Thérèse gestured to them to sit down, and after she was settled in an armchair facing them, she opened her book.

"Today is the feast day of Saint Solange," she said, looking over the top of her spectacles at the girls. "Would anyone like to tell us who this blessed martyr was?"

Delphine straightened her back so quickly that Lili thought she might fly off the chair. "She was a shepherdess on the estate of the Comte of Poitiers, who had an evil son," Delphine blurted out, and though her feet were hidden under her skirt, she jiggled them so intensely that Lili felt the motion against her own thigh.

"Young ladies, wait to be called upon," the nun said. "And don't speak so quickly. It isn't becoming to sound so excited."

"*Oui*, Sister Thérèse," Delphine said, looking down at her lap. "Saint Solange took a vow of chastity because she was so devoted to God and when the count's horrid son Bernard tried to— tried to—"

"Tried to force himself on her," the nun prompted.

"*Oui*, Sister Thérèse. When he tried to do that, she resisted him with all her might, so he killed her."

Sister Thérèse frowned. "Does someone else feel they can tell the story with the dignity it warrants?"

Lili felt Delphine sit back in surprise, and knew that back in their room she would be in tears. "What did I do wrong?" she would ask. "Didn't I know the story? Didn't I care enough about that stupid saint?"

"Mademoiselle de Praslin," the nun said, "would you be so kind as to say what happened, and do so with the proper demeanor for a lady?"

Delphine pushed her hand down in the space between her skirt and Lili's. Lili's hand followed, and squeezing their interlaced fingers, they stared at the floor while Anne-Mathilde de Praslin spoke. Anne-Mathilde was the daughter of the Duc de Praslin, one of the richest and most powerful men in France. At twelve, she was two years older than Lili and Delphine, and her body was beginning to take on the curves of a woman. Her hair was pale gold and her skin, a radiant ivory, was so lacking in flaws it seemed to be made of something other than flesh. "A perfect beauty," Lili had overheard one of the nuns remarking. "A bride worthy of a great noble of France." If Delphine hated Sister Thérèse, she truly loathed Anne-Mathilde—a sentiment she could count on Lili to embellish in the darkness of their room.

"Bernard tried a number of times to grab Solange and force her to the ground," Anne-Mathilde said in a deliberately musical voice, casting a gloating look at Delphine that only Lili saw. "But Solange prayed to the Blessed Virgin, who gave her the strength to fight him off. He was angry, not just because he couldn't have her, but because she had embarrassed him in front of his friends."

Anne-Mathilde's best friend, Joséphine de Maurepas, nodded. "If I may add a detail," she said in a voice so simpering, it was all Lili could do not to grab the girl's hair and twist it until she squealed. Joséphine was also twelve, like Anne-Mathilde, but so scrawny it was hard to imagine she would ever look like anything but a little girl. The drab ash-brown of Joséphine's hair and the way she scurried around in thrall of her best friend made Lili think of the little mice she'd watched the scullery maids shoo away with a broom at home.

"I'd like to remind everyone that Bernard fell off his horse once trying to reach down and pull Solange onto it," Joséphine was saying. "To fall off a horse for a peasant girl . . . ?" Her voice curled up, as if she were asking whether anyone in the room really needed her to explain the disgrace.

Sister Thérèse gave them each a nod of approval. "And now, Stanislas-Adélaïde," she said, her eyes narrowing, "will you finish the story for us?"

I should have known Sister Thérèse would do this, Lili thought. Delphine had been ridiculed, and now Lili had to retell the part of the story Delphine relished most. Lili withdrew her hand and brushed her ear, the secret signal with which she and Delphine warned each other to keep a straight face regardless of what was said next.

"I can certainly do that, Sister Thérèse," Lili said, copying Anne-Mathilde and Joséphine's unctuous tone. "Because at home Mademoiselle de Bercy and I often discuss the important message about piety the story contains for girls our age." *A lie is a small sin*, she thought, *especially for Delphine*. "However, I find it particularly edifying to hear Delphine tell it, and I believe the others have not had that opportunity. May I ask if she might be permitted to finish the story herself?"

Lili heard the rustling of Anne-Mathilde's and Joséphine's

dresses and knew without looking that their faces were shining with anticipation of something new to disparage. Sister Thérèse stared at Lili for a moment before she spoke. "If Mademoiselle feels she can control her urge to tell it so breathlessly?" Her eyebrows arched as she turned to Delphine.

"Bernard beheaded her," Delphine said. "But even with her head on the ground, she was able to invoke the name of God three times." Though Delphine may have sounded demure and ladylike, Lili recognized the discouragement in her tone. At home, away from the nuns' disapproval, Delphine would have stood up and tapped her shoulders and neck with her hands, as if surprised to realize that her head was no longer there. "*Mon Dieu,*" she would have said in a loud voice, before repeating it more plaintively as she crumpled to the floor. "*Mon Dieu,*" she would have whispered a third time, tapping the floor like a blind person until she found her head and picked it up.

"Then Solange walked into the town," Lili heard Delphine say. "It wasn't until she reached the church that she fell to the ground and died."

"May God's holy name be praised," Sister Thérèse murmured, and everyone made the sign of the cross.

"Did I do better?" Delphine asked, her voice rising in hope of at least faint praise.

"It was an improvement," the nun said. "But it isn't seemly for a young lady to beg for approval." Anne-Mathilde and Joséphine stifled a giggle behind their hands.

"I understand," Delphine said. Lili could hear the tremor in Delphine's voice. "I want nothing more than to improve myself," Delphine added. Lili looked to see if she was touching her ear, but she wasn't.

"And with God's grace, you will succeed, my child," Sister Thérèse said. "With God's grace, and with faith, anything is possible." She crossed herself. "After all, look at our blessed Saint Solange."

"*Oui,* Sister Thérèse." Out of the corner of her eye, Lili saw Delphine cross herself. She rushed to do the same, but so quickly that she did it again, just to make sure it counted.

DELPHINE'S TEARS GAVE way to exhausted sniffles and then to light snoring in their room that night. The candle was still lit, and Lili picked up her book of fairy tales to read until her mind was quiet enough for sleep.

"Once upon a time there was a king and queen who ruled so badly they lost their kingdom, and they and their three daughters were reduced to day labor." The story of Finette Cendron was one of Lili's favorites, but tonight none of the stories in the book was likely to amuse her.

She went to the desk and took out a sheet of paper already nearly full of penmanship exercises. *I could try writing a story myself,* she thought. She touched the tip of a quill in the inkwell on the desk. Then, squinting to focus in the dim light, she began.

"Once upon a time . . ."

Once upon a time what? She thought for a moment, and suddenly it came to her.

"Once upon a time, there was a girl living in a dreary village who wanted nothing more than to travel to the stars. Her name was . . ."

Lili thought for a moment. She could call her Delphine and put some dresses in the story, but she didn't want to do that. She scratched out the last three words and dipped her quill again.

"Meadowlark had a laugh like a songbird, so everybody called her Meadowlark. Every night Meadowlark would sneak outside and hope with all her might that her wish could come true. And then, to her surprise, one night a horse made of starlight appeared in front of her. 'Are you the girl named Meadowlark?' the horse asked. When she said yes, the horse snorted and reared up. 'My name is Comète,' it said. 'Climb on my back.' Before she knew it, Comète had galloped

off with her into the night sky, leaving behind a trail of stars wherever its hooves touched."

Lili's eyes ached in the flickering candlelight. She would have to
stop. Dipping her pen one more time, she wrote in big letters at the
top of the page, "Meadowlark, by S.-A. du Châtelet."

Emilie

1716

"GABRIELLE-EMILIE!"

Emilie de Breteuil stopped at the entrance to the dining room, turning her eyes in the direction of her mother's angry voice. What had she done wrong? Most likely a loose strand of hair. Emilie reached up to tighten the pins on a dark lock drooping at her neck, but it would be too late to avoid a tongue-lashing tomorrow. "I'm sorry, madame. I was reading and I neglected to prepare myself for dinner."

Gabrielle-Anne Froullay du Châtelet would not be so ungracious as to frown in the presence of guests at table, but her ten-year-old daughter felt her hard stare piercing through the candlelight. A servant placed a small piece of confit and several bits of pickled vegetable on Emilie's plate. The others were finishing their first course, and the guest had resumed his conversation with Emilie's father, Louis-Nicholas. "Space is so vast," Bernard de Fontenelle was saying, "that the white band you see across the sky is actually millions upon millions of stars, some of them as big as our sun." He turned to Emilie with a patronizing lift of his eyebrows. "Did you know that?"

Emilie nodded. "It's in a book Father and I are reading." She put down her fork. "Do you think it's really possible that thousands of stars have planets orbiting around them? If that's so with our sun, wouldn't natural law require that it also be the case anywhere similar conditions exist in the universe?" Her hand brushed against the fork poised on her plate and it clattered onto the table, depositing a small brown morsel she absentmindedly put back onto her plate with her fingers. Emilie cast a sidelong glance at her mother and saw, to her dismay, that she had noticed.

A smile played at the edge of Fontenelle's mouth. His friend Louis-Nicholas had told him Emilie was a very bright girl who acquired knowledge as easily as iron shavings flew toward a magnet. But Louis-Nicholas's young daughter had obviously done more than pack facts in her head. She was asking questions—and precisely the right ones.

"Yes, I'm sure that is the case," he went on. "Monsieur Newton has made a convincing argument for his law of attraction, and I think his work shows there is no end to what we might know if we set our minds to study as devotedly as he did. I, for one, believe we are not far off from the day when we will be able to determine mathematically what distant planets are composed of, and even how much they weigh."

Gabrielle-Anne rang for the dishes to be cleared for the second course. "My daughter's mind could be better used pondering other matters," she said. "I really must insist that the subject be changed."

Emilie's face brightened. Surely another of her favorite subjects would be different enough. "Do you think, Monsieur Fontenelle, that it is possible God sprinkled creations all over the universe?"

This conversation had gone in the most horrifying and sordid of directions. Gabrielle-Anne glared at her husband. If he hadn't insisted otherwise because he enjoyed having Emilie to talk to, they would long ago have sent her to a convent to get such foolishness out of her head. What future husband would put up with this? Just look at the girl and Monsieur Fontenelle, acting as if no one else were at the table! This wasn't precociousness; it was impertinence, and it would have to stop.

2

THE ONLY good thing about the abbey, Lili thought, was that it protected her from Baronne Lomont. Whenever Lili was at Hôtel Bercy for more than a few days, a sedan chair inevitably arrived to take her to Île Saint-Louis, for a visit at Hôtel Lomont. One fall morning shortly after Lili's eleventh birthday, she presented herself at the baroness's town house to make her way through the thicket of expectations attached to a simple breakfast.

"Tell me, Stanislas-Adélaïde, what did you study in catechism this week?" Seated across from Lili, Baronne Lomont set her bony chin slightly forward as if it might enable her to snap heretical thoughts out of the air before they reached the ear of God.

The baroness broke off a small piece of bread and placed it in her mouth with the deliberate manner of someone setting an example. Bread, she often reminded Lili, should never be cut at the table, but broken off just so. Only stale bread required a knife, and one should never be served anything but the freshest loaves from a host. Above all, appearing hungry by tearing off a bite with one's teeth was the mark of a peasant.

"Works of perfect Christian virtue spring from love, and have no other objective than to arrive at love," Lili recited, putting in her mouth a piece of bread so small it dissolved without requiring her to swallow. *It's a good thing Corinne made sure I had breakfast at home*, Lili thought, *since I won't get a single real mouthful until I'm back for dinner.*

Baronne Lomont leaned forward from the hips with the rigidity imposed by a tightly laced corset. Lili almost certainly was exposed to guests in a shocking state of disarray when she visited Julie de Bercy, and that was all the more reason the baroness herself needed to set an example. She had told Lili as much, pointing out with great frequency how exhausting it was for her, ailing with nearly everything that could afflict a woman in her sixties, to fulfill her duty not just to Lili, but to France itself.

And, of course, to God. "What, my dear child, do you take that to mean?" the baroness asked, putting the proper upward inflection on the last word, to convey that she expected the pleasant reply that was the mark of good conversation.

"Sister Thérèse says it means that we must show our disapproval of sinners, as a way of urging them back to the church," Lili said. "Since that is the only way to salvation, she says we help save the souls of those we love when we reject their bad ideas and behavior, even if they don't appreciate our efforts."

"And what is your response to that?"

"I find it hard to argue against that logic," Lili said, shrugging her shoulders.

"My dear girl, finding something to argue with in anything is most unattractive." The baroness rang a small bell, and the servant appeared immediately. "You may bring us our eggs," she said, before turning back to Lili. "A young lady is not to follow personal logic, but to accept what the church teaches, and learn it well. A proper girl is always thinking of the impression she is making. You may not be aware of it, but good families are already watching girls your age to see who might make a suitable match for their sons in a few years time."

"*Oui*, madame. I only meant that I had arrived at the same conclusion as Sister Thérèse," Lili lied. "I am sorry I phrased myself so poorly."

"Phrasing is an essential part of gracious communication," Baronne Lomont went on. "You must ask yourself whom your words may offend, and take pains not to do so. Women considered charming rarely reveal their thoughts. That is because their real pleasure comes from making the men with whom they are conversing sound intelligent even when they are not. You will be most praised for your conversation when you let others speak and do not force attention on yourself." Baronne Lomont removed the top of a soft-boiled egg with a single, almost noiseless flick of her knife. "Do you see how just one tap should suffice?"

Lili banged the egg harder than necessary, and the top broke off in a jagged tear, splattering tiny beads of yolk on her hand. A grimace flashed across the baroness's usually expressionless face. Pursing her lips, Lili dabbed at her fingers with her napkin in a show of what she hoped was exquisite delicacy.

I'm being impossible again, Lili thought with a mixture of pride and chagrin. *Maybe she'll give up on me.* She held her napkin to her lips so she could smile without being noticed. *Wouldn't that be wonderful?*

"WAS YOUR VISIT with the baroness pleasant?" Julie de Bercy asked that afternoon at dinner.

Delphine snickered.

"I hate going there," Lili said with a ferocious shake of her head.

"Ahhh." Julie's ample bosom rose and fell over her loosely laced dress as she sighed. "It's best to reserve hatred for things that are worse than merely unpleasant. And it does appear you survived." Her voice was so sweet that the resolve with which Lili was holding in her feelings was broken, and she reached for her napkin to capture a sudden flood of tears.

"Not your napkin, *ma chérie*," Julie said, pulling a lavender-scented lace handkerchief from her bodice and handing it to her. "It would make the baroness truly furious!"

"The more empty-headed I am, the more she likes me," Lili said with a loud sniff. "She's just awful, Maman!"

"Maybe you need stupid lessons!" Delphine broke in. "Excuse me, Monsieur Book Seller, but do you have anything on how to be completely addle-brained? Mademoiselle needs your help!"

Julie laughed with them, but her face quickly turned grave. "This kind of talk is fine when it's just the three of us, but you cannot afford to get out of practice with your manners."

"We know, Maman," Lili said. "It's just that being home with you is the only time we have any fun."

Julie's face sobered, and she reached over to stroke Lili's hand. "I know it's hard at the convent, and you have Baronne Lomont on top of that, but things will get better in time. Someday you'll be grown women, with husbands who know better than to interfere with what you enjoy most. At least that's my hope."

Julie rarely spoke of her husband, Alphonse de Bercy, an officer in King Louis's army, who died when typhoid swept through his regiment shortly after Delphine was born, but whenever there was any talk of husbands, the normal cheer of Hôtel Bercy vanished.

They stared at the crumbs on their plates, not knowing what to say. Delphine broke the silence. "Would you like me to play for you, Maman?"

Pushing back their chairs, they went into the music room. Delicate green floral wainscoting complimented the shimmering silk upholstery on the chairs; and stucco reliefs of violins on the cheery, lemon-yellow wall panels made the music room everyone's favorite place in the house. Delphine took her place at a small piano and Maman sat at a small stool in front of a gilded harp.

Julie's voice was beautiful, as supple and soft as firelight, and some nights the three of them would sing and play until they were all too tired to go on. Tonight, however, after several songs, Delphine put her fingers heavily on the keys. The harsh dissonance smothered the room. "I'm sad that I don't have a papa," Delphine said. "I haven't been able to think about anything else."

A papa, Lili thought. *I'm not sure who's better off—Delphine with a father who's dead, or I with one who's never cared enough to visit.* "I know," Julie said. "I could tell." She looked at Lili. "And I think I know what's on your mind, too. But I've decided what would cheer us all up. How about letting us know what Meadowlark is doing?"

"Oh, yes!" Delphine's melancholy evaporated. "I saw you writing pages and pages, and I have to know how Meadowlark escaped from the Spider King!"

Maman brushed Lili's hair out of her eyes and kissed her forehead. "Would you, *ma chérie?*"

Lili jumped up, glad that some things, like snuggling over Meadowlark with Delphine and Maman, weren't as difficult as eggs with Baronne Lomont, or as painful as reminders of how little her father cared.

1761

THE PLACE ROYALE, home to Hôtel Bercy, was one of the few places in Paris fit for a stroll. Even the gardens of the Tuileries were thick with the stench of garbage, and haunted by beggars and thieves. On dry and pleasant afternoons, those who lived behind the harmonious, arcaded mansions ringing the four sides of the Place Royale could leave behind the sedan chairs they used for calling on their neighbors elsewhere in the city, and cross the quiet garden on foot.

One bright winter day, Lili laced her arm through Maman's elbow as they walked back from the home of one of Julie's friends. Delphine had woken up that morning with a sore throat, and she was spending the day in bed, with Tintin for company. Neither Lili nor Maman felt any urge to hurry back indoors, so they made every pretext to stop—to find the whereabouts of a bird chirping from a hidden perch in a chestnut tree, and to inquire about the health of a passerby's ailing mother.

"Watch yourself, you swine!" The voice carried from the street to where Lili and Julie were standing near the statue of Louis XIV at the center of the square. Julie clamped Lili's arm against her side to keep her close, as they turned in the direction of the angry shouts. Beyond the trees Lili could see a man in the simple coat and hat of a merchant, who was struggling to stay on his feet while two others in aristocratic dress pounded him on his shoulders and back with their walking sticks.

"How dare you bother Madame de Martigny?" one asked, landing a blow that knocked the man to his knees.

"I only came to collect a debt," the man cried out. "My family is starving, and she owes me more than three hundred louis for the dresses I've made her!"

One of them grabbed him by the collar and pulled him to a stand. "You should be glad we don't have you thrown in the Bastille! Get out of here, and don't come back!" Then he gave the tailor a shove so forceful it knocked him to his hands and knees, but the tailor managed to stumble down the street to one of the alleys between the mansions and was soon gone from view.

Lili's eyes followed the two men as they continued to amble down Rue de l'Écharpe out of the Place Royale, as if such a beating was all in the course of an afternoon. "Maman, what was that about?"

Julie turned away from the scene and began walking toward Hôtel Bercy, still gripping Lili's elbow in her own. "It's terrible, really," Julie said. "People run up huge bills at the shops of people like that man, not caring if they pay them what they owe." She sniffed. "I wouldn't be surprised if Madame de Martigny is back in his shop next week expecting him to take a new order from her."

"Why would he do that?"

"He may think keeping her as a client improves his chances of getting paid in the end," Julie said. "Madame de Martigny may be short of funds just now—perhaps gambling debts, perhaps a loan to someone who hasn't paid her back, perhaps the loss of some other income—it could be any number of things. And she probably plans to make good on her debt, although many women I know would be quite tempted to order new dresses from someone else rather than pay what they owe for ones they've already worn."

The subject caused Julie to pick up the pace, and they were soon at the far end of the square from where the altercation had occurred. "People of noble rank usually behave honorably among ourselves when it comes to debts," she said, turning to walk along the arcaded street toward home. "But those who do the actual work in our lives . . ." She nodded with her chin toward the corner where the beating had taken place. "You saw for yourself what some people think of them."

"That's not right." Lili envisioned the tattered storefronts and dark alleyways she passed on the way to the abbey. Perhaps that man lived in one of them. Perhaps his children were ragged and thin, as they all seemed to be in the most frightening parts of Paris. "He said his children were starving." Her voice trembled. "He's going home with nothing to feed them."

"It could be worse," Julie said, pausing in front of Hôtel Bercy. "They could have insisted on throwing him in prison for his affront to French nobility. His family would truly suffer then." She gestured toward the door. "These are hard truths," she said, "and they're best discussed inside."

ONCE IN THE parlor after checking on Delphine, Maman sent for tea and a few bites of cake to cheer Lili up, but Lili sat stonefaced, eating nothing. "At the convent they tell us that works of Christian virtue spring from love and have no other objective than to arrive at love," she said. "Were those men Christians, Maman?"

Maybe they're Musulmans, or Jews. Though Lili had never laid eyes on either, as far as she knew, she had heard from the nuns about their devious ways and their vile intentions toward any good Christian woman they encountered.

"Of course they're Christians. At least if by that you mean that they go to mass often enough not to risk the disapproval of their wives, and go to confession whenever something they've done is about to become unpleasant."

"But don't they know that Christians are supposed to love their neighbors?"

"I'm afraid some people's neighborhoods are very small."

Lili thought for a moment. "Baronne Lomont tells me that everything the church teaches comes directly from God," she went on, "and that I must accept his will if I'm to be a good wife and mother some day."

"I'm sure she did. And what do you think?"

Lili scowled. "The baroness told me I should think less. Or argue less at least, and keep my thoughts to myself. She said no one will want to marry me if I demand attention for my ideas all the time."

Julie's cheeks flushed. "Well," she said, "I wouldn't suggest saying this to Baronne Lomont, but I find your ideas, and Delphine's, the most beautiful things about you. And if you ever decide not to have any more thoughts, I think you might as well go live with the baroness. I'm sure it would be pleasant having her full approval." She smiled at Lili's consternation. "I was trying to be funny," she said. "Of course, you're staying right here, thoughts and all."

Julie stood up. "I have a suggestion. Why don't you come down this evening to my salon? Delphine can come too if she's feeling well enough. I think you may understand things a little better if you have a chance to discuss them with my guests. There's one in particular I'd like you to meet before he leaves Paris."

One of the kitchen servants had appeared in the door and stood waiting for Julie's attention. "I have to see about supper now," Maman said, "and you need to put on a pretty dress and have Corinne arrange your hair." As Julie walked toward the servant, she glanced back over her shoulder at Lili. "And don't forget to bring your mind."

Emilie

1721

S HE DID what?" Gabrielle-Anne Breteuil whirled around to face her husband.

"Emilie spent half what she won playing trictrac on books," Louis-Nicholas repeated. "But at least they were reputable—science and math mostly."

"I don't care how reputable they were. Surely you don't think the host will be amused that she can't play next time because she has no money left to wager."

"I think fifteen-year-old girls are likely to be forgiven most anything," Louis-Nicholas said.

His wife scowled. "But her parents are not. We're being ridiculed even as we speak! We don't provide our daughter with sufficient money and she must gamble to have the funds for what she wishes? We have a disobedient child who does what she pleases whenever we're not watching? How can you bear to think people are saying those things?"

Gabrielle-Anne sat at the dressing table in her bedchamber, the easiest way to turn her back on her husband, and began running a brush through her hair so violently its silver frame banged against her scalp. "Wagers are to avoid being bored to death by the game, not because one cares about the money. How could our daughter not know that?"

Louis-Nicholas sighed in defeat. "I'll replace what she spent, and I'll go with her next time to make sure she loses all of it." He thought for a moment. "She told me she wasn't trying to be greedy, but that she couldn't manage to lose. She said she understood it was unseemly to appear excited about money."

"I'm not sure Emilie understands anything of importance at all, since you've filled her head with such nonsense."

Such criticism had been hurled at Louis-Nicholas so often that he accepted it without comment. "I've tried to explain to her that her intelligence was charming in a girl, but not in a young lady. I've told her more than once that no man of quality will choose to marry someone whose head is buried in a book all day. Every time, she insists she'd rather have the book than the man." He thought for a moment. "I was wrong to indulge her. I admit it. And I have come to agree with you that we should send her to be presented at court, and have her remain long enough at Versailles to improve her manners."

Finally hearing something that pleased her, Gabrielle-Anne turned toward her husband. "And we must make it clear that while she is there, she must attract at least one suitable offer of marriage." She sniffed. "Books, indeed!"

3

"YOU WANT to know how to arrive at love? Real love? Not just self-serving charity or cheap sentiment?" Jean-Jacques Rousseau's face flushed a deep red and tiny flecks of spittle flew from his mouth as he spoke with Lili in a quiet corner at the salon. "A divine light is inside everyone, and only those who don't give in to pretention and falsity can experience the love at the heart of God's creation."

Though she had just turned twelve, and his intensity would have frightened people much older, Lili leaned in closer to meet his gaze. "But how can I not give in to falsity if I don't know what's true?"

"The mind is easily deceived," he said, tapping the side of his head with one finger. "Start by suspecting anything your heart doesn't want to believe. And if you are seeking truth, you will find it in the natural order of things, not in your catechism."

How can he say something so dangerous? And interesting. "Yes, that may be," Lili said, looking down for a moment to think before turning her solemn brown eyes back toward him. "But I don't really know for myself if what Newton says about gravitation is true, any more than I know for myself if God rested on the seventh day. We can be wrong about the natural order of things, too, can't we?"

Rousseau smiled as he tucked his loose gray hair behind his ears. "You are young my dear. Children recognize truth and they will follow it naturally, even if they don't fully understand. Frightening and bullying are necessary only to force false ideas onto them."

The loose end of an upholstery nail stabbed one of her fingers, and only then did Lili realize she had been gripping the frame of the chair. She let go and clasped her hands together in her lap. "Many of the things they teach at the convent don't make sense to me, but they say people who don't believe them are damned. Aren't you afraid of that?"

Rousseau shook his head. "Truth dictates that there can be no inconsistency between natural law and religion. If they clash, it's because one of them is wrong."

"But the church says it is the one true faith, and straying from its teachings imperils one's soul." *A golden door slamming shut at the entrance to heaven,* Lili thought. *Tumbling into the flames of hell, with wild-eyed demons clutching at his legs. Doesn't he care about such things?*

"The one true faith!" Rousseau hissed with scorn. "Any religion is as good as another as long as it honors God as the creator. That it must do, because anything else denies the great truth at the core of everything, and nothing but falsehood can come from that. One faith is as good as another if it calls 'moral' what accords with natural law, and respects the dignity and freedom of everyone."

He chopped the air with his hand to emphasize his point. "None of this false piety and priggishness and none of this 'Thank you, Lord, for making me better than other people.' That is the biggest waste of your spirit I can imagine."

"So Musulmans and Jews aren't despised by God?"

"What do you think?" Rousseau leaned toward her and his voice calmed almost to a whisper.

"I don't know any," Lili said.

"But if you did?"

"I think I would try to see them as people first." An image of the man being abused by the two noblemen in the square came into her mind, but before Rousseau could answer, Julie came up beside them and he got up from his chair to acknowledge her.

"Monsieur Rousseau," Julie said in a voice that was at once firm and teasing. "I am certain you have been telling Lili wonderful things about listening to her own heart, and I wanted her to hear you say them. But I hope you are also reminding her of the power others have over young lives, and that you are cautioning that whenever she listens to her own heart, she should think twice before speaking her mind, since most people are more receptive to something other than the natural and unencumbered truth." She looked at the gray-haired man. "Am I not correct?"

"Sadly so," he said, nodding to Lili with a sly smile. "And you are now duly cautioned." He took in a quick breath. "I almost forgot that I brought madame a gift." He went off for a moment and returned with a book that he handed to Julie. "It's just been published."

"*Émile*," Julie said, tracing the embossed letters on the leather cover.

"It's about the proper way to raise children." He nodded in Lili's direction. "I think you will find in it much of what I have said to mademoiselle this evening."

"I am truly touched," Julie said, letting out a breath that emphasized the softness of not just her bosom, but the heart underneath. "Not many people are honored to receive a new work straight from the hand of one of France's great men of letters."

She hooked her arm around Lili's elbow. "But now I really must get Lili off to bed. Despite your fears that such education is ruinous"—she gave him a teasing smile—"she is returning to the Abbaye de Panthémont tomorrow."

Lili made a sour face at the mention of the convent. "I thought for a moment we had reasoned the abbey out of existence," she said, "but I'll try to think about what you've told me while I'm there." She gave Rousseau a small, quick curtsey, and after wishing him a pleasant evening and giving Maman a kiss on the cheek, she bolted up the stairs to see if Delphine was still awake.

LILI'S MIND WAS in turmoil the following morning as she jostled in the carriage heading to the Abbaye de Panthémont. She'd liked what

Monsieur Rousseau said at first. It was encouraging to think that her own ideas could be right even if the church said otherwise, but Rousseau had truly gone too far. The cathedral of Notre-Dame wasn't just a building. It was God's house, and the Abbaye de Panthémont was too. They weren't built to enshrine false ideas. The sheer size of them ought to prove that. They had to honor something right and true. They simply had to. And what about all those martyrs' gruesome deaths—it wouldn't be fair at all if the religion they died for wasn't the true one.

Annoyance flickered across Lili's face. Maman had promised she could bring her questions to the salon whenever she wished, and now, when just one visit had given her hundreds more things to ask about, she was on her way back to the abbey instead. And worse, Delphine wasn't there to grumble with her about it. Delphine's sore throat had developed into chills and a fever, and she was so listless that Maman allowed her to stay home a few more days. To avoid dealing with Baronne Lomont, who kept a close eye on Lili's whereabouts, Maman had sent Lili back alone.

She glanced down. She had gotten no further that the first page of *Émile*, which she had taken from the table where Maman had left it. "Everything is good as it leaves the hands of the Author of all; everything degenerates when it falls into the hands of man," he had written. *Everything?* A vision of Maman singing at the harp while Delphine played the piano came to mind, and Lili shook her head. Monsieur Rousseau was obviously wrong about a great number of things.

The carriage slowed to a stop, and a moment later the footman opened the door. "Horse came up lame," he said. "I'm going to bring another from the abbey. It's not far. Mademoiselle would prefer to stay in the carriage?"

The golden light beckoning through the open door on a beautiful fall morning made her put the book down. "I'd like to wait outside," she told him.

Descending from the carriage, she stood in front of the walls of a large building she did not recognize. "Where am I?"

"We had to come another way," the driver answered. "Some disturbance near Saint Benoit, so I took Rue de l'Université instead."

Lili walked around to the other side of the carriage. Small, open fields with low fences and tiny buildings lay in front of her, extending as far as she could see in the direction of the Seine. *This is Paris?* she wondered, making a full circle that revealed nothing but a jagged line of gray rooftops in every direction.

Along the usual route, walls and buildings cast permanent shadows, and rattling carriages and boisterous voices made a constant din all the way to the abbey gate. Here, the air was dreamlike in its quiet. A harvest bonfire on the far side of the field permeated the air with a scent that seemed more holy to Lili than the incense at mass. The horse nickered and bobbed its head, as if it were blessing her thought.

Perhaps I've made a wish without knowing it. If life were a fairy tale, Lili thought, perhaps a magic spell caused the horse to come up lame, so that she didn't ride by without noticing that an enchanted field had suddenly appeared on the way to the abbey. But reality seemed magical enough, producing this small patch of the natural world just when Rousseau had made her want to think in new ways about exactly such things. *It's like the whole city is my mind,* Lili thought. *It's all been built by others, except this one spot where I can try right now to see things for myself.*

She knew she wasn't in a fairy tale, but she was going to make a wish anyway. "I wish to understand what Monsieur Rousseau means by the inner light," she said, softly enough so the driver could not overhear. She shut her eyes. Larks warbled. Rooks squawked in a stand of trees. The odor of mown hay carried by a puff of breeze wove itself into the spicy scent of windfall apples from a garden on the other side of a stone wall. Then she opened her eyes again and took in the azure sky, where clouds bloomed into great explosions of white over flat, gray bases.

Had Rousseau meant that the inner light was a way of seeing beyond oneself and recognizing holiness everywhere? Even in places where the buildings and streets had overtaken all but the last patch of open ground?

Lili took in one more deep breath and sent it back into the air. "Man is born free and everywhere he is in chains," Rousseau had told her. She looked at the distant outline of the abbey over the rooftops. *I'm not sure I understand "free,"* she thought. *So far I've learned more about chains.*

When servants from the abbey arrived with Abbess Marie-Catherine's sedan chair to transport Lili the rest of the way, she didn't want to get in. *If the street isn't fit for walking, these servants shouldn't have to do it either,* she thought, *especially carrying a gilded box with another human being inside.* She had legs she wanted to use, feet that suddenly wanted to take off and pirouette down the street, but that wasn't the way things were supposed to be done. She settled for giving each of her carriers a broad smile Baronne Lomont would have found most inappropriate, and then she climbed in and sat back on the black velvet seat for the ride.

ARRIVING IN HER room at the abbey, Lili missed Delphine with such intensity that the hair on her scalp prickled and her heart seemed to forget a beat. Since she had turned twelve in September, Delphine would be quick to follow; by now they slept in the same bed less and less, because Lili stayed up late with her books, and Delphine complained about the light from the lamp. At the abbey, just like at home, Lili usually finished her toilette as quickly as she could, then sat watching Delphine dawdle over her own. Delphine always wanted her hair and dress just so, fussing over the tiniest details of her appearance so as not to risk Anne-Mathilde and Joséphine's scorn—though anyone could see that was hopeless. But despite how unlike they were, she and Delphine went through their days side by side, and tonight, for the first time since they came to the convent, Lili would be sleeping in their room alone.

She went to Delphine's bed and picked up a small white pillow in the shape of a dog—a gift from Maman after Delphine cried about having to leave Tintin behind when she stayed in the abbey. Lili put the dog pillow on her own bed and gave it an affectionate pat. Then it was time for the routine: hat and boots off, dress changed, soft shoes buttoned. Go down the hall, greet Abbess Marie-Catherine, make the sign of the cross, pray, feign interest in catechism. Then, finally, hours later, the moment of release, when she could lie down in her room to sort out her thoughts in blessed privacy.

THE PRESENCE OF someone in her room was so oppressive that Lili sensed it as she walked down the hall after her lessons. Sister Jeanne-Bertrand stood up when Lili entered. "I am to take you directly to the abbess," she said.

"But I greeted her already, when I came back," Lili protested.

"With deceit in your heart!" Anger pushed the nun's voice so forcefully through her nose that it sounded as if her skull was vibrating. She stood up, and with the full force of her hand, she slapped Lili across the face.

"What deceit?" Lili's voice trembled more with rage than pain. She touched her hot cheek, feeling the welt rise. *Mon Dieu, can these nuns read my mind?* She had barely spoken a word since she returned, and now it seemed even silence wasn't going to protect her.

"This!" Sister Jeanne-Bertrand hissed, picking up *Émile* and shaking it. "How did you come to have a forbidden book?"

A forbidden book? She'd gotten into the sedan chair without a thought to what she had left behind in the coach. The momentary thrill of having conversed at Maman's salon with someone important enough to have his work banned by the church gave way to panic. "I—"

Think first. Lili could sense Maman whispering to her. *Most people are not receptive to the truth.* She took a breath and looked squarely at the nun. "Someone left it on a table in our parlor.

Maman doesn't know I took it, and I'm not even sure she knew it was left there."

Her cheek was throbbing, but she managed to swallow, despite what felt like a rock in her throat. "I didn't know it was a bad book. I only looked at the first few words in the carriage. And I always bring something from home to read in the evenings, that's all." The nun's eyes glinted and narrowed. "Before I say my prayers," Lili added, hating herself for pandering, but desperate to banish the terrifying pall the nun had cast over the room.

"Prayers indeed, with your immortal soul in peril!" Sister Jeanne-Bertrand shook with indignation. "Bringing a book that blasphemes our Lord into a place dedicated to His glory?"

Lili touched her hot and swollen cheek as her anger boiled up toward the loveless nun who had invaded her room, toward Sister Thérèse for disrespecting someone as gentle and sweet as Delphine, and toward all the girls like Anne-Mathilde and Joséphine, who composed their faces in pious contemplation one minute and whispered malicious gossip the next. *I felt closer to God on that road than I ever have here,* Lili thought.

Say it. Tell her.

She bowed her head and shut her eyes, hearing Maman's words again. *Whenever you listen to your own heart, think twice before speaking your mind.* "*Oui,* Sister Jeanne-Bertrand," she murmured before falling silent and letting the nun lead her down the hall to the abbess.

WITHIN AN HOUR Lili had been banished to a tiny basement room, furnished with a rickety cot, a low stool, and a chamber pot that stank from years of poor cleaning. The room had been permanently darkened by a heavy curtain drawn across the only source of light, a high window just above ground level. A painted crucifix with an agonized Jesus, dripping blood from his crown of thorns, hung on the far wall at an angle that made him appear to be looking right at Lili as he died for her sins. Unnerved, she stepped away from his gaze.

Sister Jeanne-Bertrand placed a single lit candle on the stool and handed Lili a catechism. "As the abbess said, you will receive nothing to eat until you have memorized 'The Means of Sanctifying Study' and recited it to her satisfaction. I will come back in a few hours to check on your progress. You should be able to master the first part by then."

"How long will I be here?" Lili's voice trembled.

"Until you have been rescued from error," the nun replied. A chill went down Lili's spine. Sister Jeanne-Bertrand stood at the door, brandishing a large iron key. "It's up to you," she said, locking the door behind her.

The air compressed. *I'm completely alone*, Lili realized. *Not even Delphine knows where I am.* So far Lili had managed to keep back most of her tears, but now she sobbed so deeply her stomach convulsed. She lay down on the bed and shut her eyes, thinking that if she could sleep, she could forget where she was.

How could life turn around so suddenly? Just a few hours before, she had sensed the holy light of the world, and now, in the name of God, that light was reduced to a thin ray seeping below the curtain onto the gray wall. She was hurt and imprisoned, and no one knew— at least no one who would care.

She shivered. Every one of her thoughts frightened her. Best to get away from them by beginning her penance. She stood up and moved the candle closer to the bed, trying not to think about Jesus hanging above her, watching. "Sanctifying Study," she murmured, leafing through the pages until she found her assignment. "As your studies are now among your chief duties, it is of great importance that you sanctify them by directing them to the glory of God and your own spiritual advantage," the text read. On and on it went. "Godly pursuits . . . spiritual treasure . . . divine mercy. Your thoughts are bad. Your soul is in peril. Read, and save yourself."

Lili took in the words for a moment and then, keeping her finger on the page, she closed the book over it. "As your studies are now among your chief duties, it is of great importance that you sanctify them by directing them to the glory of God and your own spiritual advantage," she recited from memory. Reopening the book, she checked the text and found she had remembered it perfectly.

"To sanctify your studies you should observe three things. First, you should view them as next in importance to your spiritual duties. Submitting to the will of God, obeying your parents, and doing justice to your own God-given soul require that you do all you can to acquire useful knowledge, which, next to virtue, is your most valuable possession." *Useful knowledge?* Lili thought back to the world she had glimpsed that morning. *I can make more use of what I saw in that field.* "Wasting time and laziness are very serious faults," she read on.

Wasting time? That's what this is. She put the book down but picked it up again after a moment. "It's not a waste if it buys my way out of here," she said in a low voice, surprised at how even a whisper filled the tiny cell.

Lili's voice rose as she added to her recitation. "Consult God more than your books," the catechism said. "Do not commit the error of vanity when you see the fruit of your learning. Knowledge is a gift from the Almighty, and should not be attributed to your intellect or hard work." *Dear Monsieur Rousseau*, she dictated mentally to the air. *I thought I should let you know I have just learned that God wrote Émile. And right now, I certainly wish he hadn't.*

She felt her black mood sliding into giddiness and let it happen. "Pride, vanity, and a desire to be better than others, or to attract admiration, are motives that reason and religion should teach you to renounce," she said, marching three steps across her cell and then back again, as if to the drumbeat of a military band. She checked the text. "Oh, sorry—that's <u>despise</u> and renounce. Mustn't forget the importance of despising!"

The thud in her chest was so sudden and strong it pushed Lili down onto the bed. "What am I doing?" She put her hands in front of her face. "I believe in you, dear God," she whispered, feeling her hot breath trickle through her fingers. "And in your Son." She let her eyes go up to the crucifix she had been deliberately avoiding. "With all my heart I know you are there, but these words don't have your love in them at all."

Wiping away with her fingers the tears making their way down her face, she looked up at Jesus. "If what the nuns say is true, and this is really what you want of me, please help me understand, and I'll accept. But if it isn't, can you please help me get out of this horrible place?"

Lili got up and paced the few steps of the cell, solemnly reciting the text she had now learned in its entirety. When she said it a second time without mistakes, she banged on the door until her hands ached, but no one answered. With nothing more to do, she lay down on the cot and fell asleep.

She woke to the sound of a key in the door. "I've brought a new candle," Sister Jeanne-Bertrand said. "So you can continue your work."

"It must have gone out when I dozed off," Lili said, rubbing her eyes to see the nun better in the dim light.

"You were asleep?" Sister Jeanne-Bertrand sounded as horrified as if she had just walked in on the devil hovering over Lili's bed. "You were supposed to be working."

Lili got up and smoothed her skirt. "I finished," she said, casting a glance up at Jesus for support. "I'm ready to see the abbess."

A predatory glint flickered in the nun's eyes.

"Well then," she said, "let's find out."

ABBESS MARIE-CATHERINE LOOKED up from the papers on her desk. "Is there some problem?" Her eyes darted between Lili and Sister Jeanne-Bertrand in search of an explanation for Lili's return in only a few hours.

"She says she's memorized the whole thing," the nun said.

The abbess stood up. "If this is a ploy—"

"To sanctify your studies you should observe three things," Lili broke in. She droned her way through the essay, and when she got to the end, she cast a quick glance at Sister Jeanne-Bertrand. Her face was flushed and her eyes had narrowed to slits. "Is this some kind of trick?" she hissed, looking at the abbess as if she too might be sensing an evil presence lurking in the room.

Marie-Catherine's face was expressionless behind her black patch. "You are quite a clever girl," she said. "But you haven't finished."

"That's the end," Lili protested. "That's all you asked me to do."

The abbess arched her eyebrows and wagged her finger as she read from the catechism. "I offer to you, My God, in honor of the actions and grievous sufferings of our Lord Jesus Christ . . ." Sister Jeanne-Bertrand crossed herself. The abbess looked at Lili. "You did not memorize the prayer also?"

"I didn't know I was supposed to," Lili said, in a husky mix of pleading and rage.

Abbess Marie-Catherine stared at her without a flicker of emotion. "If you had taken pains to think about what you were memorizing, you would have wanted to pray," she said, "and you would have been grateful to see the prayer right below. From what I've observed, if you had read it a few times you would be able to recite it. Can you?"

"I prayed in my own way to understand God's message." Lili stared at her feet.

The abbess frowned. "That is unwise. Look at me." She waited for Lili to raise her eyes. "When you keep your prayers to yourself, we in the church have no means to know when you are falling into error." She glanced down at her papers. "I'm quite busy. Go back to the room and say the prayer twenty times. And—" She consulted the catechism. " 'Pride, vanity, and a desire to be better than others, or to attract admiration, are motives that reason and religion should teach you to renounce and despise.' It's clear you were not moved by this advice. You have not fulfilled your task until you show me you have been improved by it." She closed the catechism. "You may go."

* * *

ALONE IN HER cell, Lili slumped to the floor under the crucifix, leaning her back against the cold stone wall. Her mind felt as dark and blank as the curtain blocking the fading afternoon light. *I can't memorize any more*, she thought. *I just can't make myself do it.* And even if she did, was there something else the abbess would tell her that anyone truly repentant would have discovered without being told? *Is this just a game to keep me here? Will I keep falling short again and again?*

"I won't do it," Lili said aloud into the gloom. "I'm not repentant, and I don't care who's angry with me—even Maman. Let them keep me here until I rot. I'm not memorizing another word."

Emilie

1716

EMILIE DE Breteuil cast a glance toward herself in a mirror in one of the hallways at Versailles. The outfit she had chosen to go horseback riding that afternoon flattered her body's newly acquired curves and set off the blue-gray of her eyes and her neatly curled black hair. She loved dressing the part of a young lady at court, especially since she had never expected to be the beauty she had turned out to be. The problem was that her looks now attracted men who had nothing whatsoever of interest to talk about, and she was bored to death with everything about the palace except her wardrobe and the amusing ways young ladies could arrange their hair.

Jacques LeBrun, the captain of the king's household guard at Versailles, was the worst of the lot. All the appeal of a honking goose. But the chance to go riding was worth enduring a little more of his company. Or was it?

After an hour she wanted nothing more than to get rid of him. "So, Monsieur Lebrun," she said, in a tone born of desperation, "I have a proposal for our entertainment this afternoon. What would you think if I challenged you to a swordfight?" Emilie cocked her head. "I promise I won't hurt you."

Such cheek was too charming to resist. Just as she planned, within a few minutes LeBrun came back with two épees. When Emilie took a practiced fencing stance, his eyes widened in delight. "This will be most entertaining," he said, assuming the stance himself. Almost too swiftly to see, her épee clicked on a button of his jacket.

"Touché!" she cried out, to the cheers of LeBrun's friends, who had gathered to watch.

LeBrun got into position again. Emilie feinted, but this time he was quick enough to counter. Before long, however, he was being forced backward and doing all he could to avoid another hit.

"Have you had enough?" she asked, backing away. His amused smile was gone.

"I don't believe I can continue, since I cannot engage you with the seriousness you intend without running the risk of harming you."

Harming her? She didn't think so. "All right then," Emilie said, handing him the épee. "Call it a draw." The years of fencing lessons no one at court knew about, which her father had given her to help overcome her childhood clumsiness, had finally paid off.

Within a few days, her embarrassed parents brought her home from Versailles. Someone of high rank and considerable money, they agreed, must be looking for a chance to marry into a family with Louis-Nicholas's close connections to the king. Emilie would marry the first wealthy nobleman willing to have a wife so willful and out of control. For the time being, let her savor her short-lived triumph alone in her room with her books. At least there, she could not humiliate her family any further.

4

1761

THE SOUND of the key turning in the lock woke Lili as she lay on the cot in the penance room. "Is it morning?" she asked, seeing the weak light leaking again from the gap in the curtain.

"I am to bring you to the abbess," Sister Jeanne-Bertrand said, ignoring the question.

"I haven't memorized anything more," Lili said, rolling over to turn her back to the nun. "And I'm not going to."

"Get up," the nun snarled so vehemently that Lili stumbled over her blanket as she got out of bed. With her hair disheveled and the laces of her dress untied, she followed the nun down the corridor. *What now?* she wondered.

Inside the office of the abbess, a woman in traveling clothes sat with her back to the door. At the sound of footsteps on the stone floor, she turned around. "Maman!" Lili cried out, rushing toward her.

Julie de Bercy leapt to her feet and held Lili in her arms before pulling back to look at her. "What did they do to you?" she asked, making a vain attempt to smooth Lili's hair. Only then did she notice the bruise on Lili's cheek. "What is this?" she asked, wheeling around to face the abbess.

"I disobeyed, Maman," Lili murmured.

"We make no apologies for what we consider necessary to protect the young souls in our charge," Abbess Marie-Catherine said.

"Surely you don't expect we would stand by when we saw the abbey befouled by the presence of a forbidden book."

Her one eye narrowed. "Really, Madame de Bercy, I should be asking you why you permitted such a vile piece of writing in the home of impressionable girls. Stanislas-Adélaïde said guests leave things for you that you might not know are there, but if that is the case, you should be thanking us that it has been removed."

"I feel no need to defend what I choose to have in my home." Julie put her arm around Lili's shoulder. "What are you so afraid of, that the mere presence of a book inside your walls makes you do this to a young girl?"

The abbess sat in pursed-lipped silence so long that Lili had to struggle not to squirm. "You know very well what true Christians are afraid of," she said in a voice so low it was almost a snarl.

Maman took in a breath as if she were about to respond. Then, ignoring the abbess's comment, she spoke. "I am withdrawing my two girls from the Abbaye de Panthémont as of today."

Lili looked at Maman in disbelief and felt a cool, firm hand enclose her own. "Would you please ring for help emptying their room?" Julie said. "My carriage is waiting." Without another word, she turned and strode toward the door, bringing a stunned Lili in her wake.

NEVER HAD A person recovered from a cold as quickly as Delphine did upon hearing that her days at the abbey were over. She danced around her bedroom, while a confused Tintin barked and pawed at her nightdress. "I want to hear everything," she said, when she finally could be coaxed back into bed.

Maman laughed. "Since you're well enough for me to cancel the order for your coffin, you're well enough to put on a dress and brush your hair for supper. Lili and I will meet you downstairs." Maman motioned Lili toward the door. "I have something to share with you," she said.

The two of them waited in the parlor while the servants set the table and improvised an unexpected supper for three. Julie had already opened a desk drawer and taken out a letter. "I'm curious why you haven't asked me how I knew what had happened to you."

Lili thought for a moment. "I guess I always feel you're somehow watching over us."

Julie smiled. "I must say I prefer it your way." She handed Lili the letter. "Baronne Lomont will be most unhappy when she learns she is responsible for your liberation."

Lili unfolded the letter and saw the cramped and perfectly written date and salutation. "I write to inform you of distressing news I have just received from the abbess at Panthémont," the baroness had written.

Lili looked up at Maman. "The abbess wrote to her instead of you?"

"I'm afraid so," Julie said. "Marie-Catherine and Baronne Lomont are cousins, or so I've been told, and the baroness always seemed to know more about your activities there than I did. But read on."

"This situation has come about entirely because of the laxity with which you manage your household. Stanislas-Adélaïde has apparently smuggled in a book by a M. Roskeau of whom I was fortunate enough to be entirely ignorant until today. We have agreed she must be monitored most closely for evidence of such willfulness. I intend to visit the convent tomorrow to attend the examination Marie-Catherine plans for the girl. I urge you to leave this situation to me, with my assurances that I will apprise you more fully upon my return."

Maman waited until Lili had finished. "I came right away," she said. "I prayed the entire way I would get there first and we would be gone before the baroness arrived." She got up to put the letter back in the drawer. "Of course now I must wait for her response. I imagine it won't be long in coming, or in the least bit pleasant."

* * *

"ABBESS MARIE-CATHERINE HAS unfinished business with Lili and she must be returned to the convent immediately." Baronne Lomont glanced at her priest confessor, who had accompanied her to Hôtel Bercy the following afternoon. "This is the most profound of insults."

"She won't be returned, and the insult is to my family." Julie rang for the maid. "Would you like some coffee and a bit of the cake we have today, Madame?"

The older woman ignored her. "Surely you can't feel Stanislas-Adélaïde's education is already at an end. There is still quite a lot she has not yet—" The baroness locked her eyes on Lili as she formed her thought. "Fully absorbed." She arched her eyebrows in rebuke.

"I think it is quite time for her education to begin," Julie replied. "I intend to get the girls a tutor. They will study those subjects that will make them an interesting companion to an intelligent husband, not just catechism-squawking parrots with no minds of their own."

The priest and Baronne Lomont sat back, speechless.

"If you are concerned about whether Stanislas-Adélaïde will receive proper religious instruction, you may examine her yourself when she visits Baronne Lomont," Julie said to the priest. "I've given my word to the Marquis du Châtelet that the baroness will be involved in his daughter's upbringing until she is married. And we will continue, as we always have, to go to mass twice a week and confess our sins regularly."

She reached for her teacup without the slightest quaver in her hands and took a delicate sip. "Is there something more either of you would ask of me?" The priest and the baroness exchanged glances. "She is *my* ward," Julie continued, with a firmness that ended the discussion.

"Well, then." Baronne Lomont rose to her feet and turned to Lili. "See that you are at my home the day after tomorrow, in the morning." She looked at Julie with a haughty thrust of her chin. "If, of course, that meets with Madame's approval."

Julie repaid her with the same icy tone. "I'll see that she's there," she said, as the baroness swept from the parlor.

THE WINDOWS OF the Hôtel Bercy rattled as the wind from the first cold storm of fall banged the shutters. Julie had gone out despite the weather, but not before ordering that a small fire be lit in the room, where the girls were spending the afternoon. Delphine had tired of playing the piano and was moving around in her stocking feet, imitating dancers at a ball. She worked her way over to where Lili sat at the desk, intent on her notebook.

"Read me what you've written," she pleaded. "I promise I'll be your slave forever if you do."

Lili snorted. "You're already my slave for the next century, at the rate you promise things." But her concentration was broken, and with a sigh she stood up. "At least let's sit closer to the fire."

Delphine wiggled her hips next to Lili's in a chair meant for one person, looking at the pages while Lili read.

"When Comète galloped to a stop on Venus, Meadowlark was surprised to find people weeping and laying flowers in front of a long row of rocks.

"'I can't imagine any rock that could make me cry,' Meadowlark said to Comète. 'Wait here—I'm going to see what's happening.' Comète nodded his head and snorted fireworks from his white nose.

"'Why are you crying over a rock?' Meadowlark asked the first person she came to.

"'It's not really a rock,' he said. 'It's my daughter.'

"'Was she born that way?' Meadowlark asked.

"'Of course not! Who would have a rock for a baby?'"

Delphine giggled and looked up at Lili with shining eyes. "A rock for a baby!" Lili grinned and went on.

"'The Evil Queen lined all the children up,' the man said. 'If the girls couldn't curtsey perfectly and the boys didn't bow just right, they would be turned into stone with her magic wand. My little girl didn't keep her back upright enough, and now look at her!'

"Just then a few apples fell from a tree behind Meadowlark, and she looked up. A boy sat in the branches. 'Why aren't you a rock?' she asked.

"'I told her I had a stomachache and couldn't bow properly until later,' the boy said. 'She said she would come back and turn me into stone this afternoon. That's why I'm hiding.'

"'Well, hiding doesn't help if she's not here,' Meadowlark said. 'You'd better come down and practice bowing if you know what's good for you,' Meadowlark said.

"'Why bother?' the boy answered. 'Even if I were perfect, she'd turn me into stone anyway. She does it for fun and no one has the power to stop her.'"

Lili had come to the end of what she had written and closed her notebook with a clap. "What's going to happen now?" Delphine's eyes were wide.

"The Evil Queen is going to come back, and Meadowlark and Tom—that's the boy's name—are going to escape on Comète."

Delphine wiggled out of her seat. "I wouldn't let the Evil Queen turn me into stone. I would curtsey so perfectly she couldn't bear to harm me." She went to the center of the room and bit her lip as she concentrated on dropping her back exactly as she had been taught at dancing lessons. "Just like that."

Lili watched as she did it again. "Well," she said, "what would it be like to be the only one not turned to stone?"

Delphine thought for a moment as she continued to curtsey. "I wouldn't be alone for long. I would be so nice and kind that the Evil Queen would change her ways and set the others free."

"I suppose," Lili said. "But I don't think Meadowlark curtseys that well, and she's the one who's got to save everyone. I'm going to have her come back with Tom and steal the Evil Queen's wand and turn her into stone and rescue the children. Do you like it?"

Delphine lost her balance on her fourth curtsey and had to take a quick step to avoid banging against a side table. "Oops," she said, collapsing into a chair. "I guess maybe a wand really is better."

JULIE SET OFF with Lili the following morning in Hôtel Bercy's double-seated sedan chair, carried by four servants in livery. She would leave Lili at Hôtel Lomont before continuing on to the home of one of her friends, then return to cut short Lili's torment by whisking her home for dinner at midday.

Lili splayed her fingers in front of her as if she were counting something in her head. "I'm twelve years old," she said. "And I've been going to Baronne Lomont's since I was six. Once a week for six years, minus the weeks I was at the abbey, I must have visited her more than two hundred times."

"You seem oddly cheerful about it," Julie said, giving Lili a quizzical look.

Lili grinned. "Meadowlark has to defeat the Evil Queen in my new story, and Delphine gave me an idea. I'm going to disappoint Baronne Lomont by giving her nothing to criticize—even though she'll probably find something anyway." She thought for a moment. "I've always thought visiting her was like going into battle, but now I think if I curtsey well enough and manage myself just so, maybe she'll leave me alone. And that's what I really want. To be able to be myself—at least inside me where no one else sees—without having to spend all my time thinking about how I'm supposed to be."

"You are a very wise girl, *ma chérie*." Julie patted Lili's knee. "When you don't shock her anymore, just watch how quickly she'll lose interest. But still, being gracious to people you don't enjoy is one of the most important things you can learn." She winked. "Besides sipping consommé without making any noise."

Julie's face grew solemn, and she turned to look out the window of the coach. "Things are changing, Lili. When Baronne Lomont was young, a girl's independence of mind was seen as an affront. It's too late for someone her age to change, but people coming along now see things a little differently. At least some do."

She turned back toward Lili. "Monsieur Rousseau says that the restraints put on children deform their natural character, and they grow up being comfortable only in a society that's been deformed to match. He says we're suffering the consequences of that now, and I think he's probably right."

The carriage pulled up in front of an austere gray building untouched by the morning sun yet to penetrate the densely packed buildings of the Île Saint-Louis. "We're here," Maman said, pulling Lili to her in a quick embrace. "I love you, *ma petite*," she said. "Now go wield your new sword."

1764

"*CORPUS OMNE PERSEVERARE in statu suo quiescendi vel movendi uniformiter in directum.*" Fourteen-year-old Lili traced her fingers over the words as her tutor, Louis Nohant, looked on. Firelight danced off the glass of the book cabinets in the wood-paneled library of Hôtel Bercy on the dreary winter afternoon. "I can't understand this," she said. "The Latin is so—odd."

Delphine put down her pencil on the rail of the portable easel she had moved near the fireplace. "Lili! I can't draw you with your mouth all grumpy like that!"

Lili looked across the room at her. "Sorry," she said. "I forgot you were sketching, with this Newton driving me so crazy."

"Well, why do you care so much?" Delphine whined. "It makes

me cross when you get so involved neither of you wants to say anything to me."

Lili put her finger in the fold of Newton's *Principia*. "I just want answers, that's all. Don't you think we ought to care about how things really are?"

"If you mean the 'we' that's somebody else, yes. But if it's the kind of 'we' that means I have to go over there and study physics rather than sketch or play the piano, that's different."

Monsieur Nohant, a thin and nervous young man of twenty-two, rapped his knuckles on the desk. "Mademoiselle de Bercy," he said with an officiousness negated by the pimples on his chin. "You are free to stay, but not to disturb us." When he turned his back, Delphine stuck out her tongue and Lili suppressed a giggle. "I can explain, Mademoiselle du Châtelet," he said. "Newton's first law says that every object will remain in its current, uniform state of motion unless an external force is applied to it."

"Well, why didn't he just say that?" Lili demanded. She rolled her pencil across the table. "And look—it doesn't even seem to be true. The pencil is obviously going to stop moving at some point." It fell off the table onto the intricately patterned Savonnerie carpet, and Lili heard Delphine snicker.

"But you see, the table is creating friction," the tutor said. "If the pencil were moving through space unimpeded, it would never stop. And if it weren't moving, it would never start unless something hit it."

"All right," Lili said. "I can understand that, but—" She ran her finger across the next line. "*Nisi quatenus a viribus impressis cogitur statum illum mutare*? Latin is hard enough without someone so strange writing it." She pushed the book toward him. "*You* translate!"

Monsieur Nohant's eyes flitted. "I'm afraid I can't explain better than I have."

"Well, why not?" Lili had grown exasperated with this new tutor, who seemed to know little more than she did.

The door to the library opened and Julie entered. Both girls stood up. "Bonjour, Maman!" they chirped.

"Bonjour, *mes chéries*," she said, coming over to give each of them a light caress on the shoulder. "My goodness," she said, looking at Delphine's sketch. "That's a very good likeness!" She looked more closely. "But why did you erase Lili's mouth?" Delphine shot an annoyed glance at Lili as Maman came over to her.

"What's wrong," she asked, seeing Lili's knit brow.

"I can't understand this!" Lili's voice was husky with frustration.

The tutor shifted his feet. "I'm not able to explain it using the Latin," he said.

Julie picked up the book. "This is—" She looked at Lili. "You're already reading Newton?"

"*Oui*, Maman. And I really want to understand, but I can't seem to manage." Maman's eyes were oddly bright against her suddenly pale cheeks. "What?" Lili asked. "Did I do something wrong?"

"I said nothing to her," the tutor insisted.

Lili looked back and forth between the two of them. "What are you talking about?" she demanded. "Said nothing about what?"

Julie de Bercy looked away, her lips disappearing into a thin line as she pondered what to say. "I think it's best if you leave us for the day," she said to the tutor. "And you too, for a little while, *ma chérie*," she said to Delphine. "I need some time with Lili alone."

"WHAT DO YOU know about your mother?" Julie asked when the others had left.

"Nothing but the little you've told me," Lili replied. She thought for a moment. "I've always sensed I wasn't supposed to ask. There were a few girls at the convent whose mothers were dead, but since they never mentioned them, I thought maybe there was something improper about bringing it up."

Julie took a deep breath as she settled back onto the couch. "I was with your mother more than anyone else in her last days. I helped her into bed when she felt her first pains with you. I knew she was gone even before your father did." She shut her eyes to gather her thoughts. The clock ticked and a carriage went by on the Place Royale while Lili waited for her to continue.

Suddenly Julie stood up. "This is the best way to show you who your mother was." She walked over to the desk to pick up the *Principia*. "It's not just you who has trouble with this Latin. No one here could comprehend what Newton was saying until Emilie translated it into French."

"My mother translated the *Principia*?"

Julie put the book back on the desk. "Yes. And it was more than the language that was the problem. I can't comprehend it even in French, but I've been told it's rewritten, not just translated, and that Emilie's commentary is what allows people like your tutor to understand Newton at all. That, and her own mathematical calculations where Newton hadn't provided them."

"Why didn't Monsieur Nohant tell me this?" Lili demanded.

"When he first started as your tutor, I told him that when you began to study physics, he was not to mention your mother. It might be hard for you to understand, but I felt it was for your own good." Julie sat down next to her. "Your mother was a very complicated person. And controversial, I must add. She had trouble limiting herself to people's expectations, and you've seen for yourself what that can be like, haven't you?" She smiled and patted Lili's knee.

"Everyone felt it was better for you to assume there was nothing special about her until you were old enough to understand. Don't blame Monsieur Nohant for obeying me, although I suppose he'll be relieved that from now on he can consult the version of Newton he actually comprehends. And you probably will be too, from what I've heard."

She got up again and went to a small, locked cabinet. She opened it and withdrew a book. "I have been so looking forward to this day," she said, handing it to Lili.

"*Principes Mathématiques*," Lili read, tracing her fingers over her mother's name on the title page. "But this was just published a few years ago, when I was ten!"

"She finished the last details in the few days after you were born, before she suddenly took ill. It took time for people to pay attention to her work. Most weren't ready for her ideas—those who could understand them. And the *salonnières* made good entertainment of ridiculing her because her brilliance made them nervous."

Julie sat down again and watched Lili leaf through the pages. "People who know the truth see your mother's great spirit, but she has her detractors. Some people say it must have been the men around her who did the difficult science and mathematics, but I saw her doing the calculations. Make no mistake of it, *ma chérie*. This"— Julie ran her finger over random lines of text—"this is your mother's work."

"'All objects remain in a uniform state of motion,'" Lili read in French. *My mother was different too.* "Until something changes," she whispered, wondering whether something just had.

Emilie
1734

EMILIE DU CHÂTELET pulled aside the curtain of her carriage and brought her face so close to the window that her nose almost touched the glass. A few men were trickling out of the Café Gradot to attend to afternoon business before a night at the theater, but she knew Pierre-Louis du Maupertuis would not be among the first to leave. It pained him, she thought with a touch of scorn, to tear himself away from the adoration of the scientists, mathematicians, and hangers-on who convened each day in a back room of the café. Honestly, couldn't they see that even though he held the mathematics chair at the Academy of Sciences, he needed to consult his students to explain what were supposed to be his own ideas?

What irked her most was not Maupertuis's pretension, but that she was left to wait for him outside, since as a woman, she was forbidden by law from setting foot inside. Once, she had suggested to one of her friends that he offer a serving girl a bribe if she would lend out her uniform, since maids were the only exception to the law against women being present. The Marquis du Châtelet was a tolerant man, but he would not have taken kindly to such a breach of rank by his wife. Still, the hilarity of a scene in which a serving wench cleared the table while discussing mathematics with members of the academy was so delightful, Emilie had considered incurring what would at worst be a mild chastisement. Instead, she settled for showing up in men's clothing, and though everyone had been most amused by a disguise that was revealed the first time she laughed, that kind of thing could only be done once. The café owner didn't need problems with the police, who were always looking for new examples of how easy it was to disappear forever into the prison at the Bastille.

She had to make do with random scraps of remembered conversation after she fetched Maupertuis and they were en route to his home. Once there, she would spend an hour or two being tutored in calculus while her carriage waited outside. Her arrangement with Maupertuis had been going on for a few months now, beginning when she was able to come out in public again after the birth of her third child. Already she could see that her questions and ideas seemed to unnerve the illustrious Maupertuis. If she were not paying handsomely for his time, he would probably have ended his tutelage, saying he was too busy to make time for someone with no prospect of contributing to the field. All that, just to cover the fact that her questions were really quite beyond him.

Despite her frustration, the chance to talk about advanced math at all, even with someone as overblown as Maupertuis, was the best part of her present life. "I'm twenty-seven years old," she whispered into the glass, making a ring of fog that immediately vanished. "And I am so bored I—" She pressed her teeth into her gloved knuckle and sighed. Motherhood was a disappointment, since aristocratic women spent little time with their children. Her daughter, Gabrielle-Pauline, now seven, had already been removed to the Ursuline Convent to begin her education. Her son Florent-Louis was five, and his father had turned his heir into little more than a toy soldier with as little imagination and humor as possible. Her infant boy, Victor-Esprit, was weak and it was best not to think too much about what his prospects were when so many children, even in families with money for doctors and medicine, did not survive infancy.

She settled back into her seat. "I do love that sweet child," she whispered. Perhaps most of all three. Society permitted a frail child to need its mother, and that gave her permission to need Victor-Esprit. She certainly didn't need her husband, nor he her, except for the social practicalities of marriage. Now that a war had broken out over the succession to the Polish throne, she rarely saw Florent-Claude, since he lived near the border with the regiment he commanded. But even before that, their marriage was always one of convenience and little more. He had few interests and even fewer ideas, excusing himself early from the dinner table when the subject turned to any of the things that so fascinated her. The marquis was not a difficult man, and she was thankful for that, but wouldn't it be nice to find oneself in bed with a man of real—

"Real appetites" she whispered. "I want someone who—" She thought for a moment. Someone who would end a discussion—even an argument—about the rarest and finest of the day's new ideas, by tearing off her clothes and ravishing her. The most erotic thing in the world had to be when minds met and bodies followed. She sat back in the coach as forcefully as if the horse had jerked it forward, at the realization of just how desperately she wanted that to happen to her. *I need a lover*, she thought. But not just any lover. That kind.

She felt the coach jiggle as the driver jumped down to open the door. Pierre-Louis du Maupertuis stepped up and settled down across from her. He was thirty-five, with a bulbous forehead and a rather large nose, but altogether he cut a pleasant enough figure, and he was much admired for his wit by the ladies at court. Emilie eyed him sidelong as the coach rumbled through the streets of Paris. Bodies meeting minds? He was not the answer to her fantasy, she was sure, but he would serve as an adequate test of her hypothesis.

5

T HE MALLET connected with an off-center *thunk*, and the ball dribbled less than a meter across the grass. "Oh, dear," Delphine said, looking up with a pretty smile at the cluster of guests playing a game of *paille-maille* on one of the lawns of the château of Vaux-le-Vicomte.

"You must hit the ball with more force," Jacques-Mars Courville said. "May I?" He came up behind and slipped his hands alongside hers. "Like this." The young man followed through with a firm whack and the ball rolled cleanly across a meter of short grass, directly through the metal arch at which he had been aiming.

The guests at Vaux-le-Vicomte clapped, as fifteen-year-old Delphine turned her face up toward Jacques-Mars and gave him an admiring smile. "Perhaps it is my good fortune to be so bad at this that I require the help of someone so charming," she said in a deliberately lilting voice.

"And perhaps it will be my good fortune that you find you cannot master it." Seeing Delphine's confusion, he went on. "So you will permit me to help you forever," he said, bowing with such dramatic exaggeration that the others broke out in amused applause.

Lili suppressed a groan. No one could be as bad at *paille-maille* as Delphine pretended to be, and it was infuriating the way she slowed everything down, as if the whole point was to call as much attention to herself as possible. Anne-Mathilde and Joséphine, those disgusting girls from the abbey, were just as bad. Of the two, it was hard to know which was worse. Anne-Mathilde's hair was curled in the latest style, and her skin was as perfect as ever, with a hint of a blush from the summer sun. At seventeen, she had gained a little weight, revealing her curves under a loosely corseted summer dress that was the latest style for a relaxing sojourn away from Paris.

Joséphine de Maurepas was still the perfect foil. She also had grown an inch or two, but remained thin and flat-chested, with no feature worth singling out for a kind remark. Joséphine's prestige lay entirely in Anne-Mathilde's preference for her, which was understandable, given that Joséphine could always be counted upon to gossip about others without the slightest shred of mercy, and even more importantly, she viewed Anne-Mathilde as perfect in every way. Lili watched as the two of them fluttered their little fans over their mouths as they bent in to make some comment or another, most likely about Jacques-Mars's obvious attraction to Delphine.

Trying not to glower, Lili stepped up to her ball. She sized it up for only a moment before hitting it cleanly through a hoop planted in the lawn at about two meters' distance. *What a waste of time this is,* she thought, grimly planting a smile back on her face before looking up.

VAUX-LE-VICOMTE HAD BEEN recently purchased by the Duc de Praslin, Anne-Mathilde's father. When Maman had made plans for a month-long respite from the sultry August heat in Paris, Lili had been eager to come, even if it meant putting up with Anne-Mathilde and Joséphine. The usually idyllic Place Royale had no special protection from the stench rising up from the sewage and rotting garbage floating in the Seine. The eye-watering odor rose up and gathered force as it wafted down the filthy streets and alleyways of the city before—at least it seemed to Lili—it sank with special malevolence over the Place Royale. She was tired of hiding in the deepest recesses of Hôtel Bercy to keep her head from throbbing. Now she could remember only the advantages of its solitude.

She looked across the sculpted gardens beyond the lawn toward the imposing yellow sandstone walls of the massive château. The jagged rows of steeply pitched sections of roof were mottled with dark verdigris, crowned by a massive dome over the main foyer. From the open arches of the cupola on top of the dome she had looked out the morning after their arrival at endless stretches of clipped boxwood hedges in beds of crushed red brick that looked more like Turkish carpets than anything found in nature.

The view from the cupola at Vaux-le-Vicomte made it clear that visitors there were to walk in straight lines up and down the *parterres* and along the walkways of the canals rather than have ideas of their own about what to do or where to go. Even flowers were not allowed to splatter their colors over such a perfect subjugation of nature, except in tight girdles around statues, which were spaced out in perfect rows in each tidy rectangle of lawn. Beyond the green moat around the château, Lili counted eight artificial, geometrically shaped lakes placed in perfect symmetry along a broad pathway that ran like a spine down the middle of the property.

It's as if the whole place is wearing a corset, Lili thought as she and Delphine stood in the cupola that morning. Lili agreed to stroll through every open room on the ground floor in return for Delphine's word they would climb what felt like hundreds of steps to the best viewpoint on the estate. Looking down, Delphine had eyes only for the strolling parties of women in shimmering gowns and ruffled parasols, accompanied by men in dark coats and fitted trousers. She could hardly wait to get back down to begin meeting whoever was presently in residence.

At fifteen, Delphine had grown from a pretty girl into a beautiful young woman, with hair as lovely as a cascading bolt of pinkish yellow silk, now caught up stylishly under a tiny hat. Though her skin was inclined to freckle in the summer, a thin coat of lotion tamed it to a soft glow. No one would be likely to glance long away from her large, green eyes to notice any imperfections. "I plan to charm everyone who will pay me any notice," she had said as they turned to leave the cupola. "I shall be scintillating." She paused a moment to search for another word. "Just impertinent enough to be endearing."

"You've been reading too many novels," Lili retorted.

"Well, why shouldn't I try to make everyone notice me?" Delphine sniffed. "The best entries into society are by girls whose reputation for charm and beauty has preceded them. I intend to surpass them all, and since you don't care a whit about any of it, I'll do it without you."

Lili scarcely noticed the snappishness in Delphine's voice. In the distance, beyond the constraints and forced perfection of the grounds, treetops of a vast forest billowed and undulated like a skirt loose and light enough for her to pick up in her hands and run laughing into another world. Equestrian trails headed off here and there, disappearing into the thick trees. *That's where I want to be*, Lili thought. *By myself. Alone with my thoughts, and maybe a book, under a tree.*

"Well?" Delphine challenged.

"Well, what?"

"Are you going to go around being a good guest with me, or just spend the next month flopping around on a couch reading philosophy, or working out pointless math problems, or whatever it is you do?"

Lili sighed. "I can't help what I am."

"Well, if you cared a little more about your hair, and not having ink stains on your fingers, you would get a lot more attention." Delphine turned again to look down at the people in the garden. "It's cold up here. Aren't you ready to go down?"

Lili ignored her. "I'm not you," she said. "I'm not dainty, or pretty—or interested, for that matter."

Delphine snorted. "You act like you're some ugly little troll, and you're not bad-looking in the slightest!" Lili would probably be better described as handsome, a word often used to describe women with no irregularities substantial enough to make them unappealing, but lacking in the delicacy and harmony of features that would warrant anything more than the occasional description of "rather attrac-tive." Her eyes were perhaps a bit too large and an imprecise shade of brown, and her hair had settled into an uncertain hue somewhere be-tween brown and black. Furthermore, as Delphine constantly pointed out, Lili didn't make the effort to maintain her hair neatly, keep her skin powdered, or put the slightest touch of rouge on her cheeks or lips. "It would make such a difference," Delphine had ad-monished, her voice trailing off wistfully, as if she were witnessing a tragedy unfolding before her eyes.

LAUGHTER FROM THE group playing *paille-maille* brought Lili's attention back to the present. What good did it do her that the woods were beckoning, since she was not permitted to walk or ride in them alone, and every possible companion seemed to have an incompre-hensible preference for hitting wooden balls for hours on end? She sighed, loud enough to be heard. Julie linked her arm in Lili's and eased the two of them out of earshot onto a gravel pathway that grumbled under their feet with each step.

"Scowling will give you wrinkles," Julie said, looking at Lili from under her parasol. Its rose-colored silk cast a warm glow over her face. "What's wrong?"

"I'd so much rather be doing just about anything else," Lili said, tossing her head just in time to see Anne-Mathilde dissolve into giggles after hitting the ball as poorly as Delphine had done. "What is the matter with those girls? Delphine could hit that stupid ball. Why is she acting like it's so much fun to be bad at some-thing?"

"Delphine is quite a flirt," Julie said. "And she seems to enjoy the attention." Her expression turned serious as she looked at Lili. "You're almost sixteen, and it's normal to start paying attention to the men around you. It won't be long until you and Delphine are the talk of the court, with everyone wondering who you'll marry. Aren't you at all curious about that?"

"I'm curious whether anyone exists who thinks *paille-maille* is as boring as I do." Lili gave her parasol a punishing twirl in her hands. "Please, can't we go riding instead?"

"Maman, look!" Delphine called out. She gave the ball a resounding pop and it careened against the metal hoop, but made it through. The crowd applauded, Joséphine and Anne-Mathilde tittered, and Delphine cocked her head in a well-practiced manner before handing her mallet to Jacques-Mars as if he were born to carry it in one hand and her parasol in the other.

Lili looked away, but felt Maman's elbow pull her closer. "Riding tomorrow," Julie said. "I promise."

SUMMER THUNDERSHOWERS SPOILED the plan for the following day, and when Julie had a headache the next, she fulfilled her promise to Lili by asking their host to arrange a riding party for the young people staying at the château.

"I'm going to practice all day on Jacques-Mars," Delphine had said the night before, as Corinne helped them out of their dresses.

"Practice what?" Lili snorted, though she needed no answer.

"Being charming. He's only twenty, and far too young to marry, but he'll be a count after his father dies, and everyone says their lands are some of the loveliest in France." Liberated from the constraints of the corset she had worn to supper, Delphine made small dance steps around their sitting room, wearing only her chemise. "Perhaps we'll be invited for a visit to his family's château this fall, if he's really smitten with me."

"I can hardly wait," Lili growled.

Delphine stopped and put her hands on her hips. "You used to be fun, but you're not anymore," she snapped. "I'd rather be reading," she mimicked, moving her jaw up and down like a marionette. "I'd rather be doing geometry." Lili's jaw dropped in disbelief at the explosive mockery.

"I'd rather be writing about Meadowlark!" Delphine tossed her head, as if to rid herself of anything so childish.

"What did you mean by that?" Lili demanded.

"Well, wouldn't you?"

It came to Lili in a stark moment of insight. For months, Delphine had played with her hair or traced with her fingertips the patterns in the fabrics of Maman's clothing while Lili read. "When are Tom and Meadowlark going to kiss?" Delphine wheedled from time to time. "That would ruin everything," Lili always replied, sometimes with such adamance that Maman had to intervene to prevent a quarrel.

Perhaps she too was growing beyond Meadowlark, Lili thought, writing new adventures as if they were for a Delphine who no longer existed. It had become work to pick up the pen, but after Delphine's insult, Lili was certainly not going to admit it. "What I'd really like Meadowlark to do, is whack the sense back into you with a *paille-maille* mallet," Lili said, refusing to soften the moment with a friendly smirk.

"*Mon Dieu*, Lili, you're making such a terrible impression." Delphine knotted her dressing gown with an angry tug on the ends of the sash.

"You sound like the nuns," Lili retorted.

"It's not funny! You act like you're so much better than everybody, and I have to work hard so people won't dislike me because of you."

"Better? I can't do any of the things you do—smile, and tease, and say witty things that make people laugh."

"Well, you could if you tried!" Delphine exhaled in frustration as she sat down on the bed. "Aren't you worried that no one will take a fancy to you, the way you grouse around and act like nothing anybody says is interesting?"

"It isn't. Besides, what is there about needing help to tap a ball that's making you more likable?" Lili said.

"Well it seems to, even if it shouldn't," Delphine said. She was quiet for a moment. "I wish things were the way they used to be," she murmured, turning toward Lili, who had gone to sit at the dressing table to brush out her hair. "Anne-Mathilde is so disgusting, but when everyone talks about her great marriage prospects because she's so pretty and charming, I don't know what comes over me, but I want to act just like her." She paused. "I'm sorry I yelled at you."

Lili looked in the mirror at Delphine's reflection behind her and saw that she was fighting back tears. "I pity the poor dunce who would be satisfied with Anne-Mathilde," Lili said, trying to lighten the mood, "or that little rabbit who hops along after her."

But Delphine was not ready to smile. "It's nothing to laugh about. I'd rather be married to a dunce than have no offers at all, or maybe get stuck with someone like that horrible Comte de Beaufort. No wonder his wife died so young." Delphine wrinkled her nose in disgust. "She had no way else to escape having to sleep with someone whose teeth are rotten down to nubs and whose breath smells like . . . like—"

"Like dogs passing gas?" Lili gave an unintentionally loud and indecorous snort as she sat down next to Delphine. "Can you imagine hopping into bed and having that big stink waft up from under the covers?"

Delphine's somber mood vanished into a gale of laughter.

"Would you like to make a baby tonight, dear? I'm feeling rather explosive!" Lili said, clutching her stomach in anticipation of how much it was going to hurt to laugh so hard.

Delphine sucked a loud squealing noise out of her fist. "I can send an extra smelly one your way. Isn't that how it's done?"

"Of course, dear," Lili simpered. "And in nine months, I'll blow out a baby Beaufort." She paused. "Would monsieur prefer a boy or girl?"

Delphine wiped her eyes. "It has to be a boy because we'll name him Gas-ton!" she said, dissolving into another gale of wet-eyed laughter before getting up in search of a handkerchief to blow her nose. "Lili, I know gas jokes are out," she said, "but can you please—please—try to be even half that funny when we're out riding tomorrow?"

Lili might have bristled at the reminder of her shortcomings, but instead she narrowed her eyes and gave Delphine a conspiratorial grin. "Want to see something I found in the library?" She got up and retrieved a book from under her mattress, waving it in front of Delphine. "*Thérèse Philosophe*," she said. "I picked it off the shelf because I thought it would be about a lady philosopher, but guess what?" She leafed through the book until she found the first picture and held it up for Delphine to see.

Delphine's eyes grew wide and she grabbed the book from Lili. "What is she doing?"

The center of the drawing was taken up with the huge exposed buttocks of a woman whose face could barely be seen at the far edge of the plate. A priest was on his knees behind her, his massive erection disappearing into her body. In the background was the figure of a maid spying on them through a keyhole, bent over from the waist, with her skirts up, while another man dressed in the clothes of a nobleman was doing the same to her.

The two girls wiggled down next to each other on a small fauteuil meant for one. They laid out the book between their laps, gaping at illustration after illustration of men and women in different positions.

"*Mon Dieu!*" Delphine gasped, putting her hand over her mouth. "Those men's things are huge. Where does it all go?"

"I can't imagine," Lili said. "The priest tells Eradice—she's an older lady who's a friend of Thérèse—that he's helping her experience a mystical vision of God. She sees his—his thing—and thinks it's the serpent from the Garden of Eden, but he tells her that isn't what he's going to put in her when she turns around. It's going to be a holy relic, a hardened piece of the cord St. Francis wore around his waist, and she believes him. Thérèse is watching from behind a curtain while he's—well, you see."

"Have you read the whole thing?" Delphine asked, wide-eyed. Lili nodded sheepishly. "I found it a few days ago."

"You wicked girl!" Delphine giggled. "Read more!"

"'I feel my mind detaching itself from matter and going straight to God. Onward! Upward! Harder! Harder! I'm seeing angels! Don't stop now. Don't deny me true bliss. Oh! Oh!'"

They looked at each other, perplexed. "That doesn't make sense," Delphine said. "It seems as if she'd be saying 'ouch,' and telling him to stop."

"Or getting up and running out of there." Lili shook her head, reading on.

"'With each backward move of the priest's behind, his member withdrew and as its head appeared, the lips of Eradice pulled open, revealing a wondrous crimson hue. As he pressed forward, the color disappeared, leaving visible only short black hairs that seemed to grasp his member as tightly as if it were being swallowed whole.'"

Delphine gasped, looking at Lili with huge eyes. "I don't think I want to hear any more," she whispered, covering her mouth.

"Me neither. I feel sick just looking at it. I tell myself to take it back to the library, but something always makes me keep it a little longer."

Delphine traced the cover with her fingers as she thought. "It's awful," she said, "but shouldn't we know these things, now that we're not little girls anymore?" She thought for a moment before dissolving into giggles. "I know! Let's ask Baronne Lomont! 'What are these hairs and crimson hue we've heard about? Please, do tell!'"

Lili ignored her. "I don't even want to ask Maman," she murmured.

Delphine stopped laughing. "I know. It's just too horrible to imagine," she said in a somber voice. "We need to get ready for supper now." She took the volume from Lili's hands and put it back under the mattress.

* * *

THE AIR REMAINED warm long after dark, creating a shroud of mist over the moonlit lawns of Vaux-le-Vicomte. Later that night, Lili awakened to loud claps of thunder, and spent an hour at the window watching lightning scratch the distant sky.

Her thoughts were elsewhere, with Delphine. *How long has it been since we laughed like that?* It felt like years.

Did the closeness of the evening mean as much to Delphine as it did to her? Lili doubted it. If Anne-Mathilde had walked in while they were lying on their backs groaning with laughter, would Delphine have scrambled to her feet and tried to cover up her childishness?

Lili fought to convince herself otherwise, but could not. In the past, an evening like this would have ended with the two of them falling asleep in one bed, after a long session of whispering in the dark. Now she felt as if she was unmoored, not knowing where she was, or what direction to turn. *The Land of the Floating People*, she thought, trying for a moment to picture the scene Meadowlark and Tom might come upon, but the effort didn't interest her.

She wishes things were the way they used to be, Lili thought. She said so. But they weren't, and it was obvious they suited someone pretty and outgoing like Delphine better than her.

Thunder boomed at the same moment a flash of lightning illuminated the jets of water in the fountains near the entrance to the château. Rain fell softly at first and then torrentially, as a couple appeared from around a corner of the courtyard, slipping and stumbling on the wet stone paving leading to the main doors.

An image of Eradice's exposed buttocks came into Lili's mind, and when the woman's laughter sounded for a moment just like Delphine's, Lili felt a shudder deep within. It couldn't be. Not yet.

Lili tiptoed into the other room and saw Delphine asleep, her hair strewn in pale rays on the pillow. The casement window was rattling and rain was collecting on the sill. Lili closed it tightly before crawling into bed next to her.

* * *

DELPHINE SAID NOTHING about finding Lili in her bed when she woke up. She hadn't turned to hug her, or brush her hair away with a tender look. She had jumped up and said something about how late it was, and asked whether Lili knew where she had put her new riding boots. Now, when what Lili had begged for was a quiet day in the woods with Maman, only the loudest squawks of annoyed birds penetrated the sound of the horses' hooves as the group of six trotted down the path.

Does everything turn into hell here? Lili wondered. *I want to go riding to get away from the people at Vaux-le-Vicomte, not bring them along with me.*

The riding party broke into a slow gallop as they left the stables, aiming to reach the shade of the forest quickly. The fresh smell of the night rain had given way to the cloying odor of blasted flowers and sour grass steaming in the hot summer sun. Lili's new riding outfit, made of velvet heavy enough to stay in place, caused her petticoats to stick to her thighs and sweat to trickle down the groove of her back inside her tight jacket.

The trail entered a glade at the edge of the forest, and the party gathered in the dappled shade. The men mopped their brows, uttering mild curses at the heat, while the girls dabbed at their faces so as not to displace the light powder and touch of rouge suitable to their age. After a moment, Delphine and Jacques-Mars Courville trotted off in the lead. Lili could see the feather on Delphine's hat bobbing as she tilted her head this way and that, just the way she practiced in the mirror. Anne-Mathilde and Joséphine were in the middle and Lili was at the rear with Anne-Mathilde's brother Paul-Vincent, who, though he was the heir to Vaux-le-Vicomte and the future Duc de Praslin, was of little interest to anyone because he was only thirteen.

"You don't smile very much." Paul-Vincent was looking at her. Lili gave him an overblown, crazed smile she hoped would convey that she didn't welcome conversation, but he just kept staring. "You always seem to be thinking about something."

"I'm thinking about how much I would like to be left alone," Lili said.

"And I'm thinking I should be insulted," he said in return.

The unexpected self-assurance in his tone caused Lili to pull up her horse and turn toward him. "I'm sorry," she said. "You've given me no cause to be so rude." Her horse snorted and tossed its head, as if it wanted to rejoin the others, but she held it firm while she looked at her riding companion.

Puberty had given Paul-Vincent de Praslin a gawkiness that made him temporarily unattractive, with a cluster of pimples on his cheeks and a coat of dark down on his upper lip. But his expression hinted at a depth she hadn't seen in any of the young people chattering away on horseback farther down the trail.

"People think I'm scowling at them," she said, "but they're flattering themselves, because most of the time I don't even notice they're there. I'm entertaining myself in my own head—or at least trying to—over all that prattle."

Paul-Vincent's adolescent laughter turned into a bray, and his cheeks reddened in embarrassment. He began sauntering along the dirt path. "Just a minute ago, I was concentrating on a math problem," he said. "Something like, if I started riding in the opposite direction right now, and none of them noticed for ten minutes, but then my ridiculous sister and that Joséphine person started chasing me, going twice as fast as I was, how long would it take them to catch up and tell me all the gossip I'd missed?"

She giggled, and he looked over at her. "You have a nice laugh," he said. "And a nice smile too. I never noticed that before."

If he were a little boy or a grown man, I'd know how to take the compliment, Lili thought, *but coming from someone who was neither?* Still, the math joke was the funniest thing she'd heard in a long time. "Where are you all day long?" Lili asked. "I never see you except at dinner. How do you avoid having to come out and play *paille-maille?*"

"No one cares where a thirteen-year-old boy is. I'm too old to be adorable and too young to be entertaining. I just wander around, or stay in my room and do what I want."

"Like what?"

"Oh, I don't know. Little science experiments. I'm setting up a laboratory at Vaux-le-Vicomte, and I look at things under the microscope mostly."

"Laboratory?" Lili's jaw dropped. "Microscope? Here?"

"It's not what you think. Right now, it's just a corner of my dressing room set up with equipment. My father's promised to build a real lab at Vaux-le-Vicomte, though I'm not sure how much I'll be here to use it."

"What do you look at?"

"Oh, whatever looks interesting. Moss, mold, leaves. I watch fleas crawl around and see little things squirming in water drops." He tapped a pouch tied to his saddle. "I was hoping to find some things to look at today. Maybe you can do it with me."

"How could a microscope fit in there?" she asked. Lili heard how childishly eager her voice sounded, but as thoughts of Delphine's disapproval flitted through her mind, she brushed them aside.

Paul-Vincent pulled up his horse again and took out a little case. Inside was a copper instrument small enough to fit in his palm. He handed it to her, and she looked up at him, perplexed. She had seen a drawing of a microscope, and it was nothing like this tiny, violin-shaped object with a large screw in place of the instrument's neck, and a glass lens where the sound hole would be.

"This is the kind Leeuwenhoek invented. I'll show you how it works." Paul-Vincent put out his hand to take back the tiny device. "The screw tightens or loosens this little bracket that presses on the lens, so whatever you've put on this little skewer"—Paul-Vincent touched his finger to a needlelike prong set just over the little circle of glass—"can come into focus when you hold it up to the light."

He looked up at the lattice of tree branches above their heads. "When there is some light, I mean." He put the tiny object back in its case and slipped it into his saddle bag. "Hooke's microscope is easier, because you look down through a cylinder onto something, but really, this one magnifies better. If you want, I'll show you how it works after lunch."

If I want? "I'd be delighted," Lili said, trying out her best imitation of Delphine's coquettish toss of the head, and instantly wishing she hadn't made the truth sound so false.

THE TWO OF them caught up with the rest of the group just before they reached the clearing in front of a hunting lodge. Tendrils of smoke rose from the chimney where a cooking fire had been laid. The interior had been dusted and a stew pot hung over a bed of glowing embers, but other than the bustle of the moment, the lodge showed no recent signs of use.

The building could hardly be called rustic, with its painted panels and gilded cherubs in the vestibule, holding up a carved banner still embossed with the crest of the Marquis du Villars, the former owner of Vaux-le-Vicomte. In fact, nothing in the lodge seemed to be about hunting at all, once they were past the stunned-looking deer and snarling boar whose heads were mounted in the antechamber. The dishes on the table were so dainty, and the crystal so fragile, that if this were a story by Charles Perrault or Madame d'Aulnoy, Lili decided, the place would surely be enchanted.

Where's the evil witch? Lili wished Delphine were beside her to share the joke. The other girls had all disappeared upstairs, and Lili trailed along afterward, mystified again by their peals of laughter.

At the table, over a ragout of venison and root vegetables, Anne-Mathilde and Joséphine chattered about how simple, and in a way cleansing and pure, the lives of peasants must be, and how disappointed they had been to find the upstairs almost entirely unfurnished. "We shall have to persuade Father to change that, now that Vaux-le-Vicomte is ours," Anne-Mathilde said. "Won't we, Paul-Vincent?"

She noticed Lili's grin. "Whatever is so funny?"

"Oh, nothing," Lili replied. "I was just picturing you here." *Stirring a poisoned pot.*

"It can be my own little house, to entertain my friends." Anne-Mathilde ignored Lili and looked back at the two other girls. "Unless you want to turn it into a silly old laboratory." She stuck out her tongue at her brother, as if to convey her confidence that she could never be unattractive, regardless of what she did. She burst out in a laugh that turned into something more like a cackle, and Lili wondered for a moment if they all would be turned into barnyard animals by her spell.

"No, my dear sister," Paul-Vincent said. "In fact it would give me immense pleasure if you spent all your time here with your friends." He looked over at Lili, and if he could have done so without betraying that he meant his comment as an insult, Lili was sure he would have winked.

Anne-Mathilde, having missed the slight altogether, put down her napkin. A liveried valet, one of a group of servants who had come shortly after dawn to prepare the lodge for its visitors, came up behind her to pull back her chair.

"Well, then," Anne-Mathilde said, standing up. "It's settled. The lodge is mine. And since I am its mistress, I make the rules. Don't disturb the ladies for the next hour, so we can rest for that beastly ride back to the château."

"I'm not tired," Lili said. "Paul-Vincent has promised me a walk."

"Lili!" Delphine implored. She came over and took Lili's elbow. "You're supposed to stay with us," she whispered. "You know. Be sociable."

It's the only attention she's paid me all day, Lili thought, fighting down anger.

Delphine's pleading smile vanished at Lili's resistance to the tug on her arm. "Oh, go then," she sniffed.

Lili felt the eyes of all three girls on her as she turned her back and went out the door with Paul-Vincent.

* * *

A PATH AWAY from the clearing led down to a stream, which by late summer had disappeared under an explosion of thick marsh grasses. Frogs bellowed and dragonflies hovered in the sticky air. Paul-Vincent slapped his face, leaving behind a tiny smear of blood where a mosquito had landed. "This wasn't such a good idea after all," he said. "But I wanted to collect some water to look at under the microscope back at the château."

He came over to her and pressed his index finger onto her forehead. "Mosquito," he said. "Got it." He peered more closely. "A little too late, I'm afraid. You're going to have a bump." Lili's fingers found the spot by the itch, and she wrinkled her nose in disgust.

"You're very pretty," Paul-Vincent said. "The prettiest girl at the château."

"Me?" She looked away, taken aback by the compliment. "That's not something I hear too often. Delphine's the pretty one."

"Yes, but in an ordinary way, if you know what I mean."

"I'm not sure I do," Lili said, trying to sound offhand as she watched two dragonflies hovering in midair.

Paul-Vincent was making his way through the weeds to the edge of the stream. "She's very nice to look at," he called back to her, "but it doesn't seem there is anything more to discover." He lifted up a collecting jar half full of cloudy green water. "Like my sister."

"Delphine is a lot more interesting than Anne-Mathilde!" Lili snorted. *Don't talk about them,* she pleaded silently. *Even if you're just thirteen, talk about me.*

He was standing next to her again. "You'd know better than I do about girls, I suppose," he said with a shrug. He examined the liquid as he swirled it in the jar. "This should be good." He slapped his cheek again before putting the collecting jar in a bag he slung over his shoulder.

"Let's not go back yet," Lili said, surprised at the quaver in her voice.

Paul-Vincent gave her a curious look. "We're being eaten alive."

"I know," she said, running her fingers over her face. "Is there anywhere else to go besides—back there?"

"Do you like wild strawberries?" he asked.

"Does anyone not?"

"Well, then, let's go," he said, making a gesture to take her arm, before changing his mind and dropping his hands awkwardly to his side. Paul-Vincent began walking in the direction of a woodland glade between the stream and the lodge. "I noticed a big patch when I was riding here by myself last week. Perhaps there are still some, though the season's almost past."

"By yourself," Lili said. "You have no idea how much of a luxury that is."

"We all have our luxuries, I suppose," he said. "At least you're not stuck babbling in Latin at boarding school. And then, next year, it's off to my regiment." He laughed. "It sounds so odd—'my' regiment. My parents bought a command for me, of course without asking whether I wanted it or not. I'll have to go off to be a junior officer soon. Learn my way around. Get to know the men." He shrugged. "All that."

He paused for a moment to observe a doe and her fawn disappearing into the glade. "So there goes any time to do the things I enjoy, though I do rather like the uniform, I have to admit. What do you do at home in Paris?"

"Not much. Read, write stories—silly ones for children. I study things most people tell me I have no use for, like astronomy. Physics."

"No use for?"

"Everyone thinks the only things that matter are what husbands view as useful. Except for Maman, of course."

"I thought your mother was dead." Paul-Vincent picked up a twig and made a full circle of his body as he threw it.

"She is. I call Madame de Bercy 'Maman,' since she's the one who raised me." Lili bent down to pick a small yellow flower poking out from the forest debris. She put it to her nose, inhaling a fragrance that was more fresh and pungent than sweet. "Delphine and I call each other sister sometimes, though it isn't actually true." She thought for a moment. "How did you know about my mother?"

"I studied a little of the *Principia* at school," Paul-Vincent replied. "When I heard your last name, I asked Anne-Mathilde if you might be related. She didn't care a whit that your mother had a brain in her head, but she certainly was ready to gossip about this and that."

"Gossip?"

"Nothing in particular that's likely to have a shred of truth to it, especially if it comes from her. I guess it was mostly that your mother was more interested in science than people thought she should be, and although it's beyond me why anyone should care whether somebody spends her time embroidering crests on pillows or working out calculus, I guess it seemed dangerous somehow. That it was bad for women in general when men saw one of them be so—"

They both turned, hearing the voices of two young children nearby. Seconds later, a girl of about eight ran into view, chasing a boy several years younger. Both were wearing grimy smocks spattered with red from the strawberries they'd eaten. Catching a glimpse of Lili and Paul-Vincent, they backed away.

"Don't be afraid," Lili said, taking a step toward the children and putting out her hand with a smile. "Did you save a few for us?"

The boy yowled as the girl yanked him by the hand. "We didn't eat any!" she said, dragging him back into the woods as fast as he could run.

Lili turned to Paul-Vincent. "What was that about?"

"They're not supposed to take anything from the estates of nobles," Paul-Vincent explained. "Their family is probably nearby with big baskets, making off with enough to sell for a loaf of bread in the village, and maybe hoping to snare a rabbit to cook over a fire somewhere in the woods tonight."

"Don't they have a home?"

"Probably not. Part of the *population flottante*." Seeing Lili's confusion, he went on. "Peasants who've lost their lands. There are many of them now. A bad harvest or two and they can't pay their debts or their taxes. They lose their homes and patch of land and wander around taking advantage of anything that's there for them to steal."

"Steal? Are we going to eat everything ourselves? And ripe fruit is rotten in a day or two anyway."

"That's not the point," Paul-Vincent said. "My father says people should only have the benefit of work they've done themselves, if France is to stay strong."

"Growing wild strawberries is work?"

"If they think no one's watching, they'll rob us blind."

An image of the beaten tailor flashed into her mind, and she didn't care how scolding her tone sounded. "The strawberries grow by themselves, and they belong as much to the birds or those children as they do to anyone else. More, really, because they need them for food and you don't."

Paul-Vincent looked at her sheepishly. "Actually, I agree. It's been beaten into me that there's a certain way the son of a duke is supposed to turn out, and I've found it easier to say what everyone expects to hear. But I didn't really mean it. It seems as if there should be a way for everyone to have enough, but I can't say I know too many people who give it that much thought."

Lili felt her heart slowing down. "I'm glad I don't have to add you to the list of people I'd rather not talk to." She cocked her head and this time her smile was genuine. "Especially since you have a microscope I have yet to look through."

Paul-Vincent laughed. "Shall we eat a little of my inheritance first? Sit down and I'll bring some berries to you, so you don't soil your hands." He took off his jacket and laid it on the ground, and once she was settled, he took a small butterfly net from his bag. Within minutes he had returned with dozens of berries nestled at the bottom of the net. Sitting down on the soft mat of twigs and leaves on the forest floor, he turned the net inside out, spilling out the tiny fruits and brushing off bits of debris as he picked a few of them up with delicate fingers and laid them on the palm of his hand.

"Here." He gave Lili four or five of the best ones and tossed the remainder in his mouth.

Lili lifted her hand to her nose. "They smell like the woods," she said, pinching the leafy top off the first berry and putting the fruit in her mouth. The tiny, soft skin broke between her tongue and palate without her needing to chew, releasing an explosion of musty sweetness so intense, she shut her eyes to savor it better.

"If you don't eat faster, you won't get your share," Paul-Vincent said. Lili opened her eyes and tossed the remaining berries into her mouth, mashing them with her tongue against the inside edges of her teeth, and letting the spicy tang work through to her cheeks.

Nice, she thought. *So nice.* The taste of strawberries lingering in her mouth, the light shimmering in the glade, birdsong in the trees, the wisp of a breeze on a warm afternoon . . .

The good company. She looked at Paul-Vincent, who was sorting through the remaining berries. No point in letting her imagination go. He was three years younger than she was, and the suitable mate for him was probably asleep in a cradle.

A dragonfly buzzed by her head, pursued by a second one. Paul-Vincent gave a whoop of excitement, and within a few seconds he had trapped one in his net. "I was hoping for this," he said, decapitating the insect with a quick motion and securing one of its wings to the microscope. He went a few steps to a better lit spot in the clearing and held the microscope up to the light, adjusting the screws until he had it right. "Come take a look," he said.

Lili peered through the lens and gasped. The wing burst out before her like a leaded glass window in a cathedral, translucent and radiant as a drop of oil on water, held together by a lattice of rectangles and hexagons, no two alike. "Spin this screw like this," Paul-Vincent said, showing her how to twirl the specimen to see it at different angles.

Lili was vaguely aware of his hand on the small of her back as she looked through the lens, but when she turned to comment, his face was so close she almost brushed his cheek with her nose. She shifted her weight back to pull away, but without knowing quite how it happened, his lips were on hers. They were warm and wet, and softer than she imagined possible, but she was too startled to linger. She pulled away, pressing her fingers to her mouth.

"I'm sorry," Paul-Vincent said. "I shouldn't have done that."

No you shouldn't, Lili thought, not sure if she believed it. *But I think I'm glad you did.* "It isn't proper," she said, trying to sound indignant. "And it shouldn't happen again."

And then it did. This kiss, longer and more confident, set off an odd but not unpleasant twinge in her belly that inched toward her groin, fading only when a hard click of teeth caused her to startle and pull away. Just then the sound of horses' hooves crackled through the twigs on the forest floor, and Jacques-Mars burst into the clearing.

"Where in hell have you been?" he said. His horse whinnied and tossed its head at the yank of the bit when Jacques-Mars pulled up next to them. "We were about to send out the guard." He tossed his head in Lili's direction. "Help her on behind me," he said to Paul-Vincent. "I've tied up your horses back at the trail."

Jacques-Mars looked back and forth between Lili and Paul-Vincent, with an expression unnerving enough to make her feel as if her chest were folding in half. *Do men just know when some things happen? Is it that obvious?*

Paul-Vincent made a stirrup with his hands and helped her up behind Jacques-Mars, whose body under his riding jacket felt as uninviting as a statue.

"Did you notice that family stealing strawberries just up the trail?" Jacques-Mars asked. "I drove them off. Gave one of their dirty little brats a whack to let them know I meant business."

Their horses were tied up only a few minutes away, and Lili avoided Paul-Vincent's eyes when he helped her back down from Jacques-Mars's horse and onto her own.

"You're going to have to start paying attention, Paul-Vincent," Jacques-Mars said. "If you don't, hundreds like them will think your lands are the solution to their empty stomachs, and soon they'll be so bold it won't be safe for you to be out here." His eyes pierced Lili with a now-unmistakable leer. "Especially with a young lady." Then Jacques-Mars kicked his horse's flanks and galloped down the trail to the château.

Lili followed, forgetting Jacques-Mars's expression and thinking of nothing but the lingering taste of strawberries and soft lips, the secrets of dragonfly wings, and what Paul-Vincent must look like riding behind her.

Emilie
1733

"FRANÇOIS!" JEAN-LUC Valmont steadied himself as he leaned out of the coach and stared up at a third-story window. "François-Marie Arouet!" he called up again in the blaring tone of a drunken reveler. "Get yourself down out of that rat hole you live in! I've got someone I want you to meet."

A pretty young woman tugged on his coat to bring him back inside the coach. "You dolt! He doesn't answer anybody that way." Since getting out of the coach was unthinkable in the filthy and decrepit neighborhoods along the quays of the Seine, the young woman stuck her head a little way out and sang to the same window in a tipsy and off-key voice. "Monsieur Voltaire! Come down! Your public is waiting!"

The window opened and a man in his midthirties leaned out. "Be quiet!" he said. "My landlady's had enough of my so-called friends—" He looked up and down the street to see if anyone had noticed the commotion. "And I can't have you up. I've nothing to eat here."

"Get dressed!" Jean-Luc leaned out again and called up to him. "Mademoiselle du Thil and I are taking a distinguished and beautiful guest to dinner, and if we don't get out of this stinking cesspool of a street in ten minutes, you can stay home with your cheap wine and day-old bread because we're leaving without you!"

"He's coming," he said to his companions, even though the man at the window had not said so. Within a few minutes, the door flung open, and a man wearing a long, loosely curled wig, black trousers, and a lacy white shirt stepped inside the carriage, carrying a jacket he had not had time to put on. "Beastly hot for a coat anyway," he said, piercing the air with hawklike eyes as he glanced at the twenty-seven-year-old stranger sitting across from him.

"Madame, may I present François-Marie Arouet de Voltaire," Jean-Luc said with a flourish. "Voltaire, this is our illustrious visitor from Semur—Gabrielle-Emilie, the Marquise du Châtelet."

"*Enchanté.*" Voltaire gave her hand a perfunctory kiss. Sitting back as the carriage moved forward, he took in the expensive fabric and perfect tailoring of her dress, and the rakish matching hat in the latest style. "You are from Semur?" The note of surprise made his contempt for small, provincial cities unmistakable.

"Not at all," Emilie du Châtelet sniffed. "I am from Paris. I have the bad fortune of being required to live part of the year where my husband is governor." She composed her face in a practiced smile. "I am sure a gentleman such as you will not hold that against me."

The insult was subtle but clear. A marquise need offer no explanation of anything to an untitled commoner who lived in a rooming house.

Salvaging what looked like the makings of a ruined party if they took a dislike to each other, Marie-Victoire du Thil intervened. "We decided that the marquise simply had to meet you, since you are the second-most-intelligent person in Paris." She held up her fan and waved the air in a playful gesture over Voltaire's damp forehead.

"Second?" Voltaire said, putting his fingertips on the top of her fan and pushing it down so he could look in her eyes. "And what man, may I ask, is there to rival me?" A shrug of the shoulders and an arched brow were not enough to mask the hint of insecurity in his voice.

Marie-Victoire du Thil giggled. "Jean-Luc and I want to spend the rest of our lives telling people we are the ones who intro-duced you. It is no man, monsieur. You are seated across from her right now."

6

"THEY CALL you 'the little *dévots*,' the way you walk around like you're deep in prayer or something, not noticing anything else." Delphine sat before the mirror in her dressing room, dusting her neck with powder in preparation for dinner. "I try to defend you, but you don't know how silly it looks to spend all your time with a thirteen-year-old, even if he is the future Duc de Praslin."

"You spend all your time with Jacques-Mars," Lili snapped, turning away so Delphine could not see the hurt on her face.

"I don't like him at all." Delphine's tone was haughty as she leaned in to examine a slight puffiness of her upper lip. "You would have noticed if you weren't always so taken up by your little admirer."

"Was Jacques-Mars a bad boy?" Lili mocked.

"Of course not!" Delphine's arm jerked and she knocked her brush to the floor. She picked it up with an indignant sniff and slapped it down on the table. "How can you say such a thing?"

"Well, Paul-Vincent may be thirteen, but that doesn't mean he knows nothing." Lili wanted to prove a point more than she wanted to keep her secret. "For example, he kissed me," she said. "More than once. And I kissed him back."

Delphine swung her legs around on the vanity stool and stared openmouthed at Lili. "You kissed him? Paul-Vincent?" She raised her eyebrows. "Why?"

"I don't know. We were standing close, looking at something with his microscope, and it just happened."

"And?"

Perhaps it was still safe to confide in her. After all, Delphine really was her only friend. "Now he tries to do it every time I see him. I have to tell him to stop, that I only want to look in his microscope, but . . ." Lili sighed. "It's not fair. I don't see why I shouldn't be able to look at little creatures wiggling in water without there being some sort of—some sort of price attached."

Delphine turned to the mirror again, and Lili watched her apply a dab of rouge to her mouth. When it was clear she wouldn't reply, Lili shrugged and went on. "It's not that I don't like the way it feels, but he's only thirteen and it doesn't seem right to kiss someone who's just a boy. Not that I want to kiss a man either, but it just seems as if once you've done it, you can't go back to being someone who hasn't."

"I know."

Delphine's voice was distant, but she was looking down now, and Lili could not see her expression in the mirror. *Maybe she's just not interested because it's not about her,* Lili thought, *but there's no one else I can tell.* "So I let him do it once every time I see him, just to use his microscope. But it's making me not like him anymore because I feel so—" She sighed in frustration. "Do you know what I mean? Do you and Jacques-Mars—"

"Perhaps you should ask Maman to get you a microscope," Delphine interrupted.

"Is that all you have to say? If it's not one of your concerns, you're not interested?"

"That's not what I meant. You know Maman would, if she thought Paul-Vincent could not be trusted to be more—more innocent." Delphine got up from the dressing table and went to the chair where her dress was laid out. "Perhaps Maman doesn't realize that just because Paul-Vincent and Jacques-Mars are too young to be suitable, that doesn't mean they don't have ideas. Do you mind if we do each other's corset? I don't feel like calling Corinne."

Delphine planted her hands around a bedpost, and Lili began tugging on the laces. "What ideas does Jacques-Mars have?" Lili asked, feeling Delphine's body go rigid.

"Worse ones than Paul-Vincent," she said. "It's embarrassing to say."

Delphine's shoulders trembled, and she stood up. "Oh, Lili, please stop. I can't bear it. This corset's sucking the life out of me. Let's plead cramps and stay in tonight. I'm desperate—"

Julie de Bercy swept into the dressing room. "Not dressed yet?" she asked, stopping herself from chiding them when she noticed their serious expressions. "What on earth is wrong?" she asked.

Delphine broke into tears. "I—I can't say."

Lili stared at her. "It's all right," she said. "You can tell Maman about Paul-Vincent—"

"It's not about that." Delphine's voice was suddenly so hoarse it could scarcely break out of her throat at all. "I promised I wouldn't tell."

What is she talking about? Lili's heart raced with worry.

Julie came to stand behind Delphine. "Grab the bedpost," she said. "I'll finish lacing your corset while you tell me what this is all about." Delphine braced herself, and Julie asked again. "Promised whom."

"Jacques-Mars," Delphine whispered. "And Anne-Mathilde."

"And what, pray, would they feel was a secret between them and you?" She let go of the corset laces and turned Delphine around to face her. Delphine looked down to avoid her eyes.

We'd been having a good grouse, like we used to on the way to the abbey, Lili thought, *and all of a sudden she's in tears and talking about something else entirely? Anne-Mathilde and Jacques-Mars? Secrets?*

Maman raised Delphine's chin with her fingers to force her to look at her. "Is this about something Jacques-Mars has done to you? Has he . . . ?" Lili's memory flashed to the pictures in the book she had recently smuggled back to the library, and her body shuddered in revulsion. *Not that. It can't be. Please, not that.*

"Maman, I didn't mean for anything to happen. Anne-Mathilde and Joséphine suggested we all go out to the grotto at the end of the gardens the day before yesterday, since it wasn't so awfully hot. Jacques-Mars asked to go along, like he always does. When we got to the terrace above the canal—you know, the one they call the Poêle—Anne-Mathilde said she had a headache and asked a servant waiting in a carriage to make a quick trip back to the château with her, and of course that stupid Joséphine had to go too."

"That left you alone with Jacques-Mars," Maman said. "You should have thought about how that might look."

"Yes, but I also thought of how rude it would be to say I wanted to go back without seeing what he had walked with us so long to get to. He pointed out the statues of the River Gods in the grotto on the other side of the Poêle, and said that the water sprays made it nice and cool there, and we'd easily find someone who could give us a ride back." Delphine's eyes welled with tears. "It all made so much sense."

"I'm not surprised you were persuaded." Julie paused. "So you went to see the River Gods?"

"Well, no. After Anne-Mathilde's carriage was gone, we walked down the stairs to the canal. There was no place to cross, except much farther down, and I told him I didn't want to walk that far. I was annoyed he hadn't told me it was still a long way from where we'd left Anne-Mathilde, but I guess I know why he didn't. He was trying to get me alone. It's so obvious now."

"So you started back."

"We walked for a few minutes, and then he said I looked a little flushed with the heat, and wouldn't it be a good idea to sit and cool off in a little alcove under some stairs. I said yes, because my stomach was feeling a bit upset and I did feel a little faint. But when we sat down, he started kissing me really hard."

Delphine touched her lip. "It hurt, Maman. My mouth is still raw inside. He pushed me back against the wall and started working his fingers inside my bodice. I tried to stop him, but he got my breasts pulled out, and he wasn't even kissing them, more like bites so hard I thought my nipples might bleed. And then he was pulling up my skirt and trying to reach under it."

By now Julie had brought Delphine over to the couch and was sitting beside her while Lili sat on the floor clinging to Maman's knee. "How far did his hand reach?" Julie asked.

"Almost to the top of my legs. I pressed them together as hard as I could, and he said if I would let him show me where women most like to be touched, I wouldn't regret it. Then he moved his hand lower on my mouth, and when I had the chance, I bit his finger hard, until I tasted blood."

She buried her head in Julie's shoulder. "Then he grabbed me by the hair, saying the only reason he didn't hit me was that it might leave a mark people could see, and that I had better not say anything to anyone, because he would make sure everyone thought the whole thing was my idea."

Lili rubbed her knuckles on her thighs so angrily that her skin grew hot under her skirt. *I'm going to get him*, she thought. *I don't know how, but I'm going to destroy him for this.*

"And what about Anne-Mathilde?" Julie asked. "Was she involved?"

Delphine's chest heaved. "When I said Anne-Mathilde and Joséphine would defend me, he just laughed. He said Anne-Mathilde had been planning the whole thing for days. The carriage was waiting above the Poèle because she had asked someone in the stables to meet her there."

"*Mon Dieu*," Julie whispered, jumping up because she was too agitated to sit.

"Anne-Mathilde wanted this to happen?" Lili's voice came out in a barking sob. "Why?"

"It was something about how Vaux-le-Vicomte was her family's new possession, and I had been acting like I owned it."

Lili threw her arms around Delphine as she took Maman's vacant seat. "Did you notice Jacques-Mars's hand?" Delphine asked. "It's bandaged. That's the only good part."

She turned to Julie. "Did I do anything wrong, Maman? Other than being stupid?"

"No, *ma chérie*. In fact I'm proud of how you handled him." She came around to the front of the couch and helped the two girls to their feet. "But I'm not happy that you've hidden this from me. And from Lili."

"I should have noticed," Lili said, pressing her fingers hard to her lips to stop the trembling.

"It's not your fault, Lili. I thought if I didn't tell anyone, we'd go back to Paris and I could just pretend it hadn't happened."

Julie was no longer listening. "I need to think about what to do, but for now, difficult as it may seem, you have to put on your dresses and go down to dinner."

"Oh no, Maman," Delphine said. "My face is all swollen—and my eyes!"

Maman silenced her by holding up her hand. "You hid this from us for two days, and you can hide it from everyone else for a few more hours." She gestured across the room. "The bedpost," she said. "If you don't show up, they win. If you behave as if you have nothing to fear, you're the conqueror—not forever, but for now." She arched her eyebrows at Delphine and pointed again. "The bedpost."

DESPITE THE IMPOSING size of the château at Vaux-le-Vicomte, arrival at dinner did not involve grand entrances through hallways glittering with mirrors and glowing sconces. Instead, guests went through a side door off the main foyer of the house and made their way through the library and a bedroom furnished for use by the king when he visited. After passing through five or six richly appointed rooms, guests came to a bathroom and skirted around a large tub that was often still wet from its latest occupant, before entering a wood-paneled corridor so narrow that women's panniers often brushed the walls.

Lili cast a glance in a paneled mirror outside the dining room and saw a reflection of a stranger walking behind her. Delphine's strawberry-blond hair had become a tangled mat from her tears, and since there was no time to fix it, she was wearing a white wig retrieved from Maman's dressing room. Her eyes were no longer bloodshot, thanks to some drops that made them sparkle in odd contrast to a furrowed brow that even Maman's secret remedies could not mask.

At the door, Julie gave Delphine a little squeeze of the hand. "Be brave," she said, before taking the honored seat next to the Duc de Praslin. "Come on," Lili whispered. She took Delphine's arm, remembering the little girl who had practiced curtseying until she fell over and then had gotten up to curtsey some more, the girl who believed that doing something perfectly was a talisman against something as powerful as an evil queen who could turn children to stone. *Believe it again*, Lili prayed. *Walk into this room believing it again.*

Entering the dining room at Vaux-le-Vicomte was like stepping into a mosaic. Paintings of mythological scenes were inset in glowing wood-paneled walls decorated with carpetlike designs in blues, yellows, and greens. Gold moldings framed the doorways and divided the painted ceiling into quadrants that glowed in the sunlight streaming through large, oak-framed windows.

Chairs upholstered in shimmering brocade lined a table set for the duke and duchess's twenty guests. To Lili's dismay the only seats that remained were on both sides of Jacques-Mars. *Did he plan it that way?* Lili wondered, as she sat down between him and Paul-Vincent. Directly across the table, Anne-Mathilde and Joséphine stopped talking to watch Delphine take her seat. Anne-Mathilde's gown of golden brocade fit the colors of the room, and her elbow-length sleeves were tipped with several layers of lace so delicate they looked like froth. She was wearing a choker of pearls extravagant enough to settle any questions of rank at Vaux-le-Vicomte.

Wanting to see if Delphine was all right, Lili turned as far as her corset and the frame of her panniers allowed. Immediately she sat back, startled by the proximity of Jacques-Mars, who had leaned in toward her. "You look lovely," he said. His eyes lowered, resting on the tops of her breasts, pushed up into ample mounds but covered by a modest swath of nearly transparent white silk.

"Where have you been hiding, Jacques-Mars?" *A rat hole?* Lili thought, as she pasted on a smile she hoped disguised the shiver of disgust that had traveled along her spine. "Still giving *paille-maille* lessons to pretty girls?"

Jacques-Mars's eyes flickered as she looked past him to Delphine. Much to Lili's surprise, Delphine was already in deep and animated conversation with the younger brother of the rotten-toothed Comte de Beaufort, who was seated farther up the table near Maman. Apparently sensing Lili's stare, Delphine turned to glance at her, revealing a glowing face that an hour earlier had looked trapped and near panic. *I'm in worse shape than she is,* Lili thought.

"Lili?" The voice was Paul-Vincent's, on her other side. "Aren't you speaking to me?"

"I'm sorry," she said. "I'm just a little distracted."

"I just thought of an excellent experiment. Look at this." He held up his wineglass. "Do you see?"

"See what?" *Not science. Not tonight.*

"The fruit flies. They're everywhere. I think they like wine, but it looks as if something about it makes them act strange."

Lili dutifully held up her own glass, trying to catch as much light as possible from the candles. "I've got two of them sitting on the rim," she said, "tipping down inside, like they're trying to get whatever's left there."

In spite of herself, she was interested. "Maybe they just don't want to fall in."

"And maybe they're a little drunk," he snickered. "I wonder if vapors coming up from the wine are doing that, or if they're actually drinking from the film around the top of the glass. I wish I'd brought the microscope."

Lili laughed. "You can't bring a microscope to dinner!"

"How about tomorrow?" He lowered his voice. "I promise I won't try to kiss you if you come to the lab."

Lili stared at him, so wrapped up in the problems of the day that it took a moment to understand what he was referring to. She had already looked at a fruit fly under the microscope and been horrified by its enormous eyes and tiny, clawlike feet. Now she felt nothing but sympathy for the little creatures hovering on her glass. Could they escape or would they just stay there, caught and confused between the forces that attracted and repelled them, until they fell in and drowned, or perhaps flew out and survived a little longer?

"I'm the one who should be upset!" Jacques-Mars's angry whisper brought her back.

"Monsieur Courville," Delphine said, pulling herself up in her seat. "I can only wish that if I have the misfortune to meet you again, I will at least have the pleasure of being able to see the scar I hope I've left you with." Her smile and lilting tone were at odds with the words spoken under her breath, as if she were daring him to be the one who called the guests' attention to their argument.

She caught Lili's eye and her own flashed with triumph before she turned to speak to Anne-Mathilde across the table. "You're so far away I can scarcely hear what you're talking about, but Joséphine seems so amused I'm sure I'd like to know!"

Temporarily taken aback, Anne-Mathilde looked to her left to exchange a glance with Joséphine, ignoring the dazed expression of the hapless male guest with the bad luck to be seated between them. Recovering, she let out a shrill laugh. "We were just discussing taking another visit to the grotto. I'm so sorry to have missed it, with my wretched headache."

Delphine's face flushed momentarily. "Yes, it's quite enchanting—don't you agree, Jacques-Mars?" she replied, turning to him. "Just meant for an afternoon with friends."

Jacques-Mars turned away from Delphine and glowered across the table at Anne-Mathilde.

"Is there something wrong?" Lili turned to ask him, in a voice as rich and sweet as syrup.

"Not at all," he said. His brow rose. "If you'd like we can take a carriage there tomorrow. I can show you what Delphine means."

Lili fought down the urge to slap him. *Pretend nothing is wrong,* she told herself. "That sounds quite pleasant," she said.

"Really!" Jacques-Mars drew out the word in pleased disbelief, as he darted his eyes at her bodice again. "So Delphine didn't—"

"Didn't what?" Lili raised her voice in mock puzzlement. *I'll plead sick every day to avoid having to spend one minute alone with him. I'll make my heart give out and die before I let him come near me.*

Jacques-Mars's nostrils flared almost imperceptibly. "Didn't tell you how very charming I find you," he said, giving her a calculated stare. "I shall pursue you until you make good on what I insist is a promise to come to the grotto with me." The coldness of his eyes and the turn of his lip belied his attempt to make it sound like a simple flirtation.

Lili picked up her wineglass as a means to look away, gently blowing a fly off the rim before taking a sip. *Mon Dieu,* she thought as her own invisible storm whirled.

"Lili." Delphine leaned forward to look around Jacques-Mars. "The Comte de Beaufort has just told me the most remarkable story about the château." She looked back at the man seated next to her. "Do tell Lili yourself," she asked. "I'm sure I can't do it justice."

Honoré de Beaufort cleared his throat and coughed into his handkerchief, examining its contents before looking down the table at Lili. "I told mademoiselle," he said, with the precise but stuffy articulation of someone certain that no one appreciates the great significance of his words, "that Vaux-le-Vicomte so incensed Louis the Fourteenth that he had the man who built it imprisoned for having a grander home than his own. Died in prison, in disgrace, I'm afraid. Of course the king claimed to have other grounds for what he did. He said that Monsieur Fouquet had used his position as the king's treasurer to embezzle money, and that's how he could afford to build the château."

Jacques-Mars sniffed. "He's the king, after all. Kings do whatever they like. Anyone would do the same, if he had the power."

"Tell me, had he embezzled the money?" Lili asked.

"Who knows?" Beaufort laughed.

"You must admit, Monsieur de Beaufort," Jacques-Mars broke in, "that even though the king had the power to do what he did, Fouquet deserved better treatment. If not, what's the point of loyalty?"

"The point of loyalty to the king?" Beaufort's voice rose, and he pulled himself up in his chair. "There doesn't need to be a point to it. Or are you one of those—"

"Oh, honestly," Anne-Mathilde said across the table, cutting them off. "We can hear you discussing politics, and that's so unpleasant over dinner." She stuck out her lower lip in an exaggerated pout. "What a great disappointment you are, Jacques-Mars," she said. "I thought we could count on you to be fun. And you, Delphine," she added, with a smirk. "Can't you control him?"

"I'll just say one thing more," Jacques-Mars said. "It doesn't really matter what should be, only what is. I'd wager that people living on the docks of the Seine have their own neighborhood kings and knaves. One knows one's place. One should guard against angering those with more power, because they will get revenge whenever it suits them and whether anyone else thinks it's fair or not. This is true whether they're a carriage driver or a king—don't you agree?" Though he addressed the question to Beaufort, his eyes rested on Delphine, before he turned the same cold stare on Lili.

If Beaufort replied, Lili didn't hear it. *Jacques-Mars is trying to scare me,* she thought. *And I'm not going to let him.* Still, more than an hour later, Lili had scarcely eaten a bite.

AFTER DINNER MAMAN escorted the two girls across the black-and-white marble foyer toward the Chambre des Muses and its adjoining game room. "We'll stay for half an hour or so, just to be polite to the duke and duchess," she said, as they entered a high-ceilinged parlor glittering with gilded mirrors. "Then we'll plead exhaustion and go to our rooms."

As Lili entered the Chambre des Muses, Paul-Vincent saw her from inside the doorway of the game room just beyond. "I've saved the trictrac table for us!" he called out. Lili groaned, but Julie gave her a nudge. "Go. It will be better than having to make conversation."

The Cabinet des Jeux was in one corner of the ground floor of the house, facing out onto the moat and a grassy slope beyond. Though it was quite small, light flooded through its many windows, making it one of Lili's favorite places to come to read in the quiet of the morning. Now, however, she was too miserable to notice its charms. She sat down at a delicately carved wood table whose lacquered game board was inlaid with alternating chevrons and pocked with tiny holes for the pegs that kept the score. Within half an hour, Paul-Vincent was doing his best to make light of how hopelessly he was losing.

Jacques-Mars had been conversing with the Duchesse de Praslin in the Chambre des Muses, but now he came to the doorway of the Cabinet des Jeux and leaned over Paul-Vincent. What he said was too soft for Lili to overhear, but Paul-Vincent got up with a shrug. "Apparently I'm needed elsewhere," he said, as Jacques-Mars took his seat.

"If Paul-Vincent doesn't want to play anymore, I'd prefer to stop," Lili said, stacking her markers.

Jacques-Mars reached across the table and put his hand over hers. "Just one match," he said. "If you win, I'll do whatever you ask. I'll even let you out of your promise to go to the grotto with me."

Lili thought for a moment. "One match," she said, without a hint of a smile.

They stacked the ivory and ebony disks in their respective corners of the board. "Three and two," Lili said, moving two disks to the proper arrow marks on the board.

Jacques-Mars shook the dice cup and threw. "Six and five," he said, moving his own markers. Turn after turn, they moved their pieces around the board, but after only fifteen minutes, Lili stood up.

"I believe I've won the match," she announced.

Jacques-Mars looked at her. "The game?"

"No, the match. You forgot to call your last score, so it goes to me, *par puissance*," she said. "Then, six points each for hitting each of five points in your *petit jan*, and eight points each for hitting each of five points in your *grand jan*, six points for hitting your *coin de repos*, and six points for filling the *grand jan* by doubles." She sat back down. "Take your time," she said, "but that's eighty-two total points, and since we already have fifteen apiece, I don't see how you are going to get to a hundred and forty-four before I do." She shrugged. "And I see no reason to sit here waiting for you to lose."

A murmur rose up in the Chambre des Muses, as word spread that Lili had just gotten the highest score anyone had heard of in a single trictrac move, and that the points had been defaulted to her by an inattentive opponent.

"Go back to school, young man," Honoré de Beaufort roared, "and don't tell anyone a young lady thrashed you so soundly."

Jacques-Mars's face flushed purple. He swiped all the game pieces to the floor and got up so abruptly that Lili had to steady the delicate table to keep it from toppling over. "Wait a minute," Lili said, watching his shoulder slam into the narrow doorjamb as he left the room. "I want to claim my prize."

Jacques-Mars whirled around and stared at her.

"You said you would do whatever I asked," Lili said. "I want you to take off that bandage. Let's see what hurt you."

He took a step back in surprise. "I can't," he said, turning hooded eyes toward Delphine. "It's far too unsightly for the ladies." He cast his eyes around the now-silent parlor. Everyone was frozen in place, watching.

Julie stood just inside the door. Her hand tightened on Lili's shoulder so severely that she cried out. "We're leaving," Julie hissed. "Now."

Lili whirled around to look at her. "But——"

Her words died when she saw the look of horror on Maman's face. She got up and followed her into the foyer, on a path cleared by guests whose puzzled faces she was too bewildered to notice.

"WHY DID YOU do that?" Julie spun around to face Lili when they were safely back in her dressing room. The mottling of her cheeks was visible even under her makeup, and her voice was hoarse with fury.

"I wanted to expose Jacques-Mars," Lili wailed, terrified at seeing Maman so angry. "I hate him. I wanted people to know what he'd done."

"And who would have paid the price for that?" Julie demanded.

Dumbstruck, Lili recalled what Jacques-Mars had said. *It doesn't really matter what should be, only what is. Those with more power will get revenge whenever it suits them and whether anyone else thinks it's fair or not.* Suddenly she pictured the scene in the Chambres des Muses a completely different way, and putting her hand to her mouth, she turned to Delphine. "*Mon Dieu*! I'm sorry."

"Sorry for what?" Delphine asked. "Then everyone would know what he——" Her eyes grew wide. "*Mon Dieu*," she whispered. "Everyone would know."

"You girls know less than you think about the world," Julie said, her voice beginning to calm. "And I suppose I'm largely to blame for that, protecting you the way I have. But now you know there are people who make a game of other people's lives, and—sad to say—some of them are very good at it."

She sniffed with contempt. "You'll find people like Anne-Mathilde de Praslin and Jacques-Mars Courville have a great deal of company at court, and"—she shook her finger at them for empha-sis—"you are going to have to be far more careful whom you trust.

You'll end up wishing you'd never started any kind of game with people like them, because they'll choose the way it ends, not you."

"So if someone says, 'Let's go riding,' I shouldn't go?" Delphine asked.

"Consider who's asking. You already didn't like Anne-Mathilde—for good reason, I might add. And I think it is best to assume that some young men will take whatever they can get young ladies to part with." She looked at Lili. "And that includes very young men too."

Lili felt her face grow hot, but if Julie noticed, she said nothing.

"I think that being a widow with young daughters doesn't help matters," Julie went on. "I doubt this would have happened if Jacques-Mars knew there would be an irate father to contend with."

What about my own father? Lili wondered. For a moment she pictured an older man striding into a room. "Who has compromised my daughter's honor?" he would say to the astonished crowd. Lili brushed the idea aside, because she had no idea what he looked like, and it hurt less not to think of him at all.

Maman turned her back. "Help me out of my dress," she said. "The corset hook is over there on the table."

Delphine worked on the dress in silence while Lili watched, relieved that Maman seemed her usual self again. "That's better," Julie sighed, as the stays loosened and her skin broke free. "And I don't blame either of you for being furious enough at Jacques-Mars to want to harm him, but take my advice—" She slipped off the bodice of her dress, and after laying it on a chair, she stood before them, her voluptuous curves visible beneath her chemise. "Women make perilous friends, since some of the most intelligent ones find their best outlet is intrigue," she said, slipping on a dressing gown. "And men have their own risks. They have strong drives you may not yet fully appreciate."

Lili and Delphine exchanged glances. Eradice's buttocks. The man disappearing inside her. The wild looks on their faces. Julie noticed and arched her eyebrows. "Perhaps you know a little more about this than I realize?"

Lili shifted her feet. "A little, Maman."

"Well." She smiled in amusement, watching the two girls squirm. "That will have to be a conversation for another time. You're going to need men as you go through life, and you'll have to use charm to get their services, and even more to keep them. Part of that charm lies in not forgetting that even the mildest of men has that rather strange-looking thing between his legs that you apparently know more about than can be gleaned from statues of naked gods in fountains." She arched her eyebrows and looked at each of them in turn. "His fondest wish is that you will let him use it, regardless of how he tries to make it seem otherwise, and your charm lies largely in keeping those wishes alive but unfulfilled."

She gave Delphine a tender smile. "You, my darling, have perhaps a bit too much natural flirtatiousness for your own good," she said. "And you, precious Lili, must care about having a little more. But more than anything else, you both must value the absolute treasure you have in each other."

Delphine found Lili's hand and laced her fingers through it. Julie noticed and smiled. "Emilie and I had a bit of what you have, but I was enough younger—and so much in awe of her—that we could never be equals. But you two are going though life as sisters. Almost twins, since you're the same age. You must promise me that you will always protect each other—hopefully more wisely than Lili tried to do today, but with no less passion."

"*Oui*, Maman," they both said, turning to look at each other. The girl with the pushed-up breasts, still tightly contained in her corset, wearing a wig now comically askew, was in some ways the same Delphine Lili had always known, but in others a stranger she might never understand again. But that didn't matter. The world seemed suddenly full of bad things that might happen, and all Lili knew was that she loved Delphine fiercely.

"*Oui*, Maman," Lili repeated, not sure exactly what such promises might entail.

"*Oui*, Maman," Delphine murmured in return.

Emilie
1734

THE OCTOBER breeze picked up the red and amber leaves and sent them dancing in gentle swirls across the grass of the Luxembourg Gardens. Voltaire shivered in his light frock coat. "Not long now, until we're forced indoors," he said.

"My dear, Monsieur Voltaire," Emilie chided. "I haven't noticed you fretting about being indoors if it's in bed." She reached over to stroke his cheek.

Voltaire looked around. "You should be more careful, Emilie. You're a married woman—and a mother!"

"God gave me a soul that cannot hide or control its passions. That's my excuse—I've told you so already." She reached up to stroke his cheek again, turning her face to his and parting her lips just enough to reveal the tip of her tongue. "And it took you, my love, to make me feel so hopelessly—and helplessly—myself."

"But still—"

"Quiet! If you become any more tiresome, I will kiss you right here, in front of everyone." She stopped and turned to him, stamping her foot in a teasing ultimatum.

"And if you don't behave"—Voltaire mocked her gesture with his own stamp of the foot—"I will force you to listen to another little verse I have written for you."

"Oh!" Emilie clapped her gloved hands. "Please!"

Voltaire unfolded a single sheet of paper and cleared his throat.

"Why did you come to me so late?
What was my life before?
I searched for love but found only illusions,
Only the barest shadow of what has been our joy.
You are pure delight,
Absolute tenderness.
What pleasure it is to be in your arms."

Voltaire refolded the paper and put it back in his jacket. "You must swear an oath you'll never tell anyone I write such doggerel." He patted his pocket. "And just to be sure, I'll burn the evidence as soon as—"

Her lips caught his before he could finish. She kissed him deeply, and after briefly pulling away, she kissed him again, teasing his lips apart and exploring with her tongue. "Umm," she said, putting her hands on the back of his pants and pressing his hips to hers.

"Emilie!" Voltaire pulled himself away, looking around with wild eyes. "You promised!"

"No I didn't," she teased with a wag of her finger. "You said you would force me to listen only if I misbehaved." She darted in quickly to peck his lips again. "So I did!"

He shook his head and took her arm to continue their stroll. "God forbid if all those prigs at Versailles ever really knew what a devious brain was under that stylish new hat," he said, "or body under your dress, for that matter." He reached up as if he were about to pinch her breast, but she spun away.

"I'm serious about Versailles," he called after her as she pirouetted down the walk. "I wish you spent less time there."

"It's my job to look out for my husband's interests!" She danced back toward him. "Strange as that may sound to the man in his bed."

"Maybe you stay at Versaille, to avoid seeing me. You know I'm too common to be allowed through the king's door."

"And I wish you would not ruin everything by pouting about what can't be helped. At least for now." She took his arm with a faraway smile. "And that you would turn your mind to more serious things. Understanding how the world is made, not just writing plays about dead kings. Imagine what you and I could accomplish then!"

7

1765

A DAY OR two later, Julie announced that she had a family matter to attend to in Paris and would have to cut short their time
at the château. Pretending to be heartbroken, the girls packed their
things and said their good-byes. When their coach passed the stables
and outer courtyard of Vaux-le-Vicomte, Delphine sighed with relief.
"*Mon Dieu,* I'm glad that's over."

"I'll miss Paul-Vincent's microscope," Lili said, thinking that in
time she might miss Paul-Vincent himself. It was unfortunate that
one part of their time together had come to overshadow all the rest,
but at least there was hope that not every male was either stuffy or vicious.

Maman patted Lili's knee. "Perhaps we should consider getting
you a microscope of your own," she said. "But I'm not going to give
you anything I'll have to drag you away from, when there's important business this fall."

Lili groaned. She had assured Maman that once they returned to
Paris she would put her full effort into making a success of her presentation at court. Not quite sixteen, she and Delphine were still
young for the rite of passage that would announce their marriageabil-
ity, but given the problems at Vaux-le-Vicomte, Julie had concluded
that securing a good offer of marriage might be best for both of them.
She would insist on a long engagement as one of the terms of betrothal, to keep Lili and Delphine at home awhile longer, but with

them spoken for, they each would now have a man—and his entire family—with an interest in keeping her safe from the likes of Jacques-Mars Courville.

Delphine's spirits had been raised considerably by such prospects, and once they were on the road back to Paris, she could not stop talking. New dresses for balls and candlelit banquets at Versailles, followed by marriage to an adoring and complacent husband in an elegant house to redecorate and maintain to her own liking—it was all she had ever hoped for, except perhaps the little daughters she was already dressing up like dolls and teaching to dance and play the piano. The wonder of it seemed to have pushed the ugliness of what happened at Vaux-le-Vicomte from her mind, and after an hour of chatter, she had exhausted herself into a contented sleep on Maman's shoulder.

"You've been very quiet," Maman said, looking across at Lili. "Although it would have been hard to get a word in between all those ball gowns and piano lessons."

"I wish I could have her dreams," Lili said. "It would be much simpler."

"Hers haven't come true yet," she said. "I hope they do." She stroked Delphine's cheek. "But what are yours?"

"My dreams?" Lili leaned back, as if the question were too heavy to catch. "I don't have any."

"Of course you do." Maman's eyes crinkled. "I mean, besides owning a microscope."

Lili let out a deep breath. "I know so much more about what I don't want than what I do."

"Well, then, what don't you want? That's a start."

"I don't want anyone to decide my life but me. And I don't want to have to give up what interests me because someone says I should care about something else instead."

Delphine turned her head and murmured in her sleep, and Julie shifted her shoulder to cradle her again. "Things aren't as dire as they sound," she said, leaning toward Lili as much as she could without disturbing her daughter. "When you were born, I fought Baronne Lomont to bring you to live with me right away. She was quite cruel in pointing out I was still a bride, and carrying a child who would need my full attention. And she was right. By giving in, I gained time alone with my baby to learn how to be a mother, and then in the end I got you too when I was ready. And you got someone who, despite her—well, difficulties—can be counted on to be loyal to you, even if you don't always appreciate her idea of how to show it."

She paused, but when there was no reply she continued in a voice so soft it seemed she was speaking as much to herself as to Lili. "You go one direction and see a fork in the road. You look back, and see all the other forks in your past, and you'll wonder if you've made mistakes or are about to make another, and the answer is maybe so. Almost certainly you will make mistakes, at least some of the time. But the best we can do is listen to our hearts, and our minds . . ." She thought for a moment before looking back at Lili. "And to our conscience and our duty. We just keep choosing—and hope we'll be satisfied with the results in the end, though we may have let ourselves in for unpleasantness along the way by not letting others make our choices for us."

Lili thought for a moment. "Choosing doesn't seem like something I've gotten to do much of yet. When does it start?"

"Some of the biggest things you don't choose. You do have to marry, for example." She gave Lili a wicked smile. "Unless of course you want to go be a nun at the Abbaye de Panthémont."

"Maman, you are horrid!" Lili giggled.

"Well," Julie said. "Count that as choice number one. And now the next fork in that road will be to marry the right person." She turned her head downward toward Delphine. "She needs a wealthy and kind man, and not much more in the way of particulars, but you are going to require an accomplice to have the life you want. And that, my darling Lili, will require a search worthy of the daughter of the woman who bore you."

She looked at the valise on Lili's side of the coach. "Hand me my bag, *s'il te plaît*."

Julie fingered her way through the bag, eventually pulling out a book covered in delicate Florentine paper. "The duchess left it in my room as a welcoming present, and I knew right away I wanted to give it to you."

Lili leafed through the blank pages, looking up only when she noticed the silence. Julie was staring at her. "I think it's time Meadowlark comes to the rescue," she said. "It seems there's a girl named Lili who could use her help."

* * *

"An old woman and a girl of about sixteen came out of a French farmhouse and started walking with Meadowlark and Tom, who had ridden Comète down from the stars. 'The stars are a spilled handful of salt,' the old woman said. 'There's a wildflower for every kind thought.'

"'What kind of talk is that?' Meadowlark asked the girl. 'Doesn't she know anything?'

"'I'm afraid not,' the girl said, bursting into tears.

"'Well, it's nice of you to cry for her, if she's as stupid as she sounds.'

"The old woman gave Tom a pinch on the cheek. 'Obedience paves roads,' she said with a toothless grin.

"'I'm not crying for her,' the girl said. 'The same thing is going to happen to me today. That's where we're headed. I have to go get my brains scrambled.'"

Lili gave a furtive glance through her lashes at the gentleman seated in the study at Hôtel Bercy. He was stroking his chin, and she saw a bemused crinkle at the corner of his eyes. With relief, she went back to her story, not glancing up again until she got to the end.

"Meadowlark saw her boots coming into view, which always happened first when her invisibility was wearing off. 'We need to go before they see us,' she told Tom. She gave the secret whistle and Comète appeared just down the road.

"As they ran and jumped on his back, Tom said, 'I think Earth is the strangest planet we've visited.'

"'I do too,' said Meadowlark, as they galloped into the blue sky, showering stars behind them."

Lili closed her notebook and looked up. "It's rather silly, Monsieur Diderot," she said. "I don't know why Maman wanted me to read it to you."

"Not at all!" Denis Diderot said. "Satire is quite the rage, in England particularly. As long as it's in a story, one can mock nearly everything without bringing the police to the door."

"Satire, monsieur?"

"*Exactement.* An amusing story that exposes the foolishness of society."

"I didn't mean to expose anything," Lili protested. "Meadowlark is just a girl strange things happen to." A burst of noise from the conversation in the salon made them both turn around, as the door to the study opened and Julie came in.

"Well, Monsieur Diderot," she said. "What do you think of this Meadowlark that strange things happen to?" She came over to where Lili was seated and gave her shoulder an affectionate pat. "And my Lili?"

"A budding *philosophe*," he said. "You should be most proud."

Lili took another furtive glance at one of the most famous men in France. He looked to be about fifty, with a wig pushed back just enough to reveal a balding head. His straight but overly large nose hovered over a mouth that seemed too fleshy for its dainty size.

"If she were not so young, and it were not still so potentially dangerous, I would ask your permission to have her try her hand at writing for my poor *Encyclopédie*." His voice boomed, as if exuberance alone could offset the impression made by his eyes that he was in a battle with the world and the world was winning. "She has extraordinary wit for one her age—"

"And her sex, Monsieur Diderot." Maman held up her hand with a smile to soften the fact she was interrupting such an esteemed guest. "Let's not forget to state the obvious."

"Yes," he said, turning back to Lili. "I have not forgotten the obvious. She is a most lovely young woman. Has she been presented to the queen?"

"Not yet," Julie said. "We're hoping for an opportunity when she returns from Lorraine some time next month."

Diderot watched Lili's face droop. "An experience I can see you are anticipating with great pleasure."

"Yes, sir," Lili murmured, feeling how the air grew heavy around her whenever she thought of it.

Julie broke the silence that ensued. "Lili is not only a wonderful writer. She is also quite talented at math and science." She paused. "Just like her mother."

Lili looked up in surprise. Maman rarely brought up her mother at all, and even then only when they were alone. And now, here she was, treating the subject as if it were as ordinary as the cake crumbs on her plate.

"Quite," Diderot said. "Tell me, Mademoiselle du Châtelet— are you like your mother in excelling at everything?"

"No," Lili shrugged. "I certainly don't excel at curtseys."

The great man's booming laugh filled the room. "Well," he said, "if you have one place to fall short, I definitely recommend something as insignificant as that."

Lili didn't hear. What did he know about her mother? She was too timid to ask. Julie had made it clear that it was better for Lili not to listen to others, since they were likely to share gossip, not facts. "I will never lie to you," she had reassured her. "You will know the whole truth in time." Lili adored Maman too much to cross her, but at times like this—

"So tell me, mademoiselle," Diderot's voice brought her back to the conversation in the room. "What do you think are the greatest books ever written?"

"Newton's *Principia*," Lili said, without pausing to think. "Buffon's *Natural History*. The works of Rousseau and Montesquieu—and of course Voltaire." Suddenly shy, Lili looked down. "And your *Encyclopédie*."

Diderot laughed. "A very politic answer, I must say!"

"But it's true. I'm working my way through it little by little. Maman has a subscription, so we have all the volumes."

"I know. Madame de Bercy has been most generous—and brave. Apparently it's fine for the *Encyclopédie* to describe the workings of a plough, but the workings of the church are another matter. I am, in fact, quite pleased that we have managed to offend almost everyone—king, minister, cardinal, bishop . . ." He looked at Julie with a wicked grin. "And a rival *salonnière* or two of Madame de Bercy."

Diderot leaned in toward Lili with the air of a conspirator. "I was waiting to see if you would include the Bible."

Startled, Lili looked up at Maman to see if she had made a mistake. "Say what you think," Julie said. "There are no official opinions in this house."

"I think—" Lili hesitated. Even though she was long out of the convent, it still unnerved her to say some things out loud. "I don't think the Bible or the church should be relied upon as a source for what is true about the world." She thought for a moment. "Stories can be good to help us figure some things out or decide what we ought to do, but there's a different kind of information the Bible doesn't tell us anything about. How the world really works, I mean."

"And, tell me—do you think if the Bible does not tell those kinds of truths, that we should question the existence of the God whose story it tells?" Diderot asked.

Lili squirmed. This was a bit like being examined by Baronne Lomont's priest, except she was more confident Monsieur Diderot was not sniffing around for something to punish. "I think we should question everything, just as Descartes says. But God would still exist even if nothing had ever been written about him. Even if no one knew he was there." She paused, pondering a new thought. "Isn't that what it means to be God?"

Diderot slapped his thigh in approval. "Spoken with the same high spirit as her mother—or should I say both of them?" He took off his glasses to wipe them clean, and Lili looked away, uncertain what to think.

Julie got up and took Lili's notebook from her lap. "I told Monsieur Diderot about Meadowlark," she said, "and he said if your stories were as witty as I claimed, a newspaper might publish them."

"Possibly the *Gazette d'Amsterdam*," Diderot said. "To avoid the censors. And under a false name, of course."

Publish? Lili thought of all the times when they were younger that Delphine had squeezed in next to her as they read each new adventure. It was difficult enough to feel close to Delphine anymore, as she whirled through each day, filling it with hours of determined practice of all the petty details she was sure would make the Queen of France, Marie Leszczynska, like her enough to make her one of her ladies-in-waiting. It was the best thing Delphine could do to ensure that her marriage prospects sunk no lower than a rich count or marquis, with quarters at Versailles, a beautiful town house in Paris, and at least one château in the country. But all of it added up to a vision of Delphine spinning away, out of reach forever.

Maman and Diderot were already discussing how to rearrange the letters in "Châtelet" to create a pseudonym, when Lili finally spoke. "Thank you for your offer, but I don't think I want to," she said, looking at Diderot to avoid seeing Maman's reaction. "I'm not trying to be witty, and Meadowlark is private."

Diderot sat back, rebuffed. "I'm sorry, monsieur," Lili added. "You've done me a great honor. It's just—"

Maman broke in. "There's no need to explain, *ma chérie,*" she said in a voice that, to Lili's relief, offered no hint of anger or disapproval. "They are your stories to do with as you please." She turned to Diderot. "The world will simply have to wait for Lili to be ready." Although Lili always kept the notebook on the desk in her room,

Julie made a show of enforcing her point by putting it in a drawer and turning the key.

Monsieur Diderot stood up. "Well then," he said, "fame will have to wait." He looked at Lili with a curious smile, before turning back to Julie to offer her his arm. "Shall we return to your guests?"

Lili followed behind, feeling as if Maman had opened a window and invited Meadowlark and Tom to fly off without her. But as she entered the salon, she felt her heart racing not so much in anger but with pride. *I could have said yes. How would I feel right now if I had?* She wasn't sure, but it was a very good secret to have, one that toyed at the corners of her mouth as she stood just inside the salon and listened to the voices of some of the great men of France.

Though they noted Julie's reappearance immediately, their heated debate resumed within a moment. "My dear Abbé Turgot," a man in his twenties was saying. "Surely you can't think that leaving everyone to fend for themselves—this *laissez faire* approach you write of—is enough protection for the poor soul who is being swindled by some merchant. Or for the merchant, come to think of it, cheated by his own suppliers."

Anne-Robert Jacques Turgot had his back to Lili, but his voice was raised sufficiently to be heard. "Monsieur Leclerc, I must have a higher opinion of my fellow citizens than you, for if there's one thing all but the dullest-witted can understand, it's self-interest. The market always works in the public interest as long as it is left alone. Buyers look for the best price, and successful sellers will be the ones offering that price. Too high and customers go elsewhere. Swindlers find themselves out of business rather quickly, I imagine."

"And go somewhere else and start again," one of the men said, to the murmured approval of his friends.

"But you are a government minister, Abbé!" the man called Leclerc replied. "As tax collector for Limoges, surely you aren't arguing that there is no role for the government in trade. We live in modern times! Everyone—the parlement and the king—agrees that progressive regulations can move our economy beyond the—shall I say it?—medieval exchanges of peasants on market day—"

"*Everyone* agrees?" Abbé Turgot arched his thick eyebrows.

"All but a few lunatics!" someone else broke in. "We need to do whatever it takes to rebuild our treasury, if we are to avoid another military defeat at the hands of the English. *Mon Dieu,* we just handed them North America!"

"My dear Monsieur Leclerc," Turgot went on. "There is nothing more important to the financial health of France than market day, and without financial health there is no such thing as military victory. And if we are going to talk about reason, let's include the first principle of it, which is to hold sacred the liberties that are the right of all men. The government should always protect the freedom of the buyer to buy, and the seller to sell, and the minute it imposes restrictions and special privileges, it stops doing that."

"How so?" Lili asked.

Monsieur Turgot turned in surprise at hearing a young woman's voice. "Mademoiselle du Châtelet," he said with a slight bow, "I am charmed to be the recipient of what I believe are your first words at Madame's salon."

The man standing next to him guffawed. "Oh, come now, Turgot—a lovely young woman is taking you seriously! You're more than charmed—you're amazed!"

Turgot joined the laughter for a moment before moving out of their circle. Standing in front of Lili, he addressed her alone, bending slightly at the waist to accommodate her smaller stature. "The price of goods should work out between any two people so that the buyer pays no more than is necessary for the seller to make a reasonable profit," he said. "Wouldn't you agree?"

"Of course," Lili said, resisting the urge to take a step back. "Although minds might differ on what is reasonable."

The men roared. "Be careful what you say, Turgot," Leclerc said. "You're not used to having an audience actually listen to you!"

Turgot ignored him. "A point well taken," he said to Lili before turning to include the group. "But it can never be as simple as that when governments get involved. Am I correct about that, gentlemen?" When they had nodded agreement he turned back to Lili. "Suppose the king wants to make the price of grain the same everywhere, and he decrees that it remain the same next year as last. That sounds like a good thing for a king to do, doesn't it?"

"Yes," Lili said, "because it would mean everyone gets enough bread."

"Precisely. But to do so would require inspectors, and reports, and possibly even the need to move grain from one place to another to ensure such a system was workable. And that would involve money. If the king promised not to raise the price of grain, the money to make such a program work would have to come from somewhere else—a higher tax on wine perhaps, or salt. Or another charge added on top of the official price of grain—an inspection fee, say, or a transportation tax. So in the end, the person buying the grain is buying it for the merchant's fair profit plus a little more, or else the merchant finds his profit eaten up by his costs. Or perhaps the buyer can't afford the price and has to substitute something cheaper—rye for wheat, perhaps. Poorer products, higher prices. It's hardly a benevolent act in the end, when the results come to that."

Seeing Lili's troubled expression, he stopped. "Do you understand?"

Lili's mind was whirling. "I've never tried to see the whole of France at one time," she said, "but I think I see your point."

"Well, then explain it to me!" another man said, but Lili didn't hear.

"Still," she said, "I've seen times right here in Paris where it wasn't a matter of reasonable profit, but whether a person would be paid at all for his work. And I understand the *population flottante* grows every year just because peasants can't avoid going into debt to feed their families. It seems only fair that the government would concern itself with those things, if it cares so much about the natural liberties of man. How can a man feel free if he has no way of knowing if his labor will be rewarded or his family will be fed?"

"*Vive Mademoiselle la Philosophe!*" Leclerc said.

Denis Diderot cleared his throat. "You, my friends, may some day say you were here when this young woman made her first mark on the world."

Lili scarcely heard him. "No—I mean it," she said, her voice piercing the levity in the room. "I want to know what you have to say about those who need the protection of the law and don't have it."

"Mademoiselle," Turgot said, with a noticeable tightness in his voice. "Should the government pay the cleaning bills for every hem that is dirtied in a city street? To demand regulations against every fraud or cheat who takes advantage of another person is to assume a perfectible society—and I, for one, will leave that to dreamers like Rousseau, who have nothing practical to offer."

Lili took in a breath. *Nothing practical?* Before she could reply, she felt an arm around her shoulder. "I think that's enough," Maman whispered.

I want to be heard. Lili felt like crying. But Maman was right. She had to know a great deal more about the world before she could win a challenge with someone like Abbé Turgot. A vision of Baronne Lomont at her breakfast flashed into Lili's mind. *If I can learn to whack the top off an egg*, Lili told herself, *I can learn how to argue in Maman's salon.* Her day would come, but now it was time to retreat. "You are right, monsieur," she said, with a demure smile. "It is most important to be practical, and I know little about that, being still so young."

Turgot's eyes softened and he cocked his head in amusement. "Well, it appears I am not going to suffer defeat today after all. But much as I fear my demise may be imminent, I await our next encounter with the most delightful trepidation."

Another intense but nice man, Lili thought, just like Rousseau and Diderot, with ideas bigger than she could comprehend. She gave him a smile Delphine would have been proud of. "I shall practice all week for it," she said, feeling Maman's hand give hers an approving squeeze.

Emilie

Château de Montjeu, Bourgogne, 15 June 1734
To Monsieur Pierre-Louis Moreau de Maupertuis
Paris

My Dear Friend,

Words cannot express my dismay at your last letter, which I received this morning by post. Monsieur Voltaire and I are still guests of the Duc de Richelieu a full month after we came to his wedding, since he knows full well the need at present to keep Voltaire safely in hiding. Things have gone steadily from bad to worse, if worse is indeed still possible. The *lettre de cachet* for Voltaire's arrest created quite a stir here, and though Richelieu did not produce his guest for the authorities—thank heavens for the continuing devotion of former lovers, among whom I most fondly include you as well!—the letter is still in effect, and my dear Voltaire is afraid even to walk the grounds lest some enthusiastic local policeman carry him off.

That such a reaction should come from a mere book! *Philosophical Letters* contains nothing that any thinking man should fear, except perhaps the truth that in some ways the English means of government is superior to our own, and that their manners are often more civilized, especially in matters of social class. Are we French so brittle that we crumble at any criticism? And could it not be soundly argued *ipso facto* that those who cannot take criticism with a mind to self-improvement are indeed of a lesser breed than those who can?

But I digress, and important matters remain. I shudder to think it is true what you have said is true, that Parlement—without the mind of a milk cow in the way they bow to the king!—made a public ceremony of burning the book and the police have now confiscated all copies they can find. "Scandalous to religion, morality, and the respect deserved by the authorities" indeed! The scandal is they, not Voltaire's book!

My treasured friend, my misery is great, since I can now no longer deny to myself how deeply I love him. I am mortified at the ridicule with which my pleas to my usual allies at court have been met. I ask only that they convey to the king that Voltaire did not authorize the book to be smuggled into France, but I am met with the cold reply that having written an evil book in England while exiled there for writing another evil book in France hardly warranted any protestation of innocence when said evil book found its way here, whether by his leave or not. My dear Maupertuis, I know there is nothing you can do, but rest assured I do not intend to see someone of such brilliance languish in prison, especially since his health is already a cause of concern, having never been strong even in his youth.

My husband has told me he intends to ask for official authorization to sequester Voltaire at his ancestral home in Cirey. It is a dull place, and house arrest there will be a dreary thing for such a sociable man. Still, Voltaire is pleased, since the house is but a two-hour ride from the border of Lorraine, which is still, thank heaven, independent enough from the reach of the king to offer safe haven should he need to escape quickly. On his end, Voltaire has agreed to use his own money to renovate the château while he is in residence. An excellent bargain according to my husband, since the place is in a terrible state of disrepair.

I have faith in the marquis as the most respectable and esteemed man I know. He continues to offer no protest at Voltaire's intimate involvement in my life. Perhaps it gives him a feeling of being in some way equal to the acknowledged genius of the age that he is willing to share something of such value as a wife. We do not speak of such things out of mutual respect for each other but it is clear his acceptance is more than grudging, since when he is home from his regiment at the front, he invites Voltaire to accompany us everywhere.

It is time to dress for dinner, and I must break off this letter. Please write again soon, hopefully with at least a morsel of better news.

Your adoring and ever-affectionate,
Emilie, Marquise du Châtelet-Lomont

8

"D ELPHINE, PLEASE choose, so I can get some of these fabrics off at least one chair. If I don't sit down I'm going to collapse."

"Please, Maman, just one more?" Delphine clasped her hands as fervently as if she were praying to a statue of the Virgin. "If I could choose five dresses instead of four, it would be so much easier!" The mercier came over to take the swatches of fabric from a chair in the corner of the shop, and Julie sat down with a resigned sigh.

"We've been here for two hours and it's almost dark," Julie said. "They're lighting the streetlamps already."

"Lili, *please*," Delphine begged. "Help me just a little more!"

Lili, whose choices had long since been recorded in the mercier's order book, put down the intricate piece of brocade she had been examining to while away the time. "They're just dresses!" She shrugged.

"Just dresses?" Delphine's eyes widened in disbelief. "They're for Versailles!"

"It's all equally beautiful, really," Lili said.

"Well, that's the problem!" Delphine said, choking back tears. "Look at this—yellow like butter." She touched one sample. "And this—yellow like daffodils." She scolded the cloth as if it were responsible for putting her in such a difficult position. "How can I choose?"

Lili shut her eyes and waved her finger back and forth, before stopping and opening her eyes. "That one!" she said.

"Don't mock me!" Delphine said, wiping her eyes. "This is supposed to be a wonderful time, and you're spoiling it."

"It was, for the first hour," Julie chided, "but I'm about ready to choose for you if you don't hurry up."

"Perhaps if Mademoiselle stood by the mirror and we held them up again to her face?" the mercier suggested, but it wasn't going to help. Delphine's fair beauty seemed to be equally accented by every color he had laid out for display.

"I know!" said Lili. "We'll pretend there's a crowd of invisible people watching—handsome men of course, and fashionable ladies from Versailles." She folded a swatch of taffeta and covered Delphine's eyes, tying it in the back. "I'll spin you around and they'll choose for you, like magic. Hold out your finger." She guided Delphine in a tight circle. "Point," she commanded. Delphine's finger picked out a lavender-colored silk.

"I love that one," Delphine whispered. "I think it was always my favorite."

Julie heaved a sigh of relief as the girls finished off the task in a few minutes. "Time to get home," she said. "Tomorrow's the milliner and the shoemaker."

Lili groaned. "Delphine—pick the hats for me," she said. "I don't want another day like this one."

"Really?" Delphine perked up. "I'll get to pretend I'm ordering twice as many for me!"

"I can hardly wait," Julie said as she shooed them both toward the door. "And I'm sorry to keep you so long," she said to the mercier, shaking her head in Delphine's direction.

Night had fallen and the lamplight from inside the shops on the Rue Saint-Honoré cast a glow over the wares behind the glass—intricate porcelain snuffboxes and figurines, delicate cakes and pastries, books in embossed leather, and feathery hats. Julie had given orders for the driver to stop at the apothecary for some chocolate to take home, and as they waited for him to come back with the package, Lili watched as a young boy scrambled up to set candles inside the glass enclosures of the lampposts. Another man, perhaps his father, followed behind with a long pole tipped with a small wick.

"The mercier will have to go home in the dark," Lili said, looking up a cross street. The overhanging roofs would have made it gloomy any time of day, but the street was already impenetrable to the eye long before the light in the sky was completely gone. "He's a nice man. I hope he doesn't have far to walk."

"*Moi aussi,*" Julie murmured. "I wish they lit the lamps all the time, instead of just at the new moon, and then only a few places. No wonder there's so much crime. People beaten and robbed in the street . . . it's black as ink most nights." She looked out the carriage window. "The light is quite beautiful, isn't it? Imagine if the whole city were lit—but I suppose taxes would be frightening if the king decreed something like that."

"We do pay our bills, don't we, Maman?" Lili asked.

Julie smiled. "Of course."

"Does the mercier pay taxes too?"

Julie exhaled, looking out the window. "Far more than we do. The nobility is exempt from most of them, and tries to get out of the rest. I guess he pays for the lights and doesn't really get the benefit, except in front of his shop."

Delphine shuddered. "I'm glad we'll be safe at home soon," she said, taking Maman's hand. "Especially with four new dresses to discuss over supper!"

Maman didn't seem to hear. "There are many things wrong with France," she said. "The reason I wanted to have a salon was that if I couldn't do anything about it myself, at least I could draw together intelligent men who might find a way."

"It doesn't look as if they have yet," Lili said. "But I'd rather put up lights than work out a philosophy about them." She turned to Julie but they were now passing the old cemetery of Les Innocents, beyond the last streetlamp of Rue Saint-Honoré, and the darkness inside the coach made her unable to see Maman's face. Lili felt the coach pick up speed, as if hurtling through the now dark and narrow streets was preferable to taking a minute longer to arrive safely in the courtyard of Hôtel Bercy.

"Am I wrong, Maman?" Lili went on. "Abbé Turgot seemed to think that helping people could have dire consequences, and I see his point. But still, if the mercier pays taxes, why isn't his own street lit?"

"It's a good question for the abbé."

"He scares me a little," Lili admitted. "He knows so much more than I do."

"Then try asking him another way. Why not use Meadowlark? I imagine others will argue for you quite forcefully after a story makes your point." She leaned across toward Lili, as the light from one of the *hôtels* along their route shone briefly on them. "Meadowlark is more than what you said—a girl whom strange things happen to. She's your voice, Lili. Don't you want it to be heard?"

* * *

"Meadowlark and Tom got off their camels in the African oasis and saw that all the people were wearing rags. 'I thought this place was supposed to be rich from trade with the Musulmen,' Tom said, as a woman wearing a tattered veil turned toward them.

" 'You there!' Meadowlark called out. 'Why are you dressed that way?'

" 'Because I don't have anything else to wear,' the woman said. 'I used to have a different veil for every day of the week, but I don't know where the rest of my clothes have gone. The only reason we're not all naked is we sleep in what we have on. Otherwise, this would probably be gone in the morning too,' she said, shaking the hem of her gown.

"Just then three philosophers walked by. 'Why are they dressed better than you are?' Tom asked.

" 'I don't know,' said the woman. 'Only ordinary people seem to lose everything the minute they get it . . . ' "

The men in the room were shifting their weight as Lili read, and the rustle of fabric caused her eyes to dart around the salon. *They don't like it*, she thought, but feeling Maman's hand on her shoulder gave her the courage to read on. A few minutes later, she came to the end:

"The three philosophers went down an alley to a grand building near the town walls. Invisible, Meadowlark and Tom tiptoed in before the doors closed. They went into a dining room where a grand meal had been laid out on dishes of gold. Through a window, Meadowlark and Tom could see trunks full of clothing, including hundreds of veils, being loaded onto camels, while the caravan driver handed a bag of coins to a servant.

"He came in and poured the coins on the table. 'Your proceeds, messieurs,' he said. The philosophers leaned back and patted their bellies.

"'It's good to live in a land of surplus,' they all agreed.

"'I guess in Africa, the more you need, the less you have,' Tom said when they were safely back among the stars.

"'And the more you have, the less you notice,' Meadowlark replied."

The room was silent, except for the clink of a brandy glass set down too hard on a table. Lili looked up at the serious faces of the guests at the salon. Finally, she heard one pair of hands clapping. "Brava!" Jean-Étienne Leclerc cried out, and slowly the others joined in.

Once his face had returned to its normal color, Abbé Turgot gave Lili a nod of acknowledgment. "Surely, mademoiselle," Turgot said, "you don't mean to imply that philosophers are some kind of parasite living off what rightly belongs to others?"

"No, sir," Lili said. "But I don't believe there's any substitute for looking around the streets at what is real for common people. With further thought to the views you expressed here a few weeks ago, I decided it would be worth the possible consequences down the road to make sure that everyone could afford bread today and rely on having it tomorrow."

Leclerc clapped again, but Lili scarcely heard him. "Abbé Turgot," she went on, "please remember this is just a silly story about a place that doesn't exist. I mean, who would go around stealing people's possessions and treating them as if they were part of their personal treasury? It's quite absurd, really."

"Not at all!" The booming voice belonged to a man in an embroidered silk vest under an elaborately trimmed velvet jacket. His eyes had the peculiar squint of someone whose excess weight had accumulated in the face, and a wattle of flesh bobbed beneath the knob of his chin as he spoke. Lili had never seen him at the salon before, and he had slipped in unnoticed while she was reading.

"Some people have more because others have less," he said. "It's a simple principle in a finite world, Turgot, and I can't say I believe it is entirely wrong that it should be that way. But it's a fact, as mademoiselle's story points out, that those who eat at a golden trough do so by impoverishing others."

"I don't impoverish anyone!" another of the guests replied. "I give to charity, and I'm certainly not guilty of gluttony."

Several other men laughed. "You're only a glutton for losing at cards," one said. "And for the ladies."

"No harm in that, is there, Comte de Buffon?" another asked over the roar of their laughter.

Comte de Buffon? The keeper of the Jardin de Roi, the King's Garden on the far side of the Seine? Why hadn't Maman told her he was coming?

"So here is the delightful prodigy Madame de Bercy has been hiding from the world," Comte de Buffon said, coming over to Lili. He bowed and kissed her hand. "I feel I must immediately write to Monsieur Voltaire at Ferney to tell him he had better return to Paris or he may find himself dethroned!"

He peered into Lili's face. "I heard your mother's wit in what you wrote, and I am charmed to see a little of her in your face."

"My mother?" Lili looked over at Maman, who was glowing with pleasure.

"Yes," Comte de Buffon said. "I knew her quite well, and I am sure she would be delighted to see grown men squirming at the truth of your words." He bowed again. "Would you do me the honor of accepting an invitation to dinner someday soon? I'm sure my nephew would be delighted to escort you around the gardens first, and show you my laboratory."

Jean-Étienne Leclerc had eased through the other guests and was standing by the count. "I'm the nephew," he said. "I hope you're not disappointed."

Lili had never had a good opportunity to look at the young man she had known only by his last name. He looked to be in his mid-twenties, with light brown hair showing underneath his powdered wig. His eyes were blue and his skin almost as fair as Delphine's. He was as slender and tall as his uncle was portly, but both of them had eyes that penetrated hers, not in an intimidating way, but curiously, as if they were trying to see whether she might be coaxed into a smile. Almost immediately she was.

Maman came over to Lili's side. "Accept if you wish, *ma petite*."

"Do you have microscopes?" Lili asked.

The count leaned back and put his hands over his belly as he laughed. "In all sizes," he said. "And drawings of what I've observed in them. But bring a strong stomach," he said, leaning in toward her with the air of a conspirator. "Nature isn't always for the squeamish."

PARROTS SQUAWKED FROM perches in the greenhouse of the Jardin de Roi. In cages reaching nearly to the ceiling, small birds of every color imaginable fluttered together, chortling and trilling. Lili barely heard them, as she moved Comte de Buffon's magnifying glass in and out until it focused on one of several orchids on a long, thin stem.

"It's like it's been painted," she said. The count smiled. "And each one unique," he added. "Look at the next one down."

Lili focused on the stippled dots at the center of the flower and the tiny lines that ran down the petals at each side. She stood up and cradled the whole stalk in her palm. "It's hard to understand why God would go to so much trouble," she said. "I know he doesn't paint them one by one, but there doesn't appear to be any need for each of them to be just a little different."

"Nor for people to look so different either, for that matter," the count said. "Each one unique, yet one species. Would you like to take a look, Madame de Bercy?" he asked, handing the glass to Julie. "In most species, offspring are almost identical, as in these orchids. In some cases, however, such as dogs and cats, we see new and quite different forms emerging all the time. It would be hard to believe, unless the alleyways of Paris gave such a clear demonstration on a daily basis, that a dog or cat of almost any type could bear the offspring of any other type, and produce an infinite variety of offspring amply prepared to inflict an even greater surplus on our city. In fact, were alien creatures to arrive from some other part of the universe, I am certain we could not convince them there was any such thing as a 'dog' at all, they would be so sure there were hundreds of names for such a creature." He cleared his throat. "My apologies. I do tend to lecture whenever I have an audience."

"No, please, I pray you," Julie said. "We came to learn, didn't we, Lili?"

Lili nodded. "From pictures I've seen in books, your visitor might conclude people were many different species too, there's so little resemblance between a Hindu and a Lapp."

"Quite so," Jean-Étienne Leclerc replied, "and Uncle has made quite clear in his papers that were it not for the fact that we are loath to breed with people who look too different from ourselves, the world would be full of people the color of caramels with brown eyes the shape of almonds." He chuckled. "I for one would prefer to leave Chinese women to Chinese men, and I suppose they would quite agree to that, although it is hard to see how they could possibly find their young women as attractive as our present company."

He bowed in Lili's direction, and she blushed and lowered her eyes.

"I think we've heard quite enough about procreation," Julie admonished, shaking her finger at the two men in a gesture more teasing than critical.

"Yes, quite," the count replied. "But I have one more thing to show Mademoiselle du Châtelet, before we go in to dinner, if you'll allow it. I believe we have left unaddressed her question about God, and why—or in fact whether—he has gone to all the trouble to paint the spots on orchids."

He guided Lili to a stool at a table on which was set a glass cage with a pink-blossomed plant inside. Opening a tiny door, he produced a small vial containing several small insects. He shook them loose inside the cage and closed it up. "Watch."

Watch what? Lili wondered. A little bug fly around a cage? Then she and Maman shrieked. The flower had come to life, reaching out with two petals to grab the insect and pull it toward its center. "That can't be!" Lili cried out.

"But it is," Buffon replied.

"Flowers don't move!" Lili tried not to sob.

"They don't eat insects either, as a rule, but that's what appears to have happened."

"No! It makes no sense!" Imagining for a moment all the plants in the greenhouse reaching out to do the same, Lili clung to Maman.

The count offered Lili his handkerchief to wipe her eyes. "You did not see a flower move," he said with an amused smile.

"I did too, with my own eyes!"

He shook his head. "What you saw is even more marvelous, because it is true." He handed her the magnifying glass again. "What do you really see?"

Lili's hands were shaking too hard at first to bring the plant into focus, but then she saw what was unmistakably a large insect scraping pincers over its mouth. Its body and legs were the shape of petals in creamy pink and white. Its face looked like the top of the column on the orchid Lili had observed under the glass, but instead of little dots of color, she saw two tiny eyes and the single line of its now-closed mouth.

Comte Buffon picked the little animal off its perch and set it on his finger. "It's called an orchid mantis, and it lives in disguise among the flowers, getting its food from any little bug that comes by. Hold it in your hand and look some more." He eased it onto Lili's palm. "It won't bite, I promise."

Lili held her palm up close to her eyes and watched the insect stretch its limbs. "It's really quite beautiful," she said, feeling her heart slow down.

"And lovable in its own way," Jean-Étienne broke in. "Uncle keeps them as pets of a sort, do you not?"

"And to remind me never to stop marveling at what nature produces. Do you know why such a creature exists, mademoiselle?" Lili shook her head. "Simply because it can," the scientist said. "Or probably, more correctly, because it must." He replaced the mantis on its perch and closed the door of the cage.

"You see," he said, taking Lili's arm to go to the house for dinner, "I don't believe for a moment that God said during the creation, 'Let there be orchids as well as mantises that look just like them.' I believe instead that different types of plants and animals came into the world and thrived where they were put."

The great man stopped for a moment once they had crossed the terrace in front of the greenhouse. They were standing in the middle of a grand walkway so long it disappeared from view before reaching the end of the garden. Lost in thought, Buffon clasped his hands as he looked up at the plane trees lining the walk. Close to the house, gardeners trimmed the hedges of the formal garden, but farther away, grounds meant for pleasant strolls gave way to the densely packed landscape of trees and medicinal plants in the working laboratory of the Jardin de Roi.

"Things alter over time," he said, picking up the subject as if his thoughts hadn't strayed at all. Jean-Étienne and Julie had caught up and were now strolling beside them. "The climate might get hotter or colder, or wetter or drier, and the perfect fit isn't so perfect anymore. So a plant might change colors or an animal grow spots, or more hair, or a tougher hide in order to adapt. Perhaps this poor little mantis was no good at capturing insects. He adapted to look like something the insects are attracted to, and *voilà*!"

"He's the master of the house now, so to speak," Jean-Étienne broke in with a laugh.

"But how do they change?" Lili looked up intently at the aging scientist. "A green mantis isn't going to lay eggs that hatch pink any more than these trees will have blue leaves next spring. I can be sure of that, can't I?"

Buffon laughed. "I think you can count on the trees not to surprise you. Time takes regular and uniform steps. Changes that at first would be imperceptible become gradually more pronounced, and at last are marked by results too conspicuous to be missed. So my dear Mademoiselle du Châtelet, we can't watch mantises turn pink in our own lifetime, but we can conclude with confidence that they have done just that in God's time."

"That's certainly not what they taught at the abbey," she said, looking up with a sly and happy smile as they skirted the edge of the formal garden and neared the iron gates of Buffon's imposing home at the end of the grounds. "Although I can't say they put much effort into practical explanations of anything."

Buffon snorted his disapproval. "It is astonishing to me that anyone could call such views as mine irreligious. Antichurch perhaps, but irreverent, never. How living creatures adapt is beyond our knowledge, but it is not beyond God's power to have given them the means. I think in the end that was the only way he could have intended things, since it was the only way his work could survive the changes he knew were inherent in the world he made. Why go to the trouble of creating life, if a change in rainfall or temperature would wipe it out? I believe he created, for example, a mantis—or to be precise, a breeding pair of mantises. Perfect mantises for the time and place, and then they devolved from that perfection—degenerated, one might say—as circumstances demanded, just as a human being might fall from honest living to thievery because he had no choice."

"I don't think that beautiful little creature was degenerate," Lili said. "I've grown quite fond of it already, and I hope I have a chance to see it again." She looked back over her shoulder at the glass windows of the greenhouse.

Buffon laughed. "You may pay a visit to my mantis any time you wish, mademoiselle."

Lili knew she was blushing but she didn't care. She stopped just outside the gate to the mansion, letting Jean-Étienne and Julie pass ahead. "Why couldn't you argue that instead of being degenerate, every creature is perfect just as it is?"

Buffon looked at her quizzically. "I shudder to think what your nuns would say to that!" Seeing her confusion, he went on. "To say that an adapted species is perfect implies that God created imperfect ones that managed to improve themselves after his will had been done." He took in the entire garden with a sweeping gesture. "Mine is a dangerous view to hold, but I am convinced that the Divine Intent was only to set nature in motion, not to create everything himself. That would mean there's no such thing as perfect species at all—including us—only well-adapted ones."

Lili's head spun. "Monsieur Rousseau says that all things are perfect from the hand of the Creator, but degenerate in the hands of man." Visions spun through Lili's mind of men splattered with excrement from carriage wheels, tattered homeless children with strawberry stains, a man beaten for wanting to be paid, the thin line of light in the penance room at the abbey.

A pair of butterflies wafted, close enough to touch, over the raked dirt of the entryway, before fluttering off into the cool green of the garden. "Nature seems different from society," Lili went on. "It seems nature is trying harder than we are to make things a little better."

"And I think society is doing the same, or I wouldn't bother working so hard here." He took her arm to go through the gate. "One must believe that progress is possible, or what's the point of using our minds at all?"

Servants opened the door when they saw them walking across the courtyard, but the count stopped Lili again before they reached the steps to the house. "People have always tried to understand the world by looking for fixed truths and hanging on to them. I believe we are seeing that way of thinking in its last hours. How will we face the future? That's what I want to know. And the answers will come from those who understand that the only truth is change, and that the only way to go forward is to think clearly and dispassionately about the world as it really is."

He took Lili's arm again. "I have guests almost every day, but I almost always let my nephew show them around, and I join them later only as a means of having my dinner. When I heard you read your story and saw how you stood up to Abbé Turgot, I wanted to see what else you were made of." He laughed. "I scared you for a minute with my pink mantis, but not for long."

His eyes scanned her face, looking so intently into her eyes that Lili was surprised she had no desire to flinch or look away. "You are a lovely girl, with your mother's spirit as well as her mind, and you are very fortunate to have someone like Julie de Bercy who supports you. Don't spend your life struggling to be satisfied with being ordinary. Whatever muse calls you—science, writing, who knows?—I hope you'll answer."

He gave Lili a rueful smile. "I'm getting near the end of my time, but if I ever had a wish to live longer it would be to see what you make of what you have been given." He glanced through the doorway. "Shall we go in?"

Emilie

1740

"DONE." MARIANNE Loir put down her paintbrush and stood up. "I think I can finish from here without you. Would you like to look at your portrait?"

"Finally," Emilie said. "I thought I might die of old age before I ever stood up again." She came around to look at Loir's work. "Oh dear, it looks as if I already have. Do I really look that ancient? I'm not even thirty."

"You don't look old at all," the painter insisted. "You're radiant, and far more beautiful now than in the portrait in your husband's study. To be sure, you were scarcely more than a bride then, but you look as if you're ready to jump up and run away. Here you exist on your own terms. I hope you are not offended that I portrayed you that way."

"My own terms?" Emilie frowned, examining the portrait more closely. "I look as if I might be nothing more than a well-decorated wife." She held her hand to her throat, fingering the diamond she saw painted around her neck.

"I'll add symbols for whatever else you'd like to convey," Loir said. "I was certain you'd have ideas about that, so I left the table next to you empty." She gestured to the still-drying paint. "And your hands too."

Emilie thought for a moment. "Something expensive on the table—a necklace perhaps—tossed aside in favor of more important things?"

"A diamond necklace?"

Emilie laughed. "I love diamonds too much for that. Crystal beads, I think. A lovely long strand, sticking out from under piles of manuscript pages. Open books too."

"And your hands?"

Emilie looked away from the painter. A smile played across her lips, as if she were remembering something that wasn't to be shared. "In the hand of the heart, a white carnation, for passion," she said. "And in the left, a compass, for my work."

"Pointed up or down?" Loir asked. "Are you a philosopher of ideas, or a measurer of the world?"

Emilie thought for a moment. "Point it sideways, for I intend to be equally both." She laughed. "And make it look as if I wouldn't mind using the points as a weapon, if I had to."

The painter's eyes crinkled in a smile. "Madame la Marquise, it will be an honor." She followed Emilie toward the door. "I'll send it to you as soon as it is ready."

"No," Emilie said. "Send it to Cirey. To Monsieur Voltaire. He'll know what it means."

9

1765

"S TANISLAS-ADÉLAÏDE BRINGS very little of consequence to a marriage," Baronne Lomont sniffed, setting her teacup on the table in the parlor of Hôtel Bercy a month before Lili and Delphine's presentation at Versailles. "To be sure, her background on the Châtelet side is beyond reproach, but the Breteuils are in a far weaker position. Of course it's true that her grandfather Breteuil had the honor of being in attendance to the king—"

"The secretary handling the schedule for the king's foreign visitors, and one of those allowed in the king's private chambers, is hardly in a weak social position." Julie's manner was controlled, as usual, but her indignation was unmistakable. "Surely you are not suggesting a man honored in that way lacks quality."

"Of course not. The Breteuil family bought their titles long enough ago to have benefited from inclusion in good society for generations now, but that will never be the same as a noble bloodline."

"I am quite aware of all the details of rank." Julie's tone was now frosty. "And though I wish I could make light of the entire subject, I know I cannot, since it is Lili's future we are discussing."

"And of course there is the matter of a dowry. I have been led to believe by her father that his contribution will be quite small. Gabrielle-Pauline made an excellent marriage to a duke of some consequence in Italy, but I recall the marquis paid a shocking dowry, especially considering he was marrying his daughter to a foreigner. Florent-Louis is the heir, and the Châtelet lands and title must pass unimpeded to him. I'm sure his wife's family would have quite a bit to say if the marquis decided to settle Cirey or another major asset on the girl."

Lili's spirits sank as they always did when the subject of her father came up. All her life she'd been told that he preferred to live the remainder of his life alone, and that his other two children had no contact with the aging recluse either. Lili's half sister lived in Italy and after their mother's death she had drifted out of contact with everyone in Paris. Lili's half brother lived somewhere in France, but he had never made any effort to meet her, and Lili no longer gave much thought to either of them.

"Respect your father's wishes," Baronne Lomont had told her time and again. After all, he had settled a stipend on her that paid for her expenses at Hôtel Bercy, and it would be thoughtless to put this support in jeopardy out of something as self-serving as mere curiosity.

Lili felt her heart press against her tight bodice. Although she accepted that her father would not be part of her life, she wondered at moments like these whether there was more to his absence than simply not wanting to be bothered with her. Had she done something wrong? Did he blame her for her mother's death? Tears sprang to her eyes.

"It's not my fault that things are as they are," she said in a tremulous voice. "Why would he want me to be a pauper?"

Julie opened her mouth to offer reassurance, but Baronne Lomont spoke first. "That demanding tone is further evidence that it would be wise to accept my offer of some final comportment lessons for Stanislas-Adélaïde before her presentation at court," she said to Julie. "I know she is proper at table and manages other simple things I've taught her, but there is so much more to having real grace. Her conversation skills certainly leave much to be desired." She stirred her tea with a tiny silver spoon. "Has she any experience using a fan?"

No one gets married without a dowry, Lili thought, digging at a cuticle until she drew blood and had to put her finger in her mouth to clean it. Just then, the baroness glanced in her direction, and her eyes flickered with disdain as Lili hastily returned her hands to her lap.

"I have a most suitable friend who will be pleased to be of assistance," the baroness went on. "And if madame is amenable, Mademoiselle de Bercy is welcome to take part."

"Thank you for coming," Julie said, standing up to clarify that the subject, and the visit, were at an end. "One of my friends has a new opera opening this evening at the Comédie-Italienne. The girls and I are going as his guests, and we need time to prepare. Perhaps you have heard of Monsieur Philidor?"

"François André Danican Philidor?" The baroness arched her eyebrows. "The chess player?"

"*Bien sûr*. We have a chess game set up for him in the salon—you're most welcome to look—and every week we lead him to the table with his eyes covered so he can't see where the game left off the week before. He says he simultaneously played three English experts while blindfolded, but we haven't enough room here to put him to such a test."

Julie was by now near the door. "I'm sure you've heard of the English novel *Tom Jones?*" She stepped aside to allow the baroness to pass. "He's written an opera based on it, and the girls and I are quite excited, since we read the book together last winter."

Lili suppressed a giggle at Maman's subtlety. The baroness did not approve of novels or salons—with or without chess—and Maman was, in her own gracious way, telling her she didn't care.

"We'll discuss your proposal tonight," Julie said, "and I'll send word tomorrow of our decision." By now the baroness was at the parlor door. "Your generosity is most appreciated," Julie added, and with a gesture of her hand, she ushered Baronne Lomont into the hallway and on her way out of Hôtel Bercy.

* * *

"*CHEZ* BARONNE LOMONT?" Delphine wrinkled her nose in disappointment as the carriage left the courtyard for the opera house. "What on earth would she know about being attractive?"

"Everyone is young once," Julie replied.

"Except Baronne Lomont," the two girls said in unison, breaking into peals of laughter.

"Really, *mes petites*," Julie said sternly enough to silence them. "You should be aware of how much is at stake here. Delphine, of course, will inherit Hôtel Bercy, and Lili, you needn't fret about those rather cruel things Baronne Lomont said about your own situation, but neither the Bercy nor the Châtelet family is terribly strong when it comes to what assets their daughters bring to a marriage."

They turned onto the Rue des Francs Bourgeois, and light from the streetlamps danced across Lili's and Delphine's solemn faces. "Why so serious all of a sudden?" Julie cajoled. "My point is simply that it is in your best interests to make the best impression you can. What if a man you fancy is interested in someone else because he perceives you as lacking in some way? You may very well end up wishing you had paid more attention to the social graces now."

Under the hard stomacher shaping her bodice, Lili felt a familiar clawing sensation. She and Delphine would be going to meet Queen Marie Leszczynska in a month, and Lili didn't feel ready at all. Though she and Delphine had spent hours in front of a mirror deepening their curtseys and practicing the subtle differences in eye contact and smiles appropriate to use with people of various ranks, most of the time she was thinking about the book she was reading, a funny story she and Delphine had shared, or perhaps nothing more than what would be served for dinner. The time had passed for resentment and disdain. Much as she bristled at the baronne's snobbery, the old woman was right that it was past time to settle down and do what had to be done.

"I *am* paying attention, Maman," Delphine said. The carriage had by now reached the end of the lighted thoroughfare and was making its way through a maze of small, dark streets. "I play the piano for hours, and I never knock anything off the table with my skirts when I walk through even the smallest space." She thought for a moment. "Although I could be quite a bit better at the minuet." She winced and adjusted her hips on the seat. The lamps from a *hôtel* cast a brief glow inside the coach as they crossed Rue Sainte-Avoie. "And I don't know how anybody can be pleasant in these awful stomachers, even if they do make one's breasts look rather nice," Delphine said, toying with a pink satin rose on the front of one of her new dresses.

"Well then, take the baroness up on her offer and ask for help with the minuet," Julie said, as darkness fell over them again. "And if she has any advice about how to make a stomacher any more tolerable, be sure to let me know."

Lili had been listening in silence. "A long time ago you told me that Baronne Lomont could be counted upon to be loyal, even if I didn't like the way she acted toward me," she said. "Is that why she's forcing me into more of her lessons?"

"She wants you to be a grand success," Julie replied. "Even if she makes it sound as if she fully expects you won't be." The carriage slowed and she looked out. "We're at Saint-Jacques de l'Hôpital already. The Comédie Italienne is on the next block. So is it settled? I say yes to Baronne Lomont tomorrow?"

The girls took in the deepest breath that their corsets allowed. "It's decided," they sighed.

"I hope she serves good cakes at least," Delphine said, pouting as the driver dismounted and opened the door to help them down. "Even if they do make me round as a ball."

VIOLINS BOWED EXCITEDLY, and bass viols and cellos joined in a delicate, climbing staccato. The strings swirled away like butterflies, only to be netted by an insistent continuo. As the curtain opened, the rows of lanterns at the edges of the stage cast their light on two women in a garden.

"A fine-looking young man can bedevil the soul of a maiden," one of the woman sang, and Lili found her thoughts already straying, as they often did, to Jean-Étienne Leclerc and the day she had spent with Maman at the Jardin de Roi. She remembered how excited he had been to tell her about his uncle's experiments to determine the age of the earth. Buffon had left the results unpublished, Jean-Étienne told her, so as not to be thought insane, since the calculations came out to three million years. Lili smiled, remembering how the young man had leaned toward her with the air of a conspirator, whispering that they both suspected it was countless years older than that.

I like Jean-Étienne, Lili thought, as a group of hunters sang a chorus onstage. *I can talk to him.* Her mind cast back to Paul-Vincent and his microscope. *He doesn't count because he was so young,* she decided. She closed her eyes and listened to the music, trying to picture in her mind the exact color and contours of Jean-Étienne's mouth.

"That must be Tom Jones!" Jarred back to the present, Lili followed the trajectory of Delphine's finger toward a man in a hunting coat in the shadows in the back corner of the stage. *Just watch the opera,* Lili told herself. "No—it's Squire Western," Delphine corrected. "It's certainly taking a long time for Tom to show up."

The baritone began a long and enthusiastic aria about the hunt from which he and the men now filling the stage were returning, and Delphine leaned forward, looking through Maman's opera glasses at each man in turn. She groaned as Squire Western put his arm around a pudgy middle-aged man who was playing the role of the young and dashing libertine. "There's no way Sophie would fall in love with him," she announced. "Just once can't the hero be handsome?"

"Delphine, quiet!" Maman put her finger to her lips and took the glasses away, part of the ritual of waiting for Delphine to get swept up in the music and forgive the cast. Finally she did, and their box was silent except for the occasional groan as Sophie endured the dim-witted meddling of her father and the simpering courtship of the toady Blilil. Finally the curtain closed on the first act, and the candlelit chandeliers were lowered to give more light in the house.

"Look, Maman," Delphine said, peering through the golden haze at a group of people in one of the boxes on the opposite side. "That's the Comte de Beaufort, isn't it?"

Maman looked through the glasses for a fleeting moment before handing them to Delphine. "I believe so," she said. "Did you notice the box to his left?" Delphine leaned forward and squinted into the eyepiece. "Don't look quite so interested, *ma petite*," Julie said, touching her shoulder to coax her back into her seat.

"It's that wolverine, Anne-Mathilde," Delphine said, sitting back. "You look, Lili, your eyes are better. Is her little pet with her?"

Lili glanced across the theater without need of the glasses and looked quickly away. "The Duchesse de Praslin is there too," she said, casting another quick look back. "And Anne-Mathilde is making sure the man next to her is enjoying the tops of her breasts. She's hiding her face behind her fan and leaning toward him."

"I heard a rumor that since she's already been presented to the queen, Anne-Mathilde is about to be engaged to the Comte d'Étoges's son," Maman said. "That would be quite a success for both families." She looked for a moment in the direction of the box. "If that's him, she's certainly doing her best to help the matter along."

The door to the box opened, and a small man with intense gray eyes and a slightly disheveled wig stepped inside. "Monsieur Philidor!" Julie said, rising effortlessly in her corset and panniers to greet him. "A triumph! The cast is excellent! You remember my daughter Delphine and Mademoiselle du Châtelet, do you not?"

"*Enchanté*." The composer bowed. "I hope you are also enjoying my little comedy?"

"Oh yes," Delphine said, turning her head at an attractive angle. "Especially the man playing Tom Jones." She touched her ear, and Lili surreptitiously lifted her eyebrows to acknowledge Delphine's lie.

"I'm afraid I had to clean up the libretto a bit too much for some people's tastes," Philidor said. "I've already heard grumbling that

Tom Jones seems more akin to the Quaker in the story than to Monsieur Fielding's rather licentious character."

"I do wish he could be a little more"—Delphine paused, parting her lips slightly to make it appear she was measuring her words— "playful," she said, turning up one corner of her mouth just before she hid it behind her fan.

"I'm afraid the original Tom Jones would be far too much for our censors," Julie said, diverting attention away from Delphine's awkward attempt at charm. "And of course it's the music people care most about, and it, my dear Philidor—" Julie took in as deep a breath as possible and let it out sensuously. "It is truly ravishing."

Lili noticed how Julie managed to turn her body toward the brightest light in the box and bend almost imperceptibly forward, so her lightly powdered breasts and bare tops of her shoulders could complete the appearance of being hopelessly in thrall to every note in Philidor's score. *No wonder everyone adores her,* Lili thought, admiring how effortless Maman always seemed, as if she were lit by some inward fire that escaped through her skin with insuppressible radiance.

Philidor looked down at the stage. "The musicians are coming back in. I must go," he said, and with a nervous and perfunctory bow he was gone. As the orchestra tuned for the second act, Delphine looked again across the theater. "There's Joséphine," she sniffed. "Are their dresses sewn together? Can't they bear to be apart?"

"I think Anne-Mathilde sees us," Lili said. "She's putting on quite a show."

"*Mon Dieu!*" Delphine gasped. "Look who just sat down between them."

Jacques-Mars Courville had taken the chair between Joséphine and Anne-Mathilde. Noticing that Joséphine's shawl had fallen, he reached for it and draped it around her shoulders. "That was a bit cozy," Lili said, as Delphine looked sharply away. Anne-Mathilde leaned forward and said something to both of them, and Joséphine cocked her head toward Jacques-Mars, flitting her fan as she laughed.

Ignoring Julie's admonition not to stare, Lili watched as Anne-Mathilde got up and stood behind them, putting one hand on Joséphine's shoulder and the other on Jacques-Mars's as she bent over and looked across the theater. "Look who's over there, Jacques-Mars," her eyes seemed to say. "Your playmate Delphine and that other one." She stood up and continued to stare across the theater to the box where Lili and Delphine were sitting. Though they were too far away to be able to see the coldness in her eyes, Lili felt it all the same, until the orchestra started up and she forgot everything but the music.

TWO DAYS AFTER Baronne Lomont issued the invitation to come to her home for a few final lessons, Lili stood in the parlor of Hôtel Lomont in panniers so large and stiff she could have balanced a teacup on each hip.

Seated in a fauteuil, wearing a prim hat in the same green as her dress, was their tutor, Madame du Quesnay, a friend of the baroness. To one side were Baronne Lomont and her confessor, and on a couch on the other was Madame du Quesnay's brother, Robert de Barras. Delphine had just sat down next to him, managing her panniers so they rested prettily around her.

"Charming," Madame du Quesnay said to Delphine. "And now, Mademoiselle du Châtelet, shall we try it again? And please do not sigh this time. A show of frustration is most unbecoming." She lifted one hand in a delicate arc. "Fluid grace. Effortlessness. That is your goal." She turned to Delphine. "But first, Mademoiselle de Bercy, show us how you rise from a low couch."

Her eyes followed every move as Delphine stood up. "You are launching yourself upward. You must look as if you are floating to your feet." Madame du Quesnay looked at the two men. "I am indeed sorry to have to say something so indelicate, but I'm afraid I must." She turned back to Delphine. "To do it properly, Mademoiselle de Bercy, you must summon your strength by drawing your toes under you to support your weight, and come up using the strength in your upper legs, *comme ça*."

Madame du Quesnay's corset kept her back rigid as she tilted her body forward just a little from the hips. "From the thighs," she said as she rose from her chair in one motion. "Mademoiselle du Châtelet, let's observe you again. Sit where Mademoiselle de Bercy just was, as if monsieur were an admirer you are delighted to see. Then get up from the couch as gracefully as if the air under your gown were setting you afloat."

Walk to couch. Rotate hips to move panniers aside so I can land on my behind. Stick out left foot enough to help shift my weight to right foot but not enough for it to show from under my petticoats. Weight on right foot, bend at hips, brace leg against couch and go down slowly. Voilà. Lili hit the seat with only a little bump.

"Quite improved," Madame du Quesnay said. "But you are showing far too much concentration. Your lips practically disappeared inside your mouth and that is, of course, most unattractive. Practice at home until you can get up and down as if you gave no thought to it."

Seated again in her fauteuil, Madame du Quesnay raised and lowered her hand in a fluid motion. "Remember, you have no thoughts at all, except how pleasant it is to have the opportunity to converse with an attractive gentleman. Now, rise as I explained, and repeat the entire motion—down, then up."

That man is a prissy old bore, and if I have to listen one more time to him talk about his dead wife, I will throw myself out the window. Lili glazed her face over and willed her mind to go blank. Her skirts billowed out around her in just the proper way, and she turned to Monsieur de Barras. "Why, monsieur, is that a hint of a smile I see?" she asked in the most lilting tone she could muster. "I believe it is!"

"I was just remembering my Clarisse, and how she carried herself. Watching you, I am just now appreciating how extraordinary she was at something I took entirely for granted," he said with the lifelessness of a priest sleepwalking through mass.

"I am so pleased that I can contribute to your appreciation of someone else," Lili said, forming her lips in what she hoped was the correct smile, and struggling to keep the sarcasm out of her voice. She turned her hips to accentuate the bows and embroidery on the bodice of her dress and the tops of her breasts pushing up from it. "And I am so sorry for your loss." *Remove smile.* "Madame de Barras sounds as if she was absolute perfection." *Restore smile.*

He opened his mouth to speak, but Lili had already pressed the balls of her feet into the floor and was tightening her thighs to come to a stand. *Get up from the couch as gracefully as if the air under your gown is setting you afire,* she thought, suppressing the urge to laugh.

To her surprise, everyone seemed pleased. "Very graceful," the priest said. "Was it not, Baronne Lomont?"

The baroness gave a nod of fleeting approval. "A man should always believe that you find him attractive," she said to Lili. "This is the best means for someone of ordinary appearance and unexceptional charm to be found attractive in return. Wouldn't you agree, Madame du Quesnay?"

"Quite." Madame du Quesnay nodded. "Successful flirtation conveys what response would be welcome, without appearing to expect any such response at all. A man will puzzle over what your words and actions might have meant, and if he discovers he has been thinking about you, he is likely to conclude that he must be in love." She looked at her brother. "Although I don't imagine most men would be willing to admit how simpleminded they are about such things. Tell me, dear brother, was Mademoiselle du Châtelet flirting with you just then, or merely being polite?"

Barras gave a small cough to clear his throat. "I did not take mademoiselle's behavior as anything more than the effort of a young woman who knows little about grief to be pleasant to a man consumed with it."

Flirt with that dried-up old prune? Lili glanced toward Baronne Lomont and saw that she was looking at her and Barras as if absorbed in some private thought. Lili felt acid rise in her throat. *Is that what she has in mind?*

RAIN BATTERED THE last of the dry leaves still clinging to the chestnut trees in the courtyard of Hôtel Bercy a few days after the girls' last lesson with Madame de Quesnay. A dozen or more chairs were arranged in Maman's sitting room to make a narrow pathway, and at the end, an upholstered stool indicating the queen's position was placed in front of a large mirror. Lili observed from the stool while Delphine made the deep curtsey known as a *révérence*.

"Maman says we won't have any more room than this because Queen Marie Leszczynska's visitors will be crowding in as much as they can without being too obvious they're making it as difficult as possible for us," Delphine said.

Although some presentations involved both the king and queen, Lili's and Delphine's would be no more than an introduction to the queen on their first visit to her chambers. Despite the relative simplicity, Lili imagined the scene as a kind of warfare, won by having the widest panniers and fitting them through the smallest space, all the while chatting and nodding as if the task were not difficult at all. *A duel by clothing*, Lili thought with a grimace.

Delphine walked a straight line between the chairs, without touching anything with her panniers or train along the way. In front of the empty stool, she gave a deep curtsey and held it until Lili could see the trembling in her thighs disturb the fabric in her skirt.

"You may rise," Lili said in an officious tone she thought sounded queenly. Delphine came up in a single fluid motion. "How did my *révérence* look?"

"Perfect, except for the shaking at the end."

"If I have to hold my curtsey that long, I'll know Queen Marie Leszczynska hated me on sight," Delphine said. "It hurts my legs to stay down that long. 'Your majesty, la-la-la,' Maman will say, and then I'll look into the queen's eyes just so." Delphine gave the empty air above Lili a look that was at once shy and eager. "Then I'll say, 'May I bring honor to your court and to France,' and then . . ." Delphine took several steps backward without catching her train underfoot, a move she had practiced for months. "All right, now for the worst part."

Delphine went up onto her toes. She brought the train cleanly around with a much practiced twist of her body, avoiding catching it on the stiff frame of her dress and leaving it in a rumpled pile at her side. She looked behind her in the mirror, satisfied that the train lay smoothly behind her. "How did I look going around?"

"Better, but still a bit hesitant."

Delphine pulled her train out of the way and sat down heavily in one of the chairs. "I'll never get it."

"Well, just remember, I will do so poorly I'll deflect all the ridicule onto me." They both tried to laugh, but two days before their departure for Versailles, nothing was amusing. More than anything else, holding what looked like an effortless *révérence*, and the neat fall of their trains behind them after a gracious turn, would set up a good stay at court. And there was no need to state the obvious, that a good stay at court would set up everything else.

Lili walked down the aisle and held her curtsey until sweat prickled on her back and her legs felt so weak she thought she might not be able to get up. Back upright, she whipped her body around so violently that the train went far beyond center.

"You'll come visit when the queen throws me in the Bastille, won't you?" Lili said with a grim smile.

Delphine giggled. "And you forgot the backward steps again too."

Lili tried the routine a second time, and then a third, before collapsing in a chair across from Delphine. She pulled a damp handkerchief from between her flattened breasts and patted her temples.

"It's hard work to be appealing, isn't it?" Delphine said, pulling out her own handkerchief. "I hope I don't perspire like this then.

Imagine what the ladies would think of a girl whose temples are drip-ping."

"I'll just be glad when it's over and I can come home," Lili said.

"Come home? Afterward will be the only good part!" Delphine shut her eyes and leaned back with a dreamy smile. "We'll go to ban-quets and balls, and go riding with handsome courtiers. Maybe there will be a ballet or an opera while we're there and we'll sit with our fans and flirt with men who are dying to kiss us."

She opened her eyes but her voice was still far away. "I want people to say, 'There goes Delphine. Isn't she wonderfully gracious and confident? Witty and spirited enough to be interesting but never so much that she frightens people off.' That's what I want to be like, and sometimes—" She leaned toward Lili as if the line of empty chairs might overhear her otherwise. "Promise you won't say a word of this because it sounds so immodest?" she said. "Sometimes I think I already am that Delphine—at least more than before." Her face grew somber. "Certainly more than last summer."

"You *are* that Delphine," Lili said. *And I'm not any of those things.* All of a sudden the intimacy in the room was so overwhelming that Lili wanted to blurt out all her fears, but before she could reply, Julie swept in. "Time to practice with you, Maman!" Delphine said, jump-ing up so quickly that her panniers caused the delicate chair to topple over.

"Oh dear," Julie murmured, picking up the chair and setting it right again. "Fortunately, most furniture is built to stand up to our wardrobes. But girls, always be sure someone has your chair securely in hand when you stand up. And don't look around to check. You must appear to expect to be attended to at all times."

She went over to the stool. "Let's see how you're doing." Then, noticing she was still holding a letter, she fluttered it in her hand. "Lili, remind me after we've finished that I need to discuss this with you. Baronne Lomont would like a private visit with you before you leave for Versailles."

"Nothing she wants can be good," Lili grumbled.

Julie held up her hand. "Not for more lessons," she said. "But we both agree that you should not go to Versailles knowing as little as you do about your—your background. It's time you knew what other people know. Or think they do."

"Baronne Lomont?" Lili pictured the sitting room in the baroness's home. Even though a fire would be lit, she shivered at the memory of how drafty and cold it always felt. "I'd rather hear it from you, Maman."

"Baronne Lomont wishes to be the one to share this information." Julie's tone made appeal useless. "And that is appropriate, since she has a family connection."

Lili's eyes stung. "You and Delphine are my family," she whispered too softly for them to hear.

Just then a sudden rain squall sent them all to the window to look out on the courtyard. A scullery maid was rushing back inside with a basket of vegetables. The man who had sold them to her was pushing his cart with no deliberate speed in the direction of the gate, shrugging off the rain as if resisting a soaking was pointless.

A gust of wind blew more wet leaves onto the cobblestones, and Julie shivered in response. "I feel cold just looking at him," she said. "I hope it's a better day than this for your visit tomorrow." Lili felt Delphine's hand cradle her waist from one side and Maman's from the other. "*Moi aussi,*" she said, wishing that the thought of a visit to Hôtel Lomont didn't require hope to make it bearable.

LILI WAS PLEASED with what she saw as she glanced in the mirror that hung in the vestibule of Baronne Lomont's home on the Île Saint-Louis. Under a jaunty hat, her hair was formed into several ringlets fixed with sugar water so they would dangle perfectly in front of one shoulder. Her face was lightly powdered, and her cheeks and lips were touched with rouge. Her cloak in dark blue wool moved with her in an attractive drape, its gold buttons secured by embroidered loops to protect against the chill of an early Parisian winter.

The servant did not lead her in the usual direction toward the parlor, but farther back into the house, to the study. Baronne Lomont sat alone by the fireplace, dressed for mass. "Come in, my dear," she said, setting aside a letter resting in her lap. "We haven't much time. I presume you were also informed we are going to Nôtre-Dame to offer special prayers for your presentation and that of Mademoiselle de Bercy?"

"*Oui*, madame," Lili said, curtseying in the precise manner appropriate for greeting an older female relative of higher rank. Not too deep, not too long, with good eye contact afterward to show that the gesture had been a courtesy toward a family member one had the pleasure of seeing often, and wasn't meant to suggest an inappropriate level of submission.

Lili sat down across from the baroness. *It's a lot to remember, but I did it right without thinking,* she realized. Her mind whirled with the tiniest details of how the greeting might change if she were meeting someone else, and suddenly she felt a wave of tenderness toward the difficult old woman in front of her. All the long hours of cracking eggs, getting up and down from chairs, and enduring forced and pointless conversation—had it been as much of an ordeal for the baroness as it was for her, and was she equally glad it was over?

"*Oui*, madame, I am honored to go with you." Lili's eyes stung with unexpected tears. "And I want you to know how grateful I am for how well you have prepared me. I hope I have not been too difficult."

And then, to Lili's amazement, Baronne Lomont smiled. "You are either entirely sincere, in which case I thank you for your kind words, or you are a very skilled liar, in which case I have done my job well. But in any case, you have grown into a handsome young woman, and I believe you will acquit yourself well."

She stood up. "Come with me. I have something to show you." On the far wall hung an ornately framed painting of a man and two boys. In riding habits, they stood in front of a magnificent horse held by an equerry dressed in the expensive livery of a noble household. "Do you know who they are?"

"*Non*, Baroness."

"It is your grandfather, and the two boys are your father, Florent-Claude, and my late husband, Édouard-Marie. I'm sure you appreciate that they are from one of the oldest noble families in Lorraine. Two families, to be precise—the Lomont branch of the Châtelets."

"*Oui*, Baroness. Madame de Bercy has told me that much."

"Your father was one of the king's Musketeers and his grandfather was one of Louis Quatorze's most trusted generals. At the end of his career, the Marquis du Châtelet was in service to the deposed King of Poland, now Duke Stanislas, of Lorraine—you are named in honor of him—and you should hear nothing but praise for your father at court, since he has earned the admiration of all who know him."

"Oui, madame." But why, if he were such a great man, had Baronne Lomont and Maman acted as if there were nothing to say about him? *What is she telling me now that I couldn't have known long ago?*

"Your father was part of the *noblesse de robe*, as you know, not the *noblesse d'épée*," the baroness went on. "You do understand the distinction, do you not?"

"*Oui*, madame. Some families are noble by ancient bloodlines, and they are called the nobility of the sword. But the king can bestow a title of noble of the robe on whomever he wishes, as a reward for service—"

"Or a large contribution to the king's private treasury," the baroness sniffed in scorn. "You're sure to meet the countess of this or the marquis of that, and just remember that in some cases the title means very little." Baronne Lomont arched her eyebrows to reinforce her point. "You must be aware of everyone's lineage, since there is proper etiquette for each relationship. And you must be aware that many people are a mix of both types of nobility, and it can be quite complex to sort out who, like our family, are closer in status to the *noblesse d'épée* than they are to *poseurs* who bought just yesterday the same titles we have had for generations."

"*Oui*, madame."

"Your maternal grandmother was Gabrielle-Anne de Froullay, who married Louis-Nicholas le Tonnelier, Baron de Breteuil. Gabrielle-Anne was of higher rank than her husband, despite his title, since she was *noblesse d'épée*."

The baroness turned away from the painting toward Lili. "It was considered a good match, since it brought together his money and her social standing. My marriage accomplished the same. Like my family, many of the sword have seen their fortunes decline, and their hopes now lie in forging bonds with the *noblesse de robe*. It's these newer families who control much of the wealth in France now, I regret to say. A noble of the sword will never earn money from any kind of trade or profession, and that practice has played a role in our impoverishment in this new France everyone speaks so highly of."

She sniffed to show her contempt. "Any noble of the sword who accepts pay for his efforts will suffer the disgrace of losing his tax exemption and be treated socially as no better than a well-dressed laborer. But I assume you know all this."

"No, Baronne. But I suppose I could have guessed as much, from the lack of occupation I've observed." Lili winced. *Do you always have to be so sarcastic?* she chided herself.

"Quite," the baroness replied. "As a result of your connection to the Breteuils, you are *noblesse d'épée*, but of lesser standing, since it is only from one grandparent," Baronne Lomont went on. "I believe you should be able to see how important this makes a good marriage for you. It would be quite tragic for your children if you were to marry someone situated no better than you, when there are good opportunities to improve your social standing."

Baronne Lomont had by now moved away from the painting and had gone to sit at a small desk. After taking a ring of keys from a pouch dangling from her waist and laying it on the desk, she motioned to Lili to sit on a nearby fauteuil. "In fact, Mademoiselle de Bercy outranks you, for her mother comes from two excellent families of the sword, although, I'm sorry to say, they are both impoverished and rural. Monsieur de Bercy was of the robe, and he supplied the fortune, down to the last coin, in exchange for the privilege of marriage to someone of madame's standing."

She looked at Lili. "I suppose you are wondering why you are only hearing these things about the de Bercy family now. You have been kept uninformed about much of it because madame did not wish rank to be a means by which you settled the quarrels that would be inevitable between girls raised together. I believe she also disapproves of the system as a whole and tries to minimize its effects in her home."

She searched Lili's face. "You are clearly troubled."

"*Oui,* Baronne. It's a great deal to take in all at once."

"I shouldn't be too concerned. At Versailles someone like you should err on the side of extreme deference, to avoid giving offense, and we will ensure that you make a match that will advance you appropriately when the time comes for you to marry. For now, just remember that at sixteen, for you it's 'deference, deference, deference,' until you have sorted it all out."

"Deference, Baronne. I shall remember that."

Baronne Lomont gave her another long, quizzical look. "Now we must turn to the most difficult subject at hand, and that is your mother."

My mother? Lili's heart punched her ribs and for a moment she forgot to breathe.

Baronne Lomont reached for the keys again and opened a small drawer. She took out an object about the size of a small book and opened it to reveal twin picture frames trimmed with elaborate gold filigree.

"It's rather a curiosity," the baronness said. "Quite foreign in style. The marquis must have seen something like it in his travels and had one made as a present for your mother. It has symbols from both family crests—the fleur-de-lys and the sparrow hawk—and it used to contain two small portraits, one of your mother and one of him."

Lili held it in both hands. "There's nothing now."

"It wasn't empty when I found it among your mother's things at Lunéville after we buried her. This was on one side." Baronne Lomont took a small, stiff card from a waxy wrapping and handed it to Lili. On it was a miniature painting of a woman with a high forehead, brown hair, and round, dark eyes. She was looking to one side, as if something just out of reach had caught her eye. "You look quite a bit like her," the baroness said.

My mother. Lili held the card as if it might crumble in her hands. *My mother.*

"Your mother's likeness was on the left when I found it, looking toward the portrait on the right," the baroness said, "which was this one." She took from the same wrapping an identically sized portrait of a small man with narrow eyes, hollow cheeks, and a sardonic curl at the corners of his mouth.

"This isn't my father," Lili said. "I've seen this man's likeness in the front of his books. This is Voltaire. I've heard she knew him, but . . ."

The baroness sniffed with contempt. "Your mother took the marquis's gift of affection and used it in this fashion, to keep the image of another man closer than her own husband."

"I don't understand!" Lili picked up the image of her mother and stared into it. *Speak to me*, she pleaded silently, but the eyes of the young woman revealed nothing.

"When you are at Versailles, you are almost certain to hear about the relationship between the two of them. And of course, since so many people at court grow bored when they have ground the latest gossip into dust, they may use your presence to resurrect what, I must warn you, was a scandal. Some people consider themselves quite the authority on it, in all its sordid and—I must say—largely fabricated details." She retrieved the portraits and put them back in the wrapping.

Baronne Lomont sat back in her desk chair, watching Lili. "Madame la Marquise was extraordinarily gifted," the baroness went on. "Too gifted, in my opinion, for her own good."

Lili's blood pounded. *I want it back. I want to hold her again, even if it's just a picture in my hand.*

She stopped for a moment, waiting for Lili to reply. "Really, my dear," she finally said. "You must remain part of conversations. You must always make some response if you are to make a favorable impression."

"I know that she translated Newton," Lili said, clearing her throat to recover her voice. "That she did it herself, and did not, as some have said, just serve as a scribe for the men around her."

"I am not in a position to know such things," the baroness said. "The difficulty was that she was never satisfied with the role to which nature destined her. To be sure, she spent countless hours at court seeing to the advancement of her husband's interests, and her attention to her children was most admirable. A convent education for her daughter, who made a good marriage at your age, and a military career for the son who survived to adulthood. And that should have been enough for her."

The baroness paused. "Look at me, Stanislas-Adélaïde." Lili struggled to face her without trembling. "We are not to fill our days with frivolous things we wish to accomplish. One of the reasons Madame de Bercy and I withheld information from you is that when we saw you had your mother's quick mind, we did not want you to be attracted to the kind of life she led. Beyond your duties as a wife and mother, it is your social role that must take up your attention. Of course you may have small edifying pursuits of your own—a charity perhaps, or a hobby. Sketching is quite appropriate, or learning to play a musical instrument. The harp is quite appealing, since it shows off the hands, and your fingers are nicely shaped."

Lili's temples were throbbing. "*Oui*, Baronne Lomont."

"I paid a short visit once to the marquis at his ancestral home at Cirey," the baroness went on. "All day he and his guests waited for your mother and Monsieur Voltaire to leave off from their experiments and their papers, and even at dinner they would talk about nothing of interest to anyone but themselves. I recall one singularly unedifying discussion about fire, and another where both of them stormed from the table over a disagreement as to whether some hidden force was at work in rocks they had been dropping all day in their lab—"

"Monsieur Voltaire lived with my parents at Cirey?"

"Monsieur Voltaire lived with your *mother* at Cirey." Baronne Lomont paused to let her meaning register. "The marquis was rarely there, since we are almost always at war now, and he spent months on end with his regiment at the front. I imagine your mother impressed upon him how prestigious it was to have the most famous writer in France living on his property, even if there were the occasional problems with the police."

"Police?" The story was spiraling beyond imagination.

"Monsieur Voltaire is in trouble with the censors all the time. Many feel his quite public problems are a stronger reason for his fame than the quality of his work. I wouldn't know since I think it is best not to waste time on authors the church has banned." The baroness looked at a small clock on her desk. "We must get ready to leave for mass. I think I've said all you need to know."

"Baronne Lomont," Lili said, swallowing hard. "Why doesn't my father care about me?" *There. I've said it.*

"What on earth do you mean? He turns over all the receipts from one of his properties to pay Madame de Bercy for your expenses. How can you fail to appreciate that?"

"Yes, but—"

"And he replies promptly when there are issues regarding your upbringing." Her expression made it clear what she thought of Lili's ingratitude.

"But he doesn't reply to me—at least I imagine he would not if I were permitted to write. He has never asked to see me, and I've never been invited to visit him at Lunéville or Cirey. He must come to Paris from time to time, doesn't he? Why have I never met him?" Lili put her hands to her face, trying to mask what she could feel was the growing scarlet of her cheeks. "I'm sorry, madame. I should be more discreet, but—"

Baronne Lomont cleared her throat and began speaking in a voice that could barely contain her disgust. "Because of his obligations to his regiment and to the Duc de Lorraine, the marquis had few opportunities to live as husband and wife with your mother. Instead, she lived in a mockery of that state with Voltaire for more than a decade."

She paused to enforce her point. "A decade, Stanislas-Adélaïde. Your mother and Voltaire took no pains to hide that they were lovers, and that led, quite naturally, to the most vicious rumors about her, even when it became clear the passion between them—if that's what you call it—was gone, and they were no more than friends."

Lili had never seen Baronne Lomont reveal anything beyond slight irritation, but now her eyes flashed and her lip was curled.

"To hear some people tell it, your mother at one point or another bedded every scientist or man of letters in France, and though nothing like that is the case, rumors themselves serve to magnify disrepute," the baroness said. "When she conceived you, there were a few who amused themselves by spreading doubt that the marquis had been at Cirey at the appropriate time. You may hear the most unseemly whispering, but your father insists on his paternity, and anyone of quality should accept his word."

What is she talking about? My mother had lovers? Whispers about paternity? Lili's mind whirled in confusion.

Baronne Lomont stood up. "Do not listen to gossipmongers," she said with a stern face. "And now we really must go." She swept toward the door, leaving an astonished Lili to follow.

ALL THE WAY to the Cathedral of Notre-Dame Lili and Baronne Lomont sat in silence while gusts of rain from an unexpected thunderstorm battered their sedan chair. Lili shivered under a lap robe in the damp air, going over everything the baroness had said, and the one thing she had not. *Why should my father be upset with me over something that happened long before I was born, something that wasn't my fault at all?*

"Baronne Lomont?" Lili inquired into the gloomy air of the coach. "How old is my father now?"

"He is nearing seventy. Why do you ask?"

"I just wondered. Did he ever marry again?"

"No. He loved your mother very much. Sometimes I think he stayed away from you because he didn't want to be reminded of her."

Maybe I wouldn't either, if I'd lost someone I loved, Lili thought, unable to take the thought further because the only death she had ever mourned was poor little Tintin, who had died the year before.

The sedan chair slowed to a stop and she felt herself being lowered to the ground. She folded the lap robe and placed it on the velvet upholstery of her seat and waited for one of the carriers to open the door. Clouds veiled the twin towers of the west portal of Notre-Dame in wisps of gray as Lili and Baronne Lomont stepped out of the chair and entered the cathedral. Night was falling, and around them the church was dark except for hundreds of candles in the chapels lining the side aisles, and flickering light from oil lamps in the nave.

"Mademoiselle du Châtelet!"

Lili turned in the direction of a familiar voice.

"I thought that was you!" Joséphine de Maurepas said, coming out of the gloom toward her. "Didn't I tell you so?" she asked the young man walking next to her.

Lili's stomach fell. *Jacques-Mars.* "What are you doing here?"

Casting a stern look at Lili for her failure in etiquette, Baronne Lomont turned to Joséphine. "I don't believe we've been introduced," she said in an uncharacteristically pleasant tone.

"Forgive me, Baronne," Lili said. "I was taken by surprise to see someone I knew. Baronne Lomont, may I present Joséphine de Maurepas, a friend of mine from the abbey. And Jacques-Mars Courville, whom I met at Vaux-le-Vicomte this summer." The baroness nodded stiffly, and Lili turned back to Joséphine.

"Where is Anne-Mathilde?" she asked. *And why are you here alone with Jacques-Mars?*

Joséphine tittered, in a manner far more lively and confident than Lili remembered. "Anne-Mathilde is at Versailles with her mother, visiting the queen."

"At Versailles?" Now? Lili's heart sank.

"Yes, and when she heard you would be coming with Delphine, she was so pleased. She said it would be so much fun to have some friends there, since I am required to be in Paris now." She turned to Baronne Lomont. "My mother is not well. Normally she comes to Notre-Dame to light candles in our chapel on the Friday nearest the feast day for St. Martin of Tours, since he is the patron saint of her family." She took Jacques-Mars's arm. "But I am doing it in her place this year, and Monsieur Courville was so kind as to bring me. We're just waiting now for the carriage to take us home."

She looked up at Jacques-Mars with a coquettish smile. "And just think, you foolish man, if there hadn't been this beastly rain we might not have seen Lili. Or met Baronne Lomont." She reached up and gave Jacques-Mars's ear a friendly tug. "You should listen to me. I think that's settled once and for all, isn't it?"

"Decidedly," Jacques-Mars replied, looking at Lili with the same hooded eyes that had so unnerved her the previous summer. "And now that I've heard you will be at Versailles, I will have to pay a visit myself. I believe I am still in your debt for a game of trictrac I lost? I'm afraid I can no longer honor your request to remove my bandage, since I'm quite healed, but"—he brandished his finger—"I'm sure you'll be pleased to know such a pitiful wound left no scar."

"Scar?" Joséphine's eyebrows rose as she turned toward Jacques-Mars with a nervous laugh. *She wasn't part of it,* Lili realized. *She was just in tow. She's always been just in tow.*

"It's just a little joke between us," Jacques-Mars said. "Isn't it, Mademoiselle du Châtelet?"

Taken aback by his ability to be sinister and jovial at the same time, Lili was too dumbfounded to reply.

"Well then!" Joséphine had grown edgy. "If we aren't all going to be in on the story, perhaps it's time to leave." She turned to Jacques-Mars. "Shall we see if our carriage is waiting?"

"Certainly," he said, bowing to Baronne Lomont. "I hope I shall have the honor of seeing you again. And Mademoiselle du Châtelet, I am so pleased to know such an opportunity is imminent. Until Versailles, then."

The baroness' eyes pierced the gray air as she watched Jacques-Mars usher Joséphine through the door of the cathedral. "I don't like that young man," she said. "He has a way about him that is not to be trusted. And I'm not sure I like the tone of his reference to his bandage. Would you care to tell me about that?"

"Jacques-Mars was bitten on the finger by some prey he had snared," Lili said, surprised by the facility with which she reshaped the truth. "He was rather embarrassed to have been so careless, that's all." Lili shrugged. "I'm surprised he remembers. And it had nothing to do with me."

Baronne Lomont searched Lili's face. "A shrug of the shoulder usually means there is more to something, not less, but I shall take you at your word." She paused. "Nothing good will come of his attention to that young woman. Mark my words. And please reassure me you will stay away from him at Versailles."

"You need not worry on that score, Baronne," Lili said. "Neither Delphine nor I want anything to do with him. He is really quite a cad."

The baroness nodded approval. "And I should make clear to you that the only time you need not defer to a social superior is when your honor is threatened. Remaining virtuous is your right, and you should keep that in mind around men like that one."

The baroness glanced toward the crossing at the end of the nave. "They're lighting the candles on the altar," she said, taking Lili's arm but not yet moving down the aisle. "I hope you understand how important it is to have a trustworthy man who can protect you. There are many who will not, and the young are so inclined to misjudge."

"*Oui,* Baronne."

"Take for example that Jacques-Mars. He might be viewed as more charming than someone such as . . ." She appeared to be searching for an example. "Someone like Monsieur de Barras. His deep regard for his wife has made him, I'm afraid, rather poor company at present, but he is an excellent man. He is both wealthy and of the sword, which as you know has become rather unusual these days."

Lili felt her heart plummet. *I should have known this was coming.* "When his time of mourning has passed," the baroness went on, "he will begin looking for a new wife, since he has two young children, and a woman is better suited to attend to the needs of the young."

Please don't say any more. Lili fought the urge to run out of the church—anywhere, even in the rain, in the dark—stumbling along the riverbank until she fell in, if that was what she needed to do to avoid hearing what she thought might be coming next.

"Do not get your head turned about your prospects when you are at Versailles," Baronne Lomont went on. "You are young and attractive enough, and I hope you will enjoy the time before you marry, but you would be well advised to keep an open mind about men like Robert de Barras, and the kind of match you will eventually be able to make with your limited assets and standing."

Lili's knees felt weak and she pulled her elbow in, tightening the elder woman's arm against her body.

"I can see you are affected by my words," Baronne Lomont said. "You are a good girl, Stanislas-Adélaïde." She extricated herself to lower one knee in front of the altar and cross herself. Lili did the same, just as the celebrant began the mass.

"*Introibo ad altare Dei,*" the priest intoned. "I will go in to the altar of God . . ."

"Who giveth joy to my youth," Lili murmured in response,

wondering if perhaps both joy and youth were gifts God had withdrawn from her in the course of a single afternoon.

THE COACH TAKING Julie de Bercy and the two girls to Versailles two days later sped through the outskirts of Paris into the countryside. In the glare of the frosty morning, Delphine's face was pallid with apprehension and exhaustion after a night of fitful sleep. Though women were not expected to travel in anything as impractical as panniers, Delphine had insisted on wearing a dress whose tailoring required a hard busk to flatten her chest and stomach, and she had been fighting back tears from the jarring of the coach as it bounced along.

From time to time gleaners in the fields looked up as the black-lacquered coach passed, but it was too modest to attract much attention compared to the ornately gilded royal carriages going to and from Versailles. Indifferent to their presence, a man checked a snare while one of his dogs sniffed the brush around him and the other urinated against a tree trunk, sending a cloud of vapor into the frosty air.

What is that man's life like? Lili wondered. *Does he come home happy, or cursing his wet feet and poor luck? Is there a baby crying while he eats his dinner and his dogs beg for scraps?* She looked across the carriage to Maman and Delphine. Both sat staring at nothing, Maman with drooping eyes as she succumbed to the sleep-inducing jostling of the coach, and Delphine wide-eyed and rigid as a pole. *We're hurtling past that man's world, and he cares as little about us as we do about him.*

Everyone's alone, she thought, wondering why this hadn't occurred to her before.

Maman falling asleep across from her, after a morning dealing with a frantic Delphine and a complicated departure from home—what was her life really like? Lili felt a sudden rush of shame. She had never considered that Maman's life might be hard in ways Lili could not understand. Delphine was silently dabbing at a wet cheek. Why was she crying? *Maybe we never really know other people*, Lili thought. *We only know what we expect of them, and sometimes only notice them at all when they do something else instead.*

Lili looked out the window again, remembering stepping down from the carriage on the way to the abbey and seeing not the block of buildings she expected but a field much like this one, though smaller and hemmed in. She shut her eyes, thinking of Rousseau and the book that had ended her convent days. "Man is born free, and everywhere he is in chains," he had said to her in the salon. It had certainly turned out to be truer than she realized. What was the difference, really, between memorizing pages of catechism in a cell and spending days sequestered upstairs at Hôtel Bercy while she practiced a perfect curtsey for the queen?

Woman is born free and everywhere she is in corsets, she thought with a rueful smile. *I'll tell him that's what he should have said, if I ever see him again.*

Delphine had shut her eyes and her head was beginning to bob with the onset of sleep. Maman's breathing was light and her jaw was slack. Lili felt suddenly overwhelmed with such love for both of them that she wanted to take them in her arms, to gather them up and fly right through the roof of the coach, off to someplace where—

Where what? Had she come to accept what Rousseau had written? On this grim December morning, hurtling toward a destiny she had not chosen, she thought she probably had. A perfect *révérence* and swing of her panniers wouldn't bring Lili anything she really wanted, but she had succumbed to such demands anyway.

Delphine moaned in her sleep. *I'm not her*, Lili thought. *I can't be. She will get through this ordeal and go off into the future like Comète trailing stars. But me . . . ?*

She had still not had a chance to ask Maman any of the questions Baronne Lomont had been unwilling to address. *My mother lived as lovers with Voltaire for years? How did that happen? Why did it end? And I still don't understand why my father doesn't care about me. I'm sixteen, and he's had time to get over his grief. If that awful Monsieur de*

Barras will remarry before too long, why can't my father lay eyes on me? Can a general be that much of a coward?

Monsieur de Barras. A new wave of fears swept over her. Was the baroness going to try to force a marriage on her? Would Jacques-Mars Courville come to Versailles to make her pay for the embarrassment at Vaux-le-Vicomte? Lili shuddered at a vision of Anne-Mathilde's smirking face. "It will be so much fun to have friends at Versailles," Joséphine reported her as saying, but Lili knew about Anne-Mathilde's idea of fun.

She rubbed her forehead, pinching the skin between her brows as if to will all her thoughts into retreat. "What am I going to do?" she whispered, leaning back and letting the hard frame of the coach seat pummel her spine. Jacques-Mars was not the only kind of man she would need to keep at arm's length. He would come away with no fingers at all if he tried to bother her, but Baronne Lomont had a far stronger hold. Could Maman stop her from locking Lili in a cage with someone as awful as Robert de Barras, like a bird with clipped wings, mated for life?

There must be a way to fight all this. An image of her mother's portrait formed in her mind. What would she do? She had once been in the situation Lili now faced. She must have made her *révérence* before the queen, flicked her train just so, smiled properly, and done everything else required by her rank.

Play your role. Go along with what you can't change. That would be part of her mother's answer, Lili was sure. Emilie du Châtelet had done just that—gotten married, had children, managed the household.

And then she had gone off to live with Voltaire.

Lili felt goose bumps on her arms, as if cold winter air had been let into the coach by an invisible spirit who had opened the door and was now settling in next to her. *Start what you can. Follow through. Live the life you set in motion, without looking back.*

An idea came into her head as clearly as if it had been whispered in her ear. *Publish Meadowlark.*

Everything made sense. "An author?" she could picture Monsieur de Barras saying. "No wife of mine would consider such a thing." One problem solved, but how many others would she create? *I don't care*, Lili thought, exhilarated by the feel of the road thundering under her. Perhaps someone would want her for her work, for her mind, for her learning, as Voltaire had wanted her mother.

Someone will. Have faith in yourself.

"Maman?" she whispered as softly as she could, wanting to share with Julie the news of her decision. To her disappointment, Maman did not stir. Lili leaned back, her mind whirling. She needed a pen name to protect herself. Monsieur Diderot and Maman had played with the letters in her name. What could she come up with? Stanislas-Adélaïde had far too many letters. Châtelet. Le chat. Tellechat. That's it. "Tellechat," she whispered.

You can do it all, she told herself. She could go to Versailles and be charming. She could get through it with enough grace and wit to win the only victory she needed, which was to go home afterward and be done with it. Go home and see what happens next.

Emilie

My dearest Voltaire,

Can you really be so cruel as to go for a week without writing?
Do you not realize I live for contact with you? Your letter for my husband arrived yesterday, and nothing in the same post for me? Am I to
settle for a casual remark that you send your regards? You must think
that because I live so much in my mind, I have none of the feelings
of a woman. You should be most ashamed if you saw how bitterly I
weep, and how I comb your old letters in search of reassurances that
you do love me. Yesterday at a salon I lost a frightening sum playing faro—all because fears of being displaced in your heart made me
inattentive. Since I rarely lose a sou, I became the subject of the most
unpleasant campaign of whispers, and had to stay far longer than I
wished, simply to prove I didn't care what they were saying. Surely
you must know what kind of toll such things take on me.

My most cherished and beloved Voltaire, I want nothing more
than to remain in your heart if not, for now, in your arms. There are
so many women and—dare I say—men who crave your companion-
ship, and you are so fond of adulation that I fear every minute that
your head is being turned against me. I shall be waiting for a satisfactory letter from you by return post. Please do not break the heart that
yearns only for you.

Your suffering but devoted,

Emilie

10

THE QUEEN'S chambers were bathed in bloodred light, casting murky shadows across the faces of the ladies-in-waiting, making their eyes hollow, black pits. "Move," a voice behind Lili said, pushing her forward. The women's mouths formed incomprehensible phrases that they whispered back and forth with mechanical jerks of their heads.

Beneath Lili's feet the floor pitched and bucked, but she managed to make it to the queen's chair. "You've forgotten to dress," a woman as thin as a skeleton said. Feeling a sudden rush of cold air, Lili looked down. She was in her dressing gown, and though she clutched it to her, it kept flapping open, revealing a thin chemise and her bare legs underneath.

"Leave my sight immediately!" the queen screeched. "And turn around properly when you go, or I'll have you thrown in prison!" Lili spun in wild, dizzying circles until all of a sudden she was yanked to a stop by a foot holding down the hem of her skirt.

"You can't escape!" Anne-Mathilde shrieked at her with her mouth wide open, like a gargoyle looking down from the roof of Notre-Dame. Lili's clothing tore away as she broke free, running with feet so heavy she hardly moved at all.

She sat up in bed, gasping for breath. Through the window of her quarters at Versailles, she could see the sky lightening. She got up and went to the adjoining room to see if Delphine was awake. The bed curtains were closed, but on a table just outside was a basin from which emanated the harsh smell of vomit.

Lili peeked through the curtain at a sleeping Delphine before going back to her room. She put on a robe and sat at the desk, still trembling from her nightmare. *Maybe writing will calm me down*, she thought. She got out some paper and tapped the excess ink from the quill:

> Meadowlark and Tom pushed open the door to a house in Uruguay. Inside a family sat, bound to chairs with ropes of gold. Over their laps were draped silver chains so heavy they could not move their legs.
>
> "Who tied you up?" Meadowlark asked.
>
> "We did," the man said. "We have to stay here all day doing nothing, just to show we're not working."

Lili dipped her quill, shaking her head with an amused sniff before continuing.

> Just then two young servants came in. "Who are you?" Meadowlark asked. "And why aren't you tied up too?"
>
> "We have work to do. And besides, we're not wealthy enough to have gold rope and silver chains. You need those to be properly tied up, don't you?"
>
> "And if you have them, you need to show them off," the chained woman tried to explain. "What good are chains if they're locked in a drawer?"
>
> A little girl with a silk bag over her head was squirming in her chair. "I want to get up and walk around," she said. "I want to go outside."

Lili heard footsteps and looked up. Delphine was standing in the doorway rubbing her eyes. "Is it time to get ready?" she asked. "I hope I'm through being sick to my stomach. I can't put on my dress if I'm going to throw up on it, but I don't suppose I have much left anyway. I was up half the night."

"Me too," Lili said. "When I came in you were asleep. I saw your basin and was worried about you."

"I'm just so terrified of ruining everything," Delphine said. "I shouldn't have gone on and on in my head about how wonderful everything was going to be." She sat down on a daybed near Lili. "What are you doing?"

"Writing a story. I'll finish it later."

"Can you write my way out of this?" Delphine tried to smile.

"I think I'm writing my own. It's pure foolishness what we have to do. It has nothing to do with anything even slightly important."

Delphine took in a deep breath and let it out slowly. "It's important because it's the rules." Lost in thought, she picked at tiny pieces of lint clinging to her dressing gown. "Remember those drawings we saw of the women in Africa who carried huge pots on their heads? Maybe men won't marry women who aren't good at it, and African girls throw up in the night worrying about their pots tumbling to the ground."

Lili smiled. "I imagine it's always something." She looked down at her notebook. "Remember when Monsieur Diderot wanted to publish my stories and I said no? Well, I've changed my mind, but you mustn't say anything to anyone. Except Maman, of course."

Delphine clapped her hands in excitement. "I always thought it would be fun to see Meadowlark and Tom in the paper, and now we will—that is, if we live through today." Her face darkened again. "I hope Meadowlark meets Anne-Mathilde someday. That little viper wouldn't stand a chance."

Lili thought for a moment. "Rousseau says that when society is deformed, people accept deformity in order to fit in. Not that I'm excusing Anne-Matilde, but I think some of what I feel for her—just a little—is pity."

"We don't have to turn out like her," Delphine said. "She chooses to be horrid, and I don't pity her at all." She pulled up her knees under her gown and patted it in place over them. "Since you're going to publish it, can I hear your new story first?"

"I thought you'd outgrown Meadowlark."

"I was stupid." She pointed to the vacant space next to her. "Please?"

Lili sat down. Pulling up her own legs next to Delphine's, she rested the foolscap sheets on her thighs. "It's set in Uruguay," she began.

Absentmindedly working her fingers through her tangled hair, Delphine listened with a melancholy expression. "No more Spider Kings," she said when Lili finished. "Your stories have grown up too."

"No more Spider Kings," Lili repeated. "Life on earth is frightening enough."

Delphine didn't seem to hear. "I had this wild urge to jump out the window last night," she said, standing up.

"You would have been killed!" Lili put her hand to her mouth. "Or was that the idea?"

"No. I just wanted to escape, like that girl in your story. I guess I thought anything else would be better than going through today. But I suppose it's best to get on with things." She thought for a moment before leaning down to kiss Lili on the top of the head. "Thank you."

"For what?"

"For making me ready to go meet the queen. I can't believe after all these years, Meadowlark is still coming to the rescue."

LILI AND DELPHINE paused in the foyer just outside the queen's apartment. Julie gave them one last inspection and, just for something to do, brushed a nonexistent stray hair away from each girl's face.

Delphine was shimmering. Her strawberry-blond curls were lifted up gently off the back of her neck and arranged in perfect, scented ringlets whose ends skimmed the ivory ruffle of her collar. Her face was heavily powdered and her lips were dark pink with rouge. A stomacher pressed her ribs flat, pushing up her breasts so that the pink of her nipples was barely out of sight under a frill of delicate lace. The lilac silk of her bodice and skirt was printed with Chinese birds whose long, drooping tail feathers were linked with pink and ivory nosegays made from thousands of tiny embroidered knots. The sleeves had been sewn on as Delphine stood in her room, as had a long train in the English style, bunched into a dozen or more tightly crimped pleats at the back of her neck, and rippling in soft cascades down to the floor.

"You look beautiful." Lili embraced Delphine as much as their huge panniers allowed.

"You too," Delphine murmured.

Lili had chosen a simpler design for her dress, with a bodice, skirt, and elbow-length sleeves in a light gray satin she had loved from first sight in the mercier's shop, because it looked as if it were made from pools of liquid silver. Her bodice was tied with green ribbons, and her train was embroidered with garlands of leaves and graceful clusters of purple and cream-colored flowers.

A group of twenty or more guests and ladies-in-waiting noticed them standing at the door and cleared a narrow path for them. Julie started forward and Delphine followed. Lili paused for a moment and looked down in horror at the small pool of water where Delphine had been standing. Delphine's hem had dragged it a few steps into the room, making a ragged smear, and Lili took a few sideways steps to cover the spot with her own skirts and blot it as she walked forward. Her panniers wobbled at the unexpected motion.

Delphine and Julie had stopped by now in front of the queen, and Lili walked quickly to catch up and stand on Julie's other side, with her eyes downcast to hide her terror. Her panniers felt uncentered, but there was nothing she could do that would be graceful enough to avoid titters and whispers among the assembled women. She watched out of the corners of her eyes as Delphine made her *révérence* and then, after a few words with the queen, took several careful steps backward. In a second, Delphine was around, glowing in the knowledge that her train was perfect behind her.

Maman turned to Lili, offering formal words of presentation that sounded as muffled as if her head were underwater. Lili made a slow and careful *révérence,* and when she stood up again she took her first good look at the queen.

Though Lili knew Queen Marie Leszczynska was in her fifties, she was still unprepared for the matronly woman seated in front of her. The queen was short, and too plump to bother with a tight corset. She wore a dress of luxurious gold and brown brocade, decorated on the bodice with columns of transparent chiffon. Rows of jagged, ornate lace draped over her arms, pulled up at the elbows by floppy satin bows. The dress was more expensive than beautiful or stylish, and at odds with the black, mantillalike head covering that rested over her tight, gray curls.

The queen smiled at her. "Stanislas-Adélaïde. You are named for my father, I believe." Even after decades in France, her voice was full of the sounds of her native Poland. "And you are the daughter of the Marquis du Châtelet and his dear, late wife."

"Yes, Your Majesty," Lili said. "Madame de Bercy has raised me since I was a small child."

"And raised you well, I can see." She held up a pair of glasses and peered through them. Tell me," she said. "Are you as good at cards as your mother was?"

"I—I don't know, Your Majesty. I never had the opportunity to know her."

"A pity. She was the most delightful company, although I must admit her intelligence frightened all of us."

"You knew my mother?" Lili blurted out. She heard the rustle of skirts and the murmur of voices behind her and instantly felt foolish. *Of course she knew her. And the queen asks the questions, not you,* she reminded herself. "Please forgive me," she said. "I forgot my manners."

"Oh, it doesn't matter," the queen said with a dismissive wave of her hand. "All this frippery is a waste of time, but everyone does seem to insist on it." She looked through her glasses again. "I can see her face in yours."

Lili glanced at Maman and saw that her eyes were shining. "I hope so," Lili said. "I'm very proud of her."

"But you still haven't told me whether you play cards. I love a good faro player with the sense to let me win some of the time." Her eyes crinkled. "After all, I am the queen."

"I will do my best to please you," Lili said, feeling a burst of perspiration under her arms. So far it had gone well, but she'd have to back up and turn around soon, and she felt everyone's eyes boring into her back.

"And now," the queen was saying, "I must get ready for dinner."

I want to do this perfectly, Lili thought with an intensity she had never felt during months of practice. *I want her to like me.* Her steps backward were small enough to avoid catching her hem, but as she twisted her body around, she felt her train catch on one of her panniers and knew without looking that it was bunched to one side behind her.

She managed to do what she had practiced to repair the situation by rote, taking a few steps forward and letting the weight of the train drag it to its proper position, but she heard the whispers around her and knew her error hadn't escaped notice.

Maman and Delphine had already begun walking away, and she started behind them, keeping her eyes glazed to avoid seeing Anne-Mathilde, whom she hadn't noticed but assumed was there.

"Please return for a moment, Stanislas-Adélaïde," she heard the queen say.

Could it get worse? Some of the women had stepped back, eager to begin gossiping with their friends, and to her relief, Lili had room to take a few steps to turn around.

"I'm so sorry," the queen said, when Lili was facing her again. "I stretched out my foot just as you turned and your train caught on my slipper." The queen's expression was stern as she surveyed the faces around her.

What she had said was untrue—anyone could see that—but what did it matter? The queen said it was not Lili's fault, and that was the end of the matter.

"You may go," the queen said, with a flicker of a smile.

She's giving me another chance, Lili realized. *I have to do it right this time*. An unexpected calm came over her as she went up on her toes and brought her train around flawlessly. Her burden lifted, she floated through the clustered women, whose fans could not hide their astonishment at the queen's intervention.

The Queen of France rescued me! She saw Delphine's exultant grin and felt as if their spirits were dancing around the glittering room. *And best of all, it's over.*

HEAVY SNOW AND swirling wisps of fog cocooned Versailles in the first days after Lili's and Delphine's presentations. "Why did we have to come in December?" Delphine complained. "It's spoiled all my plans, to be stuck inside. We haven't been anywhere but our rooms and the queen's apartment." She let out a frustrated sigh at being ignored. "Maman! You're supposed to be still when I'm sketching you!"

"I didn't know you were," Julie said. "I was too busy with my book to notice."

"It was a surprise, and now it's spoiled! Lili, will you promise to be still if I sketch you?"

Lili giggled. "No."

"Well then, sit down and write. Sometimes you don't move for hours then."

"Maman," Lili said, still ignoring Delphine's petulance. "I've been thinking about the king. Where is he? We haven't seen him once, and I've heard he's often there when young ladies are presented."

"He comes to speak for a few minutes with Marie Leszczynska every morning during her toilette, but they each have their own lives and they're busy with their own duties."

"Where does he live?" Delphine asked, looking up from her drawing.

Julie smiled. "It's a very big palace."

"Yes, but—"

"There's another château on the grounds called the Trianon," Julie went on. "Madame de Pompadour lived there, and the king spent a great deal of his time with her even after they weren't lovers anymore. People knew if they wanted something from the king it was best to get her to ask on their behalf. But she died last year, and most people say the king is quite bereft."

"That's sad." Delphine put down her sketchbook. "Even when people die too old to be attractive anymore."

"She wasn't old, unless you think I am," Julie said. "She was just a year or two older than I, and I'm just forty." She got up and, putting her hands on her hips, arched her back. "Although my bones feel older sometimes."

Delphine got up. "I'm sorry, Maman. You are the most beautiful woman at Versailles." She gave her a hug. "Except for me, of course!" She twirled around the room in tight pirouettes. "I just wish we could have a masquerade, or a big banquet, now that that awful presentation is over. I want to wear my panniers and not think everyone is watching me to see if I make a mistake." She giggled. "Now I'll be watching right back. Wouldn't it be wonderful to catch Anne-Mathilde knocking something off a table?"

Lili watched as Delphine turned here and there, charming imaginary people in the drafty air of the parlor. She loved Delphine, but she could never understand how being in a place like this could satisfy anyone with more substance than the delicate Meissen figurines on the mantelpiece, or why Delphine seemed to want nothing more than to be a living version of them.

"Was Marie Leszczynska beautiful when she was young?" Delphine had by now danced over to Julie. "She has rather nice eyes, and I'm sure she wasn't always so fat."

Out of habit, Julie looked around to make sure no one was listening. "She was always rather plain, but the king, I'm told, fell quite in love with her after they married." Julie thought for a moment. "I think everybody loves her, at least a little. She's a genuinely nice person. Humble too, considering how little she's allowed to show it. It's sad really. The king ruined her health with eleven pregnancies and now he wants little to do with her."

Delphine dropped onto the couch beside Julie. "Eleven?"

"One was stillborn and several others died in infancy. And now her oldest son, the dauphin, is ill with consumption, and the rumor is that he's unlikely to survive to become king. He stays away from Versailles, probably to keep down the gossip about how ill he looks."

By now Lili had settled on the floor, cradling her back against Julie's velvet dressing gown. She turned to look up at her. "What happens if he dies?"

"Right now the dauphin's son is only ten years old. He'd become king anyway, in time. The only question is which number King Louis he'd be—sixteen if his father never becomes king, seventeen if he does. But it is difficult at court every time the throne changes hands. Everyone has friends and enemies, and everyone scrambles around for the same favor as before, if not more."

She thought for a moment. "Whatever happens, Marie Leszczynska won't be queen anymore, but I honestly think she might be very happy to be just the king's grandmother, and rid herself of those fawning women and ceremonies she has little taste for."

Delphine sighed. "It's too bad the little son is too young for me. I'd love to be queen. I think it would be wonderful to have people pay attention to me all the time." She giggled. "Wouldn't it be a torment to Anne-Mathilde to have to make a *révérence* to me?" She got up. "Yes, Your Majesty," she said, curtseying deeply. "Right away, Delphine. And then I'd say, 'It's always Your Majesty now, and you'd better not forget it.'"

Julie laughed, shaking her head. "I think the torment would be largely yours, *ma chérie*. Do you know, I've seen that poor woman stand naked and shivering while people argued over who had the privilege of putting a clean chemise over her head? And would you really want people discussing your bowel movements as if they were affairs of state?" Lili and Delphine wrinkled their noses in disgust.

"Versailles is beautiful to visit," Julie went on, "but to be part of the royal family would be far too public for me. You'd make almost no decisions at all about your own life. Every time I see the queen's daughters, they remind me of little bees buzzing around the queen of the hive. What other life do they have?"

"Madame Victoire is quite pretty," Delphine said, picking up Maman's hand and stroking it with a fingertip. "But you're right, Maman, the others do look like fat little bees, with their chubby little faces. Especially Mademoiselle Sophie." She scrunched her face until her eyes were slits.

"That's not my point, *ma chérie*. And you should be more careful what you say. The king is particularly fond of Sophie, I've been told. It would be a very bad idea to antagonize any of them, since their reach is much farther than yours will ever be." She smiled. "At least since it appears as if Louis-Auguste is not going to be your husband."

Delphine thought for a moment. "Madame Sophie does have a beautiful voice. Perhaps I could ask to accompany her on the harpsichord in the queen's apartments some evening. We could put on a little concert. Perhaps the king would come too, if he's fond of Sophie. Then we could meet him, since I'd hate to say I'd been to Versailles and have never seen him except on his balcony during mass."

Julie's face was somber. "I would be just as happy if you didn't. He may be king, but he isn't what I would call a good man." She looked surreptitiously toward the door. "Madame de Pompadour made sure no one replaced her in the king's affections by supplying him with an endless stream of vapid little mistresses, some no older than you. They lasted a few years and who knows what happened to them after that. They weren't common prostitutes, but daughters of noblemen who used their own flesh and blood to advance themselves."

She shuddered. "Versailles is really quite an ugly place, for all its beauty. That's why I come here as little as I can." She looked away. "And why I immediately start wondering how soon I can go home."

"They offered their daughters to the king?" Delphine's eyes were wide with astonishment.

"Wives too," Julie said. "More than once a wife was sent to his bed, sometimes little more than a child bride—a gift in exchange for a favor or advancement of some sort. Now that Madame de Pompadour is dead, I doubt he'll stop wanting young bodies, and he may decide to find them for himself."

What if it had been the king under the stairs at Vaux-le-Vicomte? Lili banished the thought with a shudder.

"Don't worry, *mes petites*," Julie said. "Everything at court has to be negotiated, and he'll look around in places he'll meet with less resistance than he would get from me. But I have more peace of mind knowing he's unaware right now that two such pretty girls are in his palace."

She looked up to see one of her servants carrying a note on an ornate silver tray. Julie opened it. "Oh, this is lovely!" she said. "Up now, both of you! We're going on a sleigh ride."

THE DECEMBER SUN blazed down on the gardens and parterres stretching out from the palace at Versailles, creating a glare so blinding that Lili looked up into the cloudless sky for relief. The storm had left behind a knee-deep blanket of snow, leaving white epaulets and wigs on sculpted nymphs, and settling like modest drapery over the private parts of reclining gods. A few birds had come out from their roosts, chirping and scolding one another, knocking snow from shrubbery as they searched for a place to forage.

Since it was warm for a winter day, the queen had ordered open sleighs. Hers was a gilded tangle of swirling mythological figures and vines in interlacing arabesques. Behind it were two smaller sleighs, equally ornate and with the same red upholstered seats. Drivers stood by each, dressed in red livery.

"Well, won't this be fun?" Anne-Mathilde said as the three girls got into one of the smaller sleighs. "I haven't had a chance for a decent conversation with either of you since last summer at the château."

"And I've so missed it!" Delphine reached up to adjust her hat, avoiding Anne-Mathilde's eyes.

"You both looked so lovely at your presentation," Anne-Mathilde went on, ignoring the insincerity in Delphine's tone. "Tell, me Lili—I'm dying to know—did the queen really step on your train? It's just too amusing . . ."

Lili glanced at Anne-Mathilde and brushed away the comment with a flick of her hand. "I'm glad it's over," she said. "And you heard what the queen said about her slipper. I have nothing to add."

Anne-Mathilde's eyes flashed at Lili's dismissive reply, but she chattered on as if she hadn't noticed. "I remember my first panniers—tiny little things like a doll's clothing. I've been coming to Versailles all my life, you know. The ladies-in-waiting used to flock around me like birds." She laughed. "Oh, how I used to hate that!"

"I can imagine," Lili said, looking away. "All that attention must have been grueling."

Anne-Mathilde sniffed to convey that she would not do Lili the honor of acknowledging her comment. "My mother says this is your first visit to Versailles, and of course it does give one quite a bit to wonder about. Anything you want to know, please just ask!" She put her gloved hand to her mouth and her eyes widened. "Oh! Speaking of something you should know, I received a letter from Jacques-Mars. He said we should expect him any day." She scanned their faces for a reaction.

Delphine shrugged. "How nice."

How nice if he were lost in a blizzard and died, Lili thought, smoothing her gloves.

"Just think how amusing it would be if he were here now." Anne-Mathilde patted the empty seat next to her. "He's such good company, don't you think? Although I prefer Ambroise Clément de

Feuillet—I suppose you've heard our families are discussing marriage. He's the future Comte d'Étoges, and everyone knows their château is one of the most charming in France. It's terribly perfect, really."

Lili nodded in mock seriousness. "Terribly."

"He's off hunting with the king today. He's one of his favorite courtiers, and the queen adores him . . ." Her voice trailed off as the sleigh made a wide arc in the snow before coming to a stop.

Relieved to be temporarily spared from Anne-Mathilde's prattle, Lili got out quickly from the sleigh and walked to the viewing terrace at the far end of Versailles's formal gardens. A blanket of white covered the entire expanse, broken only by the greenish-black cones, rectangles, and undulating swirls of groomed shubbery. The melting snow had already fallen away from the tops, leaving behind what looked like black cross-stitching on a huge white pillow, set against an azure sky.

"It's lovely, isn't it." Anne-Mathilde had gone off to join the others, and Delphine was standing next to her. "And the palace looks no bigger than my hand, we're so far away."

Lili scarcely heard Delphine as she took in what looked like a vast, empty page on which a giant hand had penciled geometry notes. "Yes," she murmured, looking away with a shiver, even though the day was mild enough to make her winter cloak uncomfortably warm.

On her visit to the Comte de Buffon at the Jardin de Roi she had seen a skeleton of a field mouse, and the memory of the symmetry of its tiny bones came to her as she looked across the snow-covered gardens of Versailles. *As perfect in their beauty and as holy as a cathedral, those bones were,* she thought. These snow-covered terraces and walkways were just something to look at. They could never be more than that. They could not speak to the soul the way that mouse, that pink mantis, indeed everything at the Jardin de Roi spoke to her.

That's where I want to be. Lili shut her eyes, remembering Buffon's kind face, and the excited way Jean-Étienne Leclerc talked about science. This strange world here, with its crazy rituals and rigidity—gardens that say "Keep out," and rules that leave the queen naked while people argue over her chemise?

No wonder her mother had wanted to escape to Cirey. *I want to escape too*, Lili thought. *I want to go back to Hôtel Bercy. I want to go back to the Jardin de Roi.*

When she was younger, Lili imagined her skull was a house where her ideas existed without any need to go outside. These days her mind roamed, seeking answers and solace her interior world could not provide. In the incomprehensible world of Versailles, her thoughts flooded outward as if she were speaking wordlessly to a presence hovering just out of sight. *You have to help me through this*, she said to the air, not certain whom or what she was addressing, or exactly what she meant.

The sun went behind a cloud and Lili looked up to see several more forming. "Brrr," Anne-Mathilde said, getting back in the sleigh and pulling a travel rug up over her shoulders. "I'd so much rather be back at the palace. The queen can be so tedious with her little outings. Now there's a piece of advice for you—get used to wondering how you ended up stuck somewhere with her and her dull daughters, when you'd so much rather be just about anywhere else."

"Umm," Delphine said as she tossed part of her blanket over Lili and pulled it up under their chins. She laid her head on Lili's shoulder, radiating contentment sufficient for the two of them.

ONCE OUTSIDE THE walls surrounding the château and gardens at Versailles, the sleighs made their way down a path to a clearing in the royal forest. Servants had already arrived and set a log fire burning, so the queen and her party could warm themselves. Marie Leszczynska was the shortest woman in the party, and was dressed so plainly that a stranger coming on the scene would not have imagined she was anyone special, except for the constant hovering around her.

The queen had brought a pouch of bird feed and soon was carrying on a conversation with the birds pecking at her feet. The afternoon light was already beginning to dim, and her daughters were cajoling her to get back in the sleigh and go home, when in the distance a hunting horn sounded. Soon, two men on horseback, one carrying the king's standard, trotted into the clearing. They dismounted quickly and bowed before the queen.

"Is my husband far behind?" Marie Leszczynska asked, handing the empty pouch of bird food to a servant. "We were just leaving, but we'll wait if he's near."

Within a few seconds, the king came into the clearing on a huge chestnut-colored stallion. Behind him on an equally large horse a well-built man in his twenties dressed in an elegant riding habit came. He waited for a groom to grab the bridle and then he dismounted, handing him the reins.

The man bowed in a graceful arc before the queen. "Ambroise Clément de Feuillet!" the queen said with a warm smile. "It's so nice to see you. I heard you arrived last week, and I had hoped your business with the king would not keep you so constantly occupied."

"I am duly chastised, Your Majesty." Ambroise returned her smile with one of his own. "I shall make a point of visiting tomorrow," he said, bowing again with a flourish, "since I have now been made aware of how badly I am missed."

What a charming man, Lili thought. *And rather good-looking too. Anne-Mathilde doesn't deserve to be so fortunate.* Ambroise excused himself from the queen and came over to kiss the hand of the Duchess de Praslin, before turning to Anne-Mathilde. "We've had a disappointing hunt," he said, after a perfunctory brush of his lips on her hand. "Only one boar. And it killed one of the dogs before His Majesty got off a shot."

He turned his head at the sound of loud barks and yelps. Soon another horse trotted into the clearing with a pack of dogs scrambling around it. Lying astride the saddle in front of the rider was the limp body of a dog, and a few feet behind, tied around the neck and dragging in the snow, was the carcass of a huge wild boar. Snow had gotten trapped in its bristly hide, caking one shoulder with crystals of blood. The tusks that had taken the life of the dog stuck out from its half-opened mouth and its eyes were glazed with snow that had melted into slime. Half-crazed with the smell of the kill, the dogs growled and nipped at each other as they sniffed the carcass.

"May I ask you to control those animals?" The queen looked up at the king, who was the only one who had not gotten off his horse. The kennel hands scurried to gather the dogs in a corner of the clearing, tossing them bits of dried meat, and putting out basins of melted snow for them to drink.

Lili had shrunk back to watch from behind Maman when the king appeared. Louis's face was broad across the cheeks and rather flat overall, and his dark eyes were overwhelmed by thick eyebrows as black as ink. Other than the fact that he was quite fat and his face was florid with the cold, she decided he was not a bad-looking man. *But still . . . you sleep with young girls?* she thought. *Why do you need to do that?*

"I wish they'd go," Lili heard Delphine whimper. "The horses scare me. And that dead dog and horrid-looking boar!"

Ambroise Clément de Feuillet went over to the king, who bent down to listen. Louis nodded his head and sat back up. He turned his horse in the direction of the path back to the palace and waited while the others got on their mounts. With a tap of his heel the king left the clearing at a trot, followed by his courtiers and the pack of barking dogs. The only ones left behind from the king's party were Ambroise and the rider carrying the dead dog. Ambroise gave him the reins of his mount, and the equerry left the clearing, leading the second horse and dragging the dead boar behind.

Suddenly it was quiet enough to hear. "I have the king's leave to go back with your party, Your Majesty," Ambroise said to the queen. "I understand Mademoiselle de Praslin has room in her sleigh."

"Lucky for you I don't force you to sit with an old woman like me," the queen said in a tone so uncharacteristically teasing that Lili thought she might reach up to pinch his cheek. "And you will have two other charming young women to sit with as well." She looked in

Lili and Delphine's direction. "I don't believe you've been introduced."

Ambroise went over to Julie. "Madame de Bercy, I believe?" He
bowed, gently picking up her hand and touching it to his lips. "My
father introduced us last year—at a ball at the Luxembourg Palace, if
I recall. It's good to see you again, and looking so well." He looked
over at Delphine and Lili. "May I have the pleasure of meeting these
young ladies?" As Julie presented each of them in turn, Ambroise
bowed and took their hand, bringing his lips as close as he could
without touching their fingers.

"Is your stay at Versailles a long one?" Ambroise asked. Though
his inquiry was directed at all three of them, his eyes rested only on
Delphine. Before she could reply, they heard the commotion of the
sleighs being readied for their return. "May I?" He offered Julie his
arm and turned to wait for Delphine to fall in step beside him.

Anne-Mathilde had been watching from near the fire and was
now coming toward them. She insinuated her way between Ambroise and Delphine and took his other arm. "Have you forgotten
I'm here?" she asked Ambroise, bursting into peals of nervous laughter. Lili looked sidelong at Anne-Mathilde's face. *She doesn't want
him near Delphine,* Lili thought, suppressing a smile as they walked
toward the sleighs.

Emilie

Dearest Maupertuis,

I am sorry to have left Paris without the chance to inform you of the terrible change of circumstances in my life. My little boy, Victor-Esprit—dear God, not yet even two years old!—died last week, and I left immediately for Cirey with his tiny coffin for burial in the family cemetery. His passing was not unexpected, since he had been frail since birth, but the shock of seeing my own flesh and blood lifeless has had the most profound impact on me.

My son, Florent-Louis, is with me, since at six he is not yet boarding at school. I have sent word to my daughter Gabrielle-Pauline's convent that I want her sent to me as soon as possible at Cirey, since I plan to be here indefinitely. I shall arrange for her enrollment in the Couvent de la Pitié at Joinville, no more than an hour from here, since I could not bear to see her as infrequently as would be the case now that Paris is several hard days' journey away.

I intend to retain a tutor for my son while I am at Cirey, since I have little confidence in either the church or the military to engender in him the kind of curiosity about the world I want him to have. I hope to inspire in him a love of the sciences and a desire to cultivate his reason, and so a great deal of his education will fall on my own shoulders, and Monsieur Voltaire's as well.

Gabrielle-Pauline has just turned eight, and I must admit, as terrible as it may sound, that I have no passion for her education, since she inhabits a world where good manners and unchallenging points of view will take her further than any real knowledge. Though the love of truth should be a stronger inspiration than the fear of God, Gabrielle-Pauline has shown such a docile and pious temperament, and so little curiosity about things of the mind, that I feel any effort to provide a more liberal education would be largely wasted.

I still hear my father's admonition that it is not wise for a girl to use her mind too much, for fear of being found unattractive as a potential wife. Gabrielle-Pauline will make a good marriage someday, and since that is the measure of parents' success with a daughter, I am doing what I feel is in her best interests, though I know such a childhood would have left me in the most miserable despair.

I am certain you are wondering why I have gone on at such length without yet mentioning our visitor at Cirey. Monsieur Voltaire has been here now for three months, and though parts of the house look more in ruins than ever due to recent demolition, he has already managed to make one wing quite cozy—a word I can't say I have used for Cirey heretofore.

As you know, the *lettre de cachet* for his arrest is still in force should he leave Cirey, but it has receded considerably in importance due to the efforts of the Duchesse de Richelieu to calm the storm. Nevertheless, he says my presence negates any desire he might feel to go elsewhere, and I am, of course, in thrall to such compliments.

In any case, since I am the *châtelaine* of the estate, it falls to me to oversee projects in my husband's absence, and to arrange for proper furnishings, which will take months. Many of the windows are entirely bare, there is only one properly furnished bedchamber in the

*house—and that hopelessly unfashionable—and not a single room is
fit for serious work.*

*I will leave it to you, my dear friend, to discern for yourself how
the prospects of a life of study with Voltaire appear to me at this point,
since it would be entirely unsuitable to express anything but the most
profound grief for the loss of my young son, and resignation to the
work that lies ahead.*

I remain affectionately,
Emilie, Marquise du Châtelet-Lomont

11

"JOSÉPHINE DE Maurepas is married?" Lili and Delphine exchanged confused glances.

"I guess you haven't heard," the queen's daughter Madame Victoire said, getting up to shuffle through sheet music at the harpsichord. "She's been married to the Marquis de Ferrand."

"Quite suddenly," Madame Sophie added. "Apparently he's been to Paris and fetched her already."

"Fetched her indeed," Victoire said, exchanging a knowing glance with her sister. "She had better hope it was a quick and thorough fetching." They both tittered behind their hands.

"That's rather odd," Lili said. "I saw her only a few weeks ago at Notre-Dame, and she said nothing about a marriage . . ."

No one seemed to hear her. "Even girls as plain as Joséphine de Maurepas should have a chance to enjoy a little attention while they are being sought after for marriage. And now, not even that," Sophie murmured, shaking her head. "Poor dear!"

Delphine had gone over to examine the sheet music with Victoire. "Ferrand?" she asked. "Is that in France?"

Sophie and Victoire laughed as if Delphine were the wittiest person they knew.

"It might as well not be," Sophie said.

"Not much there except sheep and cows." Victoire smirked. "And peasants. Lots of those." She and Sophie tittered again. "Tell me, Mademoiselle du Châtelet, when you saw her at Notre-Dame, did she look"—Victoire arched her eyebrows—"perhaps a little thick around the middle?"

Lili thought for a moment. "She was wearing a cloak. It was raining, and quite cold."

"You really must notice more, if you're to be amusing." Victoire's eyebrows rose in subtle mockery. "I imagine we'll know for certain before long," Sophie said, picking up her brandy glass and holding it to her nose.

"News travels so quickly from Ferrand," Victoire replied, and both women burst into dainty peals of laughter. Sophie put the glass down without taking a sip. "This Armagnac is quite inferior. It speaks badly for the court."

Lili had had enough. "What are you talking about?"

Victoire's eyebrows shot up again, but it was Sophie who replied with a sympathetic cluck. "About Joséphine? It usually means there will be a premature arrival of the firstborn child. It's December now." She looked at Victoire. "What do you think? Sometime in May?"

"Joséphine is pregnant?" Lili gasped. And then she understood. *Jacques-Mars.* She sat stunned, as her memories reshaped themselves. Anne-Mathilde draped over Jacques-Mars and Joséphine, looking across the opera house to where she and Delphine sat. Joséphine so flirtatious and cozy with him at Nôtre-Dame. It was all so obvious. He had seduced Joséphine, and Anne-Mathilde had helped him do it. "*Mon Dieu,*" she whispered under her breath.

"Ferrand? Oh, he's forty perhaps," Sophie was saying to Delphine. "Do you remember him, Victoire?" She glanced over to her sister.

Victoire thought for a moment. "Nothing stands out in my mind. He's not a young man—I do recall that—and I don't remember him being attractive."

"Quite fat, I believe," Sophie said. "But perhaps I'm thinking of someone else." Sophie stood up and went over to the harpsichord. Lili watched Delphine's face as Sophie sang the first notes of the music they were preparing for the queen.

She doesn't understand, Lili thought. If Jacques-Mars had succeeded in his scheme at Vaux-le-Vicomte, it could be Delphine who was banished to a place she'd never heard of, and dismissed with a laugh at court.

WHEN THE KING appeared unexpectedly in the queen's parlor a few days before Christmas for the recital Delphine and Sophie had prepared for Marie Leszczynska, the surprise animated the room. The women made their *révérences* so quickly that Lili had to catch on to the fabric of Delphine's skirt to keep from stumbling as she rose. With Louis was Ambroise Clément de Feuillet, and his father, the Comte d'Étoges. Just behind were Anne-Mathilde and the Duchesse de Praslin, who was on the arm of a newly arrived Jacques-Mars Courville.

"I understand a concert with my daughter's new accompanist is not to be missed," Louis said, bending his jowled chin down to one side, to permit an attendant to dab the beads of sweat from his temples. "Which one is Mademoiselle de Bercy?"

Julie had by now stepped to Delphine's side. "Your Majesty." She made a *révérence* again. "May I present my daughter, Delphine."

Delphine made her own deep curtsey.

"Charming," the king said. "And . . . ?" He looked at Lili, standing stupefied next to her.

"May I also present Stanislas-Adélaïde, the daughter of the Marquis du Châtelet-Lomont and his late wife," Julie said.

"Emilie de Breteuil's daughter. Yes—I'd been told she was here." Lili made her *révérence* and struggled not to flinch as the king searched her face. "And will you play in this concert also?"

"It's Mademoiselle de Bercy who has the musical talent, Your Majesty," she said.

His gaze lasted just a moment too long for comfort, and Lili felt her stomach turn over. "Well then," he said, turning his attention to Delphine and motioning her toward the harpsichord.

This is worse than being presented, Lili thought. Her eyes darted to the floor as Delphine crossed the room, but this time there was no embarrassing sign of panic to scurry to hide. When Delphine played the introduction to Sophie's first song, only a slight hesitation suggested that the performance was anything but routine. *Maybe one can get rid of nerves forever all at once,* Lili thought, since that was what Delphine seemed to have done.

The king was seated in a chair that had been quickly moved for the occasion next to the queen. He suppressed a yawn behind his hand and then turned to Marie Leszczynska as if even she might be more entertaining. *He's not interested in either of us,* Lili thought with relief. But someone else was. She glanced across the room and caught Jacques-Mars watching her. He kept his eyes locked on her, and perhaps it was her imagination, but she thought she saw his lips purse as if he were contemplating what it would be like to kiss her.

She looked away and forced herself to smile, as if she were too wrapped up in the music to have noticed him. Her eyes lit upon Ambroise Clément de Feuillet, who was standing with Anne-Mathilde on the other side of the harpsichord. This time, the look in his eyes as he watched Delphine play was unmistakable. *He's smitten with her,* Lili thought, controlling the urge to break out in a most undignified grin.

When Sophie sang her last notes, Delphine finished the concert with a flurry of tinkling notes. She stood up and made another flawless *révérence* to the king and queen before going over to Lili. From behind her fan she asked, "Was he watching me?"

"The king?" Lili asked. "He's bored to a stupor."

"Ambroise," Delphine whispered. "I thought I felt his eyes piercing my back."

"He watched you the whole time," Lili said, "but I think if any eyes were making a hole in you, it was probably Anne-Mathilde's."

Delphine opened her mouth to reply, but suddenly Ambroise was standing beside her. "You played exquisitely," he said.

Anne-Mathilde was not with him, and Lili looked across the room to see her in animated conversation with her mother and Jacques-Mars. The duchess shot a fiery glance in Delphine's direction and leaned in again toward them, hiding her mouth behind her fan.

Jacques-Mars nodded his head at something the duchess said and began walking toward where Lili stood with Delphine and Ambroise. Lili saw Maman touch him on the back to get his attention. She took his arm and steered him in the opposite direction, disappearing with him into a small sitting room.

"Are you going to the king's supper?" Ambroise was asking. "There's to be dancing afterward in the Salon de Mars."

"I think a little dancing will be just perfect to settle my nerves." Delphine gave Ambroise a shy smile. "It is a bit frightening to play for the king."

"You gave no hint of it," Ambroise said, running his eyes over the soft waves of Delphine's hair.

"Perhaps it helped that I didn't know he was coming and hadn't the time to work myself into a state over it," Delphine said with a flutter of her fan.

"I'm afraid I must confess I am indirectly the source of your fright," Ambroise said. "When Mademoiselle de Praslin told me you would be accompanying Madame Sophie, I tried to excuse myself from my father's audience with the king. But when I gave the queen's concert as my excuse, His Majesty insisted upon coming, and of course that meant my father had to come too."

Just then the sounds in the room quieted to a murmur, and Lili followed Ambroise's gaze in the direction of the king. Louis was standing up and a chamberlain was adjusting his cloak over his shoulders. As he moved across the room, the women's skirts whispered as they curtseyed, like the sound of breaking waves following the contours of a beach.

"May I show you the way, mesdemoiselles?" Ambroise gestured in the direction of the door, and they followed the king out into the glittering corridor.

* * *

LILI AND DELPHINE waited with Ambroise outside the king's apartments until Marie Leszczynska had made her entrance. The Duchesse de Praslin accompanied her, along with Anne-Mathilde, who gave Ambroise a coquettish smile as they passed. Raising her chin slightly, she turned her face away without acknowledging Lili or Delphine.

Ambroise brushed against Lili's skirt as he stepped back in reaction to the snub. Lili gave him a sideways glance and saw him staring with cold eyes at Anne-Mathilde's back as she disappeared into the king's apartments. Her heart leapt in delight. *He doesn't like her either.*

"Well then," Ambroise said. "We're free to go in." His face had lost its cold look and was open and pleasant again. "Shall we?" he said, taking Delphine's arm. Her eyes shone as she glanced in Lili's direction.

She's met her prince. Lili's heart soared, brushing away the thought that stories with princesses always have evil lurking in the shadows.

The table in the king's dining room, to Lili's surprise, was no larger than the one at Hôtel Bercy. He was seated with the queen in the middle of one side, while across the table, several courtiers in powdered wigs were taking their places. Their jackets were cut close to the body and worn open to reveal sumptuous vests in velvet and brocade. Milling around the room were several dozen similarly dressed men in tight silk breeches. An equal number of women maneuvered their panniers through the crowd, as they flirted with one person before moving on to share a confidence with another.

"I thought we were invited to dinner," Lili whispered to Ambroise, gesturing to the small number of seats at the table.

Ambroise laughed. "When you're invited to the king's dinner it means just that, I'm afraid. Only a few of Louis's favorites are invited to eat with him, and I suppose you can imagine how jealous that makes most of the rest. That's my father," he said, gesturing toward Julien Clément de Feuillet, the Comte d'Étoges, who was seated across from the king. Ambroise looked at Delphine. "I, for one, am glad I won't be torn away."

He turned back to Lili. "Don't worry, Mademoiselle du Châte-let. You'd be surprised how little time this takes, since they only eat a bite or two of each course. There will be tables set up for us at the dance." He motioned toward a huge salmon servants were whisking away nearly intact, and a suckling pig being paraded in. "Including both of those, I imagine. I've never heard of anyone going away from Versailles complaining they hadn't had enough to eat."

Appearing to watch the king, Lili examined Ambroise more closely out of the corners of her eyes. Taller than she by a head, he was wearing a wig the same chestnut color as the wisps of hair Lili saw poking out at his temples. His nose was a bit too thin, though his chin was strong and his eyes, a brown touched with yellow-green, were soft and appealing. It was more a good face than a tremendously handsome one, Lili decided, suggesting someone who found life pleasant most of the time and preferred cheerful amusements to vicious ones. A man of his description but lacking in his grace and charm might not have stood out at all, and yet he was easily the most appealing man in the room. And he liked Delphine.

"Most people who come to Versailles would die for the chance to go hungry in the king's presence," Ambroise was saying, "but they won't make it halfway to the door. It's best to just stand here and appreciate being among the lucky few, even if our stomachs growl while we're doing it."

The air in the room was growing stale and hot. Corpulent men were mopping their brows, and the women were moving as subtly as they could toward the open doors and the possibility of fresh air. Finally the king's dessert, an éclair shaped like the statue of a god in one of the fountains, was brought in on an ornate, gilded tray. The pastry sat in a pool of rippling green jelly, and spun sugar burst up around it like jets of water. After the crowd applauded the artistry, the king belched loudly and waved it off uneaten.

As he and Marie Leszczynska rose from their seats, Delphine gripped Ambroise's arm. "Oh dear," she whispered before her knees gave way in a faint.

"She needs air," Ambroise said to the people nearby. "Help me get her into another room." One woman produced a vial of smelling salts from her bodice and held it under Delphine's eyes, causing them to flutter open. "Can you walk?" Ambroise asked, as another man took her other arm to support her.

"I think so," she said. "Everything went black."

"It was the hot air," Ambroise said. "It happens all the time." By now they had brought Delphine into an adjacent room and helped her onto a daybed. In the commotion of the king and queen's departure, only a few were aware of what had happened. Even Julie had been too far away to notice. The woman with the smelling salts and the other man were soon gone, leaving Ambroise, Lili, and Delphine the only people in the room.

"I'm so embarrassed," Delphine said. "Did I make a scene?"

Ambroise laughed. "It was the most charming faint in years. It's too bad so few people saw it." Delphine smiled at him before casting a furtive, pleased glance at Lili.

"Honestly," Ambroise went on, "I'm surprised any woman makes it through a day in a corset without doing herself injury. I did hear about one countess who cracked her skull on a table when she fell. Her corset was so tight and her panniers so wide that she went over like a felled tree." He looked around. "There's a decanter of brandy over there. Would you like a little? It would do you good, I think."

Delphine smiled sweetly. "A little then."

"Mademoiselle du Châtelet, would you like some too?" He went over to the sideboard and held up the decanter.

"A bit," Lili said. "And could you tell me if there's some rule that forbids you from calling me Lili?"

Ambroise laughed. "Absolutely. The law says I am to be thrown into the Bastille if I call you Lili before you call me Ambroise." Lili gave him a sly smile.

"I think your jailers might argue that you just did—Ambroise," she said, trying his name out for practice.

A soft voice came from the couch. "And call me Delphine."

The sweet breathiness of her tone brought back memories of times long ago when Delphine had laid her head on Lili's lap and listened to stories.

"What are you doing in here all by yourself?" Anne-Mathilde swept across the room toward Ambroise, who was finishing pouring the brandy. She turned around and saw he was not alone. "Oh," she said flatly. "And what is this?"

"Delphine fainted," Lili said, "and Amb—" She paused. "Monsieur Clément was kind enough to help her."

Anne-Mathilde rushed to the daybed where Delphine was reclining and sat down near her feet. "Oh, you poor dear!" she simpered, reaching for her hand. "Are you all right now?"

"We're having something to restore ourselves," Ambroise said, ignoring the unctuousness of her tone as he handed Lili a glass with a thimbleful of golden liquid shimmering in the bottom. He went to Delphine and put hers down on the table next to her. "Would you like a little as well?" he asked Anne-Mathilde. The change in his voice was so noticeable it reminded Lili of a cloud passing across the sun.

"Oh no," she said with a demure sniff. "I'm afraid it simply doesn't agree with me."

Ambroise had by now gone back to the sideboard. "I'm going to have more than a little, after the fright Mademoiselle de Bercy gave us all." He poured about three times as much into his glass and sat down in a fauteuil across from Delphine. "That's what agrees with me."

"Just don't be too long about it," Anne-Mathilde pouted. "Can you hear the musicians? They've started to play and you know I do so depend on having my first dance with you."

"I believe I'm quite recovered," Delphine said to Ambroise. "Could you help me get up?"

Ambroise leapt to his feet and took her outstretched hand to help her into a sitting position. "Stay like that for a minute," he said, watching her face. "Your color's better, but we want to be sure the blood has gone back to your head before you try to stand."

"My, my!" Anne-Mathilde's voice had taken on a frosty edge. "Versailles has no need of doctors as long as you're here."

Ambroise shrugged. "It's just a precaution. I'd do the same for you—for anyone really. It's only common sense." His eyes crinkled. "Although you know what Voltaire says, that common sense is not so common."

"Odious little man! Really, monsieur, I'm surprised you read drivel like that." Anne-Mathilde stood up with a haughty sniff. "I'm going to the dance, and I would appreciate having an escort." She gave Delphine an imperious stare. "Mademoiselle du Châtelet should be able to provide the assistance you require at this point, is that not so, Mademoiselle de Bercy?"

"Oh, please stay a little longer, Mademoiselle de Praslin," Lili said in a deliberately lilting voice. "I'm curious what you have heard from Joséphine de Maurepas."

"Joséphine?" Anne-Mathilde's eyes opened slightly and then tightened to a narrow-eyed stare. "And why do you imagine I would be the one with news?"

"Oh, come now," Lili said. "You, Joséphine, and Jacques-Mars Courville were inseparable at Vaux-le-Vicomte and that was when? Four or five months ago? I would have thought you would be the first to hear that she had arrived safely at Ferrand."

"I'm afraid you are ill-informed. I've been at Versailles almost the entire time since last summer, and Joséphine was in Paris."

"That would be, of course, after we saw the three of you at the opera. It was the premiere of *Tom Jones,* if I remember correctly. The light was dim, but now that I've met Monsieur Clément, I'm quite sure he was the one with you in your box. And Joséphine and Jacques-Mars—"

"I don't recall," Anne-Mathilde interrupted, looking away with a haughty jerk of her neck.

Ambroise looked over at Delphine and then back at Lili. "I remember," he said. "You pointed out some friends from the abbey who were sitting in the box across. They were Mesdemoiselles de Bercy and du Châtelet, I'm sure of it now."

"Really," Anne-Mathilde sniffed indignantly. "Unless there's a point to this, I'd much prefer to be dancing."

"When I saw Monsieur Clément de Feuillet in the forest today," Lili said, "it took a moment for me to recall why he looked familiar. And I saw Joséphine and Jacques-Mars without you at Notre-Dame, and they seemed such intimate friends, I simply assumed . . ." Lili endured Anne-Mathilde's cold stare without flinching. "I just assumed that the special friendship the three of you had at Vaux-le-Vicomte had continued."

"I'm quite shocked to find myself pressed in this fashion," Anne-Mathilde retorted. "Monsieur! Please!" She held up her elbow to indicate she expected Ambroise to comply with her wishes. "And I don't know what you're talking about. I was at Versailles. I really don't see how I am supposed to know what people do when I'm not with them."

Anne-Mathilde touched her hair and gave the lace on her sleeve an angry brush with her fingertips as she waited for Ambroise to come to her. *He knows what she is,* Lili thought as they left the room. *A conniving little hypocrite who bats her eyelashes while plotting against her friends. And if he didn't see that before, please let him see it now.*

"I'm sorry if I—" Lili stopped short and turned to Delphine.

Delphine was rosy-cheeked again, and the sparkle in her eyes conveyed the huge grin she was hiding behind her fan. She hunched up her shoulders and said gleefully, "What did you think of that? Anne-Mathilde was raging!"

"I wasn't going to let him leave with Anne-Mathilde until I'd gotten her to stop acting as if she's some sweet young girl he ought to hurry up and marry," Lili said, sitting down next to Delphine. "He's far too nice a man for her. Did you see how disloyal she was to Joséphine? She acted like they hadn't really been good friends at all!"

Delphine didn't seem to have heard. "He *is* a nice man," she said dreamily. Turning toward Lili, she took her hand. "Do you think he'll marry her anyway? Even if she is"—Delphine shuddered—"such a wolverine?" Her eyes glistened with sudden tears, but she shook them away. "It isn't right. I'd be so much better for him."

"You would be perfect for him," Lili said. "And I think you need to get to that dance so he sees nothing but that all evening." She got up. "Mademoiselle de Bercy?" She bent forward stiffly in her corset and panniers, in imitation of a courtier's bow. "May I have the honor of being your escort?"

HUNDREDS OF CANDLES in the chandeliers of the social hall known as the Salon de Mars cast their light on the gilded ceiling and red walls. Former rulers gazed over the room from life-size portraits in heavy gold frames. A fire crackled in a marble fireplace at one end, near which a chamber orchestra was playing. On a raised dais, the queen sat watching the dancers, including the king, paired with a young woman whispered to be his new mistress.

Lili and Delphine stood in the doorway, taking in the scene. "Where have you been?" Julie rushed over. "I was coming to find you. Anne-Mathilde told her mother you fainted!"

"I'm all right, Maman," Delphine said. "Lili and Monsieur Clément de Feuillet helped me." She looked over Julie's shoulder. "Have you seen him?"

"I believe he's dancing with Anne-Mathilde," Julie said. She looked closely at Delphine. "You're pale. And neither of you has had anything to eat. Come along."

She took them to the Salon de Vénus, a smaller room off the Salon de Mars, where huge platters of delicacies were arrayed. They sat at a table and after Julie motioned for a servant, plates of cheese and meats were brought to the table. "There's *chocolat* and little sweets to fortify you in the Salon d'Abondance," she said. "Wine too, and brandies. Take a little, even if it isn't a proper meal, and I'll make sure you're invited to someone's quarters for a real supper after the king and queen retire for the night."

Delphine chewed pensively on a piece of meat. "It's that little suckling pig," she said. "It's quite delicious. And it's rather special to know one is tasting what the king ate."

"Or didn't eat," Lili said, spearing a morsel of cheese. She looked up at Delphine and in a mirror behind her, she saw the reflection of the Duchesse de Praslin coming toward them.

"Madame de Bercy," the duchess said, ignoring the two girls. "May I have a moment with you privately?"

Julie looked quizzically at them. "Of course." Rising from her seat, she moved out of earshot with the duchess.

Lili's back was to them, but Delphine had a clear view. "What are they doing?" Lili asked. "Do you think she's complaining about how I treated poor Anne-Mathilde?"

Delphine moved the food around on her plate, glancing furtively toward the two women. "I think she might be," Delphine whispered. "The duchess just looked over this way and she doesn't look happy. Maman is nodding." She looked up. "Here she comes!"

The duchess had left the room by the time Julie sat down. "I understand you upset Anne-Mathilde." Lili's heart thudded at the serious look on her face.

"*Oui*, Maman," she said. "I asked about Joséphine and she was being so false that I—"

"She lied, Maman," Delphine broke in. "She forgot we'd seen her at the opera, and said she's been at Versailles the whole time."

"Her mother says you practically accused her of throwing Joséphine into Jacques-Mars's arms," Maman said.

Lili took in a breath to defend herself, but before she could reply, Maman smiled. "Congratulations. It's about time someone did. That Anne-Mathilde is a menace."

She smiled at Lili as she took a piece of cheese. "What did you say, really?"

"I don't remember exactly," Lili replied, "but I didn't let her get away with saying she had no idea Jacques-Mars was paying attention to Joséphine."

"Then she said"—Delphine broke in with a perfect imitation of Anne-Mathilde's voice—"I'm not responsible for what people do when I'm not there, am I?" She sniffed. "A bit too strong a protest, if you ask me."

Worried, Lili broke in. "Am I in trouble with the duchess, Maman?"

Julie laughed. "I don't think so. I think she sees into her daughter's—" She thought for a moment. "Her shriveled little heart. But the family is set on a marriage with Ambroise Clément de Feuillet, and I think she hopes you can be intimidated into not making Anne-Mathilde look bad in front of him." A sly smirk flitted across Julie's face. "I assume that was your plan?"

Lili looked down at her plate. "*Oui*, Maman. I must admit it was." Julie's expression was amused, but her voice was firm. "Anne-Mathilde's done herself some damage tonight. The duchess is alarmed by Ambroise's indifference to her daughter, and neither of you—I repeat neither of you—should do anything about it. The Praslin family is very powerful, and you don't know how appearing to have plotted against Anne-Mathilde will harm you in the future, but you can be sure it will."

Julie got up from the table. "And now, *ma chérie*," she said to Delphine, "I think you should go out and dance. Not with him, of course. That would be too blatant. But he'll be watching how prettily you move around the floor. Let's go strengthen you first with a little warm *chocolat*." She brushed a crumb from Delphine's bodice. "And then find you a dancing partner."

DELPHINE WAS A vision in pink and ivory as she danced a chaconne with the man who had helped her when she fainted. She smiled at him as if he were the most handsome man in the room, although he was barely taller than she was, and much older. He was an excellent dancer, however, and Delphine moved across the floor so delicately that it seemed as if she were lifted by a breeze and had no feet at all.

Lili's eyes swept the room and found Ambroise dancing with Anne-Mathilde. *She's quite graceful*, Lili thought, wishing it weren't true. When the music ended some of the dancers began to move off, but Delphine stayed in place with her partner for the next dance. Ambroise guided Anne-Mathilde back toward her mother, with more than one furtive glance in Delphine's direction. At the first notes of a minuet, Delphine took her partner's hand again.

Suddenly, before they could begin the first steps, the music stopped. A murmur arose in the crowd as everyone turned to look in the direction of the king and queen. They had risen to their feet, and Marie Leszczynska was being led away, leaning heavily on the arm of Madame Victoire. One of the king's ministers held up his hand for silence. "We've just received news from Fontainebleau. The dauphin is dead. Long live Dauphin Louis-Auguste." Without saying more, he turned and walked with the king to a side door.

When the king disappeared from view, a hush settled down over the Salon de Mars. Lili heard a few sobs, as small groups of men and women headed slowly toward the doors, murmuring among themselves. Lili turned to Julie. "You're crying, Maman!"

"Of course!" she said. "He would have been our king. And dear Marie Leszczynska has lost yet another child."

"Maman?" Delphine's ashen-faced partner had deposited her with Julie before rushing toward a group of friends waiting for him.

"Come," Julie said. "All France will be in mourning by tomorrow. We'll be going back to Paris as soon as we can pack. The queen will expect us to pay her the courtesy of not making her ask for privacy."

"Home?" Delphine gasped in disbelief. "Now?" Holding her hand to her mouth, she whirled around to look for Ambroise. Lili knew she would not find him. She had already seen him disappearing from the king's apartments with Anne-Mathilde on his arm.

Emilie
1738

FLORENT-LOUIS DU Châtelet stood on his toes and held the piece of hand-lettered paper as high as his eleven-year-old arms could reach. "Anton! Hand me the hammer!" A smaller boy of about the same age, dressed in the simple clothing of a villager, put the tool in the outstretched fingers of the heir to the Château de Cirey. Florent-Louis gave several light taps to a nail, just enough to affix the paper to the door.

He stood back to admire his handiwork. "Want me to read it to you? It says 'Tonight at the Theater at Cirey! The premiere of *Mérope* by M. Voltaire. Cast—Mérope, Madame la Marquise; Polyphontes, Monsieur Voltaire; Ismène, Mademoiselle G-P du Châtelet; Euricles, Monsieur le Marquis, et al.'"

He gestured to the copies in the boy's hand. "Come on," he said. "Help me put these up on the front gate and at the church. Race you!" Florent-Louis took off, pumping his legs in his stockings and breeches, the tail of his dark hair flopping against the back of his jacket.

Emilie watched from the window of the upstairs gallery, savoring the commotion. A play was always a good way to relieve the tedium of being the hostess to what was at the moment a houseful of dull company, and the headache-inducing clanging and pounding of the workmen renovating the château. In the four years she and Voltaire had lived at Cirey, their remote haven was rarely without at least one guest from among Europe's great men of science, but it had been months since Cirey had sparkled with that light. Now it seemed everyone was off doing something exciting, and she was reduced to receiving letters about their adventures. She couldn't go to Lapland, as Maupertuis had done, to take measurements to show that the earth was flattened at the poles. She couldn't even manage to find a way to go abroad, despite corresponding regularly with scientists from all over Europe. It would be so much better if people didn't always have to come to Cirey to talk face-to-face, but . . .

No point in fretting over it. She was a woman. She could be a helpmate to great men, but not the other way around. Thank God she had Voltaire in her life. She could talk to him about what were becoming obsessions for her—understanding the deepest principles of physics, and then going further. The God who governed the world through natural law must have had the same orderly mind when it came to shaping the human heart—a natural law for mankind that reflected his will for creation better than biblical legends could.

Of course it annoyed her that after their endless discussions, Voltaire sometimes published her ideas as if they were his own, but at age thirty-two, she'd started too late and accomplished too little to establish an independent reputation as a natural philosopher herself. She inspired the greatest writer of the age to exercise his mind, not just with history and clever satire but with science, and it was good to see her ideas in print, even if works like their treatise on Newton were in his name alone. He said flattering things about her in his dedications, and that would have to be enough.

Through the open window on the other side of the room, she heard the sound of a carriage coming up the sloping path to the château. Gabrielle-Pauline, most likely. She watched as a carriage rounded the corner and stopped in front. Emilie smiled as her twelve-year-old daughter stepped down. Holding a manuscript in her hand, she stopped to examine the playbill her brother had tacked on the door before Berthe, the downstairs maid, ushered her inside. Thank heaven for a child who could be fetched from the convent and memorize her lines in the carriage before she arrived home. She would go down to greet her, and then it was time for the house to settle in for a nap before the excitement began.

THE MARQUIS DU Châtelet walked with his wife from the dining room with their son and daughter. Florent-Louis pointed through a large window to a handful of villagers milling outside. "I told that boy who helped me with the announcement that there might be a costume he could put on and stand on the stage. May I go get him, Father?"

Florent-Claude du Châtelet nodded his approval, and Florent-Louis took off through the gallery door. The marquis summoned Lucien, the downstairs manservant, with a flick of his brow. "Tell the people outside that we're sorry, but it's just too damned hot up there to let more than a few of them in."

Florent-Louis and Anton rushed up the two flights of stairs to the attic. They went through a rough-hewn entryway, past a lattice of beams supporting the roof overhead, into another room with a wood planked floor and an open-beamed ceiling. Voltaire and the rest of the cast had already begun fluttering about amid boxes of wigs on the floor and costumes flung over benches.

Emilie came into the room and held out her arms for a maid to take off her dress. Standing with her hands on her hips and wearing only her chemise and several petticoats, she looked around in amusement at the flurry of activity. Anton stared at the breasts of the *châtelaine* of the estate, clearly visible under the thin silk, but Emilie did not notice. "Here," she said, taking him by the hand and leading him to the other side of the stifling attic room. "Let's see if Berthe has something to fit you." She left him with the servant, going off with Gabrielle-Pauline so they could pin each other into sheets resembling Greek gowns.

Even though her part tonight did not require singing, by the time the audience of household guests, servants, and awestruck villagers filed in, Emilie had begun warming up her throat with *solfège* exercises from lessons she'd once taken with a tutor from the Comédie

Italienne. Her soprano voice was so rich and full it cast a spell over the cramped attic, and everyone stopped to listen. Seeing the admiration in people's eyes, and out of the sheer joy of the moment, Emilie broke into an aria from her favorite opera, *Issé*. Voltaire, his scrawny legs covered in absurd pink stockings under his toga, and sporting a crown of leaves over his immaculately curled wig, led everyone in a raucous round of applause.

When the audience was seated, Emilie and her daughter stepped onto a tiny stage whose wings and backdrop had been painted to look like a room in a Greek palace. With a grand, tragic gesture, Emilie draped herself on a couch that had been brought up from the parlor, its flowered brocade hastily covered over with a sheet.

"Great queen," Gabrielle-Pauline said. "Set aside your sad thoughts. The gods have given us victory, and now the people cry out for your coronation as their ruler. Widow of the great Cresphonte and daughter of the king, after fifteen years of the miseries of war, you alone can be the one to lead us into happier times."

Emilie sat up. "What?" she said, holding one hand dramatically to the side of her head and looking out at the audience in dismay. "Is there no news of my son, the rightful heir? Has he been missing now so long that all pronounce him dead?"

She felt the first trickles of sweat running between her breasts in a room that now seemed airless in the heat. But what did it matter, when in the middle of nowhere, a play by her lover was being performed for the first time under her own roof? She looked up at the open beams of the attic. Under her own roof indeed.

12

T HE MUDDY tracks on the road from Versailles to Paris had frozen as solid as rock, causing the carriage in which Lili and Delphine returned with Maman to Paris to lurch so badly that Lili had trouble focusing on the words in front of her.

"From the sky, Meadowlark picked out the Great Wall of China and guided Comète down to a palace nearby," she began.

Though Lili's story about two men dueling for the hand of a princess momentarily lifted the gloom of their return to Paris, by the end Delphine was wiping her eyes again.

"The princess stamped her foot," Lili read. " 'Rules are rules!' she said.
"'Rules *are* rules,' Tom said. 'I suppose so,' Meadowlark replied. 'Even as far away as China.'"

"I didn't like that at all," Delphine said.
"Why?" Lili put down her notebook, grabbing it to keep it from slipping to the floor as the carriage wheels slid into another rut.
"I hate the rules. They say Anne-Mathilde will marry Ambroise." Delphine buried her face in Julie's shoulder. "I really like him, Maman."

"I can tell," Julie said, passing her handkerchief to Delphine. "Be careful not to muss my dress with your sniffles, *ma petite*. This velvet spots so easily." Delphine gave her nose a dainty blow and roused herself just enough to settle in a limp heap next to her mother.

"And I wouldn't be so sure about the rules when it comes to what a young man might do in his situation," Julie went on. "No one has said anything about a formal engagement to Anne-Mathilde—"

"Do you think he might break off with her?" Delphine sat up so straight her back was no longer resting against the seat.

"Break off? I saw no evidence that Ambroise thinks anything is on. But it is a good match, and quite openly talked of, so I imagine the families may be viewing it favorably even if he is not. The Praslin family is not as wealthy as it once was, and though they make gestures like acquiring Vaux-le-Vicomte to make it look otherwise, I've heard rumors that their fortune is not terribly secure."

She took back her handkerchief from Delphine and tucked it in her bodice. "Ambroise's grandfather was much appreciated by Louis XIV for his discretion as the *accoucheur* who delivered the king's seven illegitimate children by Madame de Montespan. He was made a member of the *noblesse de robe* at that time, and it was only a few years ago that the family received the king's approval to purchase the château and lands around Étoges, and to use the title of count. So the Clément de Feuillet family will make a leap in status by marrying Ambroise to Anne-Mathilde, and the Duc and Duchesse de Praslin will place a daughter in a family with profitable lands in Champagne and the wealth to support her." Julie looked at Delphine with an apologetic grimace. "It is a very favorable match."

"Except that the bride is a dragon," Lili growled.

Delphine slumped dejectedly against Maman. "I might as well become a nun right now."

Lili and Maman burst into laughter, but Lili's face grew serious again almost immediately. "People don't get what they wish for very often, do they?" she mused.

"If they go through their lives wishing and wishing, probably not," Julie replied. "Especially if they hope for unreasonable things. But there's often more than one good way a situation can work out, and I think people who understand that will be more satisfied than people who don't."

She thought for a moment. "When I was young, I used to pray for this and that, but as I saw more of life I realized how badly some of the things I wanted might have turned out, and sometimes the opposite, that a thing I didn't want had consequences I liked. Now I've learned the most important thing to wish for is that I will have the grace and good character to handle whatever comes. And that you and Delphine will also." She laughed. "And besides, can you imagine how impossible the world would be if everyone's prayers were granted? There, *ma petite,* is something for Meadowlark to consider!"

A rut in the road sent Lili bouncing to the other end of the seat, and Maman and Delphine clung to each other to avoid being thrown into the bottom of the coach. "*Mon Dieu,*" Julie said. "We're lucky we didn't lose the wheel. You'd think with all the money to build Versailles they could have made a better road to it."

Delphine had been lost in her own thoughts. "Maman?" she broke in. "Why didn't Jacques-Mars marry Joséphine, if it's true what people are saying about her?"

The mood in the coach darkened again. Julie pressed her lips into a line and looked away. "No parents in their right mind would allow their daughter to marry someone like Jacques-Mars. He cares about nothing but himself, and I imagine he is no more to be trusted with money than he is with women. I've heard that Joséphine is one of three girls, in the middle of five children, and her parents hadn't seemed to pay her much mind until now. Even a little attention would have made them realize Anne-Mathilde felt no real bond with her."

Julie's eyes clouded and she seemed not to notice the jostling of the coach. "I pity poor Joséphine," she finally said. "Obviously she was flattered by the attentions of someone as dashing as Jacques-

Mars and as pretty as Anne-Mathilde, and perhaps she wanted their friendship badly enough to do whatever they asked."

"Do you think she really did, Maman?" Delphine was sitting up again. "You know—did that—with Jacques-Mars."

"I think we'll know soon enough, and Anne-Mathilde seemed too concerned about appearing innocent for me to believe she really is. I think she's done herself a great deal of harm, especially if gossip about a scheme to ruin Joséphine gets back to the queen. Marie Leszczynska has suffered too much to take it lightly when a young girl is despoiled."

"I'm sorry about the dauphin," Delphine added. "And that his little boy doesn't have a father. Even if he is going to be the King of France someday." She thought for a moment. "If anyone told me that to become queen I'd have to lose you, I'd tell him to take his crown and throw it in one of his stupid fountains." She dabbed her eyes and sniffed. "Why does everything have to be so sad?"

"And I pity Marie Leszczynska too," Julie added. "She's lost so many of her children. I'd never choose to be queen over the life I have with both of you." She sat mulling something for a few moments. "Aren't either of you curious about why Jacques-Mars wasn't bothering you after Delphine and Madame Sophie's recital?"

Had it been just yesterday? "He wasn't at the dance," Lili suddenly realized.

Delphine scowled. "He was probably off seducing someone."

Julie smiled. "I doubt it. I saw how he and Anne-Mathilde were watching both of you, and when I saw him coming in your direction, I took him into one of the other rooms for a little tête-à-tête. Shall I say we came away with an understanding that it would be in his best interests not to pursue either of you?"

"Maman!" Delphine covered her mouth so that only her eyes showed above her gloved hand. "What did you tell him?"

"I told him that I was fully prepared to speak to the queen about the rumors regarding Joséphine, and offer what happened last summer—"

Delphine gasped. "In strictest confidence, *ma chérie*," Julie went on. "To offer it as evidence of the unsuitability of his presence in her chambers." She drew up her shoulders. "As I suspected, the ridicule to which he would be exposed at being unable to cross the queen's threshold was quite sufficient to make him agree he would have no contact with either of you whatsover. I took the fact that he did not appear at the dance to be a sign of "—her mouth turned up in a sly smile—"his sincerity about the matter."

Delphine slumped in her seat. "I'm so embarrassed."

"Why? I didn't tell the queen anything."

"But would you have, Maman?" Lili asked.

Julie cocked her head. "I was quite sure I wouldn't have to," she said with a smile. "So I guess the answer is, we'll never know."

1766

BY THE TIME the trees blossomed, Paris had put behind its sadness. The future Louis XVI was installed at Versailles with his mother, Marie-Josèphe of Saxony, and the cafés, theaters, and salons of the city were again bustling with life. Green shoots and blossoms burst out at the Jardin de Roi as well. Since her return from Versailles, Lili had been spending two afternoons a week in the private natural history museum on the ground floor of the Comte de Buffon's house, replacing with neatly written Latin labels the tattered and yellowing ones in the specimen drawers and *cabinets de curiosités*.

On days when Julie could not spare the carriage, Jean-Étienne Leclerc came to fetch Lili at Hôtel Bercy. Jean-Étienne cultivated exotic medicinal plants, going back and forth between the greenhouse laboratory and his experimental plots in the garden, and since Lili's tasks for the time being were mostly in the museum, they saw little of each other after they arrived. The twenty-minute ride to and from the Jardin de Roi was all the time they had to talk, and it was scarcely enough for a breathless summary of what each had seen and done.

"I don't think I'm really much use to your uncle, but I'm certainly learning some astounding things," Lili said to Jean-Étienne as they crossed the Pont de la Tournelle and passed under the arch of the Port Saint Bernard on the way to the garden. "Like shapes of beaks—some longer than the body of the bird, all to be able to get at food." She laughed. "I don't suppose I'd want to try to eat a saddle of lamb with the bill of a toucan or hummingbird."

"It might be rather wonderful to be able to live on nectar from flowers, or—" Jean-Étienne thought for a moment. "I don't know exactly what toucans eat, but you can be sure they would be most unhappy to have to do it with a knife and fork. But you're wrong about my uncle. Perhaps I shouldn't say this, but we're the best substitutes at hand for some rather disappointing grandchildren."

Lili smiled. "He is such a kind man. The only thing that seems to rouse his temper is the church."

"And I agree with him," Jean-Étienne said as they turned onto Rue Saint-Victor. "It's quite appalling how instead of saying 'think harder' they say 'pray harder,' as if keeping one's hands clasped and eyes closed is what God intended. I think we're supposed to use the gifts we've been given, not show our devotion to the Creator by refusing to do so."

Lili giggled. "Did they let you get away with those ideas at school?"

"I learned to keep my thoughts to myself after a few priests mistook my backside for my brain and thought a flogging would have a salutary effect on my thinking." He caught himself. "I'm sorry. The bodily reference was unsuitable for present company. I'm taking courses at the medical college, and prudery is quickly swept away."

"I'm not offended at all." A medical student?

"That's what Uncle and I like about you. You don't waste our time with demands for attention." His pleasant expression faded. "Feigning offense at every little thing so we'll have to stop what we're doing to placate you."

Struck by the bitter edge in his tone, Lili cocked her head. "You have to deal with people like that too?"

"Only one." He thought for a moment. "Well, several really." He fell silent again. *Who is he talking about?* Lili wondered, but something about his demeanor suggested that she shouldn't pry. "The work in the laboratory and museum is important," Jean-Étienne said, breaking the silence. "We're trying to understand as much as we can about the world, and leave behind a good record for others to build on."

"And that's why you're studying medicine?"

"Exactly!" The exasperation in Jean-Étienne's tone had vanished. "There's nothing people can't come to understand, and as we do, so much of what makes people suffer can be alleviated. Could there be any better use of a life than that?"

"But you'd have to pay taxes if you worked, wouldn't you?"

Jean-Étienne looked puzzled. "It seems like a small price to pay for what I'd gain, and it's only fair after all, isn't it? I'm quite sure I'd still have enough for a comfortable life, although a modest one compared to some people I know . . ." His thoughts trailed off again, and Lili saw the bitterness return to his eyes.

But only momentarily. The carriage slowed to a stop in the gravel driveway between Buffon's mansion and the greenhouses, and Jean-Étienne, as usual, did not wait for the coachman to open the door. He bounded down, his face glowing with the excitement of getting to work. *He wants to do something useful with his life*, Lili thought, as he helped her down from the carriage. *I've never heard anyone talk like that before.* She gave him a sidelong glance, suddenly interested in fixing every detail about him in her mind. He was quite tall and very thin, with fine, sandy-colored hair and pale skin with a light sprinkling of freckles. *He's rather attractive, but in a healthy rather than a handsome way*, she decided. *But most of all his heart is kind, and I love every word he says.*

* * *

DELPHINE HAD SPENT most of the winter in her own quarters, sighing, and dabbing away tears when she thought of Versailles and the lost opportunities the dauphin's death had cost her. "It's bad enough that I barely got to dance," she said, "but I never got to dance with him at all."

No one needed to ask whom she meant. The news of Ambroise was all bad. He was still a regular in the theater boxes of the Duc de Praslin, and Delphine had caught an agonizing glimpse of him with Anne-Mathilde on Easter at Notre-Dame. "I will be miserable forever," Delphine concluded, to which Lili could do no more than offer a heartfelt sigh.

As the sap rose in the trees in the Place Royale, Delphine took the first steps out of her self-imposed lethargy. "I think a new spring cloak and several new hats will go a long way to lift my spirits," she told Maman, who had hovered over her all winter and was happy to oblige. The new apparel in the end only sent Delphine to her room in tears, at the realization that the only person she wanted to wear them for was probably right at that moment amusing himself with Anne-Mathilde.

"I hate to see you like this," Lili told her one April afternoon. "The problem is you're letting other people decide whether you're going to be happy. I think that's up to you."

Am I happy? Lili wondered. She wasn't sure what she meant. Jean-Étienne's face came into her mind, how his pupils stood out against their blue-gray color like black dots of ink, and how his almost blond lashes seemed thin when he looked straight at her, but thick and luxurious when the sun caught them in profile. *I think at the very least I'm quite content*, she decided. *I have Maman and Delphine. I have my writing. I have a new friend, who likes the same things I do and has a heart as big as Paris itself.*

Still, life could not feel good with Delphine so sad. And now, at Lili's challenge, something seemed to be quickening in her eyes.

"You're right," Delphine said, with a shake of her head. "You're absolutely right. I'm sick of myself, and I'm going to be happy." She stood up and looked around the parlor as if a hidden solution to her distress could be ordered to reveal itself.

Lili could see Delphine's resolve immediately begin to crumble. "Come with me to the Jardin de Roi," she implored, clasping Delphine's hands in her own. "It will be so good for you to have something to do. And I know the Comte de Buffon could use you. He never has enough time to sketch all his specimens himself, and Jean-Étienne and I are not half as good as you would be at that."

"Jean-Étienne?" Delphine said with a sly arch of her brow. "A little familiar, *non?*"

Lili blushed. "Monsieur Leclerc."

"Monsieur Leclerc!" Delphine sang in a lilting voice as she tugged on one of Lili's curls. "Bonjour, Monsieur Leclerc," she said in her most flirtatious tone as she danced away.

Lili's temper rose at Delphine's mockery, but it felt so good to see her smile and laugh that she kept her annoyance to herself.

"And is this Jean-Étienne handsome? Unmarried?" Delphine asked. "Hmmm?"

"Delphine!" Lili felt her face grow hot. "He's—" *What is he?* "He's more like a brother than a man!" she said, regretting immediately how foolish that sounded.

Delphine laughed. "Brothers are men, you silly girl!"

Lili sighed. "I know, but that's how it feels." It wasn't entirely true, but she wasn't going to give Delphine any additional fodder.

"All right. I won't ask any more questions," Delphine said. "You invited me, and I will simply have to go see this Jean-Étienne Leclerc for myself."

WITHIN A WEEK, Julie had arranged with the Comte de Buffon for her daughter to make a visit to the Jardin de Roi to sketch. "I think I'll wear my green dress," Delphine said at supper the night before. "The one with the skirt the same color as the embroidery on the sleeves. It should look quite nice with all those plants."

"You can't wear panniers," Julie said. "One of your dresses for receiving guests at home will be fine."

"No panniers?" Delphine pouted. "Even though the count's an old man, that doesn't mean he won't appreciate a pretty girl."

"He'll appreciate a pretty girl who doesn't knock things over and break them with her skirts," Lili said.

"But I'm meeting your intended!"

"He's not my intended," Lili snapped, "and I'm staying home if you're going to embarrass me!" Lili gave Julie a pleading look. "This was a terrible idea, Maman."

Julie put down her napkin. "It's wonderful to see you wanting to flirt and be pretty again," she said to Delphine. "But the Jardin de Roi is a serious place. The Comte de Buffon has dedicated his life to science, and I won't have you treating his—his heaven on earth—as if it's just a place to drop in for cakes and tea."

"*Oui*, Maman." Delphine looked down at her plate, but Lili heard the irritation in her tone.

"It will be good for you to get some practice at being gracious among people who are different from those at court. I assure you that you will impress the count most by being quiet, and taking up as little room as you can. You'll wear a high-cut bodice and only petticoats under your skirt, or you won't go at all."

The stridency in Maman's voice was so rare that both girls turned to stare at her. "The count is one of my dearest friends," Julie explained. "He has done an immeasurable service for you, Lili, giving you a respectable place to exercise your mind and be of use. And you, *ma chérie*," she said to Delphine, "I'll wager you will soon discover that the count will stretch your mind in ways that will satisfy you far more than choosing the lace for a sleeve."

Delphine was not one to sulk or take umbrage when a bet was in the making. Her eyes narrowed and her mouth turned up slyly up at one corner. "A wager, Maman?"

Julie thought for a moment. "Two new pairs of kid gloves from LaCroix et Fils, in whatever colors you choose." She leaned over the table toward Delphine with a sly smile. "I'll wager you'll give up the gloves after the first visit, just for a chance to go back again."

"It's not much," Delphine said. "But I accept." She turned to Lili. "I'm glad to be going, really. At least I'll have some new things to sketch. And I won't embarrass you, I promise."

"And I won't let the count scare you either," Lili said.

Delphine looked first at her and then at Maman. "Scare me?"

"There's this pink flower in a cage," Lili said with a grin. "Oui, *ma petite*," Maman added. "Don't scream when it bites."

JEAN-ÉTIENNE GREETED THEM at the greenhouse door with a capuchin monkey on his shoulder. It shrieked when it saw Lili, pumping its body up and down with excitement. "Bonjour, Tatou," Lili said, reaching up to scratch its tiny head.

Lili turned to look at Delphine and saw that her eyes were not on the monkey, but on how close she and Jean-Étienne were standing. Tatou gave a loud, demanding call, and as if responding to an order, Lili leaned in to touch shoulders with the young man. The monkey immediately hopped across, riding with her as they made their way toward the greenhouse.

"You'd better slip this under there," Jean-Étienne said. Picking up Tatou by the back of the neck, he took a piece of stained linen from his shoulder and draped it over Lili's dress before gently setting the monkey back down. Lili caught Delphine's eye and looked quickly away. *This must look quite cozy*, she thought.

It is cozy. He was her only real friend, other than Delphine, and Buffon was like an eccentric grandfather of the sort who, in the novels she and Delphine read on long winter nights, would show up with candy for the children and then feign grumpiness about having his pocket emptied.

What would it be like if, as Delphine suggested, Jean-Étienne were more than just her friend? What if when she came to the Jardin de Roi, he bowed to her with a special, approving look in his eyes?

What if just once he invited her for a walk? For the last month she had been taking special pains with her clothes and hair on the days she would see him, but he hadn't seemed to notice. *What if he actually saw me not just as someone to talk to but as* . . . Lili let the thought settle in. *As a woman.*

At Maman's salon, interaction with every man seemed to require flirtation of one type or another, but Jean-Étienne never flirted. *Is there something wrong with me?* Lili wondered from time to time. *Something unattractive?* But after watching a lovesick Delphine suffer all winter, she talked herself out of feelings of disappointment. Jean-Étienne's behavior had not brought painful complications to her life, and that was something to be grateful for.

Her situation was painful and complicated enough, having to fend off a disapproving Baronne Lomont, who found the work at the Jardin de Roi unbecoming for a young lady in need of a husband. After finishing the labels in the museum, Lili now worked in the greenhouse and laboratory, learning to use calipers and other measuring devices, and keeping precise notes about the varieties of orchids the count was cataloging and crossbreeding. She assisted him in his dissections and no longer flinched when he cut into the dead animals whose anatomy he studied.

Visiting Baronne Lomont, Lili felt like a stranger who had dropped in from another world. Forced by the demands of conversation to say something about how she had spent her time since her last visit, she gave desultory accounts of things that had thrilled her—the arrival of a dozen new butterfly species from Africa, the change of color in some kinds of flowers when transplanted into different soil. Most things she didn't speak of at all, glazing over her face as she performed the rituals of visiting.

Her boredom with Monsieur Barras had to be obvious. She was certain of that, and every contact made her more uneasy. The baroness's assumption that they were suited for marriage was as relentless as water running under the bridges of the Seine. *Doesn't it matter that I feel nothing for Barras, or he for me?* Apparently not, Lili decided, stunned by Baronne Lomont's stony indifference.

Sometimes she wanted to stand up and behave as if she had suddenly gone mad, just to call attention to the deepening horror she felt. *Perhaps I* would *go mad if I married him,* Lili thought. Publishing her writing as a way of fending him off seemed to be coming to nothing. Months had passed, and Diderot had not come through. The only time she felt comfortable with her life away from home was among the orchids and monkeys, the calipers and dissecting tools, at the Jardin de Roi.

Buffon had already greeted them at the greenhouse door and was ushering Delphine toward a table where she could lay down her pencils and portfolio. "Draw whatever you like, Mademoiselle de Bercy. I will do my best not to disturb you," he said. What he really meant, they both knew, was that she was not to disturb him. All afternoon Delphine moved around so quietly that Lili often forgot she was there. Then, as the light began to dim, Buffon took off his spectacles and declared that the work was at an end for the day.

"Would you like to see what I've drawn?" Delphine asked.

"Of course!" the count said, motioning her to a desk where an oil lamp was already casting its glow into the darkening room. Turning up the flame, he sat down and bent over the first sheet of paper, leaning to one side so Lili and Jean-Étienne could see. On it, Delphine had drawn one of the cabinet tops, lined neatly with jars portrayed accurately to the smallest detail. On the following page she had drawn one of the birds, both at rest and fluttering its wings.

Lili gasped at the third sheet. Staring out at her was the monkey, its white face fading out to deep brown at its temples and crown, perfect even in the imperfection of its rumpled hair, with eyes so bright that Delphine seemed to have captured it contemplating its next prank. Jean-Étienne was standing just behind her, close enough that she heard his startled intake of air.

"It's so real, I almost expect it to jump onto my shoulder," he said.

"Or shriek at us," Lili replied. His presence so close to her made her feel odd, as if an imminent bolt of lightning was raising the hair on her skin.

"At medical school we have to be taught to observe as well as you do, Mademoiselle de Bercy," Jean-Étienne told her. "And most of us never do."

As Delphine thanked him, her eyes darted between Lili and the young man, as if she was calculating the space between them at various points from head to toe. She handed another sheet of paper to the count. "I made one more, as a special gift for you," she told him. "To express my gratitude for letting me come today."

In Delphine's drawing, Buffon was bent over his microscope, one lock of hair dangling askew, as it always did. "I put in Tatou, just for fun," Delphine said, pointing to where she had drawn the monkey sitting on the table, bent over in the same pose as it examined the spectacles Buffon had put aside. "I hope you're not offended," she said. "It's just that one can't help but notice how much they resemble us."

"Offended? Not at all! I'd rather be compared to our little friend here than many of the people I've had to suffer through a dinner with." The count took Delphine's arm. "You are most gifted, Mademoiselle de Bercy, and I can't remember having more delightful company than I've had today."

"I hope I didn't interfere too badly. And I'm quite hoping you'll invite me again." Delphine cast a triumphant glance at Lili as the count and Jean-Étienne walked them to their carriage.

"HE'S SMITTEN WITH you," Delphine said the minute their coach was back on the Rue Saint Victor.

"Who?"

"Who do you think?" Delphine retorted. "That sweet old man?"

Lili laughed. "He's *your* conquest for the day. He obviously adored you."

Delphine grinned. "Well then, that makes one for each of us. But don't you go changing the subject—you do see the way Jean-Étienne looks at you, don't you?"

"He doesn't look at me at all."

"Lili, you are as dense as a rock. He watched you all day. And I saw the two of you with the monkey. You looked like an old married couple taking care of a child. 'Let me put a cloth on your shoulder, *mon amour*. Don't want you to get a spot on your dress!' 'Oh, thank you, *mon chéri*. Isn't our baby sweet?' "

Lili shook her head, amused in spite of herself. "I think he'd do that for anyone."

"Well, I don't. And he's terribly shy—that's the only reason he doesn't say anything to you. But when he was looking over your shoulder, I saw a man not nearly as interested in anything I'd drawn as in how it might feel to kiss your neck."

"Delphine!" Lili sat back in feigned shock, but immediately leaned forward again. "Do you really think so?"

Delphine smirked and said nothing.

Lili shrugged. "Well, a lot of good it would do if he did want to kiss me." For some time now she hadn't shared what she was thinking about Jean-Étienne, afraid that saying her thoughts aloud would give her fears more substance. Now the words came tumbling out. "He complained once about having his time wasted by someone, and it sounded as if he might already be promised to a woman about as perfect for him as Robert de Barras is for me."

The gaiety vanished. Lili felt a familiar rise of acid in her throat. "What if I end up with a house full of Robert de Barras's babies, pleasing him only when I remind him of his dead wife?" A shudder came from somewhere deep within her. "I'm scared, Delphine."

The smirk disappeared from Delphine's face at the serious turn in the conversation. "Me too," she whispered. "All I really want is a good marriage—and I've accepted that it won't be to Ambroise—but I've been back from Versailles for months, and nothing's happened. Even that silly Joséphine de Maurepas seems better off now than I am, with her husband and a household to rule over, even if it is in Ferrand, wherever that is." She sniffed and pulled out a scented handkerchief from her bodice. "And a baby on the way, despite it being—"

The carriage fell silent for a moment at the thought of Jacques-Mars. "Well, you are still only sixteen," Lili reminded her. "You haven't exactly been passed over." She was a bit disappointed that as usual, Delphine had managed to turn the conversation to herself, but at the same time she was relieved she wouldn't have to talk any more about something so painful.

"Sixteen now, but seventeen is quite old enough, I think," Delphine replied. "And Jean-Étienne is perfect for you but he's too thickheaded to know it. I wish he would burst into Baronne Lomont's parlor and whisk you away from that awful corpse of a man. Tell you 'I adore you, Lili,' because he does, you know." She thought for a moment. "He never actually said he was promised to anyone, did he?"

"He didn't say, and I couldn't ask without appearing too interested." Lili thought for a moment. "And you mustn't either, for the same reason."

Delphine looked out the carriage window as they crossed the Pont de la Tourenne. "No," she said, mulling it over. "No, I suppose I can't. But we can listen and see what we might be able to find out."

"We? Does that mean you want to come back to the Jardin de Roi?" Lili's grim mood brightened. "I know you told the count you did, but I thought maybe you were just being polite."

Delphine reached over and took Lili's hand. "I loved today. And Maman is right. It's much better than a new pair of gloves."

"Two pairs."

Delphine laughed. "From Lacroix et Fils. In any colors I want."

LILI'S EYES STUNG in the bright sunlight as she and Delphine came out of the Cathedral of Notre-Dame after making special devotions on the feast day of Saint Anne, Delphine's patron saint. This ritual, performed twice a year—for Lili in December on Saint Adé-laïde's feast day, and for Delphine-Anne in June on Saint Anne's—usually involved a dinner with Maman in one of the best restaurants in Paris, but Maman was expecting an important guest during her visiting hours, and the restaurant would have to wait. Instead, Lili and Delphine were making a quick visit to the Comte de Buffon to see the progress on the labyrinth he was constructing behind the greenhouse.

Lili looked back toward the towers of Notre-Dame as their carriage crossed the Seine at the Petit Pont. "All right," she said. "Time to start." She pulled out a notebook with Delphine's name on the front and turned to the first blank page. "I brought a pencil, and we'll finish in ink later, when we're not being bounced in the coach." She looked at Delphine, poised to write. "What's happened since the last Saint Anne's Day?"

Delphine groaned. "Do we have to do this every year? Can't we just do it for the good ones—the ones where I don't nearly get raped in the summer and then have my heart broken by Christmas?"

"Someday when you're so old you can't remember where you put your false teeth, you'll still know what happened every year. You can leave out the awful stuff if you want, but I remember a spectacular presentation to the queen, and a very nice opportunity to sketch for one of the great men of France."

Delphine sighed. "I'd rather talk about next year. I'm glad this one is over." Lili's face grew serious as she looked at Delphine. "This year will be the best of your life, starting today." Delphine gave her a playful slap on the hand. "That's what you always say on Saint Anne's Day!"

"That's what I always want for you," Lili said.

"You are so good to me," Delphine replied, her voice rough with emotion. "Perhaps Saint Anne will take pity on me, and bring me a proposal of marriage this year, though she hasn't shown me much pity yet."

They had reached Place Maubert and Lili watched absentmindedly as vendors hawked their wares from wooden stalls. *I don't think*

I'd count on Saint Anne to do much of anything, she thought, wondering whether saints were now simply dry bones scattered in bits and pieces inside reliquary boxes all over Christendom, or really were off in a special part of heaven reserved for the most noble soldiers of Christ. And if they were, wouldn't they be enjoying their reward, rather than sitting on a cloud with halos and opera glasses, watching all the Delphines of the world and deciding how to help?

"Perhaps I should go to mass more often, or do something noble," Delphine mused. "Perhaps I'm not deserving enough yet— Lili, what kind of charity do you think Saint Anne might appreciate the most? Maybe the wounded soldiers at Les Invalides, or perhaps those poor souls at the Saltpetrière . . ."

Lili laughed. "How about the Society for the Liberation of Ambroise from the Clutches of Anne-Mathilde?"

"That's not funny, but I'm going to laugh anyway," Delphine said, thinking for a minute. "And for you, we need the Order for the Blessed Revelation of Jean-Étienne's Love for Lili."

"I wonder how that would sound in Latin," Lili said, trying to smile. "Have you noticed that in the last few weeks he's hardly spoken to me?"

"Or me either," Delphine said with a rueful shrug. "He finds all sorts of excuses not to work near us, and he's so grim most of the time. I asked him how medical school was going, and he said he didn't want to talk about it. Didn't want to talk about it? He could hardly stop a month ago."

The coach made a turn into the driveway of the Jardin de Roi. "We're here," Lili said, surprised by the leaden tone of her voice. The greenhouses loomed on the left side of the walkway, and for the first time, Lili wanted to tell the driver to take her home, so strong and inexplicable was the gloom that overcame her. Jean-Étienne's heart was burdened, and it was frightening not to know why.

They found the count alone at his microscope in his greenhouse laboratory. "We thought we'd come take a look at the labyrinth," Lili said, glancing around for Jean-Étienne and not seeing him. "We just came to say hello. We can look for ourselves because we know you're busy."

The count's eyes looked inflamed and he seemed uncomfortable having company, but he often acted that way when he was immersed in his work. "Please stay for a minute, if you would," he said, looking away. "My nephew told me about this new substance they use at the hospital to prevent infection, and he brought me some to experiment with. It's called ethanol, and I've just had the most interesting result." He gestured to Lili. "Sit down and I'll show you."

He took a clean slide and dropped a bead of water onto it. *That's odd*, Lili thought. *I've never noticed his hand tremble before.* Looking through the microscope, Lili saw a dozen or more familiar creatures darting and spinning. "Now watch," the count said. He touched the slide with another dropper and within seconds all the motion had stopped.

"What did you do?" Lili asked.

"It's quite perplexing," the count said. "Even in the most dilute concentration, the same substance that helps strengthen our ability to heal when we put it on our skin appears to kill organisms like these with just a touch. Ethanol is the alcohol produced by distilling, and a bit of brandy is the best medicine for most things that ail us, so why is it deadly to them?"

"I don't know," Lili said, brushing aside for a moment how flat his voice was and how agitated he seemed. "Perhaps it could be the nature of their outer surface? Alcohol is rather harsh. Perhaps it burns them, or dissolves something essential?"

"I was thinking of the odor rather than the taste," he said. "Since they lack lungs, perhaps they respire through their outer surface, and this is the equivalent of those poor souls we hear about who drink themselves to death."

Delphine gave the count a light touch on his shoulder to get his attention. "While you're working, I think I'll go look for Jean-Étienne. Is he in the gardens?"

"No," Buffon said, standing up so suddenly that his chair caught on the stone floor and nearly fell over. "He's gone to collect specimens. There's an odd spotting on the wheat in the Loire Valley." He cleared his throat again. "I'm sorry. I seem to be losing my voice. He's bringing back samples for us to analyze."

"Monsieur de Buffon?" Lili asked, alarmed by the nervous, rushed staccato of his speech. "Are you all right?"

He took in a deep breath and exhaled with a sigh. "No, I can't say I am. While I've been showing you my experiments, I've been trying to think of how to tell you some news I've had, but there isn't any good way."

"Tell me what?" *Is he dying? Is Jean-Étienne . . .*

He went to his desk and picked up a letter. "Jean-Étienne has also gone to announce his betrothal. He asked me to give this to you. I planned to give it to you when you came on Wednesday, but since you're here now . . ."

"Betrothal?" Lili's heart exploded in her chest. She took the letter from his extended hand, but her fingers were so numb it fell to the floor. No one moved to retrieve it.

"Francine, I think he said her name was," the count said. "Francine Thibaudet. The daughter of the man with the spotted wheat. I can't say I recall ever seeing anyone quite so unenthusiastic about what is supposed to be a happy event. And I'd always thought you were so naturally suited to each other that I had hoped—" Buffon stopped to dab his eyes. "Forgive me, but I've been quite overcome since I heard."

Lili put her head against Delphine's chest. Her body shook with tears she could not hold back.

"Jean-Étienne is from a rather impoverished branch of my family," the count was saying, "and the Thibaudets have made a great fortune in speculation on imported wheat in bad harvest years. They bought themselves a title, so Thibaudet's the marquis of something— I can't recall what. Now he wants to marry his daughter into the *noblesse d'épée,* and Jean-Étienne can most certainly use the dowry."

"How practical," Delphine said in a tone as harsh as breaking glass. She picked up the letter and put her arm back around Lili.

"Precisely," Buffon said, "and how miserable, at least as far as my nephew is concerned. The Thibaudet family is quite adamant that he give up his medical studies. They don't want him jeopardizing his social status over something as unbecoming as a career."

"But Jean-Étienne studies for the love of it!" Lili pulled herself away and stared at the count. "What's wrong with that?"

"It makes her family nervous. His as well. He's far too suited to medicine for anyone to think he would easily give it up—wouldn't you agree? He told me the Thibaudet family is demanding that he sign an oath that he will not pursue his schooling beyond the end of this year, and they're putting off the wedding just to be sure he doesn't go back on his word."

"Poor Jean-Étienne," Delphine murmured.

It must feel worse than death, Lili thought, *knowing you're meant to do something forbidden to you.* Walking off a cliff seemed more merciful. "It's such a loss," Lili whispered.

The count heard her. "For him most of all, of course, but also for me, since I imagine he'll be pressured to cut back his time here as well." He gestured toward the greenhouse door to usher them out for their walk. "And a loss for you, my dear, now that it's clear I was right that you cared for him."

He gave Lili a long, tender look. "I'm an old man. I've seen a great deal in my life, but I can't say I've often seen a day when so much brightness appears to have been extinguished." He touched the corner of one eye to capture a tear before it fell. "I am so sorry." His voice choked again. "For all of us."

The sun had made the damp air cloying and sultry as Lili and Delphine left the greenhouse. Cicadas screamed and the low roar of hundreds of bees added to the swirling tumult of sounds, smells, and colors of a world come back to life after a long winter. Lili saw and heard none of it. *Is anyone happy in all of France?* she wondered. *Are there people who get what they want?* Not Delphine, not Ambroise, not Jean-Étienne, not Buffon. And certainly not she.

* * *

Esteemed and Dearest Mademoiselle du Châtelet,

I believe my uncle will by now have spoken to you of my engagement. Not raising this matter the last time I saw you was in part a dreadful failure of courage, but I ask you to believe that I also desired to avoid what might have been the lasting consequences of an ungraceful parting.

My marriage to Mademoiselle Thibaudet has been discussed in both families for some time. Although I had not given my consent, I had become increasingly aware that it might not be possible for me to avoid it. Mademoiselle Thibaudet is an excellent person in many regards, but I have been unable to convince myself that we would find the contentment that comes from natural compatibility. I had set such concerns aside, believing it likely that I hoped in vain of finding a wife who shared my interests and outlook. Observing you over these months showed me otherwise and strengthened my resolve to put off my engagement. I am now forced to conclude, however, that I must choose family obligations over aspirations that might have led to a greater degree of happiness for me as an individual.

I allowed myself the vanity of thinking that expressing my true feelings about you might have kindled affection on your part toward me. It would have been most callous to have allowed that when, however much I wished to be free, I knew I was not. For that reason, I kept my feelings to myself, and now, of course, they can never be expressed, even in this letter. I take some solace in knowing that you have the peace of mind that comes from not having compromised yourself by anything you might have said or done if I had been so ungentlemanly as to have allowed or encouraged you to care for me.

Out of respect for Mademoiselle Thibaudet, I will not write to you again. I will be leaving shortly to go with the

Comte de Bougainville on the first part of his voyage around the world. I will go as far as his settlement in the Falklands and then return to be married sometime later this year.

With the utmost respect and most sincere regards,

I remain your true friend,

Jean-Étienne Leclerc

As their carriage crossed the Seine and continued toward the Place Royale, Lili handed the letter back to Delphine. "I've read it three times now," Lili said. "And I still don't know what to think."

Delphine sniffed and dabbed her eyes as she read it again. "He loves you. That's what you should think. For months I've sat around moping over Ambroise and I don't know if he even cares about me!" She thought for a moment. "Now if he'd written me a letter like that . . ."

"If he had written you a letter like that he'd be telling you he'd decided to marry Anne-Mathilde," Lili snapped. "I'm sure that would make everything better!"

"You're right, I suppose. And I don't like that Francine, even if I haven't met her."

Lili smiled wistfully. "I couldn't ask for a more loyal sister than you are to me," she said. "But if you ever meet Francine, try to like her. It isn't her fault. And maybe she's as unhappy about it as he is."

"Well if you ask my opinion, the reason Jean-Étienne is going off to South America is that he wants to put off marrying her as long as possible."

"Perhaps, but what does it matter if he marries her now or later?" Lili thought for a moment. "It's not as if I loved him. At least there's that."

"I hate everything," Delphine whispered. Lili did not reply, lost in repetition of a simple thought. *Friendship. Not love. What we had was friendship. Not love.*

They reached the Place Royale just as another carriage was coming down Rue des Tournelles, behind Hôtel Bercy. "Who was that?" Lili asked without caring.

"I don't know," Delphine said, tracing the retreat of the coach down the street with disinterested eyes. She shrugged. "Maman must have a new visitor."

The valet greeted them as they entered the house. "Madame asks that you come to see her right away," he said, as he helped them remove their light summer capes. "She is waiting in the parlor." Lili and Delphine exchanged glances. The departing coach had obviously contained someone of more interest than they had thought.

"*Mes chéries!* I have the most extraordinary news for both of you!" Julie said, getting up from a fauteuil and rushing to greet them. "Look!" She held out a copy of the *Gazette d'Amsterdam*, open to a middle page. " 'The Adventures of Meadowlark,'" she said, pointing to the top.

Lili grabbed it from her and read aloud. " 'This is the first in a series of stories by M. Tellechat, recently of Belgium, about the adventures of two young travelers and their magical horse.'" All thoughts of Jean-Étienne vanished as an astonished Lili traced her fingers over the words on the page.

Delphine bounced on her toes with excitement. "You're a published author, Lili!" Her wide eyes were the only thing visible over the tent of fingers on her face. "But why 'recently of Belgium,' Maman?" She looked at the page again, tapping the letter *M*. "And why *Monsieur* Tellechat?" She glanced at Lili and burst into laughter. "Will you have to wear breeches and a jabot when you're famous?"

"Monsieur Diderot must have put it in to protect Lili," Julie replied.

"That's no fun!" Delphine looked crestfallen. "I want to tell everyone how smart and famous Lili is!"

"You must say nothing to anyone," Maman said. "It isn't safe. If powerful people get the idea she's talking about them . . ." She didn't need to finish. Everyone in Paris knew how easy it was to land in the

Bastille, even though it was hard to picture someone like Lili there.

"Was that Monsieur Diderot's carriage we saw leaving?" Delphine asked.

"No—he came earlier," Julie said. "There's more than one piece of good news." She turned to Lili. "Put that aside for a moment, since I'm sure you'll want to hear this." She motioned both of them to sit down, and then with a smile that slowly enveloped her whole being, she looked at Delphine. "That, *ma petite*, was the Comtesse d'Étoges, Ambroise Clément de Feuillet's mother."

Delphine gasped and put her hand to her mouth. "What did she want?"

"Oh, not much," Julie said, smoothing her skirts with an overly casual air as she settled into a chair across from them. "Just to make sure I knew that Anne-Mathilde de Praslin is betrothed to the Comte de Beaufort."

"Count Rotten Teeth?" Lili burst out laughing. "With his baby Gas-ton?"

Julie looked perplexed as the girls broke into laughter that soon had them wiping their eyes. "We'll explain later, Maman," Lili said.

Julie raised her eyebrows in mock disapproval. "The countess is the reason I couldn't come with you for Saint Anne's Day. She wrote a few days ago, saying she wanted to make my acquaintance, because her son is apparently most adamant in his feelings toward you. I thought it was best to hear what she had to say before telling you anything about it."

"*Mon Dieu*," Delphine said, frozen for a moment before her shoulders began to shake. The *Gazette d'Amsterdam* fell off Lili's lap to the floor as she turned to embrace her, crying until Delphine's shoulder and her own were dark with tears.

NIGHT HAD FALLEN, and an exhausted Maman and exultant Delphine had long since gone to bed. Alone in the parlor, Lili opened the *Gazette d'Amsterdam* and began to read:

The golden domes of Kiev caught the rays of the rising sun as Meadowlark and Tom set Comète down on a grassy bank near the river that ran through the city.

"Look at all these churches!" Tom said. "They must be terribly religious here."

When she was finished, she put down the paper in a sudden wave of exhaustion and rubbed her eyes. Delphine had spent hours that afternoon playing with ideas for her personal coat of arms to stamp into the wax on her letters and carve into the frame of the portrait that would adorn her parlor at the Chateau d'Étoges. Julie had reminded her, to no avail, that interest was one thing and betrothal quite another. It wasn't at all clear whether she would have a sufficient dowry to make a match attractive to the Clément de Feuillet family, and she offered no advantage in rank.

"In the end it might all come to nothing," Julie had said. "The Comtesse d'Étoges was not specific, do remember."

"He stood his ground against Anne-Mathilde, didn't he," Delphine asked. "Why can't he stand his ground for me?"

Perhaps Delphine's excitement was like a whirlwind that caught up everything in the room, but considering how long she had waited for her first story to appear, Lili felt a surprising deadness as she sat in the empty parlor. Jean-Étienne's betrothal and his letter to her had been shoved aside by the excitement over the countess's visit to Hôtel Bercy. Even the news that Diderot had placed three more of her stories in subsequent issues couldn't raise her spirits.

Jean-Étienne was lost without her having even the fleeting pleasure of a single kiss. *I still don't know what a walk in a garden with a man I love is like*, Lili thought. *And I almost might have*. Perhaps it was love she felt—or easily could have felt, if it weren't so important to deny it. More important than ever after the events of that day.

Now, with her first published story, she'd achieved what she once hoped would release her from the destiny of a loveless marriage that now seemed both her and Jean-Étienne's lot. Barras could refuse to give her paper, or let her inkwell run dry, just to make sure she made a proper wife. Husbands could do that, Lili knew, and he seemed like the kind who might. "I haven't seen even a spoonful of imagination or compassion in that man," Maman had told her earlier that evening. "As far as I'm concerned you're not going to marry him unless you want to. And I will do my best to make sure you aren't coerced into thinking you want to."

Ambroise had stood his ground, just as Delphine said. *But you have to have ground to stand on*, Lili thought, wondering if perhaps he was the only one who did. Jean-Étienne decided he couldn't say no, and from the explanation the Comte de Buffon had given, it sounded like marrying Francine was the dutiful and noble thing to do. And what footing did Lili have against Baronne Lomont and Robert de Barras? A few stories in the paper? It had been foolish to think that would help.

Did Delphine, in her blissful sleep, understand that if the gate to her dreams closed, all the will in the world would not be enough to pry it back open again? Lili shuddered and turned out the lamp to go upstairs to bed. "Her life will be the way she wants, and so will mine," she commanded into the darkness, wishing that her thoughts were enough to power her through life, and that her voice didn't sound so tiny and afraid.

At least we have Maman, Lili remembered. Her will seemed to create enough momentum for all three of them.

AFTER HIS MOTHER'S visit, Ambroise Clément de Feuillet wrote to Julie within hours to request an invitation to her salon and to inquire whether Delphine might be present. Delphine, who almost never attended, was sick with apprehension. "I'm not smart like Lili," she moaned at supper. "What if he sees I don't have all that many thoughts in my head?"

"He'd have to be looking at someone else," Julie replied. "And you'll be amazed at how intelligent you'll appear if you just listen appreciatively." She thought for a moment. "I'll make sure the Comte de Buffon will be here. His fondness for you will go a long way with the others." She leaned forward with a sly look. "I'm sure he'll boast about your drawings, so you might have some at hand to show around, and a few more in the library to share privately with Ambroise—if he can manage to get you to overcome your modesty and permit him to see them." Lili snickered, but Delphine was too nervous to smile.

"Perhaps Delphine could play and we could sing something?" Lili suggested. "Maybe a little piece by Monsieur Philidor? He's usually there, and he would be most flattered, don't you think?"

"Oh yes!" Delphine clapped her hands. "With something to do, my being there wouldn't look quite so—" She thought for a moment. "Quite so entirely what it is. And Lili is right that Monsieur Philidor would think you were doing it out of appreciation for him."

Julie chuckled. "I think that would be lovely for both you and him. Let's go choose something." Lili and Delphine followed her into the parlor, where Julie opened a cabinet and took out some sheet music. She put one of them on the bottom after looking at it and selected another. "This is lovely," she said, humming the first bars of the melody.

"What about the one on the bottom?" Lili asked, her interest piqued by what looked like an attempt to hide something.

"Oh, not that one," Julie said. "It wouldn't do." Her cheeks colored.

"Ooohhh!" Delphine squealed, trying to snatch the music from her hand. "Something a bit too *intime*?"

"Well," Julie said, sensing a losing battle, "if you must know, it's a piece Monsieur Philidor wrote for me that is—how should I say this?—a bit too ardent for the salon." She let out a resigned sigh and handed it to Delphine.

"'Who is Julie?'" Delphine read. "'A flower in winter, a cool breeze in summer, all the things the heart remembers with delight.'" She looked up. "My, my!"

"I think that's quite enough," Maman said, holding her hand out with a look that said the impromptu reading was at an end.

"All right," Delphine said, "but I think it's most unfair that you haven't told us about this before."

"Told you about what?"

"That you have an admirer." Delphine turned to Lili. "Did you guess?"

Before Lili could reply, Maman held up a hand. "Quiet now, or I won't let you play at the salon. And Lili will ask your opinions about politics, won't you?" Maman gave Lili a conspiratorial wink. "Complicated questions, in front of Ambroise."

"Why would I do that, when I'd much rather hear about Monsieur Philidor right now?" She teased Maman with an impish smile, but the look on Julie's face said that the subject was closed.

DELPHINE WASTED NO time inviting Ambroise to come sit for a portrait after he admired her drawings at the salon. "Why don't you sketch in the garden of the Place Royale?" Maman suggested to Delphine after he arrived. "It's a perfect day for you and Lili to take a little air. And of course," she said, turning to Ambroise, "your company would be most appreciated since they can't sit out alone."

It became the first of many times they took advantage of a pleasant afternoon before the heat of late summer drove them inside. On the days he was to visit, servants set up three chairs underneath plane trees surrounding the statue of Louis XIV at the center of the square. Lili brought along her writing paper or a book, and Delphine and Ambroise bantered about the gossip of the day as she sketched. Every time, he came full of new information about their mutual acquaintances. Anne-Mathilde was expecting a child. Paul-Vincent was finishing military school and would soon join his regiment. Joséphine's first child had been safely delivered but died soon after.

"And Jacques-Mars Courville?" Delphine asked, surprising Lili with the indifference in her voice.

"Jacques-Mars, from what I heard," Ambroise said, "is preparing for a career as a royal ambassador. Bound for Venice, I've heard."

"An ambassador?" Lili looked up from her reading. "That's a rather frightening prospect."

"Quite," Ambroise said. "I've heard it's intended to keep him away from the women at Versailles. Marie Leszczynska has developed a severe dislike for him."

He looked away for a moment. Was he thinking about Anne-Mathilde and her friendship with Jacques-Mars? Lili supposed so, but Ambroise was too much of a gentleman to say a bad word about someone he was once expected to marry. "He's probably feeling quite good about Venice," he went on. "Wearing a mask, he should be able to get away with most anything."

"How nice for Venice," Delphine said with a sniff, cocking her head to make sure he understood she didn't mean it.

"He'll go with the senior ambassador, of course, to learn the ways, and if he manages not to get caught in bed with his wife, I imagine he may make a success of it." Ambroise looked away. "I can't say I've met too many people I dislike as much as I do him. Perhaps it's that he's still so young to be so—I don't know." He looked at both of them in turn. "I think I've said too much. Have I upset you?"

"No! Not at all!" Delphine gave Lili a quick, triumphant glance. "We never liked him either, did we?"

"No," said Lili. "I can't say we ever have." She touched her finger to her ear, this time to signal not a lie but a shared moment of victory.

ON A SULTRY afternoon a few months later, Lili and Delphine stood at an upstairs window looking down at two carriages waiting in the courtyard. The sun came out from behind a cloud and turned the puddles from a recent shower into mirrored reflections of the sky, as they waited for the visitors to emerge from the house.

"There's Maman's lawyer," Lili said. "And Ambroise's father and their lawyer too."

Delphine buried her head in Lili's shoulder. "I'm afraid to look. Are they acting friendly?"

"Very," Lili said, watching the men share something amusing enough to make them both laugh. "They're getting in their carriages now."

Delphine's face was pale and her eyes were huge. "Should we wait for Maman, or go down?" Before Lili could reply, they heard a familiar creak on the stairs, and within moments Julie came into the room holding a paper.

"It's official, *ma petite*," she said to Delphine. "Our families have agreed to terms. You and Ambroise will be married this fall, just before the beginning of Advent."

"Oh, Maman!" Delphine said, rushing into her arms. "*Merci mille fois. Merci. Merci.*"

"WHY ARE WE stopping?" Lili asked a week later, as the carriage taking them to the Jardin de Roi stopped in front of a shop on the Rue Saint-Antoine.

"Just wait here," Delphine said. "I have a gift for Maman I need to pick up."

Lili waited in the carriage while Delphine went inside Lacroix et Fils. In a few minutes she came out carrying an oblong box covered with shiny watered silk. Laying it on her knees when she was back inside the coach, she lifted the lid. Inside were two pairs of supple kid gloves, one in black, and the other in a deep rose that was one of Maman's favorite colors.

"You know why, don't you?" Delphine said.

Lili smiled at the sudden recollection. "The bet with Maman," she said.

"She wagered two pairs of gloves that I would prefer to go to the Jardin de Roi than have them." Delphine's eyes filled with tears.

"And she was right. I've treasured every minute of it, and I thought turning the wager around would be a way to thank her for her confidence in my better nature."

Lili smiled. "I was betting against you too. It's easy to be happy there," she said as the carriage started up again. "But I don't imagine you'll be going much anymore. You'll be too busy this fall, and then—"

"And then I'll be married," Delphine said. "I love to say those words. I can't believe it's coming true. I was so miserable just a few months ago."

The carriage was crossing the Pont Marie, where the shops built up on both sides of the bridge made a passage so narrow it was perpetually in shadow. Delphine leaned forward to see Lili better. "Are you all right?" she asked. "You know—about Jean-Étienne?"

"He did what he had to do. It would be wrong of me to wish he had done something less—" Her throat tightened, and she heard the telltale hoarseness in her voice. "Less admirable."

"Look what happened to me. You shouldn't give up." Delphine reached over to take her hand. "It's not too late yet. He still has months to come to his senses."

Lili leaned back in her seat. *Try not to care. Try . . .*

Delphine's eyes narrowed. "Or for me to search down that Francine and get her to believe he's a terrible prospect."

"You wouldn't!" Lili sat up straight, bouncing in her seat as the carriage left the bridge and went onto the rough, unpaved quay on the far side of the Seine. *Would she?*

"Well, how do you think I'd feel if Ambroise put off our wedding just so he could go off on an expedition to look for bugs or leaves or something? Maybe I can make her despise him for it. I wonder where she lives . . ."

The coach pulled up in front of the Jardin de Roi, and Lili looked out the window to see a distraught Comte de Buffon waiting for them with a letter in his hand. "I've received a note from your mother by courier," he said, handing it to Delphine through the open coach door.

She read silently for a moment before handing it to Lili.

"My dear Buffon," Julie had written. "Please tell my girls that they must not come back to Hôtel Bercy today. The scullery maid became ill with cholera in the night, and the cook is showing symptoms this morning. I learned of this only minutes after Lili and Delphine left. I have sent a message to Baronne Lomont to ask her to take them in for a day or two until the severity of the situation can be assessed. Tell them I will write to them there later. Gratefully, Julie de Bercy."

Buffon asked the driver to wait and stepped up into the carriage. It rocked with his weight, but Lili and Delphine sat immobile as porcelain dolls, absorbing the import of the letter. He sat down next to Delphine and looked across at Lili. "I think you should go to Baronne Lomont's right away," he said. "We won't be able to get any work done today."

"People die of cholera," Delphine whispered.

"It's not well understood," the count replied, clearing his throat. "Sometimes it sweeps through the entire city and sometimes it affects only a single block, or a single household. Sometimes it is fatal to almost everyone, and sometimes—" He stopped, seeing the horror on their faces. "It's important to determine how severe the situation is at Hôtel Bercy," he went on, "and your mother is quite right that you must avoid contagion."

"But what about Maman?" Delphine said. "She should come to the baroness's as well."

"She has a role to play. She must keep the household from panic. She must bring doctors in and see that their orders are followed. She would like to reassure you in person—I'm sure of that—but right now she can't. And of course, she can't be certain now she hasn't been—" Buffon stopped short and opened the coach door. "I'm keeping you from further news," he said. "You must go."

The driver cracked his whip, sending the coach at frightening speed down to the Seine and across the Pont de la Tournelle to the baroness's house. Unnoticed, the box of gloves slid to the floor, spilling its contents into the darkness.

* * *

LILI AND DELPHINE were met at Hôtel Lomont by the valet. "She is waiting in the chapel," he said. "The priest is here."

The chapel was barely large enough to contain a bench along one wall and a small prie-dieu in front of an altar. Two candles made white rings on its marble surface and sent soft light upward toward a painting of the Virgin ascending to heaven on a cloud held up by angels. Lili gave an inadvertent gasp at what for a moment looked like Maman's face under Mary's blue veil. *No*, she thought. *You can't die. You can't leave us. Not now. Not ever.*

Baronne Lomont was kneeling at the prie-dieu and the priest was in front of the altar. When Lili and Delphine entered, he helped the baroness to her feet. Her face in the dim candlelight was gray and swollen. "Maman?" Delphine whimpered. "Is there news?"

"Your mother has taken to bed," the baroness replied. "She is not feeling well, but she says she is certain it can be attributed to exhaustion."

"I'm on my way to see if I can get some information from the valet," the priest said. "I was waiting for you to arrive because the baroness thought you might be comforted by the sacrament. Of course to receive it I would have to hear your confession and absolve your sins."

Lili stepped back, aghast. *Confess my sins now? How can I even think of what they are, with Maman in a house with cholera?*

Delphine nodded her head. "I would like that," she murmured. The priest nodded his head. "Of course this must be done privately, so come with me." He turned to Lili. "And you, mademoiselle?"

You are the last person in the world I would tell my secrets to, she thought with a shudder. Despite the promise of confidentiality, that simpering little priest would find a way to tell the baroness anything he thought she needed to know. "I'd rather just stay here and pray alone," she replied. He arched his eyebrows and looked at the baroness, whose expression was hidden in the gloomy light of the chapel.

"Very well," he said, leading Delphine into the parlor.

Lili sat on the bench and crossed herself. Though she tried to focus on God in the dark and airless chapel, a swirl of memories flooded her mind. *Don't cry into your napkin,* ma chérie—*it would make the baroness truly furious . . . Your thoughts are the most beautiful thing about you . . . What are you so afraid of, that the mere presence of a book inside your walls makes you do this to a young girl? . . . You are going to require an accomplice to have the life you want, and that will require a search worthy of the daughter of the woman who bore you . . . Meadowlark is your voice—don't you want it to be heard? . . . I'm curious why you haven't asked me how I knew what had happened to you at the abbey . . .*

"You were always watching over me," Lili whispered, remembering what she had told Maman so many years ago as she rode away for the last time from the Abbaye de Panthémont. She pulled herself up and held her breath, praying with all her heart that Maman would be strong, that she would get well, and that life would resume just as it was.

When I was young, I used to pray for this and that, but now I know the most important thing to wish for is that I will have the grace and good character to handle whatever comes . . . Lili trembled, hoping that she would not need to put Maman's advice to use quite so soon.

SEVERAL HOURS LATER a note arrived from the priest. "Madame de Bercy is afflicted with cholera," he wrote, "but so far the symptoms do not appear particularly severe. I will send news again this evening."

In the middle of the afternoon, after picking at an austere dinner, Lili and Delphine went to their rooms to try to rest. As the long summer dusk dragged on, they were summoned by Baronne Lomont. "One of the servants died an hour ago," she said, "and Madame de Bercy is gravely ill."

In the windowless chapel they sat with no idea of the passage of time. "Holy Mary, Mother of God, pray for us sinners now and at the hour of our death," they recited as rosary beads slipped through the baroness's fingers. And then, just as they finished, they heard the sound of footsteps at the door. The valet's face was grave as the baroness took the letter from the small silver tray he carried.

Lili held a shaking Delphine up by the waist as Baronne Lomont read the letter silently. She refolded it before speaking. "She is unconscious and has been given last rites," the baroness said, handing the letter to Delphine. "She will not last the night."

"She can't die," Delphine whispered. "There just isn't a world without her."

WHEN THE TAILORS came to Hôtel Lomont to fit them for their mourning wardrobes, Lili and Delphine stared straight ahead, allowing the tailors to lift an arm or reposition a hip as if they were not inhabiting their bodies at all. Delphine's marriage had been postponed, and since it was out of the question for unmarried women to live alone at Hôtel Bercy, she would be leaving for the Abbaye de Panthémont after the funeral. There she would live in private quarters until her wedding the following spring. Lili would stay with Baronne Lomont until she could be married.

Robert de Barras was one of the first to pay a visit of condolence at Hôtel Lomont. His cheeks showed signs of color and his voice seemed oddly loud. *He's in his element around death*, Lili thought, heaping onto him all the rage in her heart at the unfairness of his being alive while beautiful, vibrant Maman would never charm a guest in her salon again, or offer a scented handkerchief to wipe away Delphine's and her tears, or pat their knees with a loving smile.

The night of the funeral, Lili awoke to find Delphine crawling into bed next to her. They sobbed in each other's arms until the first light ushered them into restless sleep.

Emilie

1737

THE HEAT from the forge was so intense that Emilie stepped back, pulling her ten-year-old son with her. "Don't get so close, *mon cheri*!"

"But I want to watch with Papa!" Florent-Louis whined, pulling away and grabbing the hand of the Marquis du Châtelet. Voltaire stood next to him, shouting orders over the roar of the flames. With a sigh, Emilie came to stand with them, mopping her face delicately to avoid smearing her makeup. The beauty mark pasted on her cheek slid off into her handkerchief, and she scowled at it.

"Can't he see this is pointless?" she whispered to herself. "Can anyone really be that stubborn?" The Academy of Sciences had offered a prize for the best essay on the nature of fire, and as the August deadline loomed, Voltaire was in a frenzy, trying to prove that light and heat were forms of matter by weighing and calculating their mass. Iron and lead were incessantly heated and cooled in the foundry at Cirey. Perfectly measured quantities of wood were burned to see if they expanded before being reduced to ash. Emilie was tired of it all. "Pointless!" she muttered again.

A few weeks earlier, she had stalked away from her husband, who, like everyone else, seemed to think that fire, smoke, and noise must equal science, and that Voltaire's wildly waving arms and shouted demands were signs of a genius at work. "Why don't you just burn down the forest and measure that?" she had said, and then, to her astonishment, Voltaire called that an inspired idea. While servants stood at the ready with buckets of water, he and the marquis had set a small forest fire to calculate how quickly the flames spread. And then, when Voltaire couldn't interpret the results, they had done the experiment again with a new patch of trees.

"It must work next time," Voltaire said of each experiment as they discussed it over dinner. "It has to! I'm not just a writer, you know!"

It was easier to go along. After all, Voltaire was the only truly interesting thing in her life, even when he was being a fool.

"I'm not feeling well in this heat," Emilie said, turning away from the forge. "I'm going back to the house to rest. You can tell me about it at dinner."

"Can I stay, Maman?" Florent-Louis said, jumping up and down. "Please?"

Emilie smiled. "As long as you mind your father."

"This is really no place for a woman," the marquis said, putting his arm around his son's shoulder. "We'll see you in a few hours."

"This is really no place for a scientist," she muttered as she untied and mounted her horse. "Perhaps when results make no sense, you ought to examine your assumptions, Monsieur Voltaire. Don't you think so, Hirondelle?" she said, rubbing the mare's neck. Hirondelle shuddered, and Emilie laughed. With a light touch of her heels, she sent the horse in a fast trot down the path to the château.

She was a better scientist than Voltaire was, but since she couldn't hope to be taken seriously, she would have to satisfy herself with trying to get him to give up notions so foolish they would embarrass him later. Like heat having mass. He'd burned everything he could get his hands on and gotten such conflicting results, he'd never be able to demonstrate anything persuasive to the Academy.

But how can heat have no substance? Something was scorching her face back at the forge, and how can something be nothing? Emilie rode through the dappled light of the forest, oblivious to everything as she pondered the question.

Reaching the forest edge, she winced at the sudden intensity of the light reflecting off the golden fields in front of her. Then, with a gasp, she put her hands to both sides of her head and her eyes widened. "It's so obvious!"

She dug in her heels to send Hirondelle into a gallop. Only two weeks remained before the Academy's deadline, two weeks to get her own essay finished and into the mail coach bound for Paris.

13

1766

IN THE summer heat, among fears of an epidemic, Julie de Bercy was buried quickly and unceremoniously in a family plot outside the city. A few weeks later, when danger of wider contagion in the city had passed, a requiem mass was said for her soul at Notre-Dame, with music composed by François-André Danican Philidor.

"Not a large crowd," the Comte de Buffon pointed out to Lili as they filed out, "but quite an illustrious one." Among the mourners were Denis Diderot and most of Julie's regular guests at her salon, as well as Madames Lespinasse and Geoffrin, two of Julie's rival *salonnières*. Queen Marie Leszczynska offered condolences in a letter and sent two of her daughters to represent her. They arrived with the Duchesse de Praslin, who, much to Lili and Delphine's relief, had come without Anne-Mathilde. The Comtesse d'Étoges attended with Ambroise, who supported Delphine as she went with trembling steps to receive the sacrament. Lili followed mechanically on the arm of Baronne Lomont.

The mercier was there, and the dressmaker and milliner too, dabbing tears at the loss of someone who looked them in the eye and always paid her bills. They disappeared back to their shops after the mass, most with just a nod in Lili and Delphine's direction. Private carriages took the family and close friends to the Jardin de Roi, where the Comte de Buffon had invited them to a somber dinner.

Delphine went in the carriage of the Comte d'Étoges, leaving

Lili to travel alone with Baronne Lomont. *Thank God Monsieur Barras isn't invited,* Lili thought, shuddering at the thought of his mournful, cloying look when he talked about his dead wife. *Clarisse this, Clarisse that, as if Maman scarcely matters even when she's the one newly dead.* Lili felt a sudden wave of exhaustion. Slumping into a corner of the carriage, she shut her eyes.

"You should not sit in that manner when you are being observed by others," the baroness said, "even if I am the only person to see you."

Lili opened her eyes but did not move. "Maman is dead, Baronne," she said. "Surely I am permitted some show of grief?"

"You will, of course, be forgiven almost anything right now, but that doesn't mean you won't be talked about. It's at times like this that a lady's character is most clearly observed."

Lili sat up and stared ahead, avoiding the baroness's eyes. "You should not consider yourself excused from pleasant conversations simply because you are privately sorrowful," she went on. "You should view yourself as the hostess at the Comte de Buffon's dinner, if you wish talk of you to be favorable. And you most certainly need that in your circumstances . . ."

Lili had stopped listening. *Dead. Buried. Gone.* She and Delphine had not been permitted to see the body out of fears of lingering contagion, and she still didn't quite believe that Maman wasn't simply away somewhere. There had been no time yet even to visit her grave. Perhaps Maman would be waiting outside the Jardin de Roi to run to them and tell them it had all been a mistake, that someone else was buried in her coffin, that she had just been visiting a friend and was sorry she had frightened them.

The carriage slowed to a stop. "Are we clear then?" the baroness asked.

She must have been lecturing me the whole time, Lili realized. "*Oui,* madame," she said, knowing it was always best to agree with the baroness even when she had no idea what she had said.

* * *

"AND HERE'S WHERE I drew my sketches," Delphine said to Ambroise as she showed him the greenhouse after dinner. A wilted tone in her voice and a hesitancy of step as she clung to Ambroise's arm were the only signs that Delphine was suffering, and only those who knew Delphine's natural gaiety would notice even that.

Lili hung back behind them, wanting a moment to herself. *How odd it is to be here,* she thought, taking in the chirps and trills of the birds. Death had swallowed up Maman, but here in this world so full of life, not a creature knew she had existed.

Tatou screamed, rattling the bars of his cage, and a flood of affection came over Lili for the little capuchin monkey, blessed with a life so innocent and simple. *He doesn't know I'm sad*, she thought. *He doesn't understand why he's still in his cage now that I'm here.* She draped a cloth over her shoulder and opened the door. Tatou scrambled up her outstretched arm and took his seat on the cloth.

"Do you miss Jean-Étienne as much as I do?" she asked, as tears swelled her throat. Tatou met her gaze and cocked his head. "Yes, you know who I mean, don't you?" He gave a single soft cry. "But you still have the count," she said, scratching behind the monkey's tiny ear. "He's rather like a papa to both of us, isn't he?"

She looked around at the only place that felt like home now. Hôtel Bercy was a tomb, every room waiting to ambush her with memories, and Hôtel Lomont was as arid and bleak as a desert. *If I could just spend some time here, I think I might heal . . .*

Delphine's loud cry startled Lili, and Lili rushed to her where she was standing beside the pink mantis cage. "It's dead," Delphine sobbed. "I wanted to show Ambroise, and it's dead."

Stiff, and smaller in death, the mantis lay beneath its perch. Delphine buried her head in Ambroise's coat. Her shoulders heaved and her voice came out in huge, gulping sobs. Lili stood watching alone, hands at her sides, as the monkey's insistent shrieks rang in her ears.

There's nothing but death, Lili thought. Nothing would ever be good again, whole again, bright again. "Nothing," she whispered. *Nothing.*

"OF COURSE I must insist that he accede to my wishes." Baronne Lomont placed the newly arrived letter back on the tray. "You may read it yourself if you like."

Lili's hand trembled as she unfolded the stiff, cream-colored paper and laid eyes on the familiar, meticulous hand.

> *I would be greatly indebted to you if you would permit*
> *Mademoiselle du Châtelet to visit me at the Jardin de Roi now that a*
> *suitable period of mourning has passed. Her assistance is most*
> *valuable to me. I trust that, on the occasion of the dinner after*
> *Madame de Bercy's funeral, you had opportunity to observe that the*
> *Jardin de Roi is an appropriately salutary environment for a young*
> *woman, and I assure you she would always be directly in my care. If*
> *it is agreeable to her and to you to resume her work, I will be most*
> *gratified.*
>
> > *My best regards to you and to*
> > *Mesdemoiselles du Châtelet and Bercy,*
> > *Georges-Louis Leclerc*
> > *Comte de Buffon*

"You are quite correct in that." Robert de Barras gave the baroness a somber nod of his head. "It is indeed most unseemly."

Lili bristled. *What right has he to say anything about me?* she thought. *And not even to look at me while he does it.*

"Of course you understand, I assume, why the Comte de Buffon's request must be refused, do you not?" the baroness asked Lili. "Six months is a suitable period of mourning for some things, as he says, but it serves no purpose at all for you to waste your time in that fashion."

"And if I may be so bold as to presume that you will soon honor me by accepting my proposal," Barras said, finally looking at her. He brought life to his face with a haughty arch of his eyebrows. "I want to make most clear that your responsibilities at home would make such outside interests impossible to maintain."

Were you both born dead or did you smother yourselves willingly to have people approve of you? Lili battled to keep herself under control. It had been bad enough when she had come from Hôtel Bercy to visit, but in the dreary half a year she had lived with Baronne Lomont, she had never heard laughter, never heard anyone express a thought except to disparage someone else's, never glimpsed joy in being alive.

She took in a deep breath before responding. "I have given no consideration to your proposal," she said, despising the quaver in her voice. "And I find it most unpleasant to be talked about in this fashion."

"My dear, it is my home, and I shall talk as I wish." Baronne Lomont rang a bell and a servant appeared. "Please lay out some writing paper and make sure there is ink in my well," she said, casting a glance in Lili's direction. "I have several letters I must write this afternoon. And now, I would ask you both to excuse me. The tenor of this conversation is most distressing and I prefer to be alone."

Lili stood up. "I am sorry if you find my behavior disrespectful, Baronne," she said, "and I am grateful for your generosity in taking me in, but I do not feel I am obligated to show my appreciation by marrying Monsieur de Barras." She turned to him. "I do not feel we could live harmoniously, and I will not marry you, now or ever." She made a quick, stiff curtsey, in the direction of first one and then the other, and stalked out.

Be angry with me. I don't care, Lili thought. *I hate being so strident, but she forces me to be something I'm not.*

She leaned against a wall in an alcove off the hallway and felt the cool air calm her face. "Deformity," she whispered, remembering what Rousseau had once said to her. *It's my right to resist being deformed to match what Baronne Lomont and that awful man want.*

Maman would let her go to the Jardin de Roi. If she could send a carriage from the grave, it would be outside waiting for her right at that moment. Lili went over to the window and pulled the heavy curtain aside. A lump rose in her throat not so much because the courtyard was empty, but because she had been desperate enough to entertain a fleeting hope it might not be.

A memory of the key turning in the lock in her cell in the abbey overtook her, and she shut her eyes in pain. The loss of Maman hit her with such force that she was surprised it didn't knock her to the ground. *She always rescued me*, Lili realized. *But she can't do it any-more.*

Or could she? Perhaps it was Maman who had risen up inside her, giving her courage to say things to the baroness just now that she had never dared say before. Perhaps Maman was still worrying about her, and had managed to penetrate Lili's mind and heart to tell her not to surrender. And perhaps it was more than just Maman. Was her mother whispering to her also? How else could Lili explain that all of a sudden she felt bigger than herself—and braver, almost reck-less in what she believed she could do?

It's up to me. No going home to Maman to complain, no fuming with Delphine. Just me. Something came over Lili—a launching upward from her toes, a tightening of the belly, a burst of energy that carried her back into the parlor.

"I'm sure you know I received a letter from Mademoiselle de Bercy yesterday," she said, cutting off what looked like an angry and bewildered interchange between the baroness and her guest. "Her wedding has been set for next month. I have been invited to stay with her at the abbey to help her prepare. I am accepting the invitation, with or without your approval, since I am certain it is what both Ma-dame de Bercy and my mother would have wanted, and I intend to honor them."

There. She turned and strode out of the room.

Upstairs, Lili dipped her quill in the inkwell, trying to still the trembling in her hand after leaving Baronne Lomont and Robert de

Barras in the parlor. *Nothing else*, she thought with a grim smile, *can calm me like Meadowlark.*

"They cut off your wings?" Meadowlark asked in disbelief.

"Of course," the group of children said. "It hurts a little now, but we can't wait to start decorating the stumps."

Two little girls held each other's hands as they twirled in a circle. "We'll have pearls, and diamonds shaped like teardrops, and lace made from gold thread!" they chanted, laughing as if it were a private song they had practiced for years.

"But you could have flown!"

The children looked puzzled. "What's the point in that? Everything we want is on the ground."

"But you could have flown," she whispered.

Could they? Could she? Despite the scene she had just made, she still lived at Hôtel Lomont and had no place else to go. She wiped her quill and put it down in despair.

She even depended upon Delphine to have enough ink and paper so she could keep writing her stories. Baronne Lomont had seen one of them, when Lili carelessly left it on her desk shortly after her arrival. The baroness had denounced Meadowlark as a frivolous and possibly dangerous use of time and began keeping the household's writing supplies under lock and key. "You should read instead," she had told her, giving her a book on the lives of the saints and another on female piety.

Delphine's secret supplies were hidden in a compartment in the back of a drawer, and Lili had been using the baroness's ink and paper to copy in her neatest hand what she considered the most ridiculous lines from those odious books. These she left on top of the desk for the baroness to find, in hope she would take her effort seriously and be convinced of Lili's improved temperament.

"The quarrelsome woman's society is more intolerable than living in the wilderness, or in a corner of one's own attic," she had written.

"The woman who brings shame to her house is a rottenness in the bones of her husband."

"The beautiful woman without discretion is like a jewel of gold in a swine's snout."

"The contentious wife is as annoying as the constant dripping on a rainy day."

Obviously the baroness would not be fooled by her false religiosity after her outburst today. Still, with nothing else to do, Lili picked up the book on piety and read from where she had left off.

"The Bible is the best mirror by which most accurately to know what you are, and to become what you should be," she read. "With it, you may adjust all the moral garb of the soul, and go forth adorned with the beauty of holiness, clothed with the garment of purity, and decorated with the ornament of a meek and quiet spirit."

"Try that in a corset," Lili muttered to herself.

"While the word of God protects woman from the insults, the injuries, and the oppression of the other sex, it saves her with no less benefit from the sad effects which would arise from assuming prerogatives that do not belong to her, from those excesses of ambition to which her own vanity might otherwise prompt her, and from pretensions that would only make her look ridiculous in the eyes of others . . ."

Lili tossed the book toward the desk, watching with disinterest as it skidded across the edge and fell to the floor. "At least I don't have to memorize it," she said to the empty air. Lying down on the bed, she missed Maman so badly she thought her bones might dissolve with aching.

Emilie

1737

EMILIE WAS too tired to wince as the ice water bit into her hands. She pulled them out and shook off the water, scarcely noticing how chapped and red they'd become. The chips she ordered each night from the icehouse were already melted, and it wouldn't be long, on a night now close to dawn, before the water would be too warm to shock her back into wakefulness.

Two days to finish her paper on fire. The row of candles on her worktable were by now flickering stubs, and she replaced them all before sitting down again. She held her hand above a flame and felt it warm her palm. Interesting how heat traveled so much more slowly than light, and how it diffused in all directions, whereas light always moved in a straight line. How light didn't always feel hot, though every source of illumination was.

The calculations on her sheets of foolscap were so long that they strung out over several lines, and having no time to rewrite them, she turned the paper to continue along the margins. She dipped her quill and cursed under her breath when the ink dripped onto the page. She blotted it and moved on.

Sunlight could not be made of matter, regardless of how miniature the particles. She'd figured that out riding Hirondelle back from the forge. If light had mass, the earth would be pulverized by sunbeams hitting it. Because fire consisted of heat and light, if neither of these had mass, fire could not be a material thing.

If only she could carry out the experiments she had described in her notes, she might be able to prove that heat was a property inherent in light. She would take a beam of sunlight from the big window on the far side of her as-yet-unfinished study and refract it with a prism so its colors were arrayed on a sheet she would tack onto the bare wall at the other end of the room. Then she would take all of Voltaire's thermometers and attach them to the wall, one at each end, red and violet, and the others at points in between. If the thermometers reflected differences in the heat they absorbed, that would be evidence that light carried heat, but only in part of its spectrum. And if light wasn't matter, heat wasn't either.

But the experiment wasn't possible because she wouldn't be able to hide it from Voltaire. He would view her work as a criticism of him, and he had exploded in the past when he had perceived far lesser slights. Besides, the thermometers she needed were all being used for his experiments, which were obviously going nowhere, though he refused to believe it.

"There are no mysterious nonsubstances," he had scolded her that night at dinner. "To say that something in the physical world could exist without having mass is as foolish as belief in miracles. Perhaps we could produce heat by prayer!" he said, taunting her until she had thrown her napkin at him and stormed from the room.

Well, let him laugh. She was tired of playing the dutiful assistant to the great man, tired of all the things about being a woman that did little more than drain her energy—supervising the workers remodeling Cirey, entertaining a constant stream of guests, schooling her son, being a dutiful wife to Florent-Claude, and taking care of a hypochondriac like Voltaire. If he got so much as a splinter he'd make such a fuss about the possibility of a slow and painful death from infection that he'd insist on changing a completely unnecessary bandage five times a day.

If she were a man, she'd get rid of all the useless things in her life, but she wasn't. Only when the household settled into sleep and the demands stopped could she finally work. "I won't win the prize," she said loudly enough to cause the nearest flame to bob. She was a woman and her ideas were too different from what the Academy had already decided was the truth. But the Academy was wrong. Truth was the only thing that mattered, the only thing that wasn't a waste of time.

Luckily, Florent-Claude was home from his regiment for a while. He was a kind man, and a most tolerant husband. "I didn't understand a word of what you and Voltaire were arguing about at the forge," he had told her the other night, "but I was quite proud that you did." He'd ride to the nearest postal stop at Wassy himself and send her paper to Paris without Voltaire knowing. He'd already promised.

A crash in the courtyard brought her to her feet. The painters had arrived and she would need to discuss their progress in her bedroom. She wiped the pen and put it aside. "Two more days," she whispered. The paper was almost finished. She would send word to Voltaire that she was indisposed, take a short nap, and then add her last calculations to a clean copy of the text. After Florent-Claude sent it off in the post, she would do nothing but sleep for a week.

14

THE TREES in the courtyard of Delphine's wing of the Abbaye de Panthémont were a froth of white and pink, and the puffs of breeze sent petals drifting to the ground. "If any more get in your hair," Lili said, "you could wear them instead of a headdress in the church."

Delphine smiled dreamily. "I can't believe that before the last of these has fallen I'll be Ambroise's wife." They were sharing a bench, sitting close enough together for Delphine to reach over and take Lili's hand. "Thank you for coming," she said.

Lili gave her hand a squeeze. "Thank you for being here, so I had someplace to go."

"It hasn't been so bad, really," Delphine said. "When I first got here, I would not go any farther than this courtyard because I thought the sight of anything that reminded me of my boarding days might turn my hair white or give me as many wrinkles as some of the widows who come here to die." She looked around quickly to make sure no one had overheard. "And then, over time, I started to take walks, and eventually I found I could look at the buildings and not have all the memories be bad." She smiled. "At least the ones that have you in them."

Lili stood up and loosened her shoulders with a long, deliberate shrug. "It's really quite a pleasant place to live, at least here on this wing, if you have to be alone." She tried to smile. "I'd definitely prefer it to marrying Monsieur de Barras."

Delphine's face clouded. "I hope you don't end up alone. But I pray every night I never have to go visit you at that simpering little rodent's house."

"My, my!" Lili said, smiling at Delphine. "If your face gets stuck that way, white hair will be the least of your troubles."

"You're going to find someone, Lili," Delphine said. "I know you are. Just don't marry because you feel you have to and then find that person a few months later." Her face clouded. "You know something Ambroise told me? At Versailles, just before they came in to say the dauphin had died, Anne-Mathilde suggested to him that once they'd made such an advantageous marriage, she wouldn't care if he kept me as a mistress. That's when he knew for sure he would never marry her."

"She told him that?"

"He said she was desperate to make the marriage happen, after everyone had talked about it so much." Delphine brushed away a petal that had settled on her brow. "I suppose I should feel triumphant, but I just feel sick when I think about it."

A cloud crossed the sun, darkening the courtyard and causing the temperature to drop. "Look," Delphine said. "Even the heavens object."

"I think they object to many things," Lili said. "Now that I'm here with you and can clear my head, I'm astonished to see what a sheep I've been. Even though I said I would never marry Barras, I don't know how much longer I could have held out with the two of them pressing me the way they were."

Lili picked a sprig of flowers and tucked it in her unlaced bodice. "No corset," she said. "Just me, and springtime. It's wonderful." The sun came out again, lighting Delphine's hair in a halo of reddish gold. "You look so happy."

"I am," Delphine replied. "I'm getting all I ever wanted." She took a deep breath and let it out slowly. "Except that Maman isn't with us." Her eyes glistened. "I miss her terribly."

"I do too," Lili said, "but sometimes I think she's here. Sometimes I think both my mothers are. I get waves of thought from nowhere, and I think it's them, tapping me on the shoulder, telling me not to forget who I am, not to let anyone else have any part of me I don't want to give."

Corinne came through the door. "I beg your pardon, mesdemoiselles, but your dinner is ready, and this letter just arrived."

Lili and Delphine exchanged looks. "Who is it from?" Delphine asked.

"I don't know. There's no address. It was brought by a messenger, and he's already gone."

Delphine reached out her hand. "I suppose we'd better see it right away," she said, breaking the seal of the envelope. She read a few lines and smiled. "It's really for you." She handed it to Lili. "From the Comte de Buffon."

"'Esteemed Mademoiselle de Bercy,'" Lili read aloud. "'I write because I have heard that Mademoiselle du Châtelet is no longer at Hôtel Lomont. I hope that this may be a sign that an unpleasant spell of silence has been broken and that I may again communicate with her.'"

Lili looked up. "Well, it's not exactly like breaking Sleeping Beauty's spell, but good enough!"

"'Would you please inform her, if indeed she is there, that I believe she was right about the ethanol dissolving something essential to the outer surface of the organisms we observed. I hope that she will be able to correspond with me about this and other research while she is in residence at the abbey. I will send some papers once you have confirmed they will be favorably received.'"

"Isn't that just like him to talk about those squirmy little things before anything else?" Delphine said with a laugh. "Let's invite him to come for a visit!"

Lili shook her head. "Listen to what he says next. 'I have been told that the abbess is in sympathy with Baronne Lomont over what they feel is unacceptable behavior by Mademoiselle du Châtelet, and I believe it would make things worse if we attempted a meeting either here or there. Until the situation is more agreeable, I remain, at a distance, your devoted friend, Georges-Louis Leclerc, Comte de Buffon.'"

Lili waved the letter in her hand. "And then he adds, 'Please note that I have enclosed something that came from the Falkland Islands for Mademoiselle du Châtelet.'"

Inside the sheet of paper forming an envelope around the letter was another sheet, folded in quarters. Inside was a pressed, dried flower, its bright yellow center surrounded by six overlapping white petals. Drawn as if by a paintbrush from the center to the edge of each petal were three delicate lines in a purple tinged with green. On the paper protecting it, Jean-Étienne had written a note.

"'The hand of God seems to paint flowers here as well,'" Lili read. " 'This one, called a pale maiden, is quite common on the islands, growing in the heath from the coast up into the hills. I thought you would like to know that I think of you when I see it, for I recall you had a dress in just these colors.'"

Delphine danced around the courtyard with delight. "He can't stop thinking of you!" she said. Lili folded the note gently around the flower. *Could that be true?* she wondered as she put it back inside the count's letter. *Even if it is, does it matter?*

"Why the long face?" Delphine asked. "There's nothing but good on such a beautiful day. He's going to sail home with a clear head about his future, and we have two of your favorites—new peas and crevettes—for dinner." She took Lili's arm. "Shall we go in?"

Esteemed Comte de Buffon,

I cannot begin to tell you what a joy it was to receive the letter you sent to Mademoiselle de Bercy here at the Abbaye de Panthémont. I had been in the most terrible despair over my loss of contact with you. I feel safe here for now, but I do not know what methods Baronne Lomont may have to bring me back, and your warning about the abbess makes me think staying here may be more difficult than I thought.

Delphine's apartment was bathed in the dusty light of late afternoon as Corinne and the cook finished their work and stole quietly out for their after-dinner rest. Delphine had fallen asleep on a daybed, with swatches of fabric for her wedding dress strewn over her lap.

I do believe it is within the rights of a young woman of nearly eighteen to visit a sister who is about to be married, without needing permission she is certain will be cruelly and unfairly denied. But the most hopeful aspect of my situation is that Monsieur Clément de Feuillet has agreed to rent out his home in Paris and live with Delphine at Hôtel Bercy after their wedding. He has made it quite clear that I am welcome to return to my own quarters and live indefinitely with them. There can certainly be no grounds for objection to a husband and wife offering safe haven to a maiden relative, and I shall be able to return to life almost as before.

Almost, of course, because our beloved Maman will not be there. Still, Delphine's great happiness will, I am sure, be some consolation. Perhaps we shall from time to time invite guests to a salon in our mother's honor, and I can again listen to you defend my poor arguments against the learned men who so adored her.

Lili paused to dip her quill.

Of course it would not be the same without our beloved Jean-Étienne, and I hope you will share news from the Falklands the next time you write. I presume he is still engaged to be married.

Lili stopped for a moment. "Why did you spoil the page by writing that?" she muttered, tearing the letter in half with a loud rip. She wrote on a new piece of paper:

My dear Buffon.

    I am indeed with Delphine at the Abbaye de Panthémont, but will be here only several more weeks, since she will be coming back to Paris for her wedding. Please send whatever papers you have. I am most eager to use my mind, as it has been sorely neglected the last few months.

Your devoted friend,
Stanislas-Adélaïde du Châtelet.

    She picked up the pen again.

    I forgot to mention that I am enclosing a lovely pen sketch Delphine made for you of the blossoms on the trees in her courtyard. You will see she continues to perfect the observational skills we all so admire.

    She thought for a moment before adding a second signature. Lili. The way she would sign to a beloved father.

    Lili picked up the sketch and folded it inside her letter. Then before sealing it, she took one blossom from the sprig that was still protruding from her bodice and tucked it, like a talisman, between the sheets of paper. "This is for Jean-Étienne," she whispered. "Even if he never sees it."

LILI EXTENDED HER hand through the carriage door to help a trembling Delphine mount the step. Once inside, Delphine sat with excruciating delicacy to avoid uncentering her panniers and disturbing the luxurious silk petticoats under her skirt. Since she was still in half-mourning, she wore the traditional white, with a watered-silk bodice shot with gold and trimmed with ivory lace at the cuffs and neck. The cut was modest, and the slightly visible mounds of her breasts glowed under a dusting of powder. Her skirt was the same white, with gold embroidery on the tops of the panniers, and her velvet slippers and hat had been made to match. A hairdresser and tailor had come shortly after dawn to spend the better part of the day sewing Delphine into her outfit and arranging her hair in the latest style.

The sun was reaching its apex in the May sky as Lili and Delphine set out for Hôtel Bercy. "I hope we don't keep them waiting too long," Delphine said. "I so want everything to be perfect."

"It will be," Lili said. "I know it will." Except, of course, for the one thing that needed no reminder. Delphine's wedding day had arrived, and Maman would not be there.

"It just doesn't feel right," Delphine said, dabbing at her eyes with a handkerchief.

"Please don't cry," Lili said. "Maman wouldn't want you to, and you'll spoil how pretty you look."

Delphine bit her lip. "We should just pretend she's here, perhaps. Maybe that will help it be less sad."

Lili sat back in surprise. "Sad? You've dreamed of this since I told you fairy tales in bed!"

Delphine's cheeks were drained of their color. "I don't know what I think. Right now I think I'm mostly scared."

Lili reached over to touch Delphine's fingers. "Of what?"

Delphine grabbed Lili's hand, wringing it without noticing. "Of everything. Of being a good wife. Of—" She gave Lili a terrified look. "Do you think it hurts? I've heard there's a lot of blood the first time."

"I don't know. It seems as if everyone recovers—"

Delphine didn't hear. "And then there's having babies. I heard it makes even the bravest women scream. And I'm not very brave. Not at all like you!"

"I'm not brave!"

"Oh yes you are! You stood up to Baronne Lomont. You published your stories and didn't care what anyone said. You make everybody love you for your mind. Monsieur Diderot, the Comte de Buffon . . ."

"But not Jean-Étienne," Lili said. "Apparently I had very little effect on him."

"Well, he may be good at medical kinds of things, but he's a fool when it comes to—when it comes to what his heart says."

"Not everyone can be as fortunate as you," Lili said, hearing the tightness in her voice.

"Maman should be here," Delphine said, turning to look out the window to avoid Lili's eyes.

"She'd certainly be more help with—with the things you're wondering about," Lili said with a wan laugh that died in her throat.

Delphine looked at Lili quizzically. "Do you ever wonder what that song Monsieur Philidor wrote for her was about? Do you think they were . . . ? I can't even say it!"

"Lovers?" *The chess game in the parlor, the visit at the opera, the music at the funeral*. "He adored Maman," Lili replied. "Do you think she might have loved him too?"

"No. It's just too strange. But it's sad to think she might have been lonely without Papa. I don't like that either."

"We would have known," Lili said. "Wouldn't we?"

They stared at each other until Lili broke the silence. "The truth is, we might not have known very much about Maman at all."

"And now it's too late to ask, so we never will." Delphine took out her handkerchief again.

"And what if we had? What if we'd said, 'Maman, are you—you know—with Monsieur Philidor?' If she were in this carriage right now, do you think she would tell us something she didn't want us to know?"

"I suppose not," Delphine said. "But if she took a lover—it can't hurt that much, don't you think?"

Something about the sweet hope in Delphine's voice made Lili's heart flood with memories. "It's not like those saint stories we used to have to read," she said. "All that violence and resistance. You're going to spend your life with a man who loves you, and I think you'll get used to everything, and maybe even grow to like things you're afraid of now."

A man who loves you. Visions of Jean-Étienne chattering about science as they went back and forth from the Jardin de Roi merged with another of him at the microscope, another with the monkey on his shoulder, and another of when they first met at Maman's salon. *"I'm the nephew,"* he had said. *"I hope you're not too disappointed."*

"I think it must be quite wonderful to love someone so much you want to be as close to him as you possibly can," Lili said. Knowing from the twinge in her jaw that she would not be able to stop the onset of tears, she looked out the window. "We're almost there."

Delphine sat up straight. "Have I made a mess of myself?"

Lili smiled. "You've made a splendid success of yourself."

"You know that's not what I meant! Are my eyes red?"

"Your eyes are shining. And I can't wait to see his when he sees you."

The carriage made the familiar turn into the courtyard and Lili heard the voices of the household staff come out to greet them. "I love you, Delphine," she blurted out. It was not a sentiment to which they often gave words.

"I love you too," Delphine whispered.

"I wish I could ask the driver to go around the block one more time, so this part of our life wouldn't be over quite yet," Lili said, "but what's waiting for you is even better." The footman opened the door before Delphine could respond, and she was lost in the flurry of servants welcoming her home.

Hôtel Bercy is all hers now, Lili thought as she watched Delphine being ushered inside. *And today, my heart, forget yourself and be nothing but happy for her.*

"Mademoiselle Lili?" The familiar voice was Corinne's. "Aren't you coming in?"

"Of course," Lili said. "I just wanted to wait for a moment, so I wouldn't get in the way."

Corinne gave her a quizzical look. "Does mademoiselle need something for her eyes?"

Lili accepted a starched and pressed handkerchief from

Corinne's apron pocket. "It looks as if I do," she said, dabbing away tears as she walked into the house.

LILI AND DELPHINE waited in the music room to be called in by the notary. Too nervous to sit, they paced the floor, stopping from time to time to look out the windows at nothing in particular. Delphine had changed from the hat she had worn in the carriage into the traditional fragile headdress of lace streamers and orange blossoms that symbolized a bride's virginity.

"What is taking so long?" Delphine whined. "I think I'll just dissolve right here if they don't hurry up."

"Ambroise has to go through the papers with the lawyers. Make sure everything is in order before he signs."

"Do I have to do that too? My eyes feel like they're spinning in circles."

"I don't think women read it themselves. Their father decides it's all right, or in this case, your lawyer does, and then you sign."

"Well, I suppose I should be upset they don't consult me, but right now I don't care. Just let me come in and get it over with. Please!"

A loud burst of jovial conversation came from the parlor at the far end of the hall. "I hear Ambroise's voice!" Delphine said. "Do you think he sounds happy?"

"I imagine he's as unhappy as you are about having to wait. Stop scratching your neck!"

"This sugar pomade on my curls itches!" Delphine lifted her hair. "Or maybe it's the orange blossoms. Have I made myself all ugly and red?"

"No, but I'll tie your hands behind your back if you don't stop."

"I wish it were over, that's all." Delphine heard the familiar creak of a floorboard in the passageway and grabbed Lili's arm.

"Mademoiselle de Bercy?" The notary stood in the doorway. "Are you ready to come in?"

* * *

THE PARLOR WHERE Maman's salon had once been held was cleaned and polished to a glow, and large sprays of orange blossoms adorned the sideboards. The furniture had been rearranged temporarily to create an empty space in the center of the room, around a desk that had been moved there for the occasion. A document on thick vellum was laid out on the otherwise bare surface, next to a crystal inkwell and a beautifully shaped quill Lili recognized as having belonged to Maman.

Ambroise came to Delphine's side, and Lili released her hold on Delphine's elbow. He turned to the small group of assembled guests. "Aren't I the luckiest of men?" Lili looked around as a murmur of assent filled the room. The Comte and Comtesse d'Étoges were there, as well as Delphine's invited guests, Baronne Lomont and the Comte de Buffon.

Delphine took a seat at the desk. "What do I do?" she asked.

"Sign here," the notary said, pointing to a blank space. "And be careful with the pen. I've seen more than one bride forget to tap the quill and end up dripping ink."

Delphine smiled at him. "Thank you," she said in a breathy voice so sweet and kind that Lili thought for a moment Maman had suddenly materialized in the room. And then, with a confident flourish, Delphine wrote her name.

The Comte d'Étoges went to a sideboard as the group applauded. "A toast to Monsieur and Madame Clément de Feuillet," he said, lifting a bottle of wine.

Delphine by then had risen and accepted a delicate kiss on the cheek from Ambroise. "Does this mean we're married?"

"I think so," he replied, looking to the notary.

Seeing the man nod, Delphine turned around to look for Lili. "I'm married," she said, bursting into tears as she bent toward her as far as her massive panniers allowed.

"My fairy-tale princess," Lili murmured into her ear. "You made your dream come true."

"And it will be your turn now," Delphine said, pulling back to look at her. Her face grew solemn as she bent in again toward Lili. "I promise," she whispered. "With all my heart. I swear I'll do everything I can to see you as happy as I am."

THE FOLLOWING EVENING, after the nuptial mass to sanctify the marriage and a dinner hosted by the Comte d'Étoges, a few of the guests went back to Hôtel Bercy to escort Delphine and Ambroise to their marriage bed. Since unmarried women were not included, Lili said her good-byes and went with the baroness back to Hôtel Lomont, where she would stay for another week to give the bride and groom a chance to be alone, before moving back to Hôtel Bercy herself.

Darkness had fallen by then, and they rode back in silence. "You do realize that you cannot stay at Hôtel Bercy forever," Baronne Lomont said. "It's acceptable for now, but what about when they go to Château d'Étoges, or travel abroad? You can't stay alone there as an unmarried woman, and you can't follow them around wherever they go. Or is that what you intend?"

"I hardly think that having a sister close at hand early in a marriage is a detriment, Baronne," Lili said into the darkness. "I imagine she will be glad for someone to talk to, someone who doesn't have her own husband or household to concern herself with."

Baronne Lomont sniffed in disapproval. "I could have expected as much, I suppose, trying to make excuses sound like virtues."

"If you mean my refusal to marry, I intend to wait only as long as it takes to find someone I believe will support my interests."

"And what might those be? Did your visits with the Comte de Buffon make you imagine yourself a scientist? Or perhaps you fancy yourself a novelist, with your scribbling." Though she could not see the baroness's face in the shadows, Lili imagined her lip curling with scorn.

"I don't want to fight with you, Baronne Lomont," she said, feeling a sudden wave of exhaustion, "but that seems to be all we do."

Baronne Lomont was silent for a moment. "We will stop fighting, Stanislas-Adélaïde, when you accept your destiny."

Lili sat up, feeling the hair rise on her arms. "Tell her she knows nothing about your destiny," the air around her seemed to be saying.

I'm still afraid of her, Lili argued back.

"Don't be!"

Lili took a deep breath, but as she exhaled, she lost her nerve to speak. After all, what did she know about her destiny, except what she hoped it wasn't? She took in a second deep breath.

"You're as strong as you need to be," the air commanded, and the words spilled out.

"I'm an author," she said. "That's what I intend to do with my life. And I hope to pursue science as well."

"An author?" The baroness's voice curled up with astonishment.

"I'm not just amusing myself with my writing. I'm destined to do it," Lili said, surprised at the strength in her voice and wishing she were as convinced as she was pretending to be. "Your low opinion of the story you found is not shared. I have been published in the *Gazette d'Amsterdam*. Perhaps you have heard of Monsieur Tellechat?"

"I don't read such drivel!"

"I am Tellechat," Lili went on. "Monsieur Diderot tells me I am all the rage." It wasn't exactly true, but the baroness would not know otherwise.

"Monsieur Diderot?" The baroness was aghast. "I should have known nothing good would come of growing up in a house with a salon."

Lili ignored her. "I have copies, if you'd like to see. I've hidden them from you because you made it necessary to be deceitful. I've also hidden a supply of ink and paper Delphine bought for me after you refused to let me have more."

They had turned onto a lamplit thoroughfare, and a shaft of light came through the window, illuminating the baroness's face. Her dark hat and cloak left the rest of her in deep shadow, and the pale light could not reach all the crevices of her thin face, making her appear momentarily like a disembodied skull floating in midair. Lili's heart skipped a beat at what seemed like an evil apparition from a fairy tale.

I've had enough of your poison, she thought. *And you have no more power over me than I allow.*

The light faded and the coach was again in shadows. "I will marry someone who suits me when I believe the time is right," Lili said. "And I'm not discussing it again."

"Is that so?" The inflection of the baroness's voice sounded oddly musical, as if something had just given her immense delight. "I'd like you to come with me into my study when we get home," she said. "I have something to show you that I believe will put an end to this rebelliousness once and for all."

THE LETTER WITH its broken seal was the sole object on the table next to Baronne Lomont's favorite chair. She picked it up and turned to Lili. "Sit down, Mademoiselle du Châtelet."

The formality of that name was unnerving, but Lili pressed her feet into the carpet to remind herself to stand strong. "I would prefer to stay where I am," she said in a clipped voice. "It's been a long two days seeing Delphine married, and I'd like to go to bed as soon as you've shown me whatever it is you want me to see."

"As you wish," the baroness said with a hint of a smirk, handing her the letter. "It's from the Marquis du Châtelet."

"A letter from my father?" Lili's heart pounded as she opened the tightly folded single page.

My Dear and Esteemed Sister-in-Law,

I received your letter inquiring as to my wishes in regard to Stanislas-Adélaïde after the regrettable death of Madame de Bercy. I do not wish to be involved in the search for a suitable husband, and I leave it to you to arrange for her marriage, which I agree should take place as soon as possible.

I have sent to my lawyer by separate post the document you asked me to sign, and you should by now have the legal authority to make

such decisions on my behalf. Please be advised that in the negotiations
attendant to marriage, you should not represent that there will be a
dowry from me, since I do not plan to add anything beyond the
stipend she presently receives from the rents on one of my properties.

Lili stared at his unfamiliar signature, penned with a flourish below the text. "So you see," the baroness was saying. "I have put an end to your foolishness, just as I said."

Lili stared at the words swimming on the page in front of her. "Does this mean I must marry Monsieur de Barras?" she said, feeling life flowing out of her as surely as if the letter had cut a mortal wound in her flesh.

The baroness sniffed. "Monsieur de Barras tired of you during your absence at the abbey, and he is betrothed to another. I have two suitable husbands in mind, but neither has anywhere near the same fortune—regrettable for you, but entirely your fault. They are *noblesse d'épée*, however, and that will help your situation."

I am doomed, Lili thought, wishing she could simply refuse to breathe again and die right there in the baroness's parlor.

"I have agreed to let you move to Hôtel Bercy because I am too old at this point for the burden of having you live with me. However, I will permit this only so long as you give me your word before God that you will accept the first suitable offer of marriage you receive."

Lili's heart had been pounding when she read the letter, but now, much like that of a mouse she'd once seen squeezed to death by a snake in Buffon's laboratory, it slowed until she was not sure it was beating at all. "Apparently I have no choice. I will have to do as you wish."

"Before *God*, Stanislas-Adélaïde," the baroness reminded her. "Give your word before God."

Lili's knees shook. *How will I ever get out of this now?* she wondered. "You have my word before God," she replied.

Emilie
1738

"Toss it higher, *mon chéri*—and as hard as you can this time." Emilie watched her eleven-year-old son cock his arm back and throw a ball into the cloudless afternoon sky. "Watch it come down and tell me what you observe."

Florent-Louis shielded his eyes and watched the ball's motion until it landed farther down the lawn at Cirey. He ran over to where Emilie sat under a tree. "You're right, Maman," he said. "The arc as it comes down is the mirror image of how it went up." Emilie opened the notebook on her lap. "Now if you throw it just as hard, but higher"—she drew one arc and superimposed a steeper one—"it will still come back down the same way."

"Why, Maman?"

"Because that's the nature of an object set in motion against a force of gravity too strong to resist. You can use Newton's and Leibniz's calculus to determine the exact trajectory any ball would follow. A cannonball going up like this"—she drew a curved line—"would come down like this." She drew another arc. "Or, if you aimed the cannon higher, it might come down like this. You can use the calculus to know the exact path."

"But why does it matter, Maman?"

Emilie smiled. "It will certainly matter when your regiment is aiming its cannons at the enemy—and more so when they are aiming theirs at you!" They both laughed, but Emilie quickly grew serious again.

"It matters, because the Creator examined all the ways things could possibly be before settling on the way that worked most harmoniously. 'I'll have gravity be just this strong and no stronger,' he said, and 'I'll make objects able to travel this fast and no faster.' Once he set it all in motion, everything followed, not just here, but everywhere in the universe. If gravity were different on another planet, the calculus for this arc would still hold."

She retraced with her finger what she had drawn. "The symmetry is beautiful, isn't it?" she asked, giving her son's hair a gentle tug. "Science is really the purest form of beauty, Florent-Louis. Through study, we can come to see God's hand, and I for one want to do that."

It was difficult having chosen to educate Florent-Louis herself, but his latest tutor, Monsieur Linant, had been so incompetent and self-serving that she had been forced to fire him, and she was not going to get another if he would waste the child's time with the same indefensible prattle. She had wanted to slap Linant when she overheard him tell Florent-Louis that some things in God's creation were better left as mysteries, as a sign of respect. Nonsense! God wanted to be known. That was why he had ordained the human mind.

"So what we observe with your ball," she went on, "is the effect of these laws. The force of gravity is exactly what it is, so the velocity with which you threw the ball made it go as high as it did and no higher, and that caused the ball's path to be shaped precisely as it was, because no other path was possible."

"God made it all happen," Florent-Louis said with a solemn nod.

"Yes, *mon chéri*, but not in the way many people think. He did it through math. Through physics. When God said, 'Let there be light,' he meant let there be a source of energy to warm and illuminate the world, and let it be neither too far away nor too close, and let the earth circle around it, and let the movements of the sun and earth create day and night, and the seasons of the year."

She looked up through the branches of the tree. "There's a bird's nest up there. If you follow one thing to another, you see how the birds and the nest came to be only because God said 'Let there be light.' God is the Great Mathematician and if you want to find him, look in the arc of a thrown ball. Look anywhere in his universe. Look particularly hard at things you don't understand, for that's where he hides, waiting for us to come looking for him."

She could see his attention was waning. "I brought something for you," she said, producing a glass vial and a long, thin tube open at both ends.

"What is it?"

Emilie pulled out the stopper in the vial and dipped one end of the tube into it. Holding the other end to her lips, she blew out an iridescent sphere that went wobbling off into the air before it burst.

Florent-Louis's eyes grew wide. "How did you do that?"

She laughed. "It's just one of the properties of soap. Would you like to try?" Florent-Louis took the tube and the vial. "See how the light doesn't have visible colors either inside the bubble or outside but only on its surface?" she asked. "It breaks apart there, and then comes back together inside."

Florent-Louis was blowing one bubble after another, half listening. Emilie smiled. "Run along," she said, watching him dance across the grass, sending skyward one bubble after another, as she walked back to the house.

What was God's plan? That was what she cared about. She didn't want to look only at the products of it. She wanted to see his hand move, wanted to hear what words he spoke to make a universe that functioned as one whole. Could it be reduced to two or three great principles working together, or perhaps even a single one from which everything derived? In the book she had started while waiting for the results of the Academy competition, she would do her best to show the foundations of God's world, as she understood them. She'd work on what she had decided to call "The Institutes of Physics" until the book was good enough to be published, good enough to be her message to the world.

Inside the house, two letters from Paris, one for Voltaire and one for her, lay on a tray. She examined the seal on her own. The Academy of Science! "We understand that, despite the anonymous nature of the submission, you are the author of a paper submitted to the Academy for its annual competition," it read. "We are pleased to inform you that it has received an honorable mention.

"We found your ideas promising enough that we are taking the unusual step of publishing your paper in addition to the three winning entries, so it may receive the attention it deserves and begin the discussion it will most surely generate. By separate letter we are sending Monsieur Voltaire his results as well. His work received the same special commendation as your own, coming as it does, most unusually, from a man of letters. The Academy wishes to encourage the pursuit of science by all those inclined to it. However, since there are some notable errors in his data and concerns about the validity of his conclusions, we have told him if he wishes to publish it he must do so on his own."

Emilie held the letter to her chest. "I won!" she whispered. That was what the Academy was really telling her. If she weren't a woman, she would have won.

"What did you say?" Voltaire came to the door, dressed for a walk. Emilie's hand trembled as she gave him his letter.

He scanned the terse message on the single sheet. "Honorable mention?" he sniffed. "Well, I suppose it's a good start." He looked at Emilie. "What's wrong?"

"Nothing," she said, handing him her own letter. Voltaire's face grew scarlet as he took in the meaning. "You submitted your own paper without telling me?" Emilie's heart pounded with fear as he tapped his finger on the words. "And it's being published?"

Then, unexpectedly, he laughed. "Well, this could be quite good!" he announced. "Cirey just became the most famous laboratory in France. People will beg for an invitation to visit. I'll buy more instruments and every book on physics that's ever been published." He danced a circle around her. "Just wait and see. In two years I'll be one of the most celebrated scientists in Europe!"

Emilie's heart sank. Hadn't he read the letter? Didn't he under-stand the greater honor had gone to her? Voltaire saw her stricken face. "Of course I'll never forget to point out how intelligent you are," he said, "and don't worry—I'll always say I wouldn't have achieved nearly as much without you."

15

1767

SUNLIGHT POURED through the windows onto the yellow walls of the music room at Hôtel Bercy. Delphine sat on a fauteuil next to Lili while a new dog, a bichon frise like the one they had when they were little girls, sat between them on the carpet.

Lili watched as the little creature tugged the lace on Delphine's slipper to get her attention. "Remember Tintin, how he would take over the whole bed while we played with each other's hair?"

"And you'd tell me stories," Delphine added.

Lili gave Delphine a fleeting smile. "About dresses. Lots of them for Princess Delphine."

Delphine sighed wistfully. "I used to think princesses went around—well, just being princesses." She thought for a moment. "Marriage makes me appreciate Maman. She seemed to do everything so effortlessly, but being the lady of the house is more work than I thought."

Lili barely heard. "I wonder which one she would tell me to marry."

"You wouldn't be forced to marry anyone, not even the King of France," Delphine retorted.

In the three months since the marquis's letter giving Baronne Lomont permission to see to Lili's marriage, several men had approached Baronne Lomont to express interest. One was from an impoverished family with excellent ancestry, *noblesse d'épée* on both sides. He was thirty, a good age for an aristocratic marriage. Lili would be distressingly poor, the baroness pointed out, but her children could hope to do better, because they would bear his name. Though he was reasonably attractive in appearance, simple-minded jokes caused him to laugh until he passed gas or gave himself the hiccups. Lili and the baroness visited the home where he lived with his mother, and when Lili wandered into the library, she had been amazed to find it nearly empty of books.

"But he has a regiment," Delphine offered as consolation. "That means he'd be gone a lot. You could take over the library for yourself and buy all the books you want with your stipend."

"And talk about them with whom?" Lili raised her eyebrows. "He doesn't seem to have a brain at all." Lili stood up and walked nowhere in particular before returning to sit down in the same spot. "I just don't want to hate my life," she said. "I wonder how many women dread having their husbands at home."

"Probably quite a few," Delphine said. "I'm fortunate not to be one of them—although Ambroise will soon be among those not at home, I'm afraid, since he's required at Étoges soon. I'm supposed to go with him, but I'm so nauseous all the time." She stood up and touched her stomach lightly with her fingertips. "It's supposed to pass in the next few weeks, but for now, the idea of an endless coach trip on those bumpy roads is just unbearable."

Lili smiled. "In a few months you'll be round as a ball. And by— when, March?—you'll have a baby. It's just so hard to believe."

Delphine looked at her dreamily. "If it's a girl her name will have to be Julie. And what do you think of Jules for a boy?"

"I don't think I've ever known anyone by that name," Lili said. "Maybe that's good. It hasn't been ruined by someone awful." Her smile faded. "All right, we've decided I can't marry Charles Laroche, so I guess that leaves Édouard de Rabutin."

Delphine made a sour face. "That's enough to make me throw up again right now. Just the thought of having to kiss that—that lizard." Seeing Lili's stricken face, she went back to the bed and sat down next to her. "I'm sorry," she said. "I forgot you might have to."

"Maybe he'll turn into a prince." Lili tried to smile. "I told Baronne Lomont I needed another month to decide, and she's told me that's all I have. She says if these two offers slip away due to my stalling, she'll arrange to have me committed to the Abbaye de Panthémont."

"That wouldn't be so bad, would it, compared to marrying either of them?"

Lili grimaced. "She'd have me living in poverty on the nun's end, just to punish me. I can't be forced to take vows, but I'd have to live as if I had, not in the nice wing where you were. The baroness said commital is the only thing left to do when a family decides a girl is incorrigible." Her voice trembled, and she looked down at her hands to try to force herself not to cry. "She keeps reminding me I made a promise before God, and it makes me feel so—so obligated."

"Nonsense!" Delphine retorted. "Did you ever ask God if he accepted your promise? Maybe he was waving his hands telling you to say no, or maybe he covered his ears at just that moment and didn't hear you."

Lili smiled. "I suppose you could be right. Maybe a promise before God really is no different from any other. After all, I didn't exactly give my word to God himself, just to another person, and there are good reasons to break promises sometimes." Her voice drifted off. "I just wish I could be sure it wasn't wrong this time."

"Of course it's not! We simply aren't going to have you marry either of them, promise or no promise!" Delphine's eyes flashed but her brow quickly furrowed. "But what are we going to do?"

"I don't know." Lili's words barely came out.

"You sound just like I did when I thought Ambroise was going to marry Anne-Mathilde, and I flopped around like a limp old petticoat about it." Delphine picked up the dog and nuzzled its soft coat. "You wouldn't let me get away with it, remember? And I am going to do the same for you."

Delphine stared so intently at the white moldings on the music room walls, it seemed as if she might be expecting a secret message to materialize in their frostinglike designs. "Have you ever considered trying to talk to your father yourself? If he won't come to you, perhaps you could go to him."

"How would I know if he's even in Paris?"

"That's easy enough to find out. I'll ask Ambroise to inquire."

"And if he's not?"

"Well," Delphine said, "I think you'll just have to go and pay him a visit at Cirey."

"Of course!" Lili said. "I'll just ask the baroness if I can borrow her coach. Or maybe ride there on Comète."

"No—I mean it!" Delphine put the dog back on the carpet. "Baronne Lomont wouldn't have to know. We'll all go together to Étoges, or at least that's what she'll think. You'll say good-bye to her and tell her you're going to decide on a husband at Étoges and be back in a month. We'll put you on a coach for Cirey and go on to Étoges ourselves."

"But you're having a baby! You just said you couldn't bear the trip."

"I don't care if I throw up along the entire road from here to there," Delphine said. "I said on my wedding day that it was your turn to be happy, and as long as there's one thing left in my power, you're not going to marry someone who would—" Her eyes filled with tears. "Who would destroy the person I love most in the whole world."

LILI'S COACH LEFT the station in the Rue du Braque shortly after dawn the following Saturday. For three days, as the coach continued eastward, the towns had gotten smaller and the estates dotting the countryside became increasingly modest. Late on the third day, Lili stepped down in the tiny village of Bar-sur-Aube and watched as the coach made its way out of the sleepy village in Champagne and disappeared down the road toward Geneva.

"How far is Cirey from here, I wonder?" she asked aloud, although the valet and maid sent with her from Hôtel Bercy were as much strangers to the place as she was. *No need to worry,* she told herself. Ambroise had been a willing conspirator, outlining exactly what Lili was to do when she arrived. "Take a room for the night," he told her, "and use my family's title. Pretend to be married, and have the valet make it known in the town that Madame d'Étoges has arrived from Paris."

Ambroise had written to a friend who lived not too far from Cirey, asking him to send a carriage and driver to Bar-sur-Aube to meet her. The plan left a great deal to chance, and Delphine was so fretful that she had been unable to sit down for more than a few minutes without jumping up to pace the floor. What if his friend was away and couldn't help? What if the letter was lost? What if something terrible happened to Lili on the way?

"Quite frankly," Lili had told Delphine, "getting my throat slit by a bandit would be preferable to marrying anyone Baronne Lomont chose for me." There hadn't been any bandits, or breakdowns, or depraved fellow passengers, as Delphine had imagined, only mile after mile of fields and poor roads. And now, here she was.

The Marquis du Châtelet had not been informed she was coming, for fear he would write to Baronne Lomont and ruin everything. No one at the château would pick Lili up, and she was to stay at an inn until someone came for her, or a letter arrived from Étoges telling her of a change in plans. If necessary, Ambroise would rescue her himself.

Stephane, the valet, arranged to have her trunk sent up to her room before going to see if there was a letter for Lili anywhere in town. They had not gotten off the coach since daybreak, but only when her maid, Justine, went upstairs to unpack what they would need for the night did Lili realize how hungry she was.

The inn was unlike any place she had been—a dark, timbered room with low ceilings and a large stone fireplace that gave off the sour smell of cold, blackened wood. A few people in tattered work clothes sat at a table talking with a man wiping the cups left behind by others. He put them on a shelf and came over to Lili.

"Would Madame like to sit over there," he asked, "so as not to be bothered?" He gestured to the far side of the room, and Lili followed him to a table. "Shall I bring you something to eat?" he asked as he lit a candle.

Before Lili could reply, he disappeared. A few minutes later he returned, holding a wedge of bread in the crook of a hairy arm, and carrying a bowl of stew large enough to require both hands. "Madame would like wine?" he asked, putting the bread down on the bare plank table. Taken aback at the casual arrival of her dinner while she was still expecting to hear what her choices were, Lili nodded without saying a word.

She picked up the spoon resting in the bowl. It was more like a ladle, almost as wide as her mouth and quite deep—nothing at all like the tiny consommé spoons at home. The aroma from the stew rose from the bowl, and when the man hurried off for her wine, she put her lips to the rim of the spoon and took a delicate sip. She shut her eyes, savoring the sweet, heady swirl of mutton, chervil, new onions, and carrots, before opening her mouth wide and taking in the entire spoonful. Still breaking down the tender meat with her tongue, she scooped up another spoonful, and then another, until she had polished off the entire bowl and mopped up the last bits with her remaining bread.

The innkeeper came over. "Was it to your liking, Madame?" He nodded toward the empty bowl. "Would you like a little more?" *You're behaving like a barnyard animal*, she could hear Baronne Lomont saying. *Slopping like a pig who's now grunting for more.*

She gave the man a happy grin. "Yes," she said. "*S'il vous plait*, another bowl."

STEPHANE CAME BACK just as Lili was finishing the last of her wine, with word that no one had inquired about her and no letter had arrived anywhere in the village. He went off to get a second room for himself, and feeling a sudden twinge of fear at being alone in a strange place, Lili got up from the table and hurried upstairs to her room.

The beams of the ceiling were so low she could reach up and touch them, but the bed was soft and inviting. After pouring water from a pitcher into a cracked porcelain bowl, she washed her hands slowly, thinking through her situation. She'd wait all day tomorrow, and if no one arrived, she would hire a driver the following day and go to Cirey on her own. *I haven't gone all this way just to sit in Bar-sur-l'Aube*, she told herself. *I'm going to see my father if I have to walk there and beat down his door.*

It was a long time until tomorrow. She pulled out her traveling case and opened the small vial of ink. Dipping her quill, she began to write.

The tower atop the Carpathian Mountains loomed high over the snowcapped peaks spread out below. Through a small window at the top, Meadowlark heard the sighs of a young maiden.

"What are you doing up there?" she called up.

"I've been imprisoned by my parents because I won't obey them."

Lili wrote furiously until her quill was dull and she was too exhausted to sharpen it. Heaving a deep sigh, she crawled into bed.

The following morning Lili woke up to the sound of voices. She went to her window and looked down at what had yesterday been a sleepy town square but was now filled with the cries of farmers and craftspeople hawking their wares. Young laying hens and geese squawked, and piglets squealed in their pens. Baskets were piled high with apples and pears, and racks were strung so thickly with fragrant hops, they served as arbors to shade the sweating merchants from the sun.

"Best eggs you can buy," a man was saying. "Eggs from the hen-houses at Cirey!"

Cirey? Lili's heart leapt. She dashed over to the chair where Justine had laid out her dress to air and stepped back into it. She made a quick, fumbling attempt to lace the back by herself, then gave up and threw her traveling cloak over her shoulders to cover the loose dress. After a frantic struggle to pull on her shoes without stockings, she ran downstairs, barely noticing the odd sensation of the dress flopping at her sides.

Lili hurried in the direction of the voice. "Did you say you're from the Château de Cirey?" she asked a burly man who looked to be about forty.

He took off his hat. "From the village," he said. "We don't live in the house, if that's what you mean."

"How did you get here?" Lili asked.

The man shifted nervously at the odd question. "By cart. Begging your pardon, but how else? We bring our eggs and whatever we can spare from our garden. It's just a few beets this week, and some carrots." He glanced at Lili before looking away immediately, confused by the elite Parisian accent coming from someone with disheveled hair and the blur of sleep still in her eyes. "Is there something mademoiselle is concerned about?"

"I just wondered about the market. How it works. How everyone gets here."

"Well, I told you how." The man looked again at the people passing by. "Eggs!" he called out again. "Eggs from Cirey!"

"What time do you go home?" Lili asked.

"Midday. Earlier, if we've sold everything . . . Eggs from Cirey!"

Lili searched in her pockets and found several coins. "Listen," she said. "I need to go to the château and I have no way to get there. Take these now, and I'll give you more if you'll take me with you when you go home."

His face broadened into a smile. "And I told my wife it wasn't worth coming this week, with so little to sell. Come back in two hours. My cart's not fit for a lady such as yourself, but it will get you there all the same."

"Would you like to taste my fresh butter, mademoiselle?" A woman sitting on a stool near the man cut a thick slice of brown bread. "Made before daybreak this morning. Try it with my quince jam." After slathering both on top, she handed it to Lili.

The bread was dense and tangy, unlike any Lili had ever tasted. The butter tasted like clouds, and the tiny pieces of fruit floating in the jam exploded with flavor so intense that she momentarily forgot everything else. Licking her fingers greedily, she accepted another piece. Promising to return with money to buy more, she went back in the direction of the inn, carrying the glistening crust in front of her like a crown on a pillow, and wondering whether she had ever in her life experienced a moment of such pure joy.

The tavern keeper was already at work when she walked back in. "Do you know the date?" she asked him.

"Not offhand," he said, "but I can figure it out. It's market day, so it's Thursday." He consulted an almanac he pulled from a drawer. "Thursday, the third of September, 1767."

Lili grinned. *My birthday,* she thought. *I'm eighteen today. And my present is a ride to Cirey.*

THE TWO-HORSE CART made its way down the bumpy dirt road leading to Cirey. Next to Lili sat a stout woman in an apron and an old dress frayed at the cuffs and elbows. On her other side a man of nearly seventy, with a wizened face under a white beard, held the reins. In the back of the wagon, Stephane sat on a pile of straw with the man Lili had met at the market. Justine perched on top of an empty egg crate, holding the rail of the cart as the makeshift chair slid and rocked beneath her.

"Do you know the marquis?" Lili asked the old couple.

"Know him?" the woman said. "I worked for him most of my life. Him and madame, when she was alive."

Madame? Lili's heart jumped.

"I was a laundress until my fingers went bad." The woman held out two arthritic hands. "Spent washing day in the courtyard every week. Broke my back, with those vats and wringers and lines, especially when the house was full of company." She nodded in the direction of her husband. "He tended the barnyard at the château before the marquis took sick and didn't care anymore. Most of his hens died last year, so we keep him supplied with what few eggs he needs from our own henhouse. Master don't know the difference, God bless him."

"Hardly nobody at the house now," the old man said before falling silent again.

"Did you say that my—that the marquis is sick?" Lili asked. Until then her plan to visit her father was no more real than one of her stories. As talk of him continued, her stomach churned. She would have to deal with a real person, one she knew nothing about, and the prospect unnerved her more with each passing minute. *Could I walk back to Bar-sur-l'Aube?* she wondered. *Could I ask them to turn around? Tell them I've made a terrible mistake and I'll pay them for their trouble?*

I could let the wheels go around one more time and then tell him to stop, Lili thought each time the large wooden wheels came full circle. Eventually this calmed her. *I'm going to Cirey whether I'm ready or not,* she decided. *I'll figure things out when I get there.*

She pulled her attention back to what the woman was saying. "He's a good man. Not like some who treat you no better than clods of dirt in a field. Make you work for them day in and day out, leaving your own cows unmilked and birds eating the seed in your garden." She shook her head. "No, Monsieur le Marquis is a good man, God have mercy on him." She looked at Lili. "But I thought you'd know that, coming to visit him. I thought maybe things might be worse than we know."

It hadn't occurred to Lili she would need a story of her own. "I'm his niece," she said, doing a quick mental calculation before revising her story. "His grandniece actually. I just wanted to surprise him with a visit while he's ailing."

Neither of them said anything. *Of course they don't believe me,* Lili thought. Young noblewomen didn't show up alone in a strange town needing a ride from the first person they found with a cart, but tenants on an estate weren't going to ask questions. "Tell me about those days," she said. "I love hearing stories from before my time."

The old woman harrumphed. "That's a laugh," she said. "Most young people think the world wasn't created until they came out crying from the womb. Think no one but them knows anything at all."

"Tell me about Madame la Marquise." Lili tried to keep the insistence out of her voice. "I've heard she was quite unusual." She saw the old man smile, but he said nothing.

"Unusual isn't half of it," the woman said. "She was always up to some or another kind of crazy thing, dragging everybody into it."

"I thought she was some kind of vision," the man from the market volunteered from the back of the wagon. "Not like any woman I'd ever seen."

Lili turned to look at him as the cart bounced along the road. "I was just a boy—it's about thirty years ago now—when she lived here with Monsieur Voltaire, but it was one exciting thing after another," he said with a laugh. "Papa, do you remember when they set the forest on fire?"

"Damn near burnt everything to the ground," the old man said. "Made us all stand there with buckets, roasting alive." He thought for a moment. "Not as bad as the forge, though, where they melted things over and over again, and nobody got anything important done for a week."

"But you remember the theater, don't you?" the younger man asked. "I used to help put up playbills with their son, and sometimes I'd have a costume and get to stand onstage. I used to think it was better than any feast day, being up there in that attic while she sang."

Son. Lili rarely thought about the fact that her mother had a son. The baroness had made it clear the forty-year-old brother Lili had never met saw her as nothing more than a possible threat to some tiny share of his patrimony. Of her sister, all she knew was that her name was Gabrielle-Pauline, and that she had been given a good dowry, lived very far away, and hadn't written or visited anyone in Paris for more than twenty years. They seemed little more than distractions at the moment. *It's my father I came to find*, she reminded herself, *not a family it's too late to have*.

"She did have the most beautiful voice," the woman was saying. "Sang opera for hours without forgetting nothing. And she always invited everyone, not just her rich-folks company."

"Yelled a lot too," the old man said. "Especially at Monsieur Voltaire. And not in any language they speak around here."

The old woman thought for a moment. "Can't say I ever understood the situation, how he was living there, like he was the husband. Then when the marquis was home from his regiment, it was just the three of them, like old friends." She shook her head. "Don't know nobody who would have been as patient with it all as Monsieur le Marquis was."

"Well, the nobility's different, isn't they?" the man said. "They don't have our ways."

They fell silent again. "Was she pretty—the marquise?" Lili asked.

The old woman turned to her son. "What would you say, Anton? Was she pretty?"

"She always seemed so to me," the man from the market said. "But different. She didn't care as much about her hair or her makeup as the other ladies who visited, but she always wore her diamonds, even in the bathtub."

"How would you know what she wore in the bathtub?" his mother asked.

"Because I saw her once. I had an errand in the house and Longchamp asked me to help him bring some more hot water for her bath.

She told him to pour it right between her legs, and I saw a little more than I'd be willing to say, except now that so much time has passed, there's no one to care."

"Longchamp?" Lili asked.

"Monsieur Voltaire's manservant—Maman, you remember Sébastien Longchamp, don't you? He was always full of stories about how the marquise would pull off her chemise when she changed her clothes and expose—well, all her nature, I guess you could say— without caring who was there. Did the same with me in the theater, standing around with clothes you could look through as if no one had eyes to see with. 'We're all no more than a cup of bouillon on a sideboard to people like them,' Longchamp told me, and I suppose he should know, living in the house and all."

Small stone houses now lined the road, and up ahead, Lili saw a church steeple. "Is this Cirey?" she asked, but before anyone could answer, two dogs came rushing down the street, barking excitedly. A door opened and a boy of about ten came out, followed by a younger girl, holding the hand of another child around three years old.

"Papa!" they clamored. "Did you bring us anything?"

Anton jumped down from the cart. "Nothing today," he said with a slump of the shoulders. He laughed, seeing their crestfallen faces. "Except this!" He pulled out a cloth bag full of tiny candies he had bought with some of Lili's money. The children squealed with delight, nearly knocking the package to the ground as each tried to have the first fingers into the bag.

"Who is she?" the boy asked, noticing Lili.

"Guest of the marquis," Anton said, holding the reins. "Run there now and find someone who can bring a carriage for mademoiselle," he told him, before turning back to help Lili down. "We can't have the Marquis du Châtelet's niece arriving in a wagon, can we?"

"Maman! A lady's come to see us!" Anton's little daughter ran into the house in front of Lili. The smell of fresh milk permeated the air, and in the dim light seeping through the translucent panes of two small windows, Lili could see the contents of its single room. A straw mattress sagged inside a rough bed frame, opposite a soot-darkened fireplace on which hung a cooking pot. A cradle was pushed into one corner, near a butter churn. Anton's wife got up from a wooden bench at the family table, still holding a nursing infant to her breast.

"Please forgive me, mademoiselle, for not coming outside. My baby is ill and nurses so poorly, I couldn't disturb her." She came closer, and Lili saw an infant so emaciated it would have been impossible to guess its age. It lay limp in its mother's arms in a way that suggested not a contented sleep but exhaustion at the sheer effort of continuing to live.

By now the old woman next to Lili in the cart had also come in. She came over and peered in the baby's face. "Still with us," she said. She held out her crippled hands to take the baby and, cooing softly, put it in the cradle. She sat on a stool and rocked it gently with one foot while she contemplated Lili through the gloom.

"You must be from Madame the Marquise's side," Anton's wife said. "You look like her, especially from the side."

Lili's heart leapt. "My mother . . ." She struggled to remember the story she had told. "My mother was the Marquise du Châtelet's niece. Is the baby—"

"Sickly from birth," the grandmother said. "For reasons known to God."

The little girl knelt by the cradle and crossed herself solemnly, looking up to make sure that her grandmother had noticed.

"I suppose you must be hungry after that long ride," Anton's wife said. "Célie, bring the cheese from the larder."

The little girl scrambled to her feet. "Where are you from?" she asked when she returned to lay a small round of cheese on the table.

"I'm from Paris." Lili said.

"Is that near Bar-sur-l'Aube?" Célie asked. "I went there once." She glanced over at her mother, who was scooping butter into a bowl. "I saw a warf, didn't I, Maman?"

"You saw a dwarf, *ma chérie*," the woman said, and Lili felt a pang of sadness that there was no Maman to call her that anymore.

"Are you rich?" the little girl said. Her grandmother leaned forward and hissed at her to be quiet. The baby gave a tiny cry at the jostling. "Now look what you've done!" the old woman said.

Célie's face crumpled. "I just wanted to know."

Feeling like an eavesdropper on a family spat, Lili changed the subject. "Didn't the marquis have a daughter?"

"Didn't see her much," the grandmother said. "She was away at a convent in Joinville most of the time and then was married straight from there. To someone Italian maybe—do you remember, Lise?"

Her daughter shrugged. "A foreigner from somewhere."

"No, not her," Lili said. "The other one. The one she had just before—"

"Oh, that one. Don't rightly know," the old woman said. "I guess I just assumed she'd died, since we never saw her at Cirey."

"Did you know her name?"

"Can't say I did."

I'm less real to them than a cracked egg, Lili thought. *And probably little more to the man I've come so far to meet.*

The sound of horses' hooves and squeaky carriage wheels in the road outside gave her no time to nurse her bruised feelings. She heard the driver admonish the children to be careful around the horse. "I'd best be going right away," Lili said, surprised at the gloom in her voice.

"You've had nothing to eat!" the woman protested. "We can't have you going off saying we didn't feed you!"

"I'm quite fine, thank you," Lili said, doubting that even water could have made it past a throat suddenly paralyzed with apprehension.

Emilie

1738

LIGHT STREAMED in through the windows and reflected off the glowing wood and crimson wall paneling in the gallery of the Marquis du Châtelet's ancestral home at Cirey. The doors were open, and a slight breeze wafted up from the lawn and stream below. Songbirds whistled in gilded cages, while next to a lacquered desk strewn with papers and scientific tools Voltaire sat holding court. His throne was a small upholstered armchair, because with his frighteningly thin frame, Voltaire had ordered only furniture that did not make him look even smaller. Overweight guests complained about having not a single comfortable place to sit, but no note was taken of their whispered grumblings.

The owner of Cirey was one of those who could not sit comfortably in Voltaire's gallery. Though not corpulent, the marquis was a tall man with a barrel chest, who relished the wine from his cellar and the food from his estate, especially when he had hunted it himself.

Even when Florent-Claude was at home, Voltaire did not relinquish the role of grand master of the morning gathering. Other than dinners, often followed by readings or a play in the attic theater, the main entertainment for guests at Cirey was an hour and a half of socializing over coffee before Voltaire and Emilie disappeared for a long day of work. From Voltaire's command of the room, a stranger walking through would almost certainly conclude that the scion of this quiet estate in Haute-Marne was the birdlike, middle-aged man wearing an old-fashioned wig with rows of tight curls, rather than the gallant silver-haired gentleman fond enough of his military uniform to sport it even at home.

The marquis was willing to look the other way at some of Voltaire's high-handedness. After all, the gallery—in fact an entire wing of the château—had been built with the writer's money. Someday Voltaire would move on, and the beautiful house, hopefully with the second wing completed, would be the marquis's alone. A château from a nearly uninhabitable ruin, and all for no more than having given a famous man shelter and allowing him to sleep with his wife? Let people gossip. Far better to laugh it off and remain Emilie's and Voltaire's champion, since they both needed one, God knew, and therefore needed him.

Though Florent-Claude was more discreet than his wife, he had no grounds for sanctimony. He had already decided to leave earlier than necessary to go back to his regiment via a town house in Nancy where his beautiful new mistress would keep him entertained for a week or two. He would grow weary of her too, as he had long since tired of Emilie, and he would rush off again to the world of men and war, two things he understood without having to work at it.

And now it seemed that Emilie had exhausted Voltaire, just as she had Florent-Claude, not just with her mind but with her endless relish for imaginative and almost interminable lovemaking. Of course she had never gotten that from Florent-Claude. Married sex was perfunctory. Lovers were for kissing, for undressing slowly, for sweet whispers of adoration. He had never felt inclined to give Emilie any of that, nor begrudged her getting it from someone more willing. Well, perhaps he begrudged it a little. After all, he was a man, and no man relished the thought of his wife's enthusiasm for such things.

Florent-Claude had to admit there was a degree of satisfaction in seeing Voltaire nagged and criticized as if he were the spouse. Just the other night, Emilie had told Voltaire his shirt was trimmed with too much lace. He had responded in English, the language they used when they were aching for a fight. Voltaire had stormed off and had only been persuaded to return by Madame de Graffigny, an overly sociable houseguest who had convinced him that her life was over if he would not read scenes from his newest play that evening after supper.

And then there was the satisfaction of the purloined lines of doggerel someone had copied and sent to the marquis, in which Voltaire begged off as Emilie's lover because his member was too limp for good use, a state he believed was likely to be permanent. Emilie seemed to have taken the matter in stride, and though she insisted the poem was a cruel joke by one of Voltaire's detractors, she and Voltaire did seem more like old friends than bed partners now. Perhaps her attention had already strayed elsewhere—and as long as she didn't embarrass the marquis and his family, who cared?—but it was more likely she was pleased not to be distracted from the science that now consumed her every waking moment.

"Listen to this." Emilie brandished a scientific journal as the servant refreshed the guests' coffee. "Do you want to know the size of the people who live on Jupiter? It's all terribly mathematical, so it must be true. Since the eyes are in proportion to the body, and we know the size of the pupil of the eye and the distance from Jupiter to the sun in comparison to the distance from the earth, it works out to . . ." Emilie thought for a moment before giving a number precise to several decimals.

"Let me see that." Françoise de Graffigny reached for the paper from which Emilie had read. She looked up, confused. "This is in Latin," she said, "and I don't see any numbers at all."

"I translated as I read," Emilie replied. "And the equations were simple enough to work out in my head." She looked puzzled. "I meant it to be funny. Men on Jupiter? Did you think I was serious?"

Their houseguest suppressed a sniff of indignation as she caught the marquis's eye. When Emilie wasn't boring them with science, she was ridiculing them for not being as agile-minded as she was. Isn't that what these little performances were about? If no one else but Voltaire understood, why did she inflict her physics, or whatever it was, on everyone else?

The marquis knew the vapid and tedious Madame de Graffigny's mood well. He really should talk to his wife about being better company, her eyes said. Cirey would be such a pleasant place if only the marquise's intelligence didn't make things so difficult. Well, let her think that. Did Madame de Graffigny give her husband—or her fop of a lover for that matter—anything to be proud of? Florent-Claude had a wife he could boast about, even if he didn't understand or care about the things that excited her.

Voltaire rose from his chair. The socializing was over. The coffee was cold. It would be a good day to go hunting, the marquis thought. It was usually a good day to go hunting.

16

THE CARRIAGE left the front of the cottage, turned onto another village street, went a few meters, and stopped. A grove of trees had hidden the château from Lili's view before, and she realized she had waited at least an hour to ride a distance she could have walked in a few minutes. Despite her nervousness, she smiled at Anton's insistence that she arrive in proper style.

The driver opened the gate, and the carriage made a short climb on a path that swept around the side of the château. The house was smaller than she expected and seemed lopsided. The roof was higher in some parts than others, with a flat terrace on top of one section where an attic and mansard roof would normally be. The main section, with a stone-carved arch over the door at its center, was flanked on the right with a taller structure that had no counterpart on the left. The monochromatic yellow of the stone gave the building some appearance of harmony, a look of being both finished and incomplete at the same time.

Lili heard a voice in the garden behind her. An old man in a military uniform was leaning heavily on a cane, yelling into the empty air. She hesitated before taking a few steps in his direction. "Sir?" she called out.

He turned around as quickly as his aged body would allow. "Where is my regiment?" he shouted. "They were camped here last night."

"I—I don't know," Lili said. "I've just arrived." She looked around, trying to imagine a regiment bedded down between the sculpted hedges.

"Damned lieutenant!" he spat. "They send me a boy when I need a man! There's a war to win, you know!"

France isn't at war right now. "Monsieur le Marquis?" Lili asked, not sure what to say to someone who had taken leave of his senses. He looked more closely at her, and for a moment Lili thought he might recognize her. Just then his attention was distracted by the cries of a middle-aged woman running across the lawn toward the garden. "Monsieur!" she cried out to him. "You're not to go out like this! You could get lost!"

"Oh, shut your mouth! You're nothing but an old nag." The woman ignored him. "Come along," she said, taking his limp arm. He allowed himself to be led back to the house without complaint, and when she had handed him over to a tiny young chambermaid, she turned to Lili.

"You must be the niece we were just told about. Which one are you?"

"I'm Stanislas-Adélaïde," Lili said. The servant looked momentarily confused, as if she was trying to place the name. "I'm not really his niece," Lili added. "I'm his daughter."

"Oh dear," the woman said. "I'm not sure this is good." She looked around. "Come with me." She took Lili around the house and down a slope to the basement entrance to the kitchen. "Wait here," she said. "If someone asks who you are, say you're my cousin." She looked at Lili's dress, which despite being crumpled and soiled was still obviously fashionable and expensive. "No one will believe you, but just keep saying it until I get back with Lucien."

Left alone, Lili looked around the spacious kitchen. A huge fireplace filled most of one wall, surrounded by shelves and hooks loaded with gleaming copper pans of every imaginable size and shape. The aroma of wild boar wafted from a stew pot hanging over a fire in the hearth, and on a worktable in the center of the room a loaf of fresh bread lay on a rack, next to a neat pile of vegetables still covered with bits of dirt. A larder door led to a room filled with an array of preserved and dried food, bags of flour, baskets of apples and onions, and special cupboards for cheese and pastries. In a separate area, eight places were set at the servants' table.

Just then the woman returned with a man of the same age. They hurried through the door and shut it behind them. "I'm sorry to be so disrespectful to a daughter of the marquis," the woman said, "but he rages so terribly now that we try not to upset him." She gestured to the man. "This is my husband, Lucien," she said. "And I'm Berthe. We've both worked here most of our lives. We knew your mother, God rest her soul." Berthe crossed herself.

"Knew the marquis in his better days too," Lucien added, "not like you was seeing him when you arrived." His eyes were steeped in melancholy. "He's not fit for visitors now, so far from his right mind."

Lili looked at the fading light through a small window. If he weren't able to have company, perhaps she would be asked to leave, which would mean returning to Bar-sur-l'Aube in the dark. But she was the marquis's daughter after all, so that would not happen, at least not tonight. "I have a valet and maid," she said. "They're waiting at the cottage of a man named Anton."

"I'll go now and bring them here," Lucien said, and without another word he was gone.

Berthe turned to Lili. "We'll put you and your maid in the guest room in the attic of the old wing. Your valet can stay with us tonight. It's best to keep him out of sight until the marquis has a chance to get used to him. Last month he thought the new coachman was Monsieur Saint-Lambert, and he knocked the poor man senseless with his cane."

Lili smiled courteously. "Come," Berthe said. "Let's get you up to your room before the scullery maid comes back to put the vegetables in the stew. There will be gossip enough tomorrow, I'm sure. No need to get it started tonight."

Lili followed behind her up to the main floor, then up another flight of stairs, and another. A short hallway led to an attic bedroom. "I hope you find your quarters satisfactory." Berthe scowled at a sudden memory. "That Madame de Graffigny was always complaining about how Madame la Marquise and Monsieur Voltaire spared no expense for themselves, but stuck her in the attic and couldn't be bothered to finish her room properly." She sniffed. "Her room. As if she had a right to it."

She unlatched the door to a room similar in size to Lili's bedchamber at home but more sparsely furnished and in need of a new carpet and a touch of paint on the wainscoting. "I think it's rather nice," Berthe said, opening the curtains. "And the viewpoint is the highest in the house."

Lili was only half listening as she looked out the window. To her right, through branches that had obscured the château when she had looked up from the village, she could see Lucien bringing Justine and Stephane to the château on foot. None of them would have as much as a change of clothes until their trunks could be fetched from Bar-sur-Aube tomorrow, but Lili was relieved that they were all at least safe for the night.

Turning to the left, she looked out across the golden fields to a dense forest in the distance. The blue of the sky was deepening in the early twilight, and suddenly Lili realized how long it had been since she had eaten. She had no doubt that Anton's wife had fed Justine and Stephane, but she had not eaten since the woman had handed her the bread slathered with butter and jam that morning. Could it possibly still be the same day that she had woken up and run in her unlaced dress across the square?

She sat down in a sudden rush of exhaustion. "Could you bring me something to eat?" she asked. "I'm afraid I'll be asleep in a few minutes. And could you make sure my maid and valet have been fed as well?"

Berthe smiled. "It will be my pleasure, Mademoiselle Stanislas-Adélaïde," she said, leaving the room before Lili could open her mouth to tell her that only the difficult people in her life ever called her by that name.

MOONLIGHT GLEAMED ON the white bedcovers, and when it reached Lili's face she sat up to look around the unfamiliar room. Night had softened the white stucco designs adorning the wall panels, and on the wainscoting, the pattern of the silk brocade wall covering had dissolved into a gray blur. Through the narrow opening in the casement window, cool air stroked the dust of disuse from the creases and crannies in the room, prickling Lili's nose until she broke the quiet with a sneeze.

As her eyes adjusted, Lili picked out the white *chaise percée* with a chamber pot underneath. She got up, lifting the bottom of her chemise, which had served as her nightdress since her trunk was still at Bar-sur-l'Aube. Sitting down on the wooden seat, she contemplated the soft, familiar whisper of water falling into the vessel underneath her.

For a moment she couldn't remember why she had come. The bone-bruising journey had put the world of Paris so far behind that it seemed as formless as the Meissen figurines standing in a darkened cabinet across the room, waiting, as Lili was, for the light of morning to give everything back its shape.

A cock crowed in the village and Lili got up and went to the window. The sky was beginning to lighten, and with both resignation and relief Lili decided there would be no more sleep for her that night. She went to the desk, lit the lamp, and went back to Meadowlark's world.

The steps to the cathedral in Andalusia were filled with people murmuring angrily and waving their arms. Meadowlark hid Comète in a nearby garden and went with Tom to investigate. "What is everyone so upset about?" she asked a man dressed in a bishop's robe and mitre.

"There's supposed to be a wedding today, but the bride has disappeared." He scratched his head. "We think she must have been kidnapped—after all, why would she run away when she's about to be married? Everyone's been so pleased about the match. Her family has hoped for an alliance with the Mountebank-Piquedames for years . . ."

Lili rubbed her eyes. She had a real Baronne Lomont and a father to deal with, and her own wedding to escape. Sending Meadowlark off to Spain was not going to help with that. Now that she was here, all her ideas about what to say, what to do, had vanished. It would be best to use this quiet dawn to think, before Justine got up to help her dress, and Berthe came with her breakfast.

"All right," Lili said aloud. "What do I have here?" She thought for a moment. *A father I have to persuade to let me manage my own life when he clearly has no control of his own. A father who might not know who I was if I'd lived in this house every day of my life.*" A father who said he never wanted to see me.

The hope she had carried with her from Paris, that since he had not interfered in her life to this point she could persuade him to stay out of it now, evaporated with the memory of the befuddled man in uniform looking for his troops. *Perhaps I should just leave this morning*, Lili thought. *Leave before he throws me out for being someone he imagines I am.*

She wasn't sure why he would want to do that, or who he might think she was, but if he'd attacked a coachman over a grudge with this—what was his name? Saint-Lambert?—anything was possible. If she left now, perhaps Baronne Lomont would never know she had come, but if she stayed and failed, she'd lose any chance at all to hold off the fate looming in front of her.

The glass cover on the candlestick would make it safe to carry, so she lit the stub inside and stepped out of her room. The passageway had a plank floor that looked quite new, but the paneling on the walls was rough and had been given only a hasty coat of paint. The paneling stopped where the open timbers of the roof and crossbeams protruded from the walls, low enough for her to bump her head in the dim light.

She dodged her way around a cluster of roof beams that went out in different directions like the spokes of a badly damaged wheel, and she found herself in a large room, unfurnished except for a few chairs and benches. Scattered here and there were large chests and one open crate. Inside it was a jumble of odd-looking dresses and wigs, as well as a pair of pink stockings and a tattered crown made of dried leaves. A piece of paper was wedged in among the leaves, which crumbled as she pulled it away. She held the playbill up to the candlelight:

Tonight at the Theater at Cirey! The premiere of *Mérope* by M. Voltaire. Cast—Mérope, Madame la Marquise; Polyphontes, Monsieur Voltaire; Ismène, Mademoiselle G-P du Châtelet; Euricles, Monsieur le Marquis, et al.

Lili stroked the hand-inked letters. *Madame la Marquise.* Light had begun to filter through a small window, revealing an open doorway on the other side of the room. She held the candle in front of her and went through it. Her foot hit against an upholstered bench and the flame shook, illuminating the ornate wallpaper on three sides with bobbing pulses of light. The entire fourth wall was taken up by a rounded arch in a light-colored wood, framing a stage hardly bigger than some of the massive fireplaces she'd seen at Versailles. The backdrop and wings were painted to suggest a rustic farmhouse, with a wooden door, a cuckoo clock, a cupboard, and a large window looking out onto a painted blue sky. In the center of the stage, a candlestick and a water jug sat on a wooden table, ready to be used as props for the last play presented at Cirey.

The theater! Lili remembered Anton talking about how he sometimes wore a costume and came onstage, and how his mother had said the marquise could sing forever without forgetting anything. Lili

put the candle down on one of the benches, clasping her hands behind her back and lifting her face to take in this extraordinary place.
She felt her chest broaden under her thin chemise, as if it were opening a door to a secret room inside her. She was breathing the same air
as her mother had, and making the same floorboards creak. She was
so close, Lili was sure she could almost hear her voice.

A vision. That's what Anton said she was, Lili thought as she made
her way back through the anteroom and into the passageway. A noise
overhead caused her to jump back in alarm. A pair of doves cooed
and fluttered their wings, breaking the spell. Lili watched them perch
on the sill of a tiny window before they flew out into the light of a
new morning.

JUSTINE APPEARED FROM behind a screened-off alcove as Lili
came back in. "Mademoiselle is up early." Justine curtsied. "I'm sorry
I didn't hear you."

"I couldn't sleep—but no need to disturb you."

"Mademoiselle would like breakfast?" At Lili's nod, Justine disappeared, and within a few minutes she had returned with Berthe.

"Your breakfast will be sent up on the dumbwaiter in just a moment," Berthe said. "I thought I'd come to see how you slept. Your
valet already left with Lucien for Bar-sur-Aube to retrieve your
things. I'm sure you'll be happy to have them."

"I slept well, thank you," Lili said. "I looked around already this
morning and found the theater."

Berthe gave her a wistful smile. "No one's been in there in years.
I'm surprised you didn't come out covered in dust." She looked
away, lost in thought for a moment. "How we all used to enjoy those
plays!" she said. "Madame pulled everyone in—Lucien and me, and
even the marquis, though he couldn't never remember his lines."

The marquis. Lili's brow furrowed. "Berthe," she ventured, "is
my father always like he was yesterday?"

The housekeeper looked up, surprised. "Oh *non*, mademoiselle.

It comes and goes. On good days he can sit and talk for hours about things that happened years ago and remember them perfectly. And then, just like that, he asks for madame, as if she's just stepped out of the room." Her eyes looked pained. "It's terrible to see such a great man"—she thought for a moment—"reduced like that."

Justine tightened the laces on Lili's dress as Berthe went on. "Perhaps you will be good for him. He's all alone in the world now. Don't no one visit, not even his son, and of course Gabrielle-Pauline is too far away. No one in the flesh, I mean, although I suppose one might call it a blessing that so much of the time he don't know the difference. The other day I heard him carrying on a conversation in the gallery, and when I went to see who come into the house without my noticing, he was telling Duke Stanislas that he'd be joining him for the hunting season at Lunéville." She dabbed her eyes. "I didn't have the heart to tell him again that the duke is dead."

She got up to straighten the figurines on the shelves. "He died a few months back, you know. Caught his dressing gown on fire and perished later from the burns." Berthe adjusted the curtains, for something to occupy her hands as she talked. "I don't know. Perhaps the dead do visit us. Perhaps it's just our poor eyes that can't see them."

Perhaps they do. A few hours ago, Lili had been tempted to get up and run from Cirey, afraid of what might happen if she stayed. Standing in the theater, absorbing the presence of her mother, she felt as if she had taken on the strength to see this visit through. Whatever happened with her father, she would find a way to go on from there, confident in the belief that Julie and Emilie each had an arm around her.

Justine had finished her laces, and Lili turned around. "Does he talk to my mother like he talks to the duke?"

A quick, sad smile flitted over Berthe's face. "All the time."

"Does he ever mention me when they talk?"

The housekeeper looked away. "You were just a baby then. Not even born, while she were still alive to talk about you."

She busied herself for a moment before turning to face Lili. Taking a deep breath, she let it out in a sigh of resignation. "No point in watching my words here, mademoiselle. You're likely to see for yourself soon enough what kind of conversations he has with the marquise. Much of the time they're not fit for hearing. He's angry with her, and I lost sleep last night with worry over whether he'll be angry with you as well." She looked toward the door. "Your breakfast must be waiting," she said, making a perfunctory curtsey as she left the room.

"Angry about what?" Lili asked, picking up the conversation the moment Berthe returned with the tray.

She put the tray down heavily on the fragile table. "The past is best buried," she said. "I mean no disrespect, but I'm not going to say more. Lucien is with the marquis now, and he'll tell him he has a guest, so you'd best be prepared to meet him. I think you should act as if it's the first time, since he's unlikely to remember seeing you yesterday." She looked at Lili. "You remind me so of madame, though your hair's not as dark. Best be prepared for anything, since there's no telling how he'll react."

Lili gave Berthe a long and penetrating look. She could, perhaps, force the woman to say more. She was, after all, a servant, even if she had taken on the role of mistress of the house. *I'll know soon enough what she means*, Lili thought. *Just let her be.*

Justine poured Lili a cup of coffee and was stirring in a large amount of milk. Lili watched disinterestedly, as if the breakfast were not for her. "Can you show me my mother's rooms later today?" she asked Berthe. "I liked seeing the theater and—"

"They're locked."

Lili's jaw dropped momentarily at the abruptness with which a servant had cut her off, but she closed her mouth without saying anything. Chastisement at that point would only lead to angry silence, when she wanted to hear everything the talkative Berthe might be willing to reveal.

"Have been for years," Berthe went on, "ever since Monsieur le

Marquis returned after . . ." The thought did not need finishing. "Monsieur Voltaire took away more than he should have, more than was his, but there was still enough of hers left behind to break the marquis's heart, so it's no wonder he locked her rooms up."

"I thought you said he was angry with her."

Berthe gave her a quizzical smile. "You're young. Apparently you haven't learned that a broken heart can be the angriest kind of all."

FLORENT-CLAUDE, THE MARQUIS du Châtelet-Lomont, sat in the wood-paneled antechamber in his apartment. Tucked into the top of his uniform was a large white napkin spotted with drips from the ti-sane his nurse was urging him to finish. Seeing Lili, she removed the napkin, picked up his tray, and departed with a polite curtsey to them both.

"You're my daughter, come for a visit," he said. Lili felt her armpits prickle in a flood of relief.

"Yes, I am," Lili said. "Stanislas-Adélaïde, named after your good friend, the Duc de Lorraine."

"Lorraine?" His puzzled look made Lili's heart sink, but he quickly recovered. "I was a regimental commander there. And Duke Stanislas's grand maréchal until I came back to Cirey." His eyes darted around the room, as if to confirm that Cirey was indeed where he was. "And you," he added. "Is your husband well? Have you traveled alone from Italy?"

Lili's heart, buoyed by the lucidity of his first words, sank again. "I'm not that daughter," she said. "I'm the one raised in Paris by Madame de Bercy until her unfortunate death. The one Baronne Lomont recently wrote to you about. She asked for your permission to choose a husband for me. I'm sure you will recall—"

"Why are you here?" His voice dropped to a whisper.

"I felt it was important to meet my fath—"

"Did she say I was your father?" Florent-Claude's pale face turned red.

"Excuse me, sir, but I am not sure to whom you are referring." Lili struggled to keep her voice firm and her eyes locked on his. "But whether you mean Baronne Lomont or Madame de Bercy makes no difference in the matter. Since you are my father, there is no need for anyone to tell me so."

You'll hear rumors at court. Lili's heart skipped a beat, remembering the baroness's words.

The marquis's face grew calm again, and he smiled. "I'm afraid you've missed Gabrielle-Pauline. She lives at the Couvent de la Pitié in Joinville, but if you wait a few days, I'm sure my wife will fetch her again for one of Monsieur Voltaire's plays." He chuckled. "Have you met the marquise yet? I'm sure she'll ask right away how good you are at memorizing lines."

Lili's eyes shut in despair. When she opened them, he was staring at her with fierce eyes. "You tell them I'm not fooled," he growled.

Lucien hurried into the room. *He must have been listening from the hall,* Lili realized. "Monsieur tires easily," Lucien said. "I think mademoiselle should visit him again later."

Her frustration and anxiety were tinged with relief at Lucien's rescue. "Of course," she said, standing up and giving a demure nod in the terrifying old man's direction. Then an idea lodged in her mind. "But if you should be so kind," she asked him, "your wife's chambers seem to be locked. Do I have your permission to enter?"

He looked confused. "If she doesn't mind, I don't see why I should."

"I'm sure she won't mind." Lili gave him a sweet smile. *Mind? She's been waiting for me for years.* Back in the hallway, she raced in the direction of the kitchen to search for Berthe and her keys.

BERTHE OPENED THE latch with such delicacy that for a moment Lili thought she was afraid of disturbing her mistress's sleep. "Best to wait here while I pull back the curtains so you have enough light," she said, bustling ahead. When she had gone through all the rooms, she came back to Lili, wiping her dusty hands on her apron. "I suppose you'd like to be alone," she said. "If you need me there's a cord over there that rings a bell downstairs."

As Berthe's steps receded in the passageway, Lili stood in the doorway, feeling oddly shy. Dust swirled in the gray bolts of light coming through the newly opened curtains, revealing a large blue-upholstered daybed inside the first room. Flowered pillows were strewn casually at one end, while a wrinkled dent in the middle suggested that the occupant had just gotten up for a moment and intended to settle in again. Furnished with chairs and side tables, the room looked like a typical parlor, except for a bathtub set incongruously in the middle of the marble floor, as if it were just another comfortable place to sit and chat with company.

Lili passed through the doorway into her mother's dressing room. Beneath a fancifully painted ceiling, gilt moldings framed lacquered-green wall panels. A small sofa and several chairs were arranged on a large and luxurious rug, while in the corners, matching cabinets stood emptied of whatever they had once held. The silence of her mother's quarters was so complete that Lili walked across the room with slow, delicate steps, as if to do so much as cause a board to creak would make her an intruder rather than a daughter who belonged there.

The next room was dominated by a large bed, stripped of its canopy and bedcovers. *This is where my mother slept*, Lili thought as she sat down on the mattress. She looked back toward the dressing room and tried to imagine a woman coming toward her in a beautiful dressing gown, her hair already unpinned and lying in waves on her shoulders. *You were here. You were really here.*

Everything in the room, from the wallpaper to an enameled clock on a shelf, was lemon yellow or blue, including a little basket near the bed where a dog must have slept. Lili got up from the bed and bent over to pat her hand inside it. A black dog, she decided, from the dusty hairs she brushed off her fingers.

On the other side of the room, a passageway led into a small boudoir dazzling with light from glass-paneled doors leading out onto a small terrace. A single white taffeta sofa and matching stools took up most of the space in the cozy room, next to a marble fireplace that could have kept her mother warm when short winter days left her craving every last bit of light. *A room just big enough for you*, Lili thought. *Your hideaway.*

Lili cast her eyes over the delicately painted ceiling and the miniature paintings in gold filigree frames at the center of each slender wall panel. Watteau, she decided, recognizing depictions of fables by Jean de La Fontaine in two of them. *We liked the same stories.*

Lili opened the door and gazed from her mother's private terrace across the garden and lawn, down to the stream that ran through the grounds. *It's quite a place to make a home*, she thought, imagining the green lawns covered with snow and the dainty tracks of wandering deer.

Though the rooms were silent, the people that had once animated them stirred Lili's imagination, and as she turned to go back to the main door, she could almost hear the laughter and the clink of coffee spoons. Walking again through the bedroom, a question hit her with such power that she found herself sitting on the bed without knowing exactly how she got there.

What if you hadn't died?

I would have known the people sitting in the chairs in your bathroom. They would have called me by name and asked what you were teaching me. I would have sat with you in that pretty little boudoir—perhaps on one of those little stools—playing with your dog. I might have been the only one permitted to visit you there. "It's our hideaway, Lili," you might have said, giving me a secret look we shared. I would have run across that lawn, and you would have called out to me to be careful or I'd fall. You would have let me get under the covers on this bed and you would have read La Fontaine to me.

She touched the mattress, as if to anchor herself to nonexistent memories. "I miss you," she whispered, "even if I never knew you."

Missed her even more now, she realized, after the sweet pain of going through her mother's rooms.

Something wasn't right in what she'd seen, and as she took another look around the bedchamber she realized what it was. A few chairs were scattered here and there, but where the desk should have been, the space was bare. More than a few items seemed to be gone, including all the books. What had Berthe said? That Voltaire took many things with him before these rooms were locked and left to gather dust?

Lili noticed for the first time that the two mirrored panels on the far wall were doors. They opened with a loud creak, and Lili found herself in a room entirely unlike the others. Nothing hung on its walls. Huge, glass-doored bookcases, empty except for stacks of loose papers, stood on both sides of a fireplace. A section of marble floor was incomplete, leaving the boards visible underneath.

In the middle of the room was a dainty and beautifully polished desk. Its inlays in contrasting woods and slivers of gold matched the cabinets in the other room. *She moved the desk in here,* Lili realized. Pushed up against one side was a plain wooden work table spotted here and there with congealed bumps of candle wax, and littered with papers, books, and scientific tools.

For a moment Lili felt she knew her mother, understood her deeply. She was someone who would turn her back on the beauty and grace of her other rooms to come work in here, because truth was all that mattered, all that was really permanent.

Lili looked around for a place to rest and contemplate. The chair at the desk had been removed, but the window bay was deep enough to sit on. As Lili went over to it, she saw something half-hidden under the bottom of the curtain. She picked it up and held it to the light, watching as tiny rainbows shot from a prism and danced across the walls.

She put it back down, but her fingers did not want to let it go. *Keep it.* The thought came over her so strongly that she looked around, as if she half expected her mother to be standing there, telling her she had left it as a gift. The edges of the cut crystal were so sharp, it felt as if it were heating up in her hand. *Keep it*. She tucked the prism into her bodice and held her fingers there for a moment, feeling its outline over her heart.

Lili could tell by the rough feel of the keyhole on the desk drawer that someone had once made a clumsy attempt to pick it open, but when she put the point of the compass in the opening to do the same, the lock released as if it were letting out a long-held breath.

The drawer was filled with a jumble of papers that hardly appeared worth the effort of locking it at all. On top was a draft of an essay by Voltaire covered with comments in another hand, and Lili's heart leapt at what she knew must be her mother's writing. Farther down in the drawer were some sheets of foolscap filled with carefully drawn graphs of parabolas covered with calculations so long the page had been turned to continue up the margin. A few unpaid bills were scattered near the bottom of the drawer—for jewelry, perfume, clothing, renovations to her rooms. Lili smiled. Apparently the man laying the marble floor was still waiting for his payment.

Taking out the next layer of papers, she heard the thunk of a hard object at the bottom of the drawer. She pulled out an oval-shaped picture frame in ornate silver, facing down. *Voltaire*. Lili thought as she turned it over.

She stared in confusion at the face looking out at her. It was not Voltaire, but a handsome man in his thirties, wearing an immaculate white wig with a black velvet ribbon securing the tail at the back of his neck. His eyebrows were arched and his head slightly cocked to one side, as if he was waiting for an answer to an interesting question. His eyes were as round as hers, and he had the same pronounced bow in his lip.

"What are you doing here?"

Lili whirled around so quickly that the frame flew from her hand and clattered across the marble floor. The marquis stood in the doorway of the library, his eyes flashing in anger.

"I—you gave me permission to come in, sir."

The man she had seen slumped in a chair earlier that day now pulled up his chest and thundered at her. "Do you think I can't figure out why you wanted me to come home so quickly? Do you think I believe that after all these years you're suddenly filled with desire for me?" His lip curled and his voice dripped with scorn. "Have enough servants and villagers seen me, and have enough guests come to dinner to report that I'm here?"

"I—I don't know what you're talking about."

"Oh, of course. That's always a good thing to say when you have something to hide. I suppose I should be grateful your pretense averted a scandal, and I won't be ridiculed as a cuckold at court, but if you and Monsieur Voltaire are quite finished with my services, I'd like to return to Lunéville."

Lili's mouth was agape and she stared at him, speechless. Then, almost as if he were a leaking bag of air, the marquis's shoulders began to slump and he was once again the frail old man she had seen that morning.

"Emilie," he said in a voice now more petulant than angry. "I've been most forgiving, most tolerant—how could you repay me like this? How could you get yourself with child at your age? And by that little dandy Saint-Lambert? He is so unworthy of you."

Lili's eyes darted to the portrait on the floor. *Saint-Lambert. The one for whom the coachman had taken a beating. The man with her eyes, her mouth.* "No," she whispered to herself. "It can't be true."

The marquis came closer and peered into Lili's face. "You're not my wife."

"No—I'm not," she stammered.

"Who are you, then?" He seemed more frightened than curious. "And why are you in my house?"

"Sir, I'm your daughter, Stanislas-Adélaïde. I'm—" Lili's voice was hoarse with tears she was too terrified to shed, and she was shaking so badly she had to force her knees not to buckle and send her toppling to the ground. "I'm the child you were referring to just then."

His eyes flickered again. "You're the one who killed her," he spat.

"It's not my fault!" With a sob that seemed to come from deep in her entrails, Lili rushed toward the door. He grabbed her by the forearm with a grip so strong it hurt through her sleeve. "Isn't what I've done sufficient for you?" His face was scarlet. "I've given you respectability, money—do you ask for more from someone who's not even your father?"

He pulled her close again and examined her features. Then he began to laugh, at first softly and then growing to a roar so loud, Lili thought she would be shaken to pieces. "It's written on your face," he said. "You have her nose and chin, but the eyes and mouth belong to a man so reckless with his cock that he destroyed my wife." He squeezed her arm so hard she cried out. "Destroyed me too, that little prick." He released his grip and threw down her arm. "What do you want from me? You're their daughter, not mine."

THE TRUNKS HAD scarcely been unloaded before they were back on the carriage. Berthe was in tears, but Lili was as dry-eyed as the dead. "Please forgive him," Lucien said, as Justine and Stephane settled into the backseat. "He's not right anymore. He says terrible things he don't mean."

"I imagine that's true," Lili said in a brittle voice. "But tell me one thing. Was he in his right mind when he said I'm not his child?"

Lucien and Berthe exchanged glances. "I wish I could say otherwise, but with God watching, I can't," Lucien said. "I'm sorry."

"Monsieur Lambert visited Cirey nine months before you were born," Berthe added. "He and madame stayed alone for a week or more. Monsieur Voltaire and madame took great pains to bring the marquis here as soon as she missed her monthly blood."

Voltaire? That didn't make sense. "She was carrying someone else's child, and he wasn't angry?"

"Monsieur Voltaire . . ." Berthe shifted her weight as she pondered how to answer. "He was always complaining about his health, and one day he decided he weren't fit for—I don't know how to say it any more delicately, mademoiselle—fit for serving her needs as a woman. Not that he told us that, but people in a house have a way of knowing."

"No one else understood all their books and their experiments," Lucien added. "I think they stayed together to have someone to talk to."

Berthe nodded. "And once you've been together a long time," she said, "there's no letting go."

"YOU'RE IN LUCK, mademoiselle," the man at the inn in Bar-sur-Aube told Lili. "Coach from Geneva to Paris comes through this day every week just before nightfall and leaves at daybreak." Relieved, Lili paid for herself, Justine, and Stephane. "We won't unpack," she said. "Just load all our things on the coach when it gets here."

Had it really been only two days earlier she had gone into the same inn, wondering how she would get to Cirey? Lili pondered all that had happened as she separated out the bones in the stewed chicken the innkeeper put in front of her. It was just as delicious as the meal she had when she arrived, but her mood was too grim for her to do any more than move the food around in the bowl.

What was I thinking? she asked herself, tearing off a piece of bread and chewing it angrily. *Why did I believe I could defeat Baronne Lomont with this foolishness?* All she had accomplished, she decided, was to destroy her illusions about her father. *The man who's not my father after all,* she corrected herself. *And when the baroness finds out what I did . . .*

Tears of defeat and humiliation stung her eyes. She would have to go back to Paris and choose a husband, back to a place where no one, not even Maman, had told her the truth. Lili pushed the bowl away and stood up. She needed to get upstairs before the men in the tavern saw her cry.

* * *

JUSTINE WAS STILL out having her meal with Stephane, so Lili took off her dress herself and lay down in her petticoat and chemise. Though she tried to focus her thoughts, her mind refused, and soon she drifted off to sleep. When she woke again, night had fallen and the town square was quiet except for the off-key singing of a few men staggering home after too much to drink. When they were gone, the silence was total except for Justine's soft breathing in the alcove.

Lili stood at the window looking up into a sky white with stars. *It's the same sky over Paris*, she thought, and *over Étoges*. Her heart twisted with longing to pour out her heart to Delphine. Even if the marquis was a doddering old man, it would be nice to bask in Delphine's outrage over the way she had been treated.

It's the same sky wherever Voltaire is too, she thought, wondering if he still loved her mother, and if he had ever given any thought to the child she had died after giving birth to. He had cared enough to help falsify the parentage of her unborn child, hadn't he? And who was this Saint-Lambert, and why had he never come forward to meet her? What would her life have been like if he had? What would her name be? No question of it: she owed her existence to this Saint-Lambert, but a larger debt to Monsieur Voltaire. Without his efforts to help her mother hide the truth, she might be talked about openly as a bastard child.

She wondered if Voltaire was also at a window at that moment, looking at the stars. He had settled somewhere near the Swiss border, she had heard, so he could hurry to safety if any new work displeased the French censors. After she had read her story in the salon, Buffon had said in jest that he should write to Voltaire about it.

What was it he said? "I should write to Voltaire at . . ." Lili struggled to make her mind release the memory.

Ferney. It came to her like a whisper in her ear.

"Coach from Geneva to Paris comes through this day every week," the innkeeper had said. And, Lili realized with a start, the coach in the other direction was the one she'd been on a few days before.

Once you've been together a long time, there's no letting go.

Impulsively, Lili got up, put her dress back on, and rushed downstairs. The innkeeper was wiping the tables in the empty tavern. "Is Ferney near Geneva?" she asked in a breathless voice.

"About an hour by carriage," he replied, rinsing his wet rag in a bowl of dirty water.

Lili grinned broadly. "Thank you," she said. "And would you please make sure our bags aren't on that coach after all? Have someone bring them up to our rooms tomorrow, and change our booking as well. We'll be traveling the other direction instead."

Emilie

1749

A S THE moon neared the horizon, the carriage cast a moving shadow over the snow-covered fields of Champagne. Inside, under thick lap rugs and furs to protect them from the February cold, Emilie and Voltaire curled up together.

She slid her hand over her stomach. "At least somebody's warm."

"I don't know why you couldn't have waited until spring to leave Cirey," Voltaire said. "The roads are safer then, even with the mud. And with your trunks lashed to the roof, the horses can't go faster than a trot without toppling us into a ditch." He pulled the curtain aside and looked out on the darkness. "We could walk to Paris almost this fast."

"You didn't have to come," Emilie sniffed, looking away in feigned indifference.

"Of course I did! If you insist on getting yourself killed by traveling in winter, I'm afraid I'm foolish enough to feel required to do it with you. I wouldn't let you travel alone in your condition, although getting chilled like this is likely to give me a fever." Voltaire gave her a grave look that invited her to imagine the worst. "You're likely to come out of this far better than I."

"The books I must have are in my apartment in Paris." She was so tired of repeating herself. "And the people I need to consult are not likely to come to Cirey on a road as unfit for travel as you say."

"You could have sent for the books, couldn't you?"

"I have to look through them to know which ones I want," she said, emphasizing each word to convey her annoyance. "And once we're in Paris, there's no point in going back until the last snow has melted and the mud is truly terrible, so you'll have something else to complain about."

Trying to lighten the mood, Emilie gave Voltaire a playful pinch on his chin, although almost immediately her expression darkened. "I can't afford to wait two months to get started on the *Principia,*" she said, feeling her voice stick in her throat. "It's not just a translation, you know. I'm going to have to rewrite it so people can understand, and add commentaries as I go along."

She sat up, scarcely noticing the winter air creeping down her neck. "I've decided to add a supplement with nothing but calculations too. Mathematical proof is essential for the French to accept the *Principia* and Newton didn't supply enough of that." She shuddered, only partly from the cold. "I have less than seven months to figure it all out and get it written, before my time comes. That's why I'm on this infernal coach crawling toward Paris."

"You're shivering," Voltaire said, pulling her close to him and adjusting the covers. "You drive yourself too hard, my diamond-encrusted genius." He squeezed her tight. "There will be time after your time, will there not?"

It was best not to say what she was thinking. He would scoff at her premonitions, but they were as real to her as the jarring of her bones on this coach. He knew as well as she did that childbirth was dangerous, especially at her age, but he didn't seem to want to admit that the forces of nature applied to her. She was beyond their grasp, he often said to flatter her when she worried about a crease on her brow or a sagging fold of flesh. And sometimes she thought he really believed it, as if some people could have too much in their minds, too much to offer, to be permitted to die.

Voltaire knew her better than did anyone, and even he could not comprehend what she meant when she said her time was coming. She had a few months to make her mark on the world, or die trying. That was the problem. To die, still trying.

She listened to Voltaire's breathing grow shallow. For all his litany of ailments, he had the enviable ability to drift off to sleep in even the most uncomfortable places. The moon on the horizon cast a glow into the carriage, illuminating his face. He was in his midfifties now, and starting to look old. Most of his teeth were gone—a blessing in some ways since they had caused him nothing but pain for years—and the ridiculously out-of-date wig he always wore reminded her of the floppy, paddle-shaped ears of the king's spaniels. Still, there was no one she loved more—not in the wild way she once had, but as a friend she could not imagine life without.

She was fairly certain he had a mistress in Paris, but he didn't seem to care about her all that much, and Emilie was confident no one could take her place in his heart. Still, a young woman willing to adore him as she herself once had was not an insignificant threat. After all, she had fallen victim to the charms of a younger man who adored her, hadn't she? Emilie touched her stomach and felt the sharp ache that came from thinking about Saint-Lambert. Since he found out she was with child, he had distanced himself in the most distressing and painful way, but perhaps her latest letter would touch his heart . . .

She closed her eyes, just as what sounded like an explosion erupted under her seat. She screamed, clutching at Voltaire as the carriage fishtailed on the icy road. The trunks scraped across the roof as their weight shifted, carrying the coach with them and slamming it on its side. Underneath her, Voltaire groaned loudly, pinned against one of the doors. She struggled to stand up amid the hatboxes and lap rugs, now covered with the contents of a basket of food. "You're crushing me," she heard Voltaire moan, as she pounded on the other door, now above her head.

She heard the voice of Voltaire's manservant, Sébastien Longchamp, and felt his weight rock the coach as he scrambled up to open the door. "Are you all right, madame?" he asked, peering down at her.

"*Mon Dieu*," she gasped. "What happened?"

"An axle broke. Lucky we were going so slow." She grabbed his arm to pull herself up onto the side of the carriage, where the driver and another servant helped her to the ground. The driver held Longchamp's ankles as he reached down to rescue Voltaire. Within a few minutes, all of them stood, shaken but unhurt, by the side of the road.

Longchamp had been riding ahead of the carriage since nightfall, watching for obstacles in the road as it made its way toward the nearest town, where they would rest for the night. "I'll stay with monsieur and madame," he told the driver. "Take my horse and go for help." He jumped on a snowdrift to make a flat, hard platform, and then laid furs and lap robes on top. "It will be several hours before anyone comes," he said. "You'd best bundle up."

Emilie and Voltaire lay back on the rugs, pulling the blankets over them as they looked up at millions of stars burning in the clear winter sky. The only sounds in the vast, roaring silence were the nickers and whinnies of the horses, confused why suddenly everything had stopped.

"When I was little, I thought the Milky Way looked like a horse that had galloped off to another galaxy, and all we could still see was its tail." Emilie laughed, watching her breath cloud in the blue-black night. Voltaire pointed overhead. "It's no wilder an idea than thinking those stars are an archer named Orion—as if objects in the heavens stay in their appointed spots to make a good story for us."

"And then Galileo brandishes his telescope and asks a simple question: what would happen if we preferred the truth?" Emilie said. "And voilà, that smear across the sky reveals something more wonderful than anything we could imagine."

She was silent for a moment. "I wonder what people who come later will think of us," she said, resting her head against his shoulder. "The truths we're too stubborn to accept, and the lies we're too frightened to abandon. We're so adamant about moving away from superstition and alchemy, but wouldn't it be wonderful to catch a glimpse of what we're wrong about, however hard we try not to be?"

Voltaire laughed. "Painfully wrong sometimes, if I recall a certain paper on fire whose greatest merit apparently lay in giving my critics something to disparage."

Emilie scarcely heard. "It's not impossible to send objects into space, you know." She sat up, not noticing the cold. "If a projectile could be launched at a speed great enough to get beyond the earth's gravity near the top of its arc, it would keep going unimpeded in the same direction—it would either circle the earth or go on out into space forever. I'm sure it's so."

"Or until it ran into something," Voltaire teased. "Don't forget that, Madame Newton. Perhaps it might collide with people who've launched themselves out from another galaxy. I hope they're a better creation than we've turned out to be."

"Proof that God had been equally busy elsewhere." Emilie laughed. "Imagine the stir that would cause!"

"I think there's plenty keeping God busy here," Voltaire replied, reaching up to tap a finger against her temple. "Sometimes I imagine him saying, 'Finally, here's someone to talk to! Someone who understands me, if only just a little.' He is a man, you know, and all any of us really want is to be understood." He grinned, pulling her down to lie next to him. "Me most of all."

Under the blanket, Emilie poked him in the ribs. "Stop it!" she said, secretly pleased at the compliment. She turned her face toward his and saw that his smile was gone.

"You are the closest thing to the divine I have ever known," he said. "And I can't imagine wanting to feel such love for another, for fear it might cause my memory of you to fade."

When the warmth of his compliment had died away and he released her from his embrace, Emilie spoke. "God teases us with that sky," she murmured. "He says, 'My creation is too vast for you to comprehend, but I want you to try anyway. I want you to keep looking for me.'"

The bleakness she felt so often now crept back into her mind. Death was God's cruelest joke. He made people go through life knowing they would not have enough time. "I want to live forever," she whispered, too softly for Voltaire to hear.

They lay quietly, watching the stars creep across the sky. "Your eyes are sparkling," Voltaire said, breaking the silence.

She laughed. "How can you tell in the dark?"

"I don't have to see them to know." He squeezed her hand under the blanket. "Even if you weren't here, I would know that wherever you were, your eyes were giving off the fire that makes you who you are." Emilie burrowed in next to him, wishing that everything about that moment—the brightness of the stars, the sting of the cold on her cheeks, the man holding her in his arms—did not conspire to make her feel as if she might dissolve from grief.

17

1767

"I'LL SEND my carriage to fetch you in Geneva," the note resting on the seat beside Lili said in the scrawled and unsteady hand of the seventy-two-year-old Voltaire.

She had written to him from her lodgings in the city and, to her great relief, had gotten a reply so enthusiastic it did much to displace what felt like unremittingly ugly memories of Cirey. Perhaps someday she would be able to look back and think about her mother's boudoir, the theater, the bathtub, the worktable, without immediately remembering the horrible scene that had ended her time there, and the way she had struggled all the way to Geneva to rid herself of the idea that she ought to feel guilty about a situation that had wronged her more than it did anyone else.

She touched the outside of her bodice, feeling underneath it the pouch in which she carried the prism she took as a gift from her mother. *Let the marquis think I'm a thief,* she thought. *I'm glad I kept it.* She felt a surge of bitterness, and with the rote reaction of her convent years, she offered a silent prayer for forgiveness. *He's just a confused old man. It's bad enough being trapped inside himself without me wishing him any more pain.*

The carriage came to a stop and she heard Stephane's voice as he hopped down on the gravel courtyard and opened her door. The château, modest by comparison with any she had seen, gleamed in the morning sunlight as if it were radiating warmth from within. The portico, faced in warm yellow sandstone, framed a large outer door where two servants waited. In tidy symmetry under the gray mansard roof, window shutters opened up onto the white stone exterior of the two-story building, as if every room were inviting her to come inside.

"Mademoiselle du Châtelet?" A man dressed in red and white livery bowed to her after Stephane had assisted her to the ground. "I am Germond, Monsieur Voltaire's valet. It is a pleasure to welcome you to Ferney." He looked around. "Dunan! Pernette!" The two servants standing by the door rushed to the carriage and began setting Lili's trunk and boxes on the ground.

A stout woman in her forties came through a door in one wing of the house. Wiping her hands on her apron, she approached Lili and curtsied. "If you please, I am Michon, the housekeeper, and I hope that we shall be able to provide what you need for a most amiable stay," she said in a well-practiced tone. "Perhaps mademoiselle would care to retire to her room for a rest after her journey?"

Before Lili could reply, Germond shook his head. "Monsieur Voltaire asked me to bring Mademoiselle du Châtelet to him in the library the minute she arrived."

Lili caught the surprised look on Michon's face before the servant lowered her head. "Very well," Michon said, gesturing to Dunan and Pernette to take the things from the carriage into the house. Stephane jumped to help Dunan with the trunk while Justine followed, carrying Lili's satchel. "We eat dinner at two," Michon said. "Louise—she's the upstairs maid—will make sure you have everything you need." Then, after another curtsey she hurried off behind the others.

The air felt clean and cool inside the château, as if the patterned marble walls and floor imbued a serenity too great to disturb even a speck of dust. "This way, mademoiselle," Germond said. "We'll go to the library through the salon, so you'll know where to join the others before dinner." He opened a door on the far side of the vestibule and waited for Lili to go through.

Her eyes had barely adjusted to the dim light of the entryway before they were squinting again in the dazzling sunlight of the parlor. Dreamlike landscape paintings set in gilded frames softened the plain, cream-colored panels, and the gleaming wood of the chairs and bright red patterns of the carpet were reflected in the mirrors on each wall. Lili's eyes took all this in only slightly, since her attention was immediately drawn to what lay beyond.

The far wall of the salon was almost nothing but windows and glass-paneled doors opening onto a parterre that led down to a small formal garden splashed with beds of flowers. Sunlit streams of water arched and fell from a fountain into a marble pond in the center. Raked gravel paths connected the house to the woods beyond and radiated out to each corner of the garden. It was so unlike the grounds of Versailles and Vaux-le-Vicomte in its warmth and intimacy that Lili knew instantly she was going to like Ferney, in spite of the desperation that had brought her there.

"Mademoiselle?" Germond was standing in front of a closed door to her left.

Voltaire's library. Lili's heart jumped as Germond tapped his knuckles on the door before opening it and motioning her in.

The walls were covered floor to ceiling with crowded bookcases interspersed with large windows that flooded the room with light. A sticklike man, barely taller than she was, stood on a private terrace looking out over the vineyards toward the distant outline of Mont Blanc and the Alps. "Beg pardon, monsieur," Germond said. "Mademoiselle du Châtelet is here."

Voltaire turned around. "*Mon Dieu,*" he said, coming through the door toward her. He raised her hand to his lips with a bow.

"Germond!" he said, giving Lili a wide, toothless grin. "Tell me, have you ever seen me tongue-tied?" Lack of teeth gave him a speech impediment so severe it might have passed for self-mockery if it were not so obviously beyond his control.

"*Non,* monsieur," Germond replied in the flat tone of a lifelong servant. "Shall I see to coffee?" Voltaire nodded, and the valet withdrew.

Lili averted her eyes from Voltaire's penetrating gaze, struggling to control her recoil at the sight of a man who looked as wizened as a mummy and seemed to be made of nothing but bones. He bore no resemblance to the pictures she had seen, except for the old-fashioned powdered wig that brushed his shoulders, and the equally outdated cut of his frock coat and decorated jabot underneath. *I didn't expect him to be this ancient*, she thought.

The sparkle in his eyes soon made Lili put aside his odd appearance, peeling away the present so she could see in Voltaire someone who had once been young. Before he spoke again, she was already warming to the man who had captured her mother's heart so many years ago.

Voltaire led her to a small couch and settled with a wince into the chair across from her. "You are so like her," he said. His voice caught in his throat and he cleared it noisily, pulling out a handkerchief to wipe the thin line of his lips. "It's been eighteen years now. I was thinking of that when I received your letter from Geneva. The heat of the summer always puts me in mind of that time." He shook his head in disbelief. "And here you are, the living embodiment of what those years mean. Already a lovely young woman."

"I hope I haven't hurt you somehow by coming, Monsieur Voltaire," Lili said. Suddenly she realized he was crying, and her own repressed tears broke out too, as they laughed at themselves for weeping so unabashedly in front of someone who was, after all, still a stranger.

Michon returned with a tray on which sat a small pot of coffee and two tiny porcelain cups, along with a basket of fresh madeleines redolent with the smell of butter and sugar. "It's midday, monsieur," she said. "Will you be taking a walk before dinner?"

Voltaire looked at Lili. "If Mademoiselle du Châtelet would care to accompany me?" he asked, raising his eyebrows.

"I'd be delighted, but don't I need to dress for dinner?" Lili smoothed her skirt.

He cast a quick eye over her tidy but corsetless traveling dress.

"Were you planning on going for a swim in my carp pond?" His eyes crinkled in a smile. "Because if you do, I most certainly will insist you come to the table dry, but other than that, you look quite dressed to me."

Voltaire's laugh was like a cross between a child's giggle and the bellow of a bullfrog in a summer pond. "I am far too distant from Paris to care a whit about such things, and I try my best to drive off guests who do." He stood up and motioned to her to come out onto the terrace with him. "So please, my dear, just be yourself. It's hard to imagine anything else could be half so charming."

His weight on her was like a feather that had fallen on her sleeve, as they stepped arm in arm off the terrace onto a path that disappeared into a grove dappled with autumn light.

LILI MADE HER way to the salon a few minutes before the appointed hour and found the room still empty except for a man in his twenties reading a book. He jumped to his feet and kissed her hand with the exaggerated bow of an actor. "Jean-François de La Harpe," he said, in a tone that suggested she should recognize the name. "And you must be Mademoiselle du Châtelet."

"Am I early?" Lili asked. La Harpe laughed. "Since you've just arrived today, you don't know yet that Monsieur Voltaire has a habit of keeping everyone waiting, so of course, no one ever comes down on time—which makes it necessary to push back dinner a bit more, just to make sure he still keeps everyone waiting. I imagine it will be a good ten minutes before Madame Denis appears, and Father Adam will come dashing in even later."

Despite what she had to admit was a handsome face and a natural ease of manner, Lili was well on her way to disliking him. Why would the first thing he said be tinged with criticism of his host? Cleverness at the expense of gratitude didn't speak well of anyone.

And who were these other people he'd spoken of? "Madame Denis?" Lili inquired.

"Monsieur Voltaire's housekeeper." La Harpe smirked.

"You mean Michon?" Lili asked. "The servants come to table here?" It was odd, but so much had already been different at Ferney that she supposed she should be open to anything.

"Of course not!" the young man said, in a tone that sounded like the snobbish tittering of Anne-Mathilde and Joséphine in the convent. "Madame Denis lives here. She's Voltaire's niece, who's perfected on him the role of annoying wife her husband had the good sense to avoid by dying shortly after he married her." Now Lili was certain she didn't like La Harpe at all.

"Perhaps you've heard of my plays? *Warwick? Timoleon? Pharamond?*" the young man asked. "*Warwick* was quite the success, and Voltaire invited me here to help him correct some of his own verse."

Lili shook her head. "I'm sorry, but I can't place them." *This upstart says he corrects the work of the greatest writer in France?* Lili wondered what Voltaire would say if he overheard such impudence.

"*Timoleon* and *Pharamond*—I can't say I'm surprised you don't know them. I'm afraid they were quite more than the French were prepared for, and I suppose I'll have to settle for posthumous fame." He laughed, as if he felt such modesty was charming in a man of his talents.

"What a shame you'll never know if you achieved it," Lili said, struggling to keep the bite of sarcasm from her voice.

"So you are the daughter of the Marquise du Châtelet." La Harpe ignored her comment, giving Lili a look that lingered too long for comfort. "And special enough to have the whole house talking. You weren't kept waiting in the antechamber for hours, like every other new visitor."

Lili gave him the same kind of smile she had first practiced when trying to withstand the company of Jacques-Mars Courville. "Yes," she said, about nothing in particular. "Perhaps you know my mother was the translator of Newton's *Principia*."

La Harpe looked confused. "Newton?" he asked in a way that

left Lili unsure whether he was merely surprised or had never heard of him. "I thought she was just Voltaire's—"

He looked up and rose to his feet. "Madame Denis! How lovely you look," he said, lifting the new arrival's hand to kiss it. "Have you met Mademoiselle du Châtelet?"

What was the name of the fairy tale where the king was a scrawny little thing and the queen was so big she could barely fit on her throne? Lili couldn't remember, but the middle-aged woman who had just entered the room fit the story perfectly. "Ah, *oui*," Madame Denis said. "Monsieur Voltaire has been simply beside himself with excitement since he received your letter from Geneva." She looked Lili up and down as if she were taking her measure. "Did you enjoy your walk?"

She is spying on me, Lili thought, feeling a crawling sensation along her spine. Before she could reply, Madame Denis turned away, as if it hadn't been a question as much as a statement about her rule in the house. "Where is Father Adam?" she asked La Harpe.

"Still in the village, I presume," he said, "elevating his favorite hostess."

Madame Denis burst into peals of flirtatious laughter that made the fat under her chin jiggle. "Jean-François is such a clever man," she said, turning to Lili. "Did you meet Father Adam yet? He's a Jesuit who, shall we say kindly, has made up his own mind about which of his vows it pleases God that he keep, and since he is already sixty, he is making up for lost time. And my poor Monsieur de La Harpe has a lovely bride who has yet to manage to leave her bed since she arrived." Madame Denis gave an insincere pout. "Dear little sparrow, our Marie Marthe."

He's married? Lili was sure the look he had given her was neither casual nor innocent.

"The poor thing is expecting, you know," Madame Denis said, "and that can be terribly unnerving." She laughed. "I'm afraid Monsieur de La Harpe and I are quite uninteresting by comparison, the only truly normal people here in this little menagerie."

As normal as a jackal in a frock coat and a whale in a velvet dress, Lili thought, feeling a wave of protectiveness toward the old and frail-looking master of the estate. *He lives with people like these?*

The door to the library opened, and Voltaire appeared. His face lit up when he saw Lili. Ignoring Madame Denis and La Harpe, he came to her and took her arm. Madame Denis waited for La Harpe to take hers, giving him a look so intimate and flirtatious that Lili looked away to avoid being an unwilling voyeur. *Poor man*, Lili thought. *Menagerie indeed.*

LILI RUBBED HER eyes as the stub of candle flickered. It was nearly midnight, and unable to sleep after such an eventful day, she had gotten up to read a book Voltaire had lent her from his library. His *Philosophical Dictionary* had just been published, he had told her, adding with pride that it had immediately been banned by the French censors and the church. She leafed through the opening entries, stopping at "Adam."

"The names of Adam and Eve can be found in no ancient author of Greece, Rome, Persia, Syria," he had written. "It must have been God's pleasure that the origin of every one of the world's peoples should be concealed from all but the smallest and most unfortunate part, for in the natural course of things one would think the name of the forefather of all should have been carried to the farthest corners of the earth. It must have required quite a substantial miracle to destroy all the monuments to him that must once have existed, and to shut the eyes and ears of nations to Adam's story . . ."

He's certainly clever, Lili thought, turning to a page in the middle. "Freedom of Thought," she read. " 'I've been told,' Inquistor Medroso said, 'that the Catholic religion would be lost if people began to think.' 'How is that possible?' Lord Boldmind asked. 'If the church is truly divine, how could it be destroyed?' 'Well, perhaps not,' Medroso added, 'but it could be dangerously reduced. Look at Sweden, Denmark groaning under the burdensome yoke of thinking they no

longer need to follow the Pope.' 'I suppose one might see it that way,'
Boldmind replied, 'but isn't it true there would be no Christianity if
the first Christians hadn't had freedom of thought?' 'I don't under-
stand,' Medroso replied. 'I'm not at all surprised,' Boldmind said.
'It's up to people to learn to think. You were born with intelligence.
The church has clipped your wings, but they can grow again.'"

But you could have flown . . . She and Voltaire once had the same
idea about ruined wings. Perhaps she had come to a place where she
might be truly understood. She could sleep now. Ferney was already
feeling a little like home.

"COME VISIT ME in my arbor this morning, Voltaire."

Holding the note she'd received with her breakfast tray, Lili
walked across the lawn toward a linden tree surrounded by a circular
hedge. "Are you there?" she asked, calling through the entrance.
When she heard his voice she stepped inside.

The dense mass of leaves formed a a roof over a dirt floor covered with pulverized rock. Voltaire was seated in one of a pair of
chairs upholstered in red and gold brocade, set next to a wood-inlaid
table on which lay a stack of letters. An oil lamp cast light to read by
in the deep shade. To one side, a small secretarial desk and chair sat
on a worn Persian carpet. If she could ignore the tree trunk in the
middle, Lili thought, all that would be needed to complete the impression of being indoors were a few paintings hanging from the
clipped hedge.

"Welcome to my hideaway," Voltaire said, motioning to a lap
robe covering his legs. "I hope you aren't offended if I don't get up."
He was wearing a loose coat that looked more like a dressing gown,
and on his head was a scarlet turban onto which three or four caps in
various colors had been perched. He was not wearing his wig, and
fragile-looking wisps of white hair lay in unkempt straggles around
his neck, but his eyes gleamed, untouched by sallowness or clouds.

"Do you remember the last line of my *Candide*?" he asked.

"How he finally gives up his illusions that this is the best of all possible worlds, and decides that the only thing to do is to cultivate his own garden." He gestured around the clearing. "I guess you could say that's what I've done here." He gave her a wan smile. "I need asylum from my asylum. Everyone knows to leave me alone here, or else I'll write something truly wicked about them."

"I'm afraid—for reasons I haven't yet told you—that I've fallen sadly behind in my reading in the last year," Lili said. "Except for the Bible, of course." She made a face to ensure he knew such limitations had not been by choice.

"Ah yes," he said. "I must warn you that the bread you eat here will not be at all what the Lord commanded, though we have plenty of the main ingredient." Seeing Lili's puzzled look, he went on. "Take—what was it? Wheat, barley, beans, lentils, millet?—and mix them together, and make bread with it. It sounds like something I'd rather feed my goats, but here's the thing God says will make it really special." He gave her a sly grin. " 'And thou shalt bake it with dung that cometh out of man.' "

"No!" Lili's mouth dropped open, and she made no attempt to close it.

"It's right there," Voltaire cackled. "I'm afraid I'm not one of those who carries a Bible around like a third testicle, so you'll have to wait to check, but you can read Ezekiel chapter four in Latin, Greek, French, or English in my library."

"Dung?" Lili hadn't heard him.

He snickered. " 'In our sight,' the Good Lord says, so we'll all know exactly what we're eating. But remember, God is known for his mercy. He said it would be all right to use cow dung instead. But he was firm on the rest—eat it for three hundred and ninety days and not one day less." He grinned. "Aren't you lucky you arrived on day three hundred and ninety-one? But perhaps that explains why the guests are so unpleasant to be around."

"Eat dung? I'm not sure whether I want to laugh or cry."

"Exactly," Voltaire replied. "That's why religion is the vilest form of infamy. Can you imagine some poor soul, wondering why he is afflicted with gout, or whose drinking water is killing his children, thinking the remedy is to take Ezekiel's advice about what will make God stop punishing him? Although I suppose we deserve whatever we're willing to believe."

He looked away with a bemused smile, remembering something. "Many years ago, I was living above a tavern with about ten other boarders, and the *chaise percée* sat over a pipe that went down past the tavern into—well, who knows?—somewhere underground. I was arrested for having written something treasonous, and the officer thought I was hiding copies in my room. I told him I had thrown my work down the privy, and do you know what that brainless toad did?"

Voltaire didn't wait for a reply. "He went looking for it! By the time he was done, the pipe had burst and sprayed the people all over the tavern. And it was just about then, when he was standing covered in piss and shit—including mine—that he figured out there weren't any papers there at all."

"He never found them?"

Voltaire cackled. "I never put them there. I wanted to punish him for being in thrall to a government that would arrest me for writing what I thought."

Lili shook her head slowly, marveling at his audacity.

"Why are you here?" Voltaire asked in a suddenly solemn voice.

"How nice it is to have forgotten for a little while," Lili said, taken aback by the change in subject.

Voltaire rested one bony hand on his chest and massaged his chin with the other as he listened without comment to her story about her impending marriage and her trip to Cirey. "We shall have to think of something," he said when she had finished. Setting aside the lap robe, he got slowly to his feet. "Would you like to take a walk? It always helps clear my mind."

"Perhaps I could stay here at Ferney for a while," Lili thought aloud, as they walked in the direction of a little church she had noticed on the grounds. "I can copy in a good hand, and Madame Denis might like to be relieved of some of the burdens of the house . . ." She saw a smirk flit across Voltaire's face at the mention of the corpulent niece who called herself his housekeeper but whose two burdens seemed to consist of ensuring personally that there was no food left uneaten at any meal and making Monsieur de La Harpe feel witty. "It would be temporary, of course," Lili added, "but it would keep me from having to go back to Paris in a few days and choose a husband."

"Nothing would be more charming, my dear," Voltaire replied, stopping at the gate to the churchyard. "But it would be best if your name did not become associated with mine. Although with the gossip-mongering that goes on in this house, it may already be too late for that." He stopped to look at her. "Besides, I think the solution to your problem may be right under your nose. You just haven't seen it yet."

Lili opened her mouth to ask what he meant, but he was already pointing to an inscription above the door of the church. "*Deo erexit Voltaire.*" he said. "Do you know what that means?"

"Voltaire erected this to God," Lili replied.

"That's what it says, but what does it mean?" Voltaire was too impatient to wait for her to think. "It means that I did it to honor God, not to snivel before some saint the church tells us will have a chat with God on our behalf."

"You built a church?" The incongruity was so great that it pushed all other thoughts to the back of her mind.

"Not exactly," he said with a rueful look. "I rebuilt a church. I thought the old parish church spoiled the view, and since it was on my property I tore it down. I figured nobody would mind. After all, I was building a new one with my own money just a few paces away for all the poor cannibals of this village who believe they can't live—or I guess can't die is more like it—without a taste of their Savior's flesh and blood every week. But the bishop decided to punish me for not asking his permission by insisting that I build the new one right where the old one was. So yes, my dear Lili, your friend Voltaire built a church."

He looked around. "It's a shame Father Adam isn't here at the moment. I'd like you to meet him. He's my other revenge besides the inscription. Adam's been defrocked, but he says mass anyway, and it makes me feel a bit better that the people who use my property for such foolishness at least aren't being lied to in sermons quite as badly as they might be by a priest who actually believes all that nonsense."

By now they had reached the other side of the church, where the land fell away in a gentle slope, revealing vineyards, pastures, orchards, and fields of vegetables and grains. "This is what I live for now," Voltaire said. "I'm rich, you know—the château, and the town and all the land around it belong to me. I can't think of a better use for my money than to make this little bit of France a better place. When I bought Ferney, the land was too marshy to cultivate. Now the marshes are drained and there are new farms. There's a watch-making factory, and other new businesses that bring income to the village. Life is better now—more orderly, cleaner, safer. I've given up on changing the world but I can change this." His face flushed with pleasure. "We must cultivate our garden, you know."

He took a quick look back toward the château. "We should go," he said. "It must be almost time for dinner." His laugh was gleeful. "Good thing I've trained everyone to wait."

"Would you mind if I borrowed a copy of *Candide* while I'm here?" Lili asked, taking his arm as they turned back. "I'm feeling dreadfully ignorant."

The old man smiled. "I would be most pleased. But there's something else I think you should read first."

Emilie
1749

EMILIE DU Châtelet stopped writing for a moment as she felt the baby move inside her. She rested her hand on her bulging stomach. Only three months now. Work on the *Principia* was going well, and she had time to write something else. She wasn't sure why she felt driven to write down her personal philosophy when there wasn't even enough time to deal with weightier things. A little piece, this "Discourse on Happiness" admittedly was, not even meant for publication, although of course when she was dead, she wouldn't care what happened to it.

"People commonly think it is difficult to be happy, and many reasons can be shown to justify this belief," she had written a few days before. "But the truth is that it would be much easier to be happy if people tended toward self-reflection, and if a plan of conduct preceded their actions."

Voltaire would be interested in reading what followed, although there wasn't anything she said that they hadn't discussed at one point or another. "It's up to us to make our passions serve our happiness"—surely he would find no argument in that, although he might be displeased at how frankly she had written about the end of their affair and the pain the loss of his affections had caused her. Saint-Lambert as well—he should get a copy, since the misery he'd left in his wake had certainly helped to hone her thinking.

"It isn't enough simply not to be unhappy. Life would not be worth the trouble if absence of dolor were the only goal. Truly, non-being would be preferable, since assuredly that is the state in which we suffer the least. It's necessary, instead, to *strive* to be happy."

Her dear friend Duke Stanislas would understand that. He, more than anyone, knew how to make the effort required to live well. No wonder her friends would rather spend time at his provincial court at Lunéville than at Versailles. Once she was a little further along in her work on the *Principia*, she would be leaving Paris to go to Lunéville with a few companions to help her through her lying-in and the birth of her child.

A fourth copy for one of those friends, Marie-Victoire du Thil, who so many years ago had insisted on stopping by Voltaire's boardinghouse so she could taunt him with being the second-most-intelligent person in Paris. How different her life would be if she had never met him!

"We are made happy in the present not just by the pleasures we experience at the moment, but by our hopes for the future and our reminiscences of the past," she wrote. "Appropriate self-love in contemplating these things is the wind that fills our sails, and without which our ship could not move forward." It was good to feel she had done well with the life God had given her. Though she doubted her future, the desire to speak from beyond the grave was more than wind filling a sail. It was a bellowing gale that made the rigging scream.

A new friend, Julie de Bercy, would be accompanying her to Lunéville as well. Being so young and with so much to learn, perhaps she would like to read it too. Baronne Lomont of course would not. Now there was someone whose goal in life seemed to be quite the opposite of happiness, rejecting joy and pleasure with dour sanctimony, like a magnet repelled by the force of another. Baronne Lomont would be at Lunéville too, having invited herself as insurance that no one enjoyed themselves too much.

Emilie shrugged. "It would be better to figure out how to be happy in the situation we face than try to change it," she wrote. The trick was to be happy whatever one's lot. Baronne Lomont was her sister-in-law, her husband's brother's widow, and since there was no way to rid her life of such a grim-faced bore, she should endure her company as best she could.

Emilie would keep a copy of her "Discourse on Happiness" for herself, of course, and have one more made, in case she had forgotten someone. She felt as if she had. Whoever it was would come to her in time, and then she would offer up her little work, in bound leather with a ribbon for her to keep her place, as if she had intended to give the book to her from the beginning.

Her place? Emilie thought for a moment. Why was she sure the person she'd forgotten was a woman?

The baby moved again. "Quiet now," she said. "Maman has to write."

18

How could Voltaire be so cruel? Lili set the ribbon at her place and put the book down. It would be better to figure out how to be happy in the situation she faced than try to change it? The happiest people were those who desired the least change in their lot? How could her mother say such terrible things, and why would Voltaire want her to know she had? Her mother wasn't happy with her lot, and she hadn't just gone along . . .

My mother is a hypocrite! The thought stung, as surely as if it had stood up and slapped her.

"Beg pardon, mademoiselle." Lili heard Justine's voice behind her. "You'll be late to supper if you don't go down."

"Please say I'm indisposed," Lili said. *Please say I think I'm suffocating.* "I'll ask for a tray later if I'm hungry."

The dining room was directly below her bedchamber, and she could hear the guests being seated. Madame Denis's and Voltaire's voices were the easiest to pick out, but La Harpe was there too, as were a man she assumed was Father Adam and a woman who must be La Harpe's phantom wife finally up from her bed. The sounds of silverware clinking against plates and the jocular conversation, lubricated by the tasty wine from Voltaire's estate, rose up to Lili's room.

Lili didn't hear. The book compelled her to open it again. "The foremost thing is to be well decided about what one wants to be and what one wants to do," her mother had written.

As Lili read on, the words jumped out at her as if they had been shot from cannons. Shaken, she put down the book again and went to the window. She had been wrong about what her mother had meant. *She isn't saying to accept Baronne Lomont's ideas for my life*, Lili realized. *She's saying the opposite—that I can't expect to be happy if I do. She's telling me to be who I am. That's the lot I can't change.*

The first boom of thunder from a summer storm crackled in the sky, and she felt the cool, charged air on her face. "Who I am—that's the lot I can't change," she repeated aloud.

A sudden gust of wind rattled the pages of the open book and she picked it up again. "Without knowing yourself, there can be no real happiness," she read. "You'll swim perpetually in a sea of uncertainty; you'll destroy in the morning what you made the evening before; you'll pass your life making stupid mistakes that you will then try to repair or repent."

Don't be afraid of what you want. How can you be happy without the courage to acknowledge your dreams? Her mother's message burned through her so personally that at any moment Lili thought she might turn the page and see her name. *Set your sights on what you can hope to have and do not settle for less,* she was telling her. *Unreasonable hopes will make you miserable, but reasonable ones can shape your life, if you have the courage to listen to them.*

Lili was sure she felt the soft whisper of a woman's voice. "Don't give up now," it said. "Go find out who you are, and then you will know what you need."

GERMOND STOOD ON the far side of the salon, just outside Voltaire's bedroom. He bowed stiffly to Lili as she approached.

"Is he all right?" she asked, holding the note Louise had delivered to her bedroom the following morning.

"Quite, I'm sure," Germond said. "But rainy nights in the summer always leave his chest feeling tight, and he believes it wise to stay in bed the next day. One can't be too careful, you know."

"I hear you out there!" Voltaire called from his bedchamber. "Bring Mademoiselle du Châtelet in!"

He was sitting up in bed, wearing a thin muslin nightshirt and a length of soft, cream-colored wool that had been wrapped several times around his head and secured with a twist and a tuck at the crown. His coffee and a crust of bread had been pushed aside on his lap tray in favor of the Parisian journal he had been reading.

"How are you feeling, Monsieur Voltaire?" Lili asked, approaching the bed.

"One never knows," he said, holding his thin fingers to his chest. "These summer storms create miasmas that can bring the most dreadful diseases into the house. I shall keep my head warm"—he patted his turban—"and be quiet as a mouse all day, and perhaps nothing will find me." He gave her a toothless grin. "I thought perhaps you might be willing to sit with me for a while. We're too far from Paris for tongues to wag about you being in my bedroom."

He looked toward the door. "Germond!" The valet was immediately in the doorway. "Bring mademoiselle some breakfast."

Before she could sit down, Voltaire pointed to a painting on the wall opposite his bed. A rosy-cheeked woman in a blue, ermine-trimmed gown looked out with an expression that was at once haughty and slightly mischievous. "Do you recognize her?"

Lili moved toward the portrait. "My mother?" She turned back to see him nodding.

"Marianne Loir caught her spirit," he said. "And her beauty. It's my favorite portrait of her."

Lili stood, taking in every detail. "I've never seen anything larger than a miniature," she said, "and that only once." She leaned in to look more closely. "What color was her hair? I can't tell with the dusting of powder."

"As black as a raven," Voltaire said. "Do you see what she's holding?"

"A compass and a carnation."

Voltaire smiled. "She had the portrait painted for me. I knew what it meant the minute I saw it. She was offering me her passion—that's the white carnation—but at the same time the compass was telling me she would never let anyone interfere with her right to use her mind. And of course that was what I loved most about her." He paused. "Did you read the book I gave you?"

Lili sat in the chair closest to the portrait, where the air felt bathed with her mother's presence. "More than once."

"Apparently I didn't incur the complete loss of your affection by letting you read about me. I'm afraid I didn't always behave well, and I certainly was never much of a lover," Voltaire said with a rueful smile, "although I suppose it's in poor taste to offer any of the details."

Germond came in with a tray, relieving Lili of the awkwardness of a reply. She took a sip of coffee. "She said happiness involves both living passionately and being able to let go when the passion is no longer there."

"Yes, and isn't that the trick—the letting go? We were truly excellent friends, far more satisfying than being lovers, but I don't think she lived long enough to take her own advice about Monsieur Saint-Lambert."

Saint-Lambert. "I saw his portrait in a drawer at Cirey," Lili said. "I've been trying to accept that the man I always assumed was my real father has no blood connection to me at all, and that the man who is my father gets up in the morning and takes coffee just as I'm doing now." A lump grew in her throat. "And that neither of them feels anything for me"—she swallowed hard—"or I for them."

She caught a tear before it could fall. "I take it," Voltaire said, "that the last part is something you'd like to convince yourself of." He passed her a neatly pressed handkerchief from a stack on his bedside table.

Lili wiped her eyes. "I can deal with Saint-Lambert," she said. "It feels like teasing one of the specimens at the Jardin de Roi, trying to get it to lie in place. I can think about him without feeling it has anything to do with me, however odd that may sound. But my father—" Her attempt at a laugh came out as a wilted sniff. "My not-my-father. That's harder to bear, because I suppose I spent my life hoping . . ."

Voltaire waited to see if she would continue and when she did not, he spoke. "There are many kinds of passion, and one of the most painful ones is hoping in vain. I am certain your mother would tell you that you need to let go of what isn't going to happen, if you are going to choose to be happy."

Lili sighed. "I suppose you're right. But I've been wondering about what you said yesterday—that the solution to my problem was right under my nose. Did you mean that Saint-Lambert could help me somehow? That if he acknowledged he was my father, he would have the right to contract my marriage?"

Voltaire sat up straighter. "You are a very clever girl," he said, "but that's a very distressing idea indeed, and one that I don't think your mother would approve of at all. We went to great pains to cover up your true paternity, and a scandal now would do neither the dead nor the living any good."

Lili's spirits deflated. Voltaire had rejected the only idea she had come up with. "Couldn't he just go quietly to Baronne Lomont and tell her to leave me alone?"

"She would refuse to receive him. He would know that, and he wouldn't embarrass himself by trying. The Marquis du Châtelet must be viewed as your father for propriety's sake, and you, my dear, benefit from that more than anyone. Do you really want, at this point in your life, to be reborn as the bastard child of your mother's illicit affair? If you want to destroy any chance of choosing the things that will make you happy, that's a good place to start."

"But you told me the answer is obvious, and I can't see what else it might be." Her anger flashed at what she thought was a hint of glee in Voltaire's smile. "Can't you please tell me? I feel as if I'm drowning and you won't lend me a hand."

"No, I won't," he told her. "You can figure it out yourself. God gave us the gift of life, but it's up to us to give ourselves the gift of living well. You can trust me that a solution exists right under your nose. You don't have to feel you have no choice but to go back to Paris and settle for something that runs contrary to living well. Having confidence in that is my gift to you, but I will hand you nothing more."

He was silent for a moment. "Look at me, Lili," he finally said.

She took the handkerchief away from her face and raised her eyes to meet his. The gleeful look was gone, replaced by tenderness so profound her eyes welled with tears again. "You must think things through for yourself," he said. "If I have had one message for the world in all my work, that is it. And it's my message for you too. I know I'm doing what your mother would want. You need to see yourself as more than a helpless girl, dependent on others, to have the strength to create a good life. That's what your mother did."

He looked at her with a gleeful smile. "*Mon Dieu,* at eighteen you've already had the courage to go off by yourself in search of what you need. She would be so proud."

He was right about depending on herself, much as she hated to admit it. She looked over her shoulder at her mother's portrait. "Look at my hands," the eyes seemed to say. "Your passions and your mind. You can have them both—it's the message I chose. A message for you."

The sound of a man's frantic voice echoed in the vestibule, followed by the click of boots in the salon. A man rushed into the bedroom. Over his clerical collar lay strands of hair tangled from what had obviously been a fast ride on horseback.

"They executed La Barre in Abbéville!" he said. "Those dogs!"

Voltaire had already thrown off the bedcovers. "Germond! Get me my clothes!" He hopped around on his skinny legs until Germond handed him his pants. Holding on to the back of the chair, he put them on without sitting down. He pulled off his nightshirt, revealing protruding ribs and flaccid skin the color of skimmed milk, before Germond got a clean silk undershirt on him.

When he had finished dressing he headed across the salon to the library, with Lili, Germond, Father Adam, and now Michon in his wake. "Shall I . . . ?" Michon said.

"Yes, coffee for everyone," Voltaire said, waving her off. "And bring the brandy too."

"Tell me the details," Voltaire demanded of Father Adam as he motioned him to sit. Lili sat down also, choosing a chair out of Voltaire's sight just in case she hadn't been invited.

Father Adam patted his coat over the inside pocket. "I came off without the letter, I was in such a hurry," he said. "But I remember what it said. La Barre received no royal pardon, even after the papal nuncio and the bishop requested it."

"No royal pardon from a death sentence for not doffing his hat at a crucifix in a parade?" Voltaire eyes flashed with anger. "That's the only thing the prosecutors could prove he did!"

"They took him to the scaffold wearing a sign that said he had been found guilty of impiety, blasphemy, and sacrilege—"

"Sacrilege? The judges agreed there was no evidence he was the one who smeared filth on the statue of Christ in the cemetery. It was obviously someone else and they know it!" Voltaire banged his hand so hard on his desk that the inkwell rattled. "And blasphemy for singing a few dirty songs in a tavern with his friends, and having a pornographic novel in his room? One dies for this in France?"

"What did you expect?" Father Adam said, as Michon put down the tray. She motioned to the brandy and he nodded. "Just a little. That lawyer Duval wanted him to die, and he was going to die even if all he'd done was blow his nose during mass."

Voltaire's chest heaved, as if he were trying to hold back an explosion. "This is partly my fault, you know. When they found that novel they also found my dictionary. That's what that bastard Duval really wanted to say. 'Read Voltaire at your peril. If you decide to think, you're risking your life.'"

"It is not your fault," Father Adam said. "Of course, you could always let an old defrocked priest forgive your sin with a little wave of my hand . . ." Voltaire snorted in derision but calmed a little at the priest's joke. "But really," Father Adam went on, "unless you are saying you were wrong to write it, you aren't at fault that he decided to read it."

Father Adam tossed down his coffee and poured another cup that was mostly brandy. "La Barre made that choice—and apparently he didn't regret it. The letter said he laughed when they read the sentence on the scaffold, and laughed even harder when he saw the name of the friend who was smart enough to escape written on a sign above an empty noose."

"He laughed?" Lili gasped.

Voltaire didn't hear. "What happened then?" he demanded.

"They cut off his head and threw it on a bonfire." Father Adam stared at Voltaire for a moment. "Along with a copy of your *Philosophical Dictionary.*"

The same dictionary she had found so amusing? Lili knew people got thrown in jail for crossing the authorities—Voltaire himself had—but hanging a man and desecrating his body just for having a forbidden book in his room? A memory of the nun at the abbey slapping her face for having Rousseau's *Émile* made her stomach churn. *This is France?* Lili thought with dismay. *This is the society the Comte de Buffon believes is improving?*

Voltaire spun in the direction of the door. "Germond!" he called out. "Pack my bag," he said when the valet came in. "You know that bonfire was a message for me," he said to Father Adam. "Are the police on the way?"

"No sign of them yet—but you're wise to expect them."

As he turned to leave, Voltaire seemed to notice for the first time that Lili was there. "I must get across the Swiss border," he said. "This is likely to blow over in a few weeks, but I do not intend to allow the imbeciles running this country to subject me to even one night in their jail." He looked at Father Adam. "What day is today? When does the next coach to Paris leave?"

Lili's heart sank. "Tomorrow morning," Father Adam said. "You'll be safe here, with Madame Denis and Father Adam."

Voltaire clasped his cold, dry hands over Lili's. "The authorities don't want anyone but me. Still, you should take the coach to Paris no later than next week. It isn't going to be pleasant here for a while, I'm afraid."

LILI STOOD ON the steps of the château less than two hours later, watching Voltaire's coach disappear down the road. Charcoal-colored thunderheads had gathered over the mountains behind the château, and she saw the first flash in the sky, followed by a loud, crackling boom. A gust of wind sent fallen leaves swirling across the driveway just as the first drops of rain spotted the ground. "Best get inside, mademoiselle," Michon said. "It's not good that he had to go off in this, but no need for you to get a soaking too."

Wordlessly, Lili walked back through the vestibule and into the salon. The room seemed drained of life, not just from the clouds covering the sun, but as if the house knew that Voltaire was gone. *I don't want to be here with Madame Denis and Monsieur de La Harpe,* Lili thought with an inadvertent shudder of mistrust.

She went to Voltaire's bedroom and picked up the nightshirt Germond had not yet put away. She draped it on the chair beneath her mother's portrait. Taking a candle, she held it up to examine the face more closely. "I'm still here," the eyes seemed to say. "Still waiting."

Tell me the answer, Lili pleaded silently. *If it doesn't involve Saint-Lambert, then—*

A flash of light illuminated the garden behind her, followed almost immediately by a louder and more immediate clap of thunder. Lili stood transfixed in front of the portrait, as what felt like lightning traveled through her mind. "That's it!" she said to the face in the portrait. She pressed her fingers to her lips, and stood on her toes to touch her mother's rosy cheeks and whisper her thanks.

She found Michon in the dining room. "Please ask Justine and Louise to pack my bags immediately," she told her. "And tell Stephane to go to the stables to see about a carriage. We'll be taking the Paris coach tomorrow."

DRESSED IN HER traveling clothes, Lili waited in Voltaire's library while the carriage was loaded. In Voltaire's desk, she had found a stack of vellum sheets, and she was using her last hour at Ferney to finish the story she was writing as a gift for Voltaire. Her eyes lit on what she had already written and she read it again.

"Look at those men!" Tom said, tugging on Meadowlark's sleeve.

She turned around just in time to catch a glimpse of a small group, all with crooked noses and flattened cheeks. "What happened to their faces?" she asked.

"The king fell out of a tree once and landed on his face," a girl said. "He had two terrible black eyes and a broken nose. They wanted to show how devoted they were, so they bashed their faces in with boards." The girl gave a furtive glance around. "The king healed quite nicely. Most people think those men were quite foolish to do that, since they don't look like him at all anymore, but we admire them greatly all the same. See the medals around their necks? They're Knights of the Royal Order of Self-Bashers. The king established it to honor them for their devotion."

Lili smiled, imagining Voltaire cackling as he read it. She skimmed to the end of what she had written and picked up her pen to add more.

Meadowlark and Tom left the ceremony for the Return of the Four Wanderers and found Comète in a nearby pasture. As they flew over the mighty Amazon, Meadowlark pulled back on the reins. "Who's that?" she asked Tom, pointing down toward a young man paddling a boat. She guided Comète to a landing on the banks. "Are you the missing Fourth Wanderer?" she asked.

"I am." The young man nodded with a wide grin.

"They're waiting for you back there," Tom told him. "Did you find a place where people are happier? We heard that's what they send you out to do, but you're not supposed to find any. It makes people happier at home when you don't."

"No, I didn't," the Fourth Wanderer said. "Things are much the same everywhere. But I've discovered I'm happier out here on the river, with no one telling me what to do or think, and I've decided I'm never going back." He looked at the two of them. "Do you think that's wrong? Maybe I could convince people that bashing their faces in has nothing to do with happiness at all."

Lili thought for a moment. She hadn't known exactly how to end the story, but now it came to her.

"I've wandered the world a little myself," Meadowlark said gravely, "and I can tell you something you'll probably find wherever you go."

"What's that?" the young man asked.

"It's easier to bash one's skull in than to think with the mind inside it."

Lili blotted the last words. After signing her name, she sat looking at the page for a moment. "Thank you for making me think for myself," she added. "I'm off to live well. With deep affection, your Lili."

THE COACH STOPPED overnight at Bar-sur-l'Aube, but in the morning, Lili was not on it. She, Justine, and Stephane were rattling back along the road to Cirey, not in Anton's cart, but in a carriage Lucien brought from the château. A few days later, they returned, and when the next coach came through Bar-sur-l'Aube, Lili was once more on her way to Paris.

"I pray this will work," she had written to Delphine the night before she left. "And if not, I will strive to be happy, whatever happens." From time to time for reassurance, she slipped her hand into her satchel, where, tucked next to the pouch containing her mother's prism, there were three letters with wax seals imprinted with the crest of the Marquis du Châtelet.

GEORGE-LOUIS LECLERC, COMTE de Buffon, got up from his chair at the valet's announcement that Mademoiselle du Châtelet had dropped in to see him. "Lili!" he said, opening his arms wide before kissing her cheek. "Are you back from Étoges already?"

"Not exactly," Lili replied. "At least not from Étoges. It's rather a long story. Do you have time?"

"For you, my dear, always," he said. "But perhaps I may exact a favor in kind. I have bones from a South American rodent on the table over there—"

"A gift from Jean-Étienne, I imagine," Lili said, practicing her resolve not to have unreasonable hopes.

"Indeed." The count looked at her quizzically. "It's a bit too difficult for me with my poor, old eyes. I was working on it when you were announced, and I was telling myself to stop before I destroyed it altogether, but as usual I was being rather stubborn about it."

He sat down on a comfortable armchair directly across from Lili. "I saw Baronne Lomont at a funeral last week, and she said you were coming back in a matter of days from Étoges and that you would be married by the end of the year. She wouldn't say to whom. Odd—something about not being at liberty yet to publish the bans . . ."

"If I am betrothed, I am not aware of it," Lili said icily.

The count stroked his chin and gave her a penetrating stare. "So, if you haven't been at Étoges, where, pray, have you been?"

"Cirey," Lili said, waiting to see the name register in his mind. "And Ferney."

"With Voltaire?" The count's eyes widened with astonishment.

"Yes, and with my—with the Marquis du Châtelet. Delphine concocted the story that I was at Étoges, but I was never there at all." Lili smiled. "Apparently it worked, since the whole point was to fool the baronne. I'm sure Delphine will be most delighted."

"Fool the baroness?"

Lili sighed. "Baronne Lomont told you her intentions, not mine. I went off to see if I could do anything about it, and I discovered—at least I think I did—that I can." She opened the bag she was carrying and handed the three letters to the count. "I've come up with a plan."

He sat down and read the letters. At first his brow furrowed with puzzlement, but by the time he had read them twice he was chuckling with undisguised glee. "You clever girl!" he said, wiping his eyes. "You are certainly your mother's daughter."

He paused, contemplating her for a moment. "Your mother's daughter, but with a different father than you thought, I presume you realize now."

"Did you know?" Lili asked, her heart in her throat. *Did he keep it from me? Is there anyone I can trust to be truthful?*

"No," he said, to Lili's relief. "But I can't say I didn't know either. I do recall there were raised eyebrows at the time, but it seems to me they were more over her age and her carelessness." He frowned. "I'm sorry—that was quite thoughtless. In this case, her carelessness turned out to be a wonderful gift to the world. I'd call you predestined, if I believed in such things."

He searched her face for recognition of the compliment, but Lili was too distressed and confused to smile.

"It's a rather poor use of the mind to dwell on gossip, especially when it doesn't pertain to one's own life," Buffon went on. "You were here, the marquis called you his child, and of course the truly important thing was your mother's untimely death. I grieved for her quite profoundly, for what we all had lost." His face clouded. "Not knowing at the time, of course, what we had gained."

Lili puzzled for a moment before realizing the count was referring to her. At this show of affection, the fears and anxiety she had felt since beginning her journey lifted, and words came tumbling out.

"So much of my life I'd just assumed I wasn't important, that what happened to me didn't really matter—that my obligations were only to others and that there was something bad in me if I cared too much about myself. Maman wasn't like that, but Baronne Lomont has been relentless since I was a little girl. When I went to Cirey and found out I wasn't the marquis's daughter, I felt worse than I ever had, as if I was nothing more than—" She thought for a moment. "No more than a pesty insect buzzing around the face of someone I had foolishly thought would care. And then—I'm not sure exactly how—my mother's voice was in my head, telling me that I'd have to matter to myself first, before I could expect anything good to happen. So I got the idea to go to Ferney, and Monsieur Voltaire told me to rely on myself, and if I failed to live well I would have no one to blame but me."

She sat back, wondering whether she had ever in her life spoken so many words with no more than a pause to take a breath. "I decided I owe it to myself to be happy," she said, pressing her palms into her thighs with the force of an oath.

Buffon was grinning broadly. "Your mother would be very pleased. And I would only add one thing. You owe it to her too. It's what she wants for you. And Madame de Bercy also. Go out and conquer the world, or at least whatever little piece of it you choose. Do it for yourself, Lili, and for them too."

"So you'll help me?" Lili's heart pounded with excitement.

"With all my heart," he replied. "But I think we can wait a few minutes to begin plotting. If you are up for a walk, there's something I'd like to show you in Jean-Étienne's garden—a development I think you'll find most interesting."

* * *

SHE TOOK HIS arm as they strolled the Jardin de Roi, down a tree-shaded path Lili recalled from memories that seemed both impossibly distant and as fresh as summer rain. "Did Jean-Étienne send a letter with the bones?" she asked, hoping she could take whatever followed with the equanimity she had vowed.

"No." The count turned to her. "Let's sit for a moment," he said, motioning to a bench. "We've been so busy getting caught up about you that I haven't told you the news."

News? The count's solemn face set off an explosion of fear in Lili's mind. *Jean-Étienne's married. What else could it be with such a look? Or worse. He's dead. Drowned at sea. Poisoned by some plant. Broken at the bottom of a cliff in the Falklands.*

"Lili," the count said. "You remember Francine Thibaudet, his betrothed?"

"How could I forget?"

"Well, it seems as if Jean-Étienne was gone a little too long." The count smiled wryly. "Apparently she took up with a cavalry officer, and when she—when she needed to be married quickly—Jean-Étienne was on the other side of the world. Since he'd been gone for several months already, her situation had obviously been none of his doing."

Lili's heart slammed so hard against her ribs she wasn't sure she could take a breath.

"The family had no choice but to break the engagement and marry her off quickly to whomever could be persuaded to take a less than virginal bride in return for a hefty share of the Thibaudet fortune," the count went on. "She's off already, living somewhere in Bourgogne with her new husband."

"So Jean-Étienne is—" Lili's head swam. "Free?"

The count nodded. "And, I might add, quite the richer for the experience. A broken engagement can be quite lucrative for the one not at fault. It's a business contract, like any other, with considerations of real value. So he is now at liberty to marry the woman of his choice, and I am quite certain he knows who that is."

Unreasonable hopes will make you unhappy. Lili remembered her mother's words. *But reasonable ones?* Lili's heart shook off its burden of restraint, like a winter of snow sliding from a roof. "Is he—" she stammered. "Does he—"

"If you mean, does he love you, I think the answer is decidedly yes."

She leaned in against the count on the bench, too overwhelmed to say aloud what perhaps it was now safe to acknowledge: *I love him. Can it be possible to get what I haven't even dared to hope for?* "I feel dizzy," she murmured. Buffon gave her knee a fatherly pat. "We'll rest, then, before I tell you the rest."

There was more? Lili sat up, her head instantly cleared. "No," she said. "Please go on." She gave him her best attempt at a smile. "I can always faint later."

The count laughed. "Well, if you think his misery at his engagement could not be surpassed, I assure you, when I told him I heard you were betrothed, it was far worse. I don't think I've ever seen a young man with a grimmer face." He waited for his words to register.

The development in the garden? Lili's eyes widened. "He's back?"

Buffon's face broke into a huge grin. "And about to receive some very good news." Lili didn't wait to hear. Holding up her skirt, she ran down the path.

"JEAN-ÉTIENNE?" HE WAS kneeling over a shrub, finishing a graft. He looked up at the sound of her voice.

"Lili!" A grin exploded over his face as he jumped to his feet, but it just as quickly faded. "How delightful it is to see you," he said stiffly, brushing his hands on his work trousers. "I'm afraid I'm far too dirty to greet you properly."

Lili's heart sank. Why was he being so distant? Hadn't the count just told her how he felt? Then it came to her: he'd been principled when he was betrothed, and he would be just as principled now that he thought she was.

"Jean-Étienne, I—" Tongue-tied and shaking, Lili put her hand over her mouth.

Buffon had come up beside her and put an arm over her shoulder as her eyes flooded with tears. "If perhaps I may interject?" he said. "I believe Mademoiselle du Châtelet has something important to tell you."

"I— It was a misunderstanding. I'm not engaged." Without knowing exactly how it happened, her arms were around him. "You're not lost to me," she whispered, feeling her hot breath on his neck.

"Lili . . ." They swayed together like branches of a tree when a breeze sweeps away the staleness of too long a spell without rain. When he pulled away, she saw that his face was wet.

"And you're not lost to me," he said, wiping away her own tears with a touch so soft her knees trembled and a hoarse sob broke loose from her throat.

"I'm sorry," she said, embarrassed by the coarseness of the sound. "I hope I'm not turning into a frog." She stepped back, trying to make a joke of it by giving him a crooked smile.

"No," he said, facing her and taking both her hands in his. "You will always be the fairest in the land."

Buffon gave a gleeful laugh. "And I suspect the evil fairy in the story is about to lose her power." Enjoying the moment, he rocked backed and forth between his heels and toes, clasping his hands behind his back. "My dear boy," he went on, "I think you have captured the heart of the cleverest girl in all of France."

"Not yet," Lili said. "I haven't freed myself of Baronne Lomont yet, and apparently she's decided I'm getting married this month." She shrugged and gave Buffon a wan smile. "Although no one but herself seems to know to whom."

"But what uncle said about your heart?" Jean-Étienne asked. "About my capturing your heart—?"

Yes, yes, yes. She wanted to say it again and again, to cry it out to every rooftop in Paris and to the heavens themselves, but suddenly his arms were around her and his lips were on hers. So joyfully she thought she might explode with happiness, Lili said yes with no words at all.

EXCEPT FOR THE small group of servants who remained in Paris while Ambroise and Delphine were at Étoges, Lili was alone in Hôtel Bercy that night. Her candle cast a pool of light as, unable to sleep, she roamed the house. Here was the bed where she and Delphine told stories, the stair railing where she had stood to listen to the guests in the salon, Maman's sitting room where she and Delphine practiced their curtseys, the parlor where Delphine had been married. The bedroom where Maman died alone, to protect them.

How full the mind could be! Some days were for saving every last detail—days like the one she had just passed. "Tell us how you and Papa fell in love," her children might say someday.

"Well, we were both supposed to marry someone else, so we tried to pretend we didn't care. We both went away for a while, and when we came back everything had changed. We were both free to admit how we felt, and . . ."

The swirl of images and the rush of feeling in her head and body were the real story. How Jean-Étienne had taken her up in his arms, how they buried their heads in each other's necks and wept until their shoulders were wet. How their lips came together as if they were always meant to do just that. How the sensation traveled down her body to a place deep in her groin where a feeling awakened in her she had not known before and that she wanted to feel again. How she had a glimpse of what her mother meant when she said that people must make their own happiness. How when they turned around and saw Buffon in the distance, walking back alone to the house, they knew that sometimes time really does stop, at least in one spot in the Jardin de Roi.

Memory was a strange thing. The coach ride from Bar-sur-Aube had receded in one day to nothing but a few aching bones and unpacked bags, but as she stood in the dining room of Hôtel Bercy, wishing she could conjure up Maman to tell her the news, it seemed as if the scent still lingered from her handkerchief, ready to catch Lili's tears just as it did after all those painful childhood visits with Baronne Lomont.

Baronne Lomont. "Don't get ahead of yourself," Lili whispered into the candlelight. "There's no happily ever after yet." Giving the silent room one last look, she went up to bed.

THE DOORMAN'S GREETING at Hôtel Lomont was cool and perfunctory. "This way," he said, leading them to the parlor. Baronne Lomont was sitting with a man Lili did not recognize.

"May I introduce Monsieur Brillat," she said after Buffon bowed to greet her. "From the tenor of your note, I thought it advisable to have my lawyer present." Lili's heart fell as her hopes for a quick victory evaporated.

"This is unexpected," the count said, "but if mademoiselle agrees, it is quite all right with me." He gave Lili a reassuring look, and she nodded, speechless with apprehension. "Mademoiselle du Châtelet has just returned from a trip to Cirey," the count said after they both sat down.

Baronne Lomont's eyebrows arched. "Cirey?"

He nodded. "While she was there, she met with the marquis on several occasions—"

"This is extraordinarily deceitful behavior, Stanislas-Adélaïde." The baroness's eyes flashed like a sharpened sword as she turned to look at her.

Lili's heart slammed against her tight bodice. "I'm sorry for that," she said, reaching up to touch her fingertips to the spot where the prism lay hidden under her dress. "But I believe it was also wrong of you to keep me from meeting him when it turned out he was most welcoming." *Mostly when he thought I was someone else*, she thought, *but I'll keep that part to myself.* "I believe you should have encouraged it. He is, after all, a part of my heritage, is he not?"

Had the baroness's eyes darted? Lili wasn't sure.

"Mademoiselle du Châtelet came away from Cirey with some correspondence," the count said, taking one letter from a small leather portfolio and handing it to the baronne.

"The seal is broken," she said, fixing Lili with a critical stare.

"It was not addressed to you, madame," Buffon said. "In fact, you will see it is addressed to no one, since it was given directly to Mademoiselle du Châtelet. It was her right to open it if she wished."

The baroness turned it over to look at the blank exterior and passed the vellum sheet to the lawyer. "Perhaps you could read it aloud. My eyes are not what they once were."

Monsieur Brillat cleared his throat. " 'To all those it may concern, in regard to Stanislas-Adélaïde du Châtelet: I, Florent-Claude, am the father of the aforementioned child. I recently appointed Philippe-Charlotte, Baronne Lomont, to serve as my representative in the betrothal and marriage of my daughter. I hereby revoke that appointment in favor of a representative of my daughter's choosing. Sincerely, Florent-Claude, Marquis du Châtelet.' "

"This is absurd!" the baroness said, putting down her cup forcefully enough to warrant a scolding if Lili had done it that clumsily as a child.

"Not at all." Buffon shrugged. "What he gave, he can take away." He took a sip of coffee with the utmost casualness, as if they were discussing nothing more important than the weather. "And Mademoiselle du Châtelet has chosen me."

"You are not even a relative!" she said. "I'm surprised you would accept. It's already a bit of a scandal that she spends so much time with you. It's hardly proper to have such interest in a child not your own kin."

"Well," Buffon said, setting the trap. "Perhaps that makes two of us." He pulled out the second letter and handed it to the lawyer.

"It looks the same." Brillat looked up in confusion. " 'To all those it may concern, in regard to Stanislas-Adélaïde du Châtelet: I, Florent-Claude, am——'" He suddenly stopped reading and looked up at Buffon, who was sitting back in his chair, waiting. "It says I, Florent-Claude, am *not* the father of the aforementioned child."

"What?" The baroness leaned forward, her chalky skin mottling with pink. "This is an outrage!"

The lawyer went on. " 'I recently appointed Philippe-Charlotte, Baronne Lomont, to serve as my appointed representative in the betrothal and marriage of said child. I did this with no legitimate authority, since another man, Jean-François de Saint-Lambert, is her father. As of today, Stanislas-Adélaïde is disinherited, and neither I nor any member of my family will take any responsibility on my behalf in the matter of her marriage.'"

The victory far outweighed the pain of the letter's contents. Lili had waited several days at Cirey for the marquis to be sufficiently angry to write the second one. He had already been sanguine enough to write the first, although at that moment the marquis had thought she was Emilie asking him sweetly for a favor. *Some things the baroness simply doesn't need to know*, Lili thought, lowering her head to disguise the smile playing at the corners of her mouth.

The lawyer put the letter down. "Well, that certainly makes a tangle of things. Is he or is he not her father? Even he doesn't seem to know."

"He is!" the baroness spat. "The child befuddled his mind."

"I don't think Lili played much of a role at all," Buffon said, producing the third letter, written in the childlike scrawl of someone with little opportunity to practice. He read this one himself. " 'I, Berthe Villon-Crassy, and my husband, Lucien Crassy, both of Cirey, have served all our lives at the château. Sometimes Monsieur le Marquis's memory is good but he don't recognize people from one day to the next, and thinks things are happening that aren't. He don't pass one day without saying things that make no sense or are different from what he said an hour before. He's been like this for going on two years now, and it's only living here so long that makes us know what to do with him.'" Buffon handed the letter to the baronne. "It's signed by Berthe, with her husband's *X* underneath, and witnessed by the village priest."

"Well, there you have it," the baroness said. "Just what the servants said—he doesn't know from one moment to the next—"

Buffon held up his hand to cut her off. "Precisely. And that's why the document you claim gives you permission to choose a husband for Lili is no more valid than these." The baroness looked like a duelist in the moment between the firing of the shot and the realization he has been hit. "This Berthe makes it quite clear that his condition is long-standing," the count added, "and it is no more certain he wishes your assistance than that he wishes Lili to choose for herself."

Baronne Lomont gave her lawyer a questioning look. "Your letter would be a difficult authority to enforce, madame, under these circumstances," Brillat said.

Thank you, thank you, thank you, Lili thought, picturing Voltaire's mischievous smile. It was true that the answer had been right in front of her nose: who her father was didn't matter, just the fact that the marquis wasn't. Voltaire had been right about how different she would feel if he had told her the answer. *This is my victory,* she knew, and now it Marquis's was hers to claim.

She took the Marquis's two letters back from the lawyer. Holding one in each hand, she locked her gaze on the old woman across from her. "You are correct that these letters are contradictory, Baronne Lomont. You may pick which one will be destroyed after my wedding."

"I most certainly will not be coerced into such a choice," the baroness hissed with the ferocity of a cornered animal. "My letter is as valid as either of these, and I will continue to presume it is in force until. . . ." Her voice died away.

"Until you hear otherwise from the marquis?" Buffon said softly. "My dear madame, I think you just have."

"I shall write him immediately to see if there's been trickery here." She looked away with a haughty toss of her head.

"My dear baroness," Buffon said. "I must tell you with the utmost seriousness that, given the confusion that exists about the marquis as a result of these letters, even if you were to get another letter designating you, I would be obligated to file a formal objection to any marriage I knew was not desired by Mademoiselle du Châtelet. That is, of course, why public announcements of marriage are made in advance, so reasonable objections by any party may be heard."

To Lili's surprise, seeing Baronne Lomont so agitated was excruciating rather than pleasurable. "I'm sorry it's come to this," she said, trying to put a touch of softness into what she knew had to be a strong and unwavering voice. "I truly regret having to defy you when you have put so much effort into what you thought was right for me. I *am* grateful for your concern that I marry well, but I will be the one to decide what that entails."

She struggled to hold her stare as her heart went out a little more to the anguished baroness. "And of course, any attempt to stop my monthly allowance based on a claim that I have been disinherited would require that you produce the letter naming Monsieur Saint-Lambert as my father when I bring the matter to a court of law."

The blankness in the baroness's eyes told Lili that her old nemesis would have no secret weapon to reveal this time. "And if I may interject," Buffon said, "I propose that on the day Mademoiselle du Châtelet is married, not just one but all four letters be destroyed, including yours, Baronne Lomont. Nothing is served by discussing the marquis's health or Lili's parentage or finances beyond this room, but I must be clear that keeping these matters private will depend upon your conceding you have no further role to play in her marriage."

"Shall we discuss this alone?" Brillat asked.

The baroness's face was now scarlet and her eyes singed the air. "No!" she snapped. "That won't be necessary. I wash my hands of this tawdry mess." She stood up. "Marry whomever you wish, Stanislas-Adélaïde." She did not look at her, but turned directly to the count. "I'll call the doorman to see you out."

* * *

JEAN-ÉTIENNE WAS WAITING in the greenhouse, but Tatou reached Lili and the count first, screeching as he bounded over, and scrambled up onto her shoulder. Jean-Étienne got up from the notes he was working on and rushed over.

"Well, it appears as if I misspoke again," the Count de Buffon said. "It is just a matter of publishing the bans, and Lili will be married before the end of the year." A bewildered Lili and a distraught Jean-Étienne stared at him openmouthed, and seeing the torture on both their faces, the count lost heart to toy with them. "Married to each other—at least that's what I hope you will decide to do."

It took a moment to register, but when it did, Jean-Étienne's face exploded in a grin, and he ran over to Lili, picking her up and twirling her around. He put her down and held her at arm's length to look at her beaming face. "I cannot believe how lucky I am," he said. Too shy to give her more than a perfunctory kiss in front of the count, he let her go, slipping his hand down to take hers. "Tell me everything!" he said, looking back and forth between them.

"She washes her hands of the whole mess." Lili looked at the count. "I think that's what she said, wasn't it?" Buffon rocked back on his heels, obviously pleased with himself. "I believe her exact words were 'this tawdry mess.'"

"And you, Uncle?" Jean-Étienne asked.

"Mademoiselle's representative in everything," Buffon said with a smile.

"Well then," the young man replied, "may we talk privately, sir?" He looked perplexed. "Is that what I'm supposed to say? Last time it was all said for me, so I'm not quite sure."

Buffon held up his hand. "There's a certain young lady whose feelings must be ascertained first. And for that, I shall leave you alone. When you're ready, you'll find me in my study, making a mess of those rodent bones you brought from the Falklands."

As the count took his leave, Lili gave Jean-Étienne a sidelong glance. *He'll be the father of my children,* she thought, noticing how his cheeks glowed pink under his milky skin, how his fine, light brown hair glowed in the light, how his eyes sparkled with health and intelligence. *Not the one you'd pick out in a crowd,* she thought, *but no matter who was in that crowd, he'd be the best one of all.*

Jean-Étienne bent one knee to the ground and Tatou scrambled down from his shoulder to perch on it. Jean-Étienne laughed. "This doesn't involve you, little friend." Taking a small fruit from his pocket, he threw it on the floor and Tatou scrambled after it. "Stanislas-Adélaïde," he said, "would you be so kind as to—"

Lili smiled at the formality. "Stop!" she said. "You sound as if you want me to pass you the salt. Start again—and call me Lili."

"Lili." Jean-Étienne's face grew serious. "I think I fell in love with you that day in the salon when you faced down Abbé Turgot. I am so sorry that I caused you pain with Francine, and I promise I will do my best never to hurt you again. If you agree to be my wife, I will strive every day to be worthy of you." He kissed her hand. "I will support your dreams, and together we can be more than we could ever be alone."

He started to get up. "Haven't you forgotten something?" Lili tried to tease him, but she could barely get the words out for the size of her grin. "You have to ask, remember?"

"Oh, yes." Jean-Étienne's cheeks colored. "Stanislas-Adélaïde du Châtelet, will you marry me?"

She put her hands around his face. "Get up," she said in a mock command. "That's my first order, and you'd better get used to hearing them!"

Once he had risen, she brushed his lips with hers. "Yes," she said. "I will marry you." He caught her up in his arms and kissed her firmly, passionately. "I will be by your side through whatever life brings," Lili said when he had pulled away to kiss her eyes, her forehead, her neck. "I will be your champion and your friend, and—"

"Don't forget," Jean-Étienne said, still kissing her, "the mother of our children."

"The mother of our children," Lili whispered. "If God is good to us." Tatou screeched, and Lili felt his feet tickle her back as he bounded to her shoulder. "And until then, we have you," she said, with a laugh, scratching the monkey behind the ear.

"Let's go tell Uncle!" Jean-Étienne said with the exuberance of a young boy who has found a treasure. He grabbed her hand, but Lili held back.

"I have something I want to do." She looked around and found an orchid drooping with the weight of its flowers. Taking a pair of cutters from the table, she removed one stalk.

"I want to share this moment with a person I can't run back and tell," Lili said, tearing the petals from one orchid and sprinkling them at their feet.

"Let's preserve our ambitions, and above all, know well who we want to be," she said. "Let's decide on the road we want to follow in life, and always try to scatter the path with flowers." She took another orchid and tossed the petals in the direction of the greenhouse door.

"Who said that?" Jean-Étienne asked, taking Tatou on his hand and putting him down to investigate.

"My mother. She wrote something before she died—an essay on how to be happy. She wrote it for me, I think—strange as that may sound, since she never knew me. I've read it so many times I can recite parts from memory." Facing him, she took his hands in hers and looked into his eyes. "Let's try, Jean-Étienne. Whatever life brings, let's try to be truly happy together."

"Perhaps your mother can teach us both about that," he replied. "It's not always the easiest thing, although it seems it should be."

He picked up Tatou. "Back in your cage, little fellow," he said. "It's time for Lili and me to go visit the count." The greenhouse pulsed with life as they walked out into the golden light of the Jardin de Roi.

EPILOGUE

July 1778

THE SOAP bubble grew larger and larger before it drifted off across the lawn of the Château d'Étoges toward a girl with a halo of reddish-gold curls, and another with tresses so dark that in the bright summer sun they seemed tinged with blue. They giggled as they waved at the bubble to keep it afloat. "Ahh," Charles-Anne Clément de Feuillet, the nine-year-old future Comte d'Étoges, grimaced when it disappeared in a wet pop.

"Make another!" the fair-haired girl, his older sister Julie, called out to him.

"Oh yes!" Emilie Leclerc clapped her hands. "Another—and another after that!"

Charles-Anne groaned as if he were quite beleaguered to be in the service of two girls, but he dipped his wand and started again.

In the afternoon light, the purple foliage of a magnificent copper beech created a pool of shade where Lili and Delphine sat. "Julie is becoming quite the young lady," Lili said, watching Delphine's eleven-year-old daughter practice dance steps on the newly mown grass, the outline of her legs faintly visible under her gauzy muslin dress. "Indeed," Delphine said. "It's really astonishing how quickly time has passed. I was just a few years older than she when I started thinking that all I really wanted in life was to get married." She shook her head. "It seems so different when it's your own child. I feel like saying, 'Don't you dare grow up until I'm ready.'"

"And I'm certainly not ready," Lili said, watching her own eleven-year-old daughter trying to persuade Delphine's son to give the metal straw and vial of soapy water to her. "Emilie's a little tiger," she said. "If she wants something, she won't let go. And I, for one, am happy that she's still got her nose in her books most of the time, and doesn't talk about wanting to grow up at all."

She laughed. "Emilie cares even less about hats and dresses than I did. Do you remember getting your wardrobe for Versailles? How Maman and I were about ready to drag you out by your heels, we wanted so badly to go home?"

Delphine chuckled. "Julie's like that. Now that I'm on the other side, please accept my apology. I must have driven you to distraction about so many things." Her eyes took in both girls. "It's quite something, isn't it—we have girls a few months apart in age, just like us? And they're different in the same ways, but they love each other." She reached for Lili's hand, not needing to say the rest.

"And luckier in some ways. They have fathers who adore them . . ." Lili's voice trailed off. The visit to the marquis at Cirey still hurt her to think about more than a decade later, and when he died a few months after she left, she had felt only a brief moment of sadness. As for her true father, shortly after her marriage she had arranged to meet Jean-François de Saint-Lambert. He seemed as unenthused about her as she was about him, and after making an insincere pledge to remain in touch, they had said good-bye with great relief and made no further effort.

By now, Charles-Anne had gone off to a small spring-fed pond and was lying on his stomach, reaching into the water to grab the turtle he called his pet. Emilie remained behind, sitting on the grass with her skirt billowing around her, blowing a bubble and taking the pipe from her mouth to examine the small, iridescent orb before it floated away. Lili gestured in Emilie's direction. "She'll ask me a million questions tonight," she said. "Just how I imagine her grandmother as a child." She supposed it would never go away, the twinge of sadness that Emilie's grandmother would not be pulling up in her carriage for a visit with her namesake, not see her turning out in so many ways to be just like her, from her raven-black hair to her insatiable curiosity.

Lili looked out across the lawn to the château where she and her children spent every summer with Delphine, now the Comtesse d'Étoges. The small but elegant mansion was surrounded by a moat, patrolled by three white swans and a family of ducks. Emilie and Charles-Anne's tutor Anatole was in a rowboat, making the circuit around the château with two boys, aged six and four.

Anatole, a distant cousin of Jean-Étienne's, had come into their lives when George-Louis, the older of the two boys in the boat, was born, and Lili realized she could not continue schooling Emilie herself. Anatole was more like a part of the family than an employee, and in Paris, when he was not teaching the children, he worked just for the love of it in the laboratory Jean-Étienne had set up in one of the buildings at the Jardin de Roi. Like Jean-Étienne, Anatole was the odd one in his family, intensely intelligent and progressive in his thinking, more concerned about science than status.

Emilie had been taught solely at home, first by Lili and then by Anatole, and never spent a single night at a convent. Instead, for two years she had gone with her best friend, Julie, one day a week for catechism at an Ursuline convent near Hôtel Bercy. From Emilie and Julie's secretive giggles and imitations of the nuns, Lili was quite sure the church had made little progress in impressing upon them the importance of submission and piety for future wives and mothers of France. It was important to be sufficiently informed to make one's way in a society shaped by the church, Lili and Delphine both felt, but their children could choose for themselves what to believe.

The two boys in the rowboat were as blond as Emilie was dark—the image of their father, with skin so fair their noses and cheeks were covered with freckles within days of their arrival at Étoges. Georges-Louis looked up and saw her watching them. "Maman!" he called out. "There's fish in here, and Anatole said he'd make me a net to catch them!"

"That's wonderful!" Lili called out. The younger one tried to stand up to wave. "Be careful, François! Georges—hang on to your brother!"

She had named them Georges-Louis and François-Marie, after the two men who had meant the most to her during her struggle with Baronne Lomont. The baronne was dead now, having failed to wake up one morning the previous winter. Her death was followed only a few months later by Buffon's in April, and Voltaire's in May. Lili and Jean-Étienne were pleased that both men had a chance to see while they were alive how lovingly they would be remembered.

Buffon had been buried, as he wished, not in the Pantheon but a day's coach ride from Paris, on his country estate at Montbard. Voltaire had been staying in Paris at the hôtel of the Marquis de Villette when he was struck by his final illness—this one all too real—and he had been unable to return to Ferney. Lili had gone several times in his final days to be by his side. His last conscious act was to wave away the priest who had come to hear his confession, before turning his back to reject the last rites of the church. "Let me die in peace," she had heard him say.

That was less than two months ago. A coach had set out with his body for Ferney, but the weather was too hot and the embalming inadequate for the journey. Somewhere along the way the stench grew too great, and now he lay, buried quickly under the stone floor of an abbey church in a town Lili had never heard of. She couldn't decide whether, if Voltaire knew, he would laugh or cry.

The village of Étoges was probably much like that town, little more than a row of buildings on both sides of a dirt road. The château was on a small rise, making it possible to look out from the lawn and see every cart that came along the road, filled when Lili arrived for the summer with vegetables and fruit, and by the time she left in the fall, with the first of the grapes that would be turned into champagne by the vintners on the estate. Since Étoges was not on a road connecting any cities, only the occasional coach announced itself by the clouds of dirt kicked up behind it.

Today, just such a billow of dust appeared beyond the formal gardens on the far side of the grounds. Delphine saw it first. "I think they're here!" she said, getting up. In a matter of minutes, a dusty black coach came through the gilded entry gate. Charles-Anne jumped up and joined Emilie and Julie, who were already running toward it. Anatole was rowing furiously toward the tiny dock, with the two boys bouncing in their seats.

"Papa!" they all cried out, stumbling to get there first as they ran across the gravel courtyard to the coach. Ambroise opened the door before the coachman could do it for him and stepped down into the group of excited children. Charles-Anne grabbed his father around the waist, bouncing up and down, while Julie wrapped her arms around him from behind.

Walking arm in arm with Delphine, Lili watched for her first glimpse of her husband. As Jean-Étienne's head appeared in the open door of the coach, Lili felt the familiar leap of her heart. *I love him,* she thought to herself, smiling with beatific warmth as she watched her little boys run across the drive to him, while their daughter grabbed both his hands in hers and jumped with delight.

"All right, *mes chéris,*" Jean-Étienne said. "Maman's turn." He took Lili in his arms and squeezed her tight. "Umm," he said, stepping back to look at her at arm's length. "The air at Étoges certainly agrees with you," he said, giving her a brief but affectionate kiss. "You look lovely—and I cannot wait until tomorrow, when I can join you over there on those chairs and recuperate from that awful Paris heat." The expression in his eyes said privately to Lili how much he looked forward to something else, just between them, that would take place before then. He looked down at his daughter. "The smell's been brutish this last week, *ma petite,*" he said, wrinkling his nose in disgust and pinching her nostrils.

"Papa! Papa!' The boys were tugging at his coat. Jean-Étienne picked up first one and then the other, holding the little one out for a spin before pulling him close. "I've missed you all so much!" He kissed Jean-François on the cheek before putting him down, and turned to gaze at Lili with a look that said he knew he was the luckiest of men.

They turned to walk toward the house. Ambroise was arm in arm with his wife, his children chattering noisily beside him. He reached over to put his hand gently on Delphine's stomach. "How is the new one?" he asked.

"Asleep," she replied, and then gave a little start. "Not anymore. I think we're all glad you're home."

"Papa, what did you bring me?" Julie asked, dancing backward to walk in front of him.

"Ribbons for your beautiful hair," Ambroise replied. "And a music box." With his other arm, he pulled Charles-Anne closer to him. And for you, *mon fils*, that little telescope you wanted."

"A telescope?" Emilie broke in. "Can I look? Maybe we can find Saturn tonight!"

Delphine was right, Lili knew. The day was not that far off when she and Jean-Étienne would need to discuss their daughter's future. Watching Emilie and Charles-Anne jumping up and down about the telescope, it saddened her that he was too young for her. Perhaps the beautiful and happy children crowding around their father and uncle in the courtyard could be spared the agonies all four of them had endured. She and Jean-Étienne, like Delphine and Ambroise, were doing their best to make a good life for their children, but in the end, as for everyone else, happiness was something they would have to achieve on their own.

"What did you bring me, Papa?" Emilie was asking.

"Just what you asked for," he said. "Monsieur Voltaire's *L'Ingénu*—and enough sugared almonds to make your mother complain they'll make you sick." He grinned at Lili, who gave him a poor excuse for a scowl. "I read it on the coach—I hope you don't mind. It's about a Huron Indian who comes to live in French society. It's really quite funny—and a bit sad."

Emilie got up on her toes to kiss his cheek. "*Merci,* Papa."

He smiled at her. "You're welcome, my treasure. Perhaps I should have brought you a few new handkerchiefs too, to use while you're reading it. I'm sure you'll cry at one part."

"Book cries are the good kind, Papa," she said, swinging his hand. By then they had reached the house. They went through the vestibule, greeting Corinne, now the head housekeeper at Étoges, as she came down the marble staircase from the upper floors. "It's a pleasure to see you, messieurs. I'll bring some biscuits and coffee to the parlor," she said with a curtsey before hurrying off.

"Can I play the piano for you, Papa?" Julie asked, taking off her sun hat. "I've learned a new piece by Mozart."

Ambroise stroked her flattened hair. "I'd love to hear, but your uncle and I want to talk with Aunt Lili and your mother for a little while first."

Anatole gestured to the children to come to him. "Time for your dinner," the tutor said.

Julie groaned. "Can't Emilie and I stay with you?" she pleaded to her mother. "We want to eat with the grown-ups."

"Soon," Delphine said, looking up to catch Lili's eye. *Soon enough,* their glance conveyed. "You can come back in when the little ones are down for their nap."

"And we can start *L'Ingénu* upstairs after dinner," Emilie said to a pouting Julie. "I'll read to you if you want."

"All right," Julie said with a dramatic sigh, as she and Emilie went off to catch up with the others.

The downstairs maid came back with coffee and a plate of small pastries. "Let's hear all the news!" Delphine said as the coffee was served and the sweets were passed. "People first, then politics," she said in a teasing tone that nevertheless conveyed who set the rules of conversation at Étoges.

Now that he was the count, Ambroise was at Versailles quite often and on his visits to Paris he spent time at the salons. Lili and Delphine knew he could be counted on to come back with information so fresh some people in Paris might not yet know it. "The big news," he said, "is that Joséphine de Maurepas is now a widow. She'll stay in the Auvergne at her château until fall, but renovations have begun on a hôtel she bought in Paris. All the talk is of the great expense she's incurring, and from the letters she's sent to friends inquiring about the most fashionable tailors and milliners, it's quite clear she intends to be a happy widow indeed."

"And what does Anne-Mathilde think of all this?" Delphine asked. Far away from the excitement of Paris, Joséphine had had plenty of time to wonder how she had ended up in a place as remote as Ferrand, with a dull and rather crude husband twice her age. When she finally realized Anne-Mathilde's treachery, she had broken off all contact with her, and the two were renowned for the way they snubbed each other whenever Joséphine was in Paris.

"She won't know," Ambroise said solemnly. "That's the other big piece of news. Anne-Mathilde died last week in childbirth."

"Anne-Mathilde dead?" Delphine said, furrowing her brow in disbelief. She and Lili exchanged a stupefied glance.

"I'm afraid I'm at quite a loss for words," Lili said. "I never liked her, and I can't say I'm sad I won't see her again, but still . . ."

Delphine and Ambroise were both lost in thought and didn't seem to hear. What were they remembering about the unpleasant young woman who had come so close to ruining their chance for happiness together? Lili shuddered at the memories that crowded her mind, but most of all the terrible day at Vaux-le-Vicomte when, for her own entertainment, Anne-Mathilde casually put Delphine's virtue in peril.

"Well," Delphine said, "I'm going to be honest. I'm not glad she's dead, but fairly close to it."

Ambroise seemed relieved at the confession. "I've been trying to tell myself to feel some grief," he replied, "but quite frankly, I'm having trouble."

The room fell silent, and the click of a spoon in Jean-Étienne's cup sounded as loud as gunfire. "So," Lili said to break the dark mood, "did you see her brother while you were there? Any news of Paul-Vincent?"

"I saw him when I went to pay condolences to the family before I left," Ambroise said. "He's quite annoyed that he won't be permitted to go off to the American colonies to fight in their revolution. He's the Duc de Praslin's only son, and as his heir he can't take the risk of being killed."

"Paul-Vincent doesn't seem to be the kind who would be excited about going off to fight in a war," Lili said.

"Oh, that isn't it," Ambroise replied. "He wants to go to America to look around, and the war is just an excuse. What he really wants is to be a naturalist like Buffon. He sounded far more excited about seeing Indian villages than battlefields."

He paused for a moment, weighing his words. "But someone else is going. Now that Lafayette has persuaded France to enter the war on the side of the colonies, all the talk is of fighting the British. I heard just this week that Jacques-Mars Courville will be joining Lafayette's entourage."

Jacques-Mars. The name still filled Lili with disgust. "So the king has finally given up on the idea of keeping him away from Versailles by making him a diplomat?" she asked with a sardonic grin. A disastrous apprenticeship in Venice had led to a posting in Germany and one in Denmark, but Jacques-Mars had been back in Paris, without explanation and without a position, since last winter.

"Decidedly," Ambroise said. "Marie Antoinette loathes him. She wants to decide for herself how to mistreat the young ladies at court. Or more likely she's upset that he hasn't tried to bed her."

Delphine shuddered. "That Austrian woman is the worst thing that's ever happened to France."

Jean-Étienne had been sitting silently, listening to the conversation. "Oh, I think there are quite a few equally bad things that happened before her. She's silly and thoughtless, and she spends money like water when so many are suffering, but that's nothing new, is it?"

Delphine sniffed. "I suppose not."

"I think we heap blame on her because we don't want French problems to be French people's fault," Jean-Étienne said. "The poverty in Paris is a disgrace—and not just there, but everywhere in the country." As he habitually did when the subject was intense, he shoved rather than tucked a strand of loose hair behind his ear. "It's true that an obscene amount of money is wasted at Versailles, but we all should look for ways to make things more equal, to treat the poor as deserving dignity and enough to eat. It's not Marie Antoinette's fault she came to a country that already didn't care about the hunger and squalor many people live in."

"All right," Delphine said, with a good-natured smile. "She irritates me all out of proportion. I just remember how kind and unassuming Marie Leszczynska was, and I guess anyone would suffer by comparison."

"Perhaps it's not a subject for our first hour here," Jean-Étienne went on, "but I've been spending much of the time from Paris thinking about how serious things have become. There's a revolution in America because the English king is unconcerned with the burden of his taxes on the public. To finance the war against Britain in the colonies and at sea, prices have gotten higher in France for people who already can't afford bread for their table. And bad harvests have made things even worse."

Distracted, he dug at his hair again. "People won't starve quietly. They'll fight back, regardless of how much affection they have for Louis—and there's still a lot of that, despite his wife. Times are changing and he needs to change with them, or we'll have a quite unpleasant future, I fear."

"I'm afraid I must concur," Ambroise said. "Although the bickering in the salons and Parlément is partly responsible for nothing ever getting done. The king has been willing to discuss reforms for some time, though. He's not a stupid man. He knows what revolution elsewhere could mean for him—and for France."

Delphine got up to pour more coffee. "Please, let's talk about something more pleasant." She moved the plate of pastries in front of Jean-Étienne. "The cook made your favorite—the lemon ones."

"Yes," Lili said, relieved to have such a frightening subject dropped. "Is the Duc de Richelieu staying well enough not to take much of your time?" Two years after their wedding, Jean-Étienne finished medical school and went into service to the Richelieu family as one of several private physicians. In return, he and Lili lived without rent in one of the family properties, an elegant, furnished hôtel near the Luxembourg Palace. He made no money from his work, so everyone was satisfied—most of all the two of them. They had sufficient funds to live comfortably and no desire for more than that.

"They've been well enough not to need me at all," Jean-Étienne said, "except for the occasional aftermath of too many late nights with endless food and wine. I've spent almost all my time in the lab, but I certainly am missing you and Anatole."

"I haven't been there much even when I am in Paris, especially since Georges-Louis and Jean-François were born," Lili scoffed.

"True," Jean-Étienne replied, "but that doesn't mean I can't miss you. Someday when our children need you less, we'll work together all you want."

"That sounds both wonderful and terrible," Lili said. "I do want to get back to science, but I don't want my children to grow up so fast."

Jean-Étienne laughed. "I think there will still be plenty of disease and infection when you're ready to come work on it with me. Thank God the slaughterhouses have been moved back from the riverbank, so the blood and guts don't get dumped in the water people carry up from the Seine to drink. Now we just have to work on laws against throwing sewage in the streets, or in pipes that go directly to the river. We don't know how the organisms we see under the microscope from contaminated water make people sick, but we're quite certain that's what is doing it."

He looked up, and Lili followed his eyes to see Emilie and Julie standing in the doorway. "We thought you might like some sugared almonds," Emilie said, in an obvious ploy to come sit with the adults.

Lili's heart swelled as she looked at the two of them. She loved Julie as if she were her own child, and she knew Delphine felt the same about Emilie. Seeing them standing there, one dark and one fair, only a few months apart in age, she understood what Maman had thought when she looked at the two of them so many years ago. *How deeply I was loved*, she realized, feeling her throat tighten.

The two girls went to each of the parents and parceled out Emilie's sugared almonds. When they got to Lili, she stood up and held them close to her. "I love you both," she whispered.

"I love you too," they said, bewildered at the moment she had chosen to say something they already knew.

Life can be uncertain and frightening, to be sure, Lili thought, *but Voltaire was right. We must cultivate our garden, and mine is right here.* She took an almond. "*Merci, mes chéries*," she said. "How nice of you to bring these to us."

"Oh!" Jean-Étienne said, jumping up. "In all the excitement I forgot the big surprise." He left the room and came back with a package wrapped in paper and a leather braid. He handed it to Lili.

"Is this . . . ?" She looked up at him. He grinned as she pulled away the paper to see a book with a leather cover and gold trim. She opened to the title page. " 'The Adventures of Meadowlark and Tom,'" she read, " 'by S-A du Châtelet with illustrations by Delphine de Bercy, Comtesse d'Étoges.'" Her voice broke, and passing the book to Delphine, she embraced her husband.

"Someday it will be those novels you want to write," he whispered. "France needs a writer with a heart like yours."

"What is it, Maman?" Julie asked Delphine.

"They're stories Aunt Lili wrote when we were young, and she kept writing them as we grew up, until there were enough for a book," she said, handing it to Lili's daughter.

"My mother wrote this?" Emilie asked, scrunching up her face.

"I did," Lili said, remembering back to the day she first held her mother's translation of Newton in her hands, and wondering if she looked as amazed and thrilled as her own daughter looked right then.

Emilie snuggled in beside her. "Read to me," she said.

Lili opened the book. " 'Once upon a time, there was a girl living in a dreary village who wanted nothing more than to travel to the stars . . . ' "

"Do you think we can do that, Maman? Go to the stars?"

"Yes, my darling Emilie," Lili said. "Yes, we can."

"I already have," she whispered, in a voice so soft it was no more than breathing.

The Adventures of Meadowlark and Tom

by
S-A du Châtelet
with illustrations by
Delphine de Bercy, Comtesse d'Étoges

Once upon a time, there was a girl living in a dreary village who wanted nothing more than to travel to the stars. She had a laugh like a songbird, so everybody called her Meadowlark. Every night Meadowlark would sneak outside and hope with all her might that her wish could come true. Then, to her surprise, one night a horse made of starlight appeared in front of her. "Are you the girl named Meadowlark?" the horse asked. When she said yes, the horse snorted and reared up. "My name is Comète," it said. "Climb on my back." Before she knew it, Comète had galloped off with her into the night sky, leaving behind a trail of stars wherever its hooves brushed the clouds . . .

1

*In which Meadowlark visits Venus, meets Tom,
and learns about good manners . . .*

When Comète galloped to a stop on Venus, Meadowlark was surprised to find people weeping and laying flowers in front of a long row of rocks. "I can't imagine any rock that could make me cry," Meadowlark said to Comète. "Wait here—I'm going to see what's happening." Comète nodded his head and snorted fireworks from his white nose.

"Why are you crying over a rock?" Meadowlark asked the first person she came to.

"It's not really a rock," he said. "It's my daughter."

"Was she born that way?" Meadowlark asked.

"Of course not! Who would have a rock for a baby? The Evil Queen lined all the children up, and if the girls couldn't curtsey perfectly and the boys didn't bow just right, they would be turned into stone with her magic wand. My little girl didn't keep her back upright enough, and now look at her!"

Just then a few apples fell from a tree behind Meadowlark, and she looked up. A boy sat in the branches.

"Why aren't you a rock?" she asked.

"I told her I had a stomachache and couldn't bow properly until later," the boy said. "She said she would come back and turn me into stone this afternoon. That's why I'm hiding."

"Well, hiding doesn't help if she's not here. You'd better come down and practice bowing if you know what's good for you," Meadowlark said.

"Why bother?" the boy answered. "Even if I were perfect, she'd turn me into stone anyway. She does it for fun and no one has the power to stop her."

Meadowlark thought for a moment. "The way I see it," she said, "you have two choices—learn to bow perfectly in the next few minutes, or get away from that Evil Queen."

"How do I get away? She has too much power."

"Not over me!" Meadowlark said, stamping her foot to show she meant it. Comète heard her and came prancing over, sprinkling starlight whenever he shook his mane.

Tom jumped down from the tree. "Is that your horse?" he asked. "Can I have a ride?"

"Only if you're brave enough to leave home forever. That's what I did, even though we don't have an Evil Queen in France."

Tom drew a line in the dirt with his toe. "I don't know," he said. "I've never been anywhere else. All my friends are here."

"All your friends are rocks."

Just then Meadowlark's ears perked up at the shrill sound of a woman's voice. "Where's that boy with a stomachache?" the Evil Queen screeched.

Just as she entered the clearing and raised her magic wand, Meadowlark pulled Tom up behind her on Comète and they flew away in a blaze of light.

Tom sighed with relief. "I'm glad to be away from there. I might be a rock by now."

"Just a minute," Meadowlark said. "It isn't right to leave like this."

She guided Comète to a landing in a field behind the Evil Queen and sneaked into the clearing. "Where is that boy?" the queen was saying as she looked behind each rock. "I'll teach him to mind his manners."

"And I'll teach you to mind yours!" Meadowlark said, jumping from her hiding place. She grabbed the queen's wand and waved it three times. "Let the ones with good manners be people and the others be stone!" she cried out, hoping whatever spirit lived inside the wand cared more about justice than queens.

The Evil Queen's clothing hardened around her as she cried out for help. "Please!" she whimpered. "I'll curtsey just right for you, I promise! Just make it stop!"

In front of Meadowlark's eyes the rocks in the field began to crumble, and from each emerged a child. When they had dusted themselves off they all cheered, and they cheered louder yet when they realized the boulder in the middle of the clearing was the Evil Queen. They rushed over and began crawling all over it, kicking it and calling it names.

A boy spat on the rock before coming back over to look at the wand. "Can I have that?" he asked, looking as if he might steal it if Meadowlark refused.

"It's too much power for anyone to have," she said, "especially boys who spit." She scowled at him as she picked up the wand. "I'll take care of this myself," she said, looking at Tom. "You have your friends back. What do you want to do?"

"Living here is so dull we might as well be rocks," Tom said, jumping back on Comète. "Let's go!"

When they were back in the reaches of space, Meadowlark took the wand and broke it in half. Together they watched as the two shooting stars burned out in the black night.

2

*In which Meadowlark and Tom
visit France and learn about the mind . . .*

eadowlark and Tom looked down at the earth from the moon. "It's very pretty," Tom, said. "Especially the blue part. I've never seen rock that color before."

"Rock?" Meadowlark said. "That's not rock, that's ocean."

"What's ocean?"

"Well," said Meadowlark, "why don't you go see for yourself." They hopped on Comète, and with a shake of his tail he bore them through the sky and landed outside a village somewhere on the coast of France. Comète trotted off to find a field of oats, and Meadowlark and Tom started walking toward the houses they could see in the distance.

An old woman and a girl of about sixteen came out of a farmhouse along the way and started walking with them. "The stars are a spilled handful of salt," the old woman said. "There's a wildflower for every kind thought."

"What kind of talk is that?" Meadowlark asked the girl. "Doesn't she know anything?"

"I'm afraid not," the girl said, bursting into tears.

"Well, it's nice of you to cry for her at least, if she's as stupid as she sounds."

The old woman gave Tom a pinch on the cheek. "Obedience paves roads," she said with a toothless grin.

"I'm not crying for her," the girl, whose name was Piret, said. "The same thing is going to happen to me today. That's where we're headed. I have to go get my brains scrambled."

"Why don't you turn around and run while you still have them?" Meadowlark asked.

"Because I have to get married, and that's what they do to you first. No one will marry me until I'm fixed."

"It sounds like quite a fixing to me," Meadowlark said. "Let's go see what we can do."

In the middle of the village square, a crowd of men was already gathered near a huge oak tree. A straight-backed chair had been hoisted to the highest branch. Tied inside was a girl Piret's age. When the men in the tree let the chair go, it spun around so fast that the girl was a blur as they slowly lowered her to the ground.

She got up and staggered over to the mayor. "He's going to say something really stupid," Piret said, "and if she repeats it instead of laughing at him, the bachelors will go to the priest over there to make bids on her and she'll be married this afternoon."

"Ice is cold butter," the mayor said.

"Ice is cold butter," the girl said, nodding her head gravely. The men all cheered and crowded around the village priest, offering their bids.

"The best price goes to the girls who are so addled they answer the mayor backward, though that doesn't happen very often," Piret said. "The most scrambled ones are supposed to make the best wives."

"Tom and I go around the universe saving people," Meadowlark said. "And we're going to try to save you. But first we have to make ourselves disappear." The Philosopher King of Saturn had given Meadowlark a pair of magic boots that made her and whomever she was touching invisible, but the spell only lasted an hour. Meadowlark grabbed Tom by the hand and tapped her right toe twice, followed by a hard stamp of her left heel on the ground.

Piret and the old woman looked around. "Where did they go?" Piret asked. "Fingers are roots," the old woman replied.

Unseen, Meadowlark and Tom scurried to the top of the tree. "We have to untie the rope and turn it the other way," she said. "If it spins backward, maybe the magic won't work." They finished just as Piret was hoisted in the chair. They watched from a nearby branch as she was spun down to the ground. She stood up and staggered over to the mayor. "Dizzy so am I, *Dieu Mon,*" she said.

"Oh, no," Tom said. "It looks like it didn't work."

"Potatoes' eyes are watching in the dark," the mayor said.

"Dark the in watching are eyes potatoes," Piret said. All the men cheered and made such a rush for the priest, they ended up tripping over each other and falling in a heap on the ground. Meadowlark and Tom hopped down from the tree and pulled Piret behind the tree to ask her what happened.

"I'm fine," she said, once she figured out where they were, since they were still invisible. "It worked perfectly. I just don't want anyone to know, so I can tell all the girls to do the same thing. If our husbands think our brains are scrambled but they're not, whose brains actually are? I have to go get married now. Thanks!" She turned back to them. "And don't forget not to trust the potatoes!"

Meadowlark saw her boots coming into view, which always

happened first when the invisibility was wearing off. "We need to go before they see us," she told Tom. She gave the secret whistle and Comète appeared just down the road.

As they ran and jumped on his back, Tom said, "I think Earth is the strangest place we've visited."

"I do too," said Meadowlark, as they galloped into the blue sky, showering stars behind them.

3

*In which Meadowlark and Tom visit Africa
and learn about philosophy . . .*

The camel on which Meadowlark and Tom had been riding got to its knees, and they dismounted inside the walls of an oasis town somewhere in North Africa. They spat sand from their mouths. "I always wanted to see what it would be like to ride a camel," Meadowlark said, "but I definitely prefer Comète."

"Me too," Tom said, "but there are some adventures you just have to have on the ground." He looked around. "Why are all these people wearing rags? I thought this town was supposed to be rich from trade with the Musulmans."

A woman wearing a tattered veil over her face was walking toward them. "You there!" Meadowlark called out. "Why are you dressed that way?"

"Because I don't have anything else to wear," she said. "I used to have a different veil for every day of the week, but I don't know where the rest of my clothes have gone."

"Well, don't you have children or friends who can help you find them?"

"That's just it—they can't find any of their things either. We're sure we used to have more, so it must be a genie's spell, though no one's seen any of them for years. The only reason we're not naked is we sleep in what we have on. Otherwise, this would probably be gone in the morning too," she said, shaking the hem of her gown.

Just then three philosophers walked by. "Why are they dressed better than you are?" Tom asked.

"I don't know," said the woman. "Only ordinary people seem to lose everything the minute they get it."

"The problem in this town," said the first philosopher, "is that people don't take enough responsibility for themselves. They want the government to solve their problems for them, but they don't want to pay for it."

"If they worked harder and saved, they'd have more," said the second. "Like this beggar needs to," he said, pointing in the direction of the woman.

Meadowlark and Tom were by now invisible, leaving her looking around in confusion. "Have I lost you too now?" she asked the empty air.

The men shook their heads at her. "And suppose the government did give them all a change of clothes?" the third said. "If you alter one thing, you'd best be prepared for unintended consequences, especially when some of them are as crazy as she is."

"I'm not crazy—I'm just confused!" the ragged woman called after them. "You would be too if you were half-naked and didn't know why!"

"Let's follow them," Meadowlark whispered to Tom.

The three philosophers went down an alley and soon they were at a grand building near the town walls. Meadowlark and Tom tiptoed in behind them before the doors closed. They went into a dining room where a grand meal had been laid out. The servants were dressed in gowns of velvet, the crystal was cut from huge diamonds, and the dishes were made of gold. Behind them, through a window, Meadowlark and Tom could see trunks and boxes full of clothing, including hundreds of veils being loaded onto camels, while the caravan driver handed a bag of coins to a servant. He came in and poured the coins on the table. "Your proceeds, messieurs," he said.

They all leaned back and patted their bellies. "It's good to live in a land of surplus," the first one said. "And even better when it's made you rich," said the second.

"I guess in Africa, the more you need, the less you have," Tom said when they were safely back among the stars.

"And the more you have, the less you notice," Meadowlark replied.

4

*In which Meadowlark and Tom go to Uruguay
and learn about liberty . . .*

"So this is Uruguay," Meadowlark said. "But where are all the people?"

"I don't know," Tom said, "but there's smoke coming from every chimney." He ran ahead and banged on the first door he came to.

"You'll have to let yourself in," a muffled voice said. "We can't get up."

Meadowlark and Tom pushed the door open and went inside. A family sat, bound to chairs with ropes of gold, and with their faces and mouths covered with finely woven cloth embroidered with family crests. Over their laps were draped silver chains so heavy they could not move their legs.

"Who tied you up?" Meadowlark asked, but the man could only mumble through the cloth in his mouth. "Who tied you up?" she repeated, after pulling it away.

"We did. What did you think?"

"Why in the world would you do that?"

He shook his head, dumbfounded. "It's obvious. We have to stay here all day doing nothing, just to show we're not working."

"You could just stay inside, minding your own business. You don't have to be tied to your chair!"

"But this way we're sure people will believe us."

Just then two young servants, a girl and a boy, came in dressed in peasants' clothing. "Who are you?" Meadowlark asked. "And why aren't you tied up too?"

"Tied up?" They laughed until they clutched their sides. "We can't sit around all day. We have work to do. And besides, we're not wealthy enough to have gold rope and silver chains. You need those to be properly tied up, don't you?"

"I suppose," Meadowlark said.

"And if you have them, you need to show them off," the chained woman tried to explain, though her voice was muffled almost beyond comprehension. "What good are chains if they're locked in a drawer?"

A little girl with a silk bag over her head was squirming in her chair. Meadowlark pulled it off. "I want to get up and walk around," the little girl said. "I want to go outside."

"You can't do that," her parents said.

"Why not?" Tom asked.

"Because we can't tie her up when she comes back."

"Aha!" said Meadowlark. "And if that's the case, who will stop her from leaving?" She pulled the girl's chains off her lap and untied her ropes. "You're free!" she said.

"Free?" the girl asked. "What's that?" She turned to the servants. "Do you know what that means?"

"No," they both said. "Maybe it just means different from before."

"Well, that would be enough for me," the girl said, running toward the door. "Anything has to be better than this!"

Meadowlark went to the door to watch the girl jumping in the air as she ran down the street. Her legs were not very strong from having spent so much time in chains, and before she had gone very far she fell down, exhausted.

"Help me up," Meadowlark heard her order the people passing in the street. "Don't you know I'm one of the Chained People? You're supposed to obey me."

"The Chained People never help us," one of them said. "Around here, you learn to do everything for yourself."

The girl looked around, not sure what to do. She spied Meadowlark, who was now standing next to her. "Can you help me up, please?" she asked, fluttering her eyelashes.

"You'd better learn to stand on your own, unless you want to go back there," she said, pointing in the direction of the house. The girl looked at the house and then at the road out of town. She sighed, and with a great effort, she pulled herself up and dusted off her skirt.

"I'll be going, then," she said. Her hand flew to her mouth. "I think I forgot to close the door behind me!"

Meadowlark laughed. "I'll do it for you," she said. "I'm more than happy to help the Chained People with that."

5

*In which Meadowlark and Tom go to China
and learn about love . . .*

From the sky, Meadowlark picked out the Great
Wall of China and guided Comète down to a palace nearby. In the garden, twenty paces apart, two
men at small desks faced each other. Above them
on a terrace, a princess sat with her ladies-in-waiting.

One of the men rolled what he had written into a scroll,
which he put on a gilded platter to be delivered to the man at
the other end. The servant bobbed his head like a chicken pecking for scratch as he carried the scroll, and when he reached
the other man, he bowed vigorously for several minutes before
extending the platter to him.

As the man read it, his nostrils flared upward and his lips
pursed, as if the words smelled too rotten for a delicate nose to
bear. He tapped his nose and turned his face sideways in profile, lifting his chin skyward. The first man sniffed indignantly
and did the same. Meadowlark saw their eyes darting toward
each other, waiting to see who would break the pose first.

The second man wiggled his fingers and a servant handed
him his pen. Without moving his head, he scribbled something on the scroll. When he was finished, he flicked his wrist
in the direction of his adversary, and the servant scurried off
with his reply.

"Who are those people?" Meadowlark asked a servant standing nearby.

"They're Ting and Tang," the man said. "Two great nobles of the realm. They're fighting a duel."

"A duel?" she exclaimed. "In France they fight those with guns or swords."

Ting looked up at the sound of an unfamiliar voice. "I suppose we could do that," he said. "After all, we invented gunpowder. But"—he motioned Meadowlark to come closer so no one else could hear—"we're only fighting over a princess, and there are too many of those in China to care terribly much who wins this one."

"Well then, how do you fight?" Meadowlark asked.

"We exchange notes about the ways we wish the other would die," Ting answered. "For example, I told him I would like to see him fall through a crack in the ice and drown, and now"—he took back the scroll, which had just been returned to him—"Tang has written that he'd like my ship to be lost at sea."

By then the princess had come down to see what the commotion was all about. "Lost at sea?" she said, looking at the sun lowering on the horizon. "It's getting late. Don't you think someone should be drawing blood by now? We need a winner before supper."

She looked at Meadowlark and Tom. "You're rather strange-looking. Where are you from?"

Her attention was distracted by the servant, who had delivered the scroll to her instead of to Tang. "What's this?" the princess said, raising her eyebrows.

"I thought you might like something different," Tang said. "So I wrote directly to you. It's a poem."

The princess unrolled the scroll. "'I planted a rose garden for you,'" she read.

White for your skin, like cool ivory
Pink, for the lips I long to kiss
Yellow for your flowing hair—

"Wait a minute," the princess said. "My hair's not yellow. I'm Chinese."

"I know," Ting said, pointing at Tom. "But his is, and I needed another color for a rose. It isn't a very good poem, but I did write it for you."

"It certainly isn't," the princess said. She read again, " 'Blue for your eyes—' "

She scowled at Ting, who gave a helpless shrug and gestured toward Tom's eyes. "My eyes are brown and there isn't even such a thing as a blue rose."

"There is in my garden," Ting said.

The princess sniffed. " 'Red for the blood I'd rather not shed.' Well at least that makes sense." She squinted. "What's this word? Your penmanship isn't very good."

"Garden. 'My garden will grow only if watered with your love,' " Ting said. "That's the last line."

Tang came over to them. "Have I won?" he asked. "It is rather late, and I'm quite hungry."

The princess ignored him. "This is most out of the ordinary, and I don't like it at all," she said to Ting. "You'll have to come back tomorrow and have your duel according to the rules."

Meadowlark was puzzled. "I rather liked the poem," she said. "It sounds as if he really loves you."

"What does that matter?" the princess said. "If I let him write a poem to me once, what would stop him from doing it again?" She stamped her foot. "Rules are rules!"

"Rules are rules," Tom said to Meadowlark.

"I suppose so," she replied. "Even as far away as China."

6

In which Meadowlark and Tom
go to Kiev and learn about free will . . .

The golden domes of Kiev caught the rays of the rising sun as Meadowlark and Tom set Comète down on a grassy bank near the Dnieper River running through the city.

"Look at all these churches!" Tom said. "They must be terribly religious here."

"Except there's no one in them," Meadowlark said. "It looks as if there's nobody here at all." They wandered down empty streets for almost an hour until they ran into a little boy hiding something wiggling under his cloak. "What do you have there?" Meadowlark asked.

"Nothing!" the boy said as he dashed past them. Tom grabbed his cloak, which came off in his hand.

"It's a puppy!" Meadowlark said.

"No it isn't!" the boy replied tearfully.

Meadowlark pointed at the little animal cradled in his arms. "I can see it right there."

The boy looked down at the little dog blinking in the bright sunlight. "I've lost him for sure now!" he said, breaking out in sobs.

"Why? Did we catch you stealing him?" Tom asked.

"No, but he's the last one in the litter and I've been hiding him because I don't want the Court of Good Choices to hear about it."

"The Court of Good Choices? What's that?"

"Here in Kiev everyone believes in free will. We have to. It's the official opinion. If you say 'I'm going to eat the last apple in the basket' and someone else gets to it first, that's not free will. You're supposed to get what you wish for. Everyone is. Otherwise there's no free will, and that isn't possible because it's the law."

"That's not what free will means!" Meadowlark said, shaking her head.

"It means that here," the boy replied. "Parlément voted on it. And now it's the Court of Good Choices' job to make sure it's enforced. Suppose somebody else sees the dog and wills it to be theirs. We'd have to go to court, and there can't be a loser because that person wouldn't have free will. So they'll decide neither of us can have the dog, so it has to be drowned. Or at least I think that's what happens. They don't tell us exactly, because then someone might say, 'It's my will that it not be drowned.'"

"But if neither of you get what you want, how is that free will?" Meadowlark asked.

The boy scratched his head. "It doesn't make sense to me either. They call it the doctrine of adjusted happiness. You have to adjust what you want until you get it, and then you'll be happy. If you both want the last apple, it has to be laid on the ground halfway between you, and you can't move until one of you decides you don't want it. Tennis has been banned altogether, because both players want to win. But it doesn't work as well as that all the time. If a husband wants to live on one side of the river and his wife wants to live on the other, they have to live on a boat in the middle."

"So free will actually means never getting what you want," Meadowlark said.

"It seems to work out that way. Nobody's ever satisfied, but nobody can complain that someone else is freer." The boy looked around him at the empty street. "That's why hardly anybody lives here anymore. They've all moved to places where you don't get what you want most of the time, but you stand a chance of getting it once in a while."

"They have crazy ideas about free will here," Meadowlark whispered in Tom's ear, "but I know I'm not waiting around here long enough for anyone to will me to stay." She called for Comète, and they jumped on his back and were gone. Below them they could just make out the boy's voice.

"Wait a minute!" he yelled. "I will you—" but they were too far away to hear the rest.

7

*In which Meadowlark and Tom go to Carpathia
and learn about obedience . . .*

The tower atop the Carpathian Mountains loomed high over the snowcapped peaks below. Through a small window at the top, Meadowlark heard the sighs of a young maiden.

"What are you doing up there?" she called.

"I've been imprisoned by my parents because I won't obey them."

"What do they want you to do?"

"It's what they don't want me to do." A girl of about sixteen pushed huge tangles of thread aside and looked out the window. "I love to spin, and they say it's not fitting work for a princess."

"Well, what do they think is?"

"I'm supposed to sit around all day and talk to people about things that don't matter. If anything's too complicated for my father, he outlaws it, so it means that anything worth talking about has been forbidden."

"Why does he do that?"

"Because he thinks people are plotting against him. He thinks if people use a word he doesn't know, they're sending a secret message. Just before he locked me up, some people were talking about Newton. When they told him Newton had lived very far away and he had been dead a long time, he said, 'Well then, why do you disturb my sleep with talk of him?' and threw them all in a dungeon."

"Did he know who Newton was?"

"He thought he did. He said Newton was from China and he had swept eastward and conquered us a long time ago. I told him I thought he meant Attila the Hun, but he said that since the two names sounded so much alike, they must be related."

"So how did you end up here?"

"I love to spin. Maybe it's because you can see the connection between what goes in and what comes out. Don't you think that's rather reassuring?"

Meadowlark nodded. "And rare."

"And the best part is that *I* matter," the princess added. "What I do to the wool is what makes it come out the way it does. But the problem is that I'm supposed to let the servants do it. It's beneath me, my parents say. First they locked me up here with nothing to spin, and then when that didn't work they gave me everything I needed and told me to keep spinning until I was so sick of it I would beg them to let me stop." She pushed the tangles of thread out of the way. "The room's full to the ceiling again, and they'd better come cart it away soon, or they'll find me dead of suffocation."

She leaned out even further. "Can you help me?"

"What do you want me to do?"

The princess pulled a letter from her bodice and let it float to the ground. "Can you deliver this? It's to someone I love, but I was afraid to tell him when I could, for fear it would become complicated, and that always ends up badly." She shrugged. "My father—I guess I'm a little like him after all."

Meadowlark took the letter. "Where can I find this person?" she asked.

"That's the hard part," the princess said. "I hope it's not too late. He's in the dungeon. He's the one who mentioned Newton."

8

In which Meadowlark and Tom
go to the Brazilian Rain Forest
and learn about happiness . . .

D eep in the Brazilian rain forest, Meadowlark and Tom dangled their feet in the waters of the Amazon, just outside the walls of a fabled city of gold. From every direction, people appeared from the jungle, waving palm fronds and singing chants as they made their way toward the city gate.

"What's that on their right cheeks?" Tom asked. Meadowlark squinted in the bright sun. "I don't know," she said. "It looks like a birthmark in the shape of Corsica." She scanned the crowd. "And they all have the identical one."

"There's no such thing as identical birthmarks," Tom said. "That's the point of having them, isn't it?"

Meadowlark nodded. "You there," she called out to a young girl at the edge of the crowd. "Where are you going with those red stains on your faces?"

The girl looked bewildered. "We paint them on every morning. It takes a long time too, since they have to be perfect." Seeing Meadowlark's confusion, she went on. "It's the king's birthmark. We try to look as much like the king as we can to show our respect and appreciation. He always has our best interests at heart, you know."

Her eyes darted around and when she was sure no one could hear, she bade Meadowlark to come closer. "But it can't be permanent, because the next king will have our best interests at heart too, and we'll all have to change to look like him."

"How do you know he has your best interests at heart?" Tom asked.

"Because he says so," the girl replied. "And because we are happier here than people anywhere else on Earth. Doesn't that prove it?"

"Who says you're happier?" Meadowlark inquired.

"The king does!" The girl threw her hands up in exasperation. "Really, what is wrong with you? Are people where you come from happier than we are?"

"I don't know," Meadowlark said. "I'll have to look around next time I'm in France."

"We don't have to look around," the girl said proudly. "We already know. But you've come on the perfect day if you need convincing. This is the Festival of the Four Returning Wanderers. Every year the king sends young men out in each of the four directions, and today is the day they give their report on whether they found happier people anywhere." Her face clouded. "Only this year we've been told only three returned. It's dangerous out in the world, you know—and that makes us appreciate being here all the more."

"Maybe he didn't come back because he found a happier place and decided to stay," Meadowlark said.

The girl's eyes darted around to see if anyone might have heard. "You can be put to death for saying something like that! It causes discontent, and that ruins everything."

"Look at those men!" Tom said, tugging on Meadowlark's sleeve. She turned around just in time to catch a glimpse of a small group, all with crooked noses and flattened cheeks. "What happened to their faces?" she asked.

"The king fell out of a tree once and landed on his face," the girl said. "He had two terrible black eyes and a broken nose. Most of us just irritated our eyes with sand to make them as bloodshot as his, and ringed them with soot until his bruises were gone, but they wanted to show how much more devoted they were, so they bashed their faces in with boards."

The girl gave a furtive glance around. "The king healed quite nicely. Most people think those men were quite foolish to do that, since they don't look like him at all anymore, but we admire them greatly all the same. See the medals around their necks? They're Knights of the Royal Order of Self-Bashers. The king established it to honor them for their devotion."

By now Meadowlark and Tom had arrived in a large public square. A dais had been erected in the middle, upon which the king and queen sat under brightly colored umbrellas. Since it was a hot day, young girls and boys waved fans made of parrot feathers over their royal heads and mopped their royal faces with the soft undersides of gigantic jungle leaves.

Three young men climbed the steps and stood in front of the royal couple. The girl pointed to another man on the stage. "He's the Official Bellower," she said. "He'll repeat whatever the travelers tell the king."

"He said, 'I have searched far and wide and found nothing but misery and unhappiness,'" the Bellower called out after the First Wanderer was finished. The crowd burst into loud cheers. The Second Wanderer stepped forward and after he had spoken with the king, the crowd hushed, waiting to hear. "He has searched far and wide and found nothing but misery and unhappiness," the Bellower called out to another burst of applause.

"Hooray for the misery of others," a few sang out, and the crowd joined in with what must have been a familiar song.

The happiest are best, the best are happiest.
Praise to the Returning Wanderers!
They make this truth shine clear.
The happiest are best, the best are happiest.
Hooray for the misery of others!
They make this truth shine clear.

Meadowlark was standing near the dais, and when it was the Third Wanderer's turn, he stood at a different angle and she could see the words he formed with his lips. "Your Majesty, everywhere I went I found that some people were happy enough, while others did nothing but complain," he said. "I believe that people are as contented here as anywhere, and as happy as possible, short of heaven."

"He said, 'I have searched far and wide and found nothing but misery and unhappiness,'" the Bellower shouted to the crowd.

"What?" Meadowlark's jaw dropped as she turned to Tom.

"Shh!" The girl glared at her. "Isn't anything sacred where you come from?" she said, turning to join in the song.

Meadowlark and Tom found Comète in a nearby clearing and jumped on his back. As he flew over the mighty Amazon, Meadowlark pulled back on the reins. "Who's that?" she asked Tom, pointing down toward a young man paddling a boat. She guided Comète to a landing on the sandy shore. "Are you the Fourth Wanderer?" she asked.

"I am," the young man nodded with a wide grin.

"Did you find a place where people were happier?" Tom broke in.

"No," the Fourth Wanderer said. "Things are pretty much the same everywhere. But I've discovered I'm happier out here on the river, with no one telling me what to do or think." He touched the place on his cheek where the red stain once had been. "And I've decided I'm never going back."

He looked at the two of them. "Do you think that's wrong? Maybe I could convince people that bashing in their faces or painting birthmarks on their cheeks has nothing to do with happiness after all."

"No," Meadowlark said. "Things like that are too good a substitute for real happiness for most people to be willing to give up."

The young man's lip trembled and Meadowlark thought for a moment that he might burst into tears. "You don't think they would want to know that they're not really the best or the happiest? That they'd be better off deciding for themselves who they are and what they want?"

"I've wandered the world a little myself," Meadowlark said gravely. "And I can tell you something you will probably find wherever you go."

"What's that?" the young man asked.

"It's easier to bash in one's skull than to think with the mind inside it."

AFTERWORD

HISTORICAL NOVELISTS strive to make a time and place more real by weaving the factual and the imagined together. We start out knowing what we are inventing and what we are taking from our sources, but the end product becomes so complex that the boundaries are blurred. Lili and Delphine are more real to me than the characters who actually lived, since I spent so much more time with them, and the most "real" things about the biographical characters are the details and dialogues I invented.

The fabric of the story can be teased apart quite easily, however, to answer the question, "What happened next?" For my fictional characters, the best response is that the reader's imagination is as good as mine. Lili and my other creations are dear friends of a season whom I have now lost track of and know nothing further about. The real-life characters, however, are another matter.

The epilogue is set in 1778, the year the French openly allied themselves with the American colonies in the war for independence from Britain, and the year in which both of Lili's mentors, Buffon and Voltaire, died. Eleven years later, the French Revolution would sweep away Lili and Delphine's world almost as quickly as the soap bubbles bursting over the lawn at Étoges. If the novel had continued, Lili and Delphine would have been forty when the revolution broke out, and their daughters would have been young wives starting families of their own.

Their future, like that of all those of their class, would not have been pretty. Their husbands would have been particularly vulnerable, for even socially conscious noblemen supportive of the revolution's goals lost their heads to the guillotine. Emilie du Châtelet's only surviving son, Florent-Louis, was guillotined during the Reign of Terror. One prominent scientist, Antoine Lavoisier, on whom Jean-Étienne is loosely modeled, had his pioneering work on the conservation of mass and the role of oxygen in combustion cut short by the executioner's blade. When Lavoisier asked the judge at his trial if his execution could be stayed long enough for him to complete some scientific work, the judge told him, "The Republic has no need of scientists."

Like Lavoisier, Jean-Étienne might have finished his time in this world as a headless corpse thrown into a common grave. Lavoisier's wife, Marie, was his chief assistant, and Lili's desire to be of service to science in Jean-Étienne's lab might have come to the same abrupt end as Marie's did when her husband died. Though Marie lived into her seventies, many women also ended their lives on the guillotine, so Lili's fate could have been worse than widowhood.

Lili's and Delphine's best protection lay in being figments of my imagination, but among the real-life characters, even the dead were not immune. In the furor over eradicating the nobility, the people of Lunéville desecrated graves, including Emilie du Châtelet's. Bones believed to be hers and her child's were reinterred later. Estates were looted and their goods stolen or destroyed. Places like Étoges and Vaux-le-Vicomte fell into disrepair as they passed from hand to hand over the generations.

Within the confines of the book, the boundaries between documented fact and authorial license can also be fairly easily delineated. I believe that a historical novelist has an unwritten pact with readers to be as truthful as he or she can. Though in the end it is up to readers to remember the difference between a novel and a scholarly treatment of a subject, I want my audience to be confident I present people, events, and eras accurately. Because historical records are often so short on intimate and mundane details, it's necessary to invent a great deal to fill out a story, but as long as these inventions are consistent with what is documented and don't misrepresent critical truths, I embellish freely on the known.

In fact, there would be no historical fiction without doing this, and those who prefer their history straight will probably be happier reading nonfiction. For the rest, I offer the argument that more things are true than are ever written down. Even the famous don't often leave behind much of a record of their day-to-day lives, and sometimes the imagination brings us closer to the whole truth than documented sources can.

That said, I would like to acknowledge a few places where I have made minor adjustments to nonessential facts. First, it isn't clear when Emilie and Voltaire first met. There was almost certainly a brief introduction when she was a child, but it registered on neither of them. Judith Zinsser places their first meeting at the opera, but I chose to base my scene on the alternative account in David Bodanis's book. I also adjusted the time frame for Emilie leaving Paris for Cirey after the death of her son. In reality, she didn't go for several months. I changed by a few months the premiere date for Philidor's opera based on *Tom Jones* to make it consistent with the purchase of Vaux-le-Vicomte by the Duc de Praslin. I also adjusted the date of La Barre's execution. It actually occurred a year before Lili's visit to Ferney, but I thought the incident was so instructive about Voltaire and his times that it would be valuable to include it. Finally, it isn't clear with whom Emilie du Châtelet shared her "Discourse on Happiness." All that is known for certain is that Saint-Lambert preserved a copy, waiting until after the deaths of both the Marquis de Châtelet and Voltaire to publish it. The marquis died in the same year as Lili's fictional visit to him, but Voltaire lived until 1778. The essay wasn't published until 1779, a year after the epilogue of the book is set.

ACKNOWLEDGMENTS

A NOVEL BASED around the life of Emilie du Châtelet would probably have remained just one of a number of ideas in my head if it weren't for two authors who discovered her long before I did. My sincerest gratitude goes to David Bodanis and Judith Zinsser, whose biographies of Emilie became the bedrock of my own research. Roger Pearson's biography of Voltaire also helped greatly to get the facts right about that part of the story.

A number of people gave of their time and expertise to help me bring this book to life. Madame de Salignac-Fenélon opened the du Châtelet estate out of season to give me a special, lengthy tour of the château and grounds at Cirey. Madame Filliette-Neuville allowed me to interrupt her busy day as owner and host at the Chateau d'Étoges to clarify the lineage of her family and the history of the château. Ambroise Clément de Feuillet is not a fictional character but was indeed the heir and soon-to-be Comte d'Étoges when Delphine marries him, a fact I would not have known without Madame Filliette-Neuville's help. Mahdjer Bhat Charilla gave me an extensive private tour of Voltaire's home at Ferney, and her knowledge brought a new depth and accuracy to the details about Lili's stay there.

Jane Birkenstock, whose website www.visitvoltaire.com is a great resource for those interested in Voltaire and his life, provided background knowledge and gave me advice that helped me make the most of my research time in France.

Natalia Denisenko helped me steer the last chapter in the right direction, and Severiani Salvagno explained points of math and physics that this science-avoiding English major might otherwise have misrepresented.

And let me proclaim this to the stars (Meadowlark, are you there?): I have the best possible agent in the best of all possible authorial worlds. Meg Ruley of the Jane Rotrosen Agency supports me and my writing with enthusiasm, thoughtfulness, and integrity. All the people at the Jane Rotrosen Agency are a joy to work with and give me a feeling of a home away from home when I am in New York.

My editor at Gallery Books, Kathy Sagan, worked with tenacity and good humor to help me improve the manuscript, and her assistant, Jessica Webb, has been an enthusiastic supporter throughout.

As always, I want to single out the three people who know me best and support me day in and day out. My "bossy big sister" Lynn is still proving a half century after our childhood that bossiness can be a good thing—at least when her little sister needs a thorough critique of her writing. My partner and dearest love, James Fee, has spent countless hours and untold energy to help me endure the rough patches of being an author. And finally, the enthusiastic support of my son, Ivan Corona, always makes me feel on top of the world.

And, to all of this, I must add my gratitude to Emilie du Châtelet herself, and to François-Marie Arouet de Voltaire, for walking the walk. Their lives gave added joy to my own as I wrote.

PRONUNCIATION GUIDE AND WHO'S WHO

NOTE: TYPICALLY, French words ending in one or more consonants leave those consonants almost but not entirely unsounded, one of a number of subtleties it is not possible to convey in this guide. These pronunciations approximate the French but are not exact. Real-life characters are shown in bold.

Barras, Robert de (bah-RAHS, Row-BAIR de): Widowed suitor of Lili.

Bar-sur-Aube (bar-soor-OBE): Coach stop between Paris and Geneva.

Bercy, Delphine (bare-SEE, del-FEEN): Lili's adoptive sister.

Bercy, Julie (bare-SEE, zhoo-LEE): Emilie's friend and Lili's adoptive mother.

Breteuil (bray-TOY): Emilie du Châtelet's last name at birth.

Buffon, Georges-Louis, Comte de (boo-FOH, ZHORJ-loo-EE, KOMT de): Naturalist and philosophe, creator of a comprehensive illustrated work of natural history using up-to-date scientific principles, and an early advocate of the concept of evolution and an ancient date for the creation of the world.

Châtelet, Emilie du (SHA-te-lay, Eh-mee-lee): Aristocratic mathematician and physicist, most widely known for being Voltaire's longtime lover.

Châtelet, Florent (floh-RAHN): Name of Emilie's husband and son.

Châtelet, Stanislas-Adélaïde du (stahn-ee-SLAHS-ah-deh-lye-EED): Emilie du Châtelet's daughter.

chéri(e)(s) (shay-REE): Dear one(s).

Cirey (see-HRAY): Village in Lorraine where the Marquis du Châtelet's ancestral home is located.

Comète (koh-MET): Meadowlark's horse.

Courville, Jacques-Mars (koor-VEEL, jahk-MAHRS): Friend of Anne-Mathilde.

Crassy, Berthe and Lucien (kras-SEE, BAIRT and loo-see-YEN): Servants at Cirey.

Danican Philidor, François André (dahn-ee-KAHN fee-lee-DOHR, frahn-SWAH ahn-DRAY): French composer and famous chess genius.

Denis, Madame (de-NEE): Voltaire's niece, a widow who lived with him for many years at Cirey and elsewhere.

Diderot, Denis (dee-de-ROH, de-NEE): Philosophe and author/editor of the first comprehensive encyclopedia.

Encyclopédie (anh-see-klo-pay-DEE): Compilation of all scientific, philosophical, practical, and vocational knowledge considered important to the philosophes.

Étoges (eh-TOWJ): Village and château of the Clément de Feuillet family.

Germond (zhair-MOHN): Voltaire's valet at Ferney.

Graffigny, Françoise de (grah-fee-NYEE, frahn-SWAHZ de): Frequent houseguest at Cirey, whose letters are a significant source of knowledge about Emilie and Voltaire's activities and relationship. Later in life she wrote several highly successful novels and is now acknowledged as one of the significant writers of her era.

hôtel (oh-TELL): The name by which Parisian town houses were known.

Île de la Cité (EEL de lah see-TAY): Island on the Seine where the cathedral of Notre-Dame is located.

Jardin de Roi (jahr-DAH de RWAH): The King's Garden, known today as the Jardin des Plantes.

La Harpe, Jean-François de (lah ARP, Zhan-Frahn-SWAH de): Minor playwright who was a frequent guest at Ferney and styled himself as a consultant to Voltaire.

Leclerc, Jean-Étienne (luh-KLAIR, ZAHN-eh-TYEN): Nephew and protégé of the Comte de Buffon.

Leszczynska, Marie (leh-ZIN-skah): Polish-born wife of King Louis XV and sister of the Duc de Lorraine.

Lomont, Baronne (loh-MOHN, bah-RONE): Widowed sister-in-law of the Marquis du Châtelet.

Longchamp, Sébastien (lohn-SHOM, say-bas-tee-YEH): Voltaire's manservant, whose diary provides intimate information about Voltaire's life and habits.

Lorraine, Duc de (loh-REHN, Dook de): Formerly King Stanislas of Poland, who, after being deposed, was granted by King Louis XV the semi-independent Duchy of Lorraine to rule for life. Marie Leszczynska, the Queen of France, was his daughter.

Lunéville (loo-nay-VEEL): City in Lorraine and site of Duke Stanislas's palace, where Emilie du Châtelet died and is buried.

Maman (mah-MAH): Mother.

Maupertuis, Pierre-Louis (moh-per-TWEE, pee-YAIR loo-EE): Famous French mathematician and physicist. His work in Lapland established that the earth is flattened at its poles, and his other works confirmed or refined many of Newton's ideas.

Maurepas, Joséphine de (moh-re-PAH, zho-say-FEEN de): Young noblewoman from Lili and Delphine's days at the convent.

pannier (pan-EER or pan-YAY): Frame attached to each hip to create skirts extended to the sides.

Panthémont, Abbaye de (pahn-thay-MON, ah-BAY de): Convent where Lili and Delphine boarded as children.

philosophe (feel-oh-SOHF): General term for French Enlightenment thinkers.

Place Royale (PLAHS roy-AHL): Square in Paris where Lili lives. Now called the Place de Vosges.

pont (POHN): Bridge.

population flottante (poh-poo-las-SYO floh-TANT): "Floating" people of France, i.e., the homeless and dispossessed.

Praslin, Anne-Mathilde de (prah-LEHN, AHN-mah-TILD de): Young noblewoman from Lili's and Delphine's days at the convent.

Praslin, Paul-Vincent (POHL vahn-SAWN): Son and heir of the Duc de Praslin, owner of Vaux-le-Vicomte.

Richelieu, Duc de (rish-LYOU, Dook de): Powerful noble and friend of Emilie du Châtelet.

Rousseau, Jean-Jacques (hroo-SOW, zhan-ZHAK): Philosopher and author, precursor to the Romantic Era in his ideas about personal liberty and the need to raise children without societal interference.

Saint-Lambert, Jean-François (sahn-lam-BARE, zhan-frahn-SWAH): Emilie's lover and father of Lili. He was a contributor to the *Encyclopédie* and a well-known poet later in his life.

Thérèse, Jeanne-Bertrand (tay-REHZ, zhan-behr-TRAHN): Nun at the convent.

Thibaudet, Francine (tee-bow-DAY): Jean-Étienne Leclerc's fiancée.

Thil, Marie-Victoire du (TEEL, mah-REE veek-TWAHR doo): Close friend of Emilie du Châtelet, possibly the one who introduced her to Voltaire.

Tintin (tan-TAH): Lili and Delphine's dog.

Turgot, Abbé (toor-GOH, ah-BAY): Philosophe and economist famous for his support of free market capitalism.

Vaux-le-Vicomte (VOH-le-vee-COMT): Large country estate near Paris owned by the Duc de Praslin.

Voltaire, François-Marie Arouet de (vol-TAIR, frahn-SWAH-mah-REE ah-row-EH de): Renowned Frenchman of letters and Emilie du Châtelet's lover and confidant.

FINDING EMILIE

Laurel Corona

DISCUSSION GUIDE

1. What does the reader learn about the two great influences on Lili's life, Baronne Lomont and Julie de Bercy, from the letters in the prologue? About the Marquis du Châtelet and his relationship with Emilie?

2. Early in the book, Delphine is victimized by her social environment, but also masterful at triumphing over it. What in her personality and behavior accounts for this? How does Lili's temperament make her also a victim and victor?

3. Why is the Jardin de Roi so important to Lili? Have you ever had a place of refuge? What effect did it have on your life?

4. Do the political and scientific views discussed in Julie's salon and elsewhere in the novel resonate in our world today?

5. "The truth is all that matters, all that is really permanent." Do you agree? Did Emilie apply her philosophy well in real life? Can anyone?

6. What do you think of Rousseau's idea that our upbringing is deliberately intended to deform us to fit the society we live in? Is this the source of much of our own unease and discomfort?

7. Emilie du Châtelet says in her "Discourse on Happiness" that it would be better to figure out how to be happy in the situation we face than try to change it, and that the happiest people are those who desire the least change in their lot. What does she mean? Is it good advice?

8. Toward the end of the book Lili realizes, "I'd have to matter to myself first, before I could expect anything good to happen." Is this true?

9. When Lili sees Delphine's and her own daughter standing in the doorway in the closing scene of the novel, she understands how much Julie must have loved them both. If you are a parent yourself, how did having your own children affect how you saw your own parents?

10. Have you ever had the feeling you were helped by departed loved ones? If so, how?

11. Lili's Meadowlark stories reflect her fears and dilemmas. What are some of these, and how do they shape what she writes?

ENHANCE YOUR BOOK CLUB

1. View Marianne Loir's portrait of Emilie du Châtelet, which she gifted to Voltaire, at http://commons.wikimedia.org/wiki/File:Le_Tonnelier_de_Breteuil,_Emilie.jpg.

2. Go to www.visitvoltaire.com for information about Voltaire, Emilie du Châtelet, and the Château de Cirey. There are also links to hotels and restaurants in the area if you feel like taking your book club on an adventure to France!

3. Set the scene by meeting with your book club at a French restaurant, or make your own fête françois with recipes at www.francethisway.com/frenchfood and www.epicurious.com/recipesmenus/global/french/recipes.

4. Visit the author's website, www.laurelcorona.com, to read about her adventures in France researching *Finding Emilie* and to find out more about her other historical novels.

A CONVERSATION WITH LAUREL CORONA

Julie de Bercy is a fascinating character who created a balance between adhering to conventions of society and advancing modern thinking in the novel. Did you base her character on a historical figure?
Julie de Bercy is entirely my creation. One of the main outlets for aristocratic women of great intellect in this era was to host a salon, and many of the most renowned women in their day were salonnières. Madame de l'Espinasse and Madame Geoffrin, who attend Julie's funeral, are real people, as is Madame de Graffigny, the houseguest at Cirey whom Emilie found so tedious. It's a challenge for historical novelists to set up a plot that has their protagonists, especially the female ones, interacting plausibly with a wide range of interesting and important real-life figures, and Julie's salon seemed a good way to accomplish this.

While Lili is the main character in Finding Emilie, *it is also Emilie du Châtelet's story. Did you originally intend to intersperse scenes from the past and the present, depicting both Emilie and Lili, or is this dual narrative something that developed during the writing process?*
I knew from the outset that I needed to find a way to bring in Emilie's biography, because her mother is what makes Lili's story singular. The challenge was that the reader has to be far more informed about Emilie than her daughter is. I decided the only way to do this was to intersperse vignettes about Emilie with the main narrative of Lili's story. This way, the reader is finding Emilie before Lili does, realizing how important that knowledge is to Lili, and cheering her on to find Emilie herself.

What was it about Emilie that first captured your interest? What can modern-day women learn from her?
I first heard of Emilie du Châtelet only as a footnote to Voltaire, but when I learned she had played a significant role in introduc-

ing Newtonian science to the French intelligentsia, I wanted to know more about her. I assumed she would fit the stereotype of the corseted-and-bewigged snob I imagine from portraits of aristocratic women of her time, but instead I found a flawed and fabulous woman surging with life, intellect, and passions of all sorts, blazing through life prepared to regret some of her decisions but making them anyway.

The main thing I think modern women can learn from her is gratitude. We inhabit not only a much more open, tolerant, and inclusive world, but the tools we have for exploring that world are so much more advanced. Every time I hear about a breakthrough in physics, I wonder what Emilie would make of it. Today she might be a Nobel Prize winner in a state-of-the-art laboratory, instead of having to do her work in near-secret and watch others take credit for it because her interests were not considered proper for a woman. I particularly enjoyed adapting from Voltaire's servant Longchamp's memoir the incident of the broken axle and the night spent looking up at the winter sky. In it Emilie and Voltaire talk about the ignorance their era had surmounted, and what the future would make of their own errors. That's always a good vantage point to have—that we too must be prepared for our most cherished views to be proven wrong.

Tell us about your research trip to France. What did you find most striking about the Château de Cirey, where Voltaire and Emilie lived together for so many years?
The immediately striking thing about Cirey is how remote it is. I'd traveled in France before, mostly to heavily visited areas, but I'd never been to the Champagne region in northeastern France, and I was surprised at how tiny and scattered the villages were. Many of them are little more than a few buildings on both sides of a road passing through, but even these roads are not going to towns of appreciable size. It must initially have been very difficult

for the highly sociable and urbane Emilie and Voltaire to adjust to life there, but eventually they found it suitable for their work and they kept it full of lively company.

The most striking things about the château were its modest size (Voltaire's home at Ferney is even smaller) and its rather odd shape. The house belonged to Emilie's husband's family, and he apparently didn't mind his wife living with her lover there, because Voltaire was using his own money to expand and refurbish the house. I guess they considered it a fair trade! The château looks half-finished in some ways. It has a second story that goes only halfway across the main part of the house, and the last wing in the architectural plans was never built. This sense of a work in progress added to the feeling that at any moment Voltaire or Emilie might come bursting through the door to see who's come for a visit.

The owner of the house gave me a private tour before the summer season, when it is open to the public, and told me that the few tourists who visit are mostly American or Korean. I suppose I shouldn't have been surprised that most know little to nothing about Emilie. They come because they want to see the house where Voltaire lived, close enough at the time to the French border so he could escape in a hurry from the law. Perhaps now that readers are "finding" Emilie, the purpose of visits to Cirey will change!

Why did you decide to include the tales of Meadowlark and Tom in the narrative? At what point did you write these adventures?
I hadn't originally intended to use these stories so extensively, but when I got about fifty pages into the first draft, I realized that the story I saw ahead was really quite dark. I decided I needed to lighten it up both for myself as I wrote, and eventually for the reader as well. I saw the Meadowlark stories both as comic interludes and as a means of watching Lili grapple with the concerns of each stage of her life.

Lili spends time with the Comte de Buffon and Jean-Étienne in the Jardin de Roi, the king's garden, in Paris. Did such a place actually exist? What was its purpose?

It is very much there, renamed the Jardin des Plantes after the French Revolution. It is bigger than in Buffon's day, but still laid out essentially the same. Its original purpose, medical research, is still honored by some plantings in the area where I imagined Jean-Étienne's garden, but for most visitors, it's a pleasant place for a stroll, ringed by museums and the Paris zoo.

In the novel you write that some of Voltaire's published ideas, in fact, came from Emilie du Châtelet. Were you aware of this aspect of the philosopher and his work, or did it come as a surprise to you? To what extent did Emilie contribute to Voltaire's work?

I was not aware that Voltaire took himself very seriously as a scientist. He saw recognition as a man of science as adding to, or surpassing, the status he could gain as a man of letters. Most scholars now are comfortable with attributing the difficult and complex scientific thinking in his papers to Emilie. In the case of any collaboration where conflicting claims of authorship are made, the simplest way to sort it out is to ask what each accomplished independently of the other. In Voltaire's case, he produced no work as a scientist before or after he lived with Emilie. Emilie was the only one of the two who had spent years studying the sciences and mathematics before they met, and she went on, after their relationship became more distant, to produce her greatest works without his help.

One of Newton's laws of physics states that an object at rest will remain at rest unless an external force is applied to it. What was the force that set you on the path to novel writing?

What sent me off on a different trajectory (and at much greater speed) was my experience writing my first full-length book, *Until Our Last Breath* (St. Martin's Press 2008). I had written a number of shorter books for younger readers, and I felt very comfortable moving up to the length and scope of the new book, but I was unhappy with the constraints of the genre of narrative non-fiction. Having to accept the limitations of known facts was a constraint I wasn't comfortable with, because I think the truth is sometimes better served by a mix of imagination and research. I wanted to be creative about filling in what no one thought to document, and historical fiction is the perfect way to do that.

On your website, you state: "My goal as a historical novelist is to provide . . . the reader with high-quality fiction about women and the forgotten and undervalued roles they played in their societies." Why is sharing the stories of women in particular something you're inspired to do?

I have always asked, "where were the women?" when learning about any historical era. There were so many of us, and I don't believe for a minute we were nearly as invisible, or as limited in our roles, as most histories would suggest. It makes more sense that our stories have been forgotten than that they were never there to be told. Women of every era I have researched were far more adventurous, intellectual, heroic, and accomplished than we have been led to believe. We have to make a choice whether to accept that women's stories won't be told because we lack sufficient facts, or tell them anyway, using our imaginations and our ability to make strong inferences from what is known. There's a difference between the facts and the truth, and when the facts are not known, the truth must served by fiction, or not be told at all.

Why do you think historical fiction is so popular with readers?

People today are so busy, and they want to get high value out of what little discretionary time they have. Good historical fiction is by nature a "smart read," because one is learning about people, places, and events in the past within the context of a compelling story. Historical fiction, in the hands of an author who takes the factual foundation of his or her work seriously, is the perfect illustration of Horace's ancient adage, that literature should both delight and instruct.

What time period will you be exploring in your next book?
My next novel is set in Spain and Portugal in the fifteenth century. People know the year 1492 because of Columbus, but many do not know that several other momentous events involving Ferdinand and Isabella also happened that year. The first was the fall of the Muslim Caliphate of Granada and the end of centuries of Muslim political presence in Iberia. The second was the expulsion of the Jews from Spain. My novel covers the period from Henry the Navigator in Portugal, to Ferdinand and Isabella in Spain, from the point of view of a Jewish woman who is witness to those tumultuous times.